"Ms. Grafton writes a smart story and wraps it up with a wry twist."
—*The New York Times Book Review*

Wendell Jaffe has been dead for five years—until his former insurance agent spots him in a dusty resort bar. Now California Fidelity wants Kinsey Millhone to track down the dead man. Just two months before, his widow collected on Jaffe's $500,000 life insurance policy—her only legacy since Jaffe went overboard, bankrupt and about to be indicted for his fraudulent real estate schemes. As Kinsey pushes deeper into the mystery surrounding Wendell Jaffe's pseudocide, she explores her own past, discovering that in family matters as in crime, sometimes it's better to reserve judgment. . . .

"The best first-person-singular storytelling in detective novels."
—*Entertainment Weekly*

"Grafton not only does it right—she's flat-out the best in the business. . . . *J Is for Judgment* [is] another winner."
—*The Detroit News*

" 'J' is for 'just gets better'. . . . Read it!"
—*Houston Chronicle*

A Main Selection of the Literary Guild®

By Sue Grafton:

**KINSEY MILLHONE MYSTERIES**
*A Is for Alibi*
*B Is for Burglar*
*C Is for Corpse*
*D Is for Deadbeat*
*E Is for Evidence*
*F Is for Fugitive*
*G Is for Gumshoe*
*H Is for Homicide*
*I Is for Innocent*
*J Is for Judgment*
*K Is for Killer*
*L Is for Lawless*
*M Is for Malice*
*N Is for Noose*
*O Is for Outlaw*
*P Is for Peril*
*Q Is for Quarry*
*R Is for Ricochet*
*S Is for Silence*
*T Is for Trespass*

*Keziah Dane*
*The Lolly Madonna War*

# J
## IS FOR
## JUDGMENT

### A NOVEL

# SUE GRAFTON

BALLANTINE BOOKS • NEW YORK

FOR TORCHY GRAY,
*in honor of a friendship that began
with a green bean collage . . . hers, not mine.*
Western Kentucky State Teacher's College
Bowling Green, Kentucky
1958

2008 Ballantine Books Mass Market Edition

Published in the United States by Ballantine Books, an imprint of The Random House Publishing Group, a division of Random House, Inc., New York.

BALLANTINE and colophon are registered trademarks of Random House, Inc.

Originally published in hardcover in the United States by Henry Holt and Company, Inc., in 1993.

This edition published by arrangement with Henry Holt and Company, Inc.

ISBN 978-0-345-50312-1

Printed in the United States of America

www.ballantinebooks.com

OPM 9 8 7 6 5 4 3 2 1

# Acknowledgments

The author wishes to acknowledge the invaluable assistance of the following people: Steven Humphrey; Jay Schmidt; B. J. Seebol, J.D.; Tom Huston, Seacoast Yachts; Chief Deputy Richard Bryce, Sergeant Patrick Swift, and Senior Deputy Paul Higgason, Ventura County Jail; Lieutenant Bruce McDowell, Custody Division, Ventura County Sheriff's Department; Steven Stone, Presiding Justice, State of California Court of Appeal; Joyce Spizer, Insurance Investigations Inc.; Mike Love and Burt Bernstein, J.D., Chubb-Sovereign Life; Lynn McLaren; William Kurta, Tri-County Investigations; Lawrence Boyers, Virginia Farm Bureau Insurance Services; John Mackall, Attorney-at-Law; Jill Weissich, Attorney-at-Law; Joyce McAlister, Associate Attorney, Legal Bureau, Police Department, City of New York; Diana Maurer, Assistant Attorney General, State of Colorado; Janet Hukill, Special Agent, FBI; Larry Adkisson, Senior Investigator, Eighteenth Judicial District Attorney; Peter Klippel, Doug's Bougs Etc.; Frank Minschke; Nancy Bein; and Phil Stutz.

With special thanks to Harry and Megan Montgomery, whose boat, *The Captain Murray*, plays such a central role in both the novel and jacket photograph.

# 1

ON THE FACE of it, you wouldn't think there was any connection between the murder of a dead man and the events that changed my perceptions about my life. In truth, the facts about Wendell Jaffe had nothing to do with my family history, but murder is seldom tidy and no one ever said revelations operate in a straight line. It was my investigation into the dead man's past that triggered the inquiry into my own, and in the end the two stories became difficult to separate. The hard thing about death is that nothing ever changes. The hard thing about life is that nothing stays the same. It began with a phone call, not to me, but to Mac Voorhies, one of the vice-presidents at California Fidelity Insurance for whom I once worked.

My name is Kinsey Millhone. I'm a licensed California private investigator, working out of Santa Teresa, which is ninety-five miles north of Los Angeles. My association with CF Insurance had been terminated the previous December, and I hadn't had much occasion to return to 903 State. For the past seven months I'd been leasing office space from the law firm of Kingman and Ives. Lonnie Kingman's practice is largely criminal, but he also enjoys the complexities of trials involving accidental injury or wrongful death. He's been my attorney of record for a number of years, stepping in with legal counsel when the occasion arises. Lonnie is short and beefy, a body-builder and a scrapper. John Ives is the quiet one who prefers the intellectual challenges of appellate work. I'm the only person I know who doesn't express routine contempt for all the lawyers in the world. Just for the record, I like cops, too: anyone who stands between me and anarchy.

Kingman and Ives occupies the entire upper floor of a small building downtown. Lonnie's firm consists of himself; his law partner, John Ives; and an attorney named Martin Cheltenham, Lonnie's best friend, who leases offices from him. The bulk of the day-to-day work is attended to by the two legal secretaries, Ida Ruth and Jill. We also have a receptionist named Alison and a paralegal named Jim Thicket.

The space I moved into used to be a conference room with a makeshift kitchenette. After Lonnie annexed the last available office on the third floor, he had a new kitchen built, along with a room for the copying equipment. My office is large enough to accommodate a desk, my swivel chair, some file cabinets, a mini-refrigerator and coffee maker, plus a big storage closet stacked with packing boxes untouched since the move. I have my own separate phone line in addition to the two lines I share with the firm. I still have my answering machine, but in a pinch Ida Ruth covers incoming calls for me. For a while I made a pass at finding another office to rent. I had sufficient money to make the move. A sidebar to a case I was working before Christmas resulted in my picking up a twenty-five-thousand-dollar check. I put the money in some CDs—the bank kind, not the music—where it was happily collecting interest. In the meantime I discovered how much I liked my current circumstances. The location was good, and it was nice to have people around me at work. One of the few disadvantages of living alone is not having anyone to tell when you're going someplace. At least now at work I had people who were aware of my whereabouts, and I could check in with them if I needed any mothering.

For the past hour and a half, on that Monday morning in mid-July, I'd sat and made phone calls on a skip trace I was working. A Nashville private investigator had written me a letter, asking if I'd check local sources for his client's ex-husband, who was six thousand dollars in arrears on his child support. Rumor had it that the fellow had left Tennessee and headed for California with the intention of settling somewhere in Perdido or Santa Teresa counties. I'd been given the subject's name, his previous address, his birth date, and his Social Security number with instructions to develop any lead I could. I also had the make and model of the vehicle he was last seen driving, as well as his Tennessee license plate number. I'd already written two letters to Sacramento: one to request driver's license information on the subject, another to see if he'd registered his 1983 Ford pickup. Now I was calling the various public utility companies in the area, trying to see if there were any recent hook-ups in the guy's name. So far I hadn't hit pay dirt, but it was fun anyway. For fifty bucks an hour, I'll do just about anything.

When Alison buzzed me on the intercom, I leaned over automatically and depressed the lever. "Yes?"

"You have a visitor," she said. She's twenty-four years old, bubbly and energetic. She has blond hair to her waist, buys all her clothes in size 4 "petite," and dots the "i" in her name with a heart or a daisy, depending on her mood, which is always good. Somehow she sounded as if she were calling on one of those "telephones" kids make with two Dixie cups and a length of string. "A Mr. Voorhies with California Fidelity Insurance."

Like a comic strip character, I could feel a question mark form above my head. I squinted, leaning closer. "Mac Voorhies is out there?"

"You want me to send him back?"

"I'll come out," I said.

I couldn't believe it. Mac was the man who supervised most of the cases I'd worked for CF. It was his boss, Gordon Titus, who'd fired my sorry ass, and while I'd made my peace with the change in my employment, I could still feel a flush of adrenaline at the thought of the man. Briefly I entertained a little fantasy that Gordon Titus had sent Mac to offer his abject apologies. Fat chance, I thought. I did a hasty survey of the office, hoping it didn't look like I'd fallen on hard times. The room wasn't large, but I had my own window, lots of clean white wall space, and burnt orange carpeting in an expensive wool shag. With three framed watercolors and a leafy four-foot ficus plant, I thought the place looked very tasteful. Well, okay, the ficus was a fake (some sort of laminated fabric tinted with accumulated dust), but you really couldn't tell unless you got up real close.

I would have checked my reflection (Mac's arrival was already having that effect), but I don't carry a compact and I already knew what I'd see—dark hair, hazel eyes, not a smidge of makeup. As usual, I was wearing jeans, my boots, and a turtleneck. I licked my palm and ran a hand across my shaggy head, hoping to smooth down any stick-up parts. The week before, in a fit of exasperation, I'd picked up a pair of nail scissors and whacked all my hair off. The results were just about what you'd expect.

I hung a left in the corridor, passing several offices on my way to the front. Mac was standing by Alison's desk out in the reception area. Mac's in his early sixties, tall and scowling, with a flyaway halo of wispy gray hair. His brooding black eyes are set slightly askew in a long bony face. In lieu of his usual cigar, he was smoking a cigarette, ash tumbling down the front of his three-piece suit. Mac has never been one to plague himself with attempts at fitness, and his body, at this point, resembles a drawing from a child's perspective: long arms and legs, foreshortened trunk with a little head stuck on top.

I said, "Mac?"

He said, "Hello, Kinsey," in a wonderful wry tone.

I was so happy to see him that I started laughing out loud. Like some great galumphing pup, I loped over to the man and flung myself into his arms. This behavior was greeted by one of Mac's rare smiles, revealing teeth that were tarnished from all the cigarettes he smoked. "It's been a long time," he said.

"I can't believe you're here. Come on back to my office and we can visit," I said. "You want some coffee?"

"No, thanks. I just had some." Mac turned to stub out his cigarette, realizing belatedly that there weren't any ashtrays in the area. He looked around with puzzlement, his gaze resting briefly on the potted plant on Alison's desk. She leaned forward.

"Here, why don't you let me take that?" She removed the cigarette from his fingers and took the burning butt directly to the open window, where she gave it a toss, peering out afterward to make sure it didn't land in someone's open convertible in the parking lot.

Mac followed me down the hall, making polite responses as I filled him in on my current circumstances. When we reached my office, he was properly complimentary. We caught up on gossip, exchanging news about mutual friends. The pleasantries gave me time to study the man at close range. The years seemed to be speeding right along for him. He'd lost color. He'd lost about ten pounds by the look of him. He seemed tired and uncertain, which was completely uncharacteristic. The Mac Voorhies of old had been brusque and impatient, fair-minded, decisive, humorless, and conservative. He was a decent man to work for, and I admired his testiness, which was born of a passion for getting the job done right. Now the spark was missing and I was alerted by the loss.

"Are you okay? You don't seem like your old self somehow."

He gestured peevishly, in an unexpected flash of energy. "They're taking all the fun out of the job, I swear to God. Damn executives with all their talk about the bottom line. I know the insurance business . . . hell, I've been at it long enough. CF used to be family. We had a company to run, but we did it with compassion and we respected each other's turf. We didn't stab each other in the back and we didn't short-change any claimants. Now, I don't know, Kinsey. The turnover's ridiculous. Agents are run through so fast, they hardly have a chance to unpack their briefcases. All this talk about profit margins and cost containment. Lately I find myself not wanting to go to work." He paused, looking sheepish, color coming up in his face. "God, would you listen? I'm beginning to sound like a garrulous old fart, which is what I am. They offered me an 'early retirement package,' whatever the hell that means. You know, they're maneuvering to get some of us old birds off the payroll as soon as possible. We earn way too much and we're too set in our ways."

"You going to do it?"

"I haven't decided yet, but I might. I just might. I'm sixty-one and I'm tired. I'd like to spend time with my grandkids before I drop in my tracks. Marie and I could sell the house and get an RV, see some of the country and visit the clan. Keep making the rounds so we don't wear out our welcome." Mac and his wife had eight grown kids, all of them married with countless children of their own. He waved the subject aside, his mind apparently focused on something else. "Enough of that stuff. I got another month to decide. Meantime, something's come up and I thought about you."

I waited, letting him get around to the subject in his own good time. Mac always did better when he set the stage for himself. He took out a pack of Marlboros and shook a cigarette into view. He dried his lips with one knuckle before he put the cigarette between his teeth.

He took out a pack of matches and lit up, extinguishing the match flame with a mouthful of smoke. He crossed his legs and used his pants cuff as an ashtray, leaving me to worry he'd set his nylon socks ablaze. "Remember Wendell Jaffe's disappearance about five years back?"

"Vaguely," I said. As nearly as I remembered, Jaffe's sailboat had been found, abandoned and adrift, off the coast of Baja. "Run it by me again. He's the guy who vanished out at sea, right?"

"So it appeared." Mac seemed to wag his head, casting about for a quick narrative summary. "Wendell Jaffe and his partner, Carl Eckert, put together limited partnerships for real estate deals to develop raw land, build condominiums, office buildings, shopping centers, that kind of thing. They were promising investors a fifteen percent return, plus the return of their original investment within four years before the two partners would take a profit. Of course, they got in way over their heads, taking off big fees, paying huge 'overhead' expenses, rewarding themselves handsomely. When profits failed to materialize, they ended up paying old investors with the new investors' money, shifting cash from one shell company to the next, constantly soliciting new business to keep the game afloat."

"In other words, a Ponzi scheme," I inserted.

"Right. I think they started with good intentions, but that's how it ended up. Anyway, Wendell began to see that it couldn't go on forever, and that's when he went off the side of that boat. His body never surfaced."

"He left a suicide note, as I recall," I said.

"That he did. From all reports, the man was exhibiting all the classic symptoms of depression: low spirits, poor appetite, anxiety, insomnia. He finally goes off on his fishing boat and jumps overboard, leaving a letter to his wife. In it, he says he's borrowed every cent he can, pouring it into what he now realizes is a hopelessly failing business. He owes everybody. He knows he's let everybody down and he just can't face the consequences. Meantime, she and his two sons were in a hell of a situation."

"What ages were his kids?"

"I believe the older boy, Michael, was seventeen and Brian was about twelve. Jesus, what a mess. The scandal left his family reeling and forced some of his investors into bankruptcy. His business partner, Carl Eckert, ended up in jail. It looked like Jaffe jumped just before his house of cards collapsed. The problem was, there really wasn't any concrete proof of death. His wife petitioned for a court-appointed administrator to manage his assets, or the few he had left. The bank accounts had been stripped and the house was mortgaged to the hilt. She ended up losing that. I felt sorry for the woman. She hadn't worked in years, since the day she married him. Suddenly she had these two kids to support, not a cent in the bank, and no marketable skills. Nice lady, too, and it was rough on her. Since then, we've had five years of dead silence. Not a whisper of the man. Not a trace."

"But he wasn't dead?" I said, anticipating the punch line.

"Well, now I'm getting to that," Mac said with a touch of irritation. I tried to silence my questions so he could tell it his way. "The question did come up. Insurance company wasn't anxious to pay off without a death certificate. Especially after Wendell's partner was charged with fraud and grand theft. For all we knew, he was a skip, taking off with the bucks to avoid prosecution. We never said as much, but we were dragging our feet. Dana Jaffe hired a private investigator who initiated a search, but never turned up a shred of evidence pro or con." Mac went on. "Couldn't prove he was dead, but you couldn't prove he wasn't, either. A year after the incident, she petitioned the court to have the man declared dead, citing the suicide note and his depressed mental state. Presented affidavits and whatnot, testimony from his partner and various friends. At that point, she notified CF she was filing a claim as his sole beneficiary. We launched our own investigation, which was fairly intense. Bill Bargerman handled it. You remember him?"

"Name sounds familiar, but I don't think we ever met."

"He was probably working out of the Pasadena office back then. Good man. He's retired now. Anyway, he did what he could, but there was no way we could prove Wendell Jaffe was alive. We did manage to overcome the presumption of death—temporarily. In light of his financial problems, we argued successfully that it was unlikely, if Jaffe was living, that he'd voluntarily appear. Judge ruled in our favor, but we knew it was only a matter of time before he reversed himself. Mrs. Jaffe was plenty mad, but all she had to do was wait. She kept the premiums on his policy paid and went back into court when the five years were up."

"I thought it was seven."

"The statute was changed about a year ago. The Law Revision Commission modernized the procedure for probate in the estate of a missing person. Two months ago, she finally got a finding and order from the superior court and had Wendell declared dead. At that point, the company really had no choice. We paid."

"Ah, the thick plottens," I said. "How much are we talking?"

"Five hundred thousand dollars."

"Not bad," I said, "though maybe she deserved it. She sure had to wait long enough to collect."

Mac's smile was brief. "She should have waited a little longer. I had a call from Dick Mills—another retired CF employee. He claims he spotted Jaffe down in Mexico. Town called Viento Negro."

"Really. When was this?"

"Yesterday," Mac said. "Dick was the agent who sold Jaffe the original life insurance policy, and he went on to do a lot of business with him afterward. Anyway, he was down in Mexico, dinky little place, midway between Cabo and La Paz on the Gulf of California. He says he saw Wendell in the hotel bar, having drinks with some woman."

"Just like that?"

"Just like that," he echoed. "Dick was waiting for the shuttle on his way out to the airport and he stopped off in the bar to have a quick one before the driver showed. Wendell was sitting on the patio, maybe three feet away, a little trellis arrangement between the two of them. Dick said it was the voice he recognized first. Kind of gravelly and low with a south Texas accent. Guy was speaking English at first, but he switched to Spanish when the waiter came over."

"Did Wendell see Dick?"

"Apparently not. Dick said he never was so surprised in his life. Said he sat there so long he nearly missed his ride to the airport. The minute he got home, he picked up the phone and called me."

I could feel my heart begin to thump. Put me anywhere close to an interesting proposition and my pulse accelerates. "So what happens next?"

Mac tapped a length of ash into his pants cuff. "I want you to go down there as soon as possible. I'm assuming you have a valid passport in your possession."

"Well, sure, but what about Gordon Titus? Does he know about this?"

"You let me worry about Titus. This thing with Wendell has been sticking in my craw ever since it happened. I want to see it settled before I leave CF. Half a million dollars is nothing to sniff at. Seems like it'd be a nice way to close out my career."

"If it's true," I said.

"I've never known Dick Mills to make a mistake. Will you do it?"

"I'd have to make sure I can clear my schedule here. Can I call you in an hour and give you an answer then?"

"Well, sure. That's no problem." Mac checked his watch and stood up, placing a thick packet on the corner of my desk. "I wouldn't take much more time if I were you. You're on a flight leaves at one for Los Angeles. Connecting flight's at five. Tickets and itinerary are in there," he said.

I started laughing. California Fidelity and I were back in business.

# 2

ONCE MY COMMUTER flight landed at LAX, I had a three-hour delay before the Mexicana flight took off for Cabo San Lucas. Mac had given me a folder full of newspaper articles about Jaffe's disappearance and its aftermath. I settled myself in one of the airport cocktail lounges, sorting through the clippings to educate myself while I sipped a margarita. Might as well get into the spirit of the thing. At my feet I had a hastily packed duffel bag, including my 35-millimeter camera, my binoculars, and the video recorder I'd given myself as a thirty-fourth birthday present. I loved the impromptu nature of this trip, and I was already feeling that heightened sense of self-awareness that traveling engenders. My friend Vera and I were currently enrolled in a beginning Spanish class through Santa Teresa's adult education program. So far, we were confined to the present tense, short, mostly declarative statements of little known use—unless, of course, there were some black cats in the trees, in which case Vera and I were prepared to point and make remarks. *¿Muchos gatos negros están en los árboles, sí? Sí, muchos gatos.* I saw the trip as an opportunity to test my language skills, if nothing else.

Along with the clippings, Mac had included several eight-by-eleven black-and-white shots of Jaffe at various public functions: art openings, political fund-raisers, charity auctions. Judging by the events he attended, he was certainly one of the select: handsome, well dressed, a central part of any group. Often, his was the one blurred face, as if he'd pulled back or turned away just as the camera shutter clicked. I wondered if even then he was consciously avoiding being photographed. He was in his mid-fifties and big. Silver hair, high cheek-bones, jutting chin, his nose prominent. He seemed calm and self-possessed, a man who didn't care much what other people thought.

In a curious way, I felt a fleeting bond with the man as I tried on the idea of changing identities. Being a liar by nature, I've always been attracted to the possibility. There's a certain romance in the notion of walking out of one life and into another, like an actor passing from one character role to the next. Not that long ago I'd handled a case in which a fellow, convicted of murder, had walked away from a prison work crew and had managed to create a whole new persona for himself. In the process, he'd shed not only his past, but the taint of the homicide conviction. He'd acquired a new family and a good job. He was respected in his new community. He might have continued pulling off the deception except for an error in a bench warrant that resulted in a fluke arrest some seventeen years later. The past has a way of catching up with all of us.

I checked my watch and saw that it was time to go. I packed away the clippings and grabbed my duffel bag. I moved through the main terminal, cleared security, and began the long trek down the concourse to my posted gate. One immutable law of travel is that one's arrival or departure gate is always at the extreme outer limit of the terminal, especially if your bag is heavy or your shoes have just begun to pinch. I sat in the boarding area and rubbed one foot while my fellow passengers assembled, waiting for the gate agent to call our flight.

Once I was seated on the plane with my duffel stowed in the bin above, I pulled out the glossy hotel brochure Mac had enclosed with the tickets. In addition to my flights, he'd booked accommodations for me at the same resort where Wendell Jaffe had been seen. I wasn't convinced the guy would still be in residence, but who was I to turn down a free vacation?

The picture of the Hacienda Grande de Viento Negro showed a three-storied structure with a stretch of dark beach faintly visible in the foreground. The blurb under the photograph boasted of a restaurant, two bars, and a heated swimming pool, with recreational activities that included tennis, snorkling, deep-sea fishing, a bus tour of the town, and complimentary margaritas.

The woman in the next seat was reading over my shoulder. I nearly shielded my paper as if she were cheating on a test. She was in her forties, very thin, very tanned, and sleek. She wore her black hair in a French braid and was dressed in a black pants suit with a tan shell underneath. There was not a hint of color on her anyplace. "Are you headed for VN?"

"Yes. Do you know the area?"

"Yes, I do, and I hope you're not planning to stay *there*," she said. She was pointing at the brochure with a little moue of distaste.

"What's the matter with the place? It looks fine to me."

She pushed her tongue along the inside of her cheek as though she were checking her gums. Her brow lifted slightly. "It's your money, I guess."

"Actually, it's someone else's money. This is business," I said.

She nodded, clearly unconvinced. She occupied herself with her magazine, a look on her face like she was trying not to butt in. After a moment I saw her murmur a comment to the man on her right. Her traveling companion, in the window seat, had a wad of Kleenex hanging out of one nostril, stanching a nose bleed that had apparently been induced by increasing cabin pressure as the plane prepared for takeoff. The twist of tissue looked like a fat hand-rolled cigarette. He leaned forward slightly to get a better look at me.

I turned my attention to the woman again. "Really. Is there a problem?"

"I'm sure it's fine," she said faintly.

"Depending on how you feel about dust, humidity, and bugs," the man interjected.

I laughed . . . heh, heh, heh . . . on the assumption that he was kidding. Neither one of them cracked a smile.

Belatedly, I learned that *viento negro* means "black wind," a fair description of the blizzard of dark lava soot that swirled up from the beach late every afternoon. The hotel was modest, an upside down U-shape painted apricot yellow with little balconies across the front. Alternate patios had planters affixed to the railings with bougainvillea tumbling down in a waterfall of magenta. The room was clean but faintly shabby, looking out across the Gulf of California to the east.

For two days I cruised both the Hacienda Grande and the town of Viento Negro, looking for anyone who even halfway resembled the five-year-old photographs of Wendell Jaffe. If all else failed, I could try to quiz the staff in my amateur Spanish, but I worried that one of them might tip him off to the inquiry. If he was there, that is. I hung out by the pool, loitered in the hotel lobby, took the shuttle into town. I tried all the tourist attractions: the sunset cruise, a snorkling expedition, a bumpy ass-agonizing jaunt on a rented all-terrain vehicle, roaring up and down dusty mountain trails. I tried the two other hotels in the area, local restaurants, and bars. I sampled the nightly entertainment at the hotel where I was staying, all the discos, all the shops. There was no sign of him.

I finally managed to get a call through to Mac at home and filled him in on my efforts to date. "This is costing a lot of money if he's already blown out of here . . . assuming your friend actually saw Wendell Jaffe in the first place."

"Dick swore it was him."

"After five long years?"

"Look, just keep at it for another couple of days. If he doesn't turn up by the end of the week, you can head home."

"Happy to oblige. I just like to warn you when I don't get results."

"I understand that. Keep trying."

"You're the boss," I said.

I learned to like the town, which was a ten-minute taxi ride from the hotel down a dusty two-lane road. Most construction I passed was in a state of incompletion, raw cinder block and rebar abandoned to the weeds. A once stunning view of the harbor was obscured now by condominiums, and the streets were filled with tots selling Chiclets for a hundred pesos apiece. Dogs napped in the sunshine, sprawling on the sidewalks wherever it suited them, apparently trusting the local citizens to leave them unmolested. The storefronts that lined the main street were painted harsh blues and yellows, bright reds and parrot greens, as gaudy as jungle flowers. Billboards proclaimed farflung commercial influences from Fuji color film to Century 21 real estate. Most cars were parked with two wheels on the sidewalk, and the license plates suggested an influx of tourists from as far away as Oklahoma. The merchants were polite and responded with patience to my halting Spanish. There was no evidence of crime or civil rowdiness. Everyone was too dependent on the visiting Americans to risk offense. Even so, the goods in the market stalls were shoddy and overpriced, and the fare in the restaurants was strictly second-rate. Restlessly, I wandered from one location to the next, scanning the crowds for Wendell Jaffe or his look-alike.

On Wednesday afternoon—day two and a half of my stay—I finally gave up the search and retired to the pool, where I lathered myself with a glistening coat of sunscreen that made me smell like a freshly baked coconut macaroon. I had donned a faded black bikini, boldly exposing a body riddled with old bullet holes and crisscrossed with pale scars from the assorted injuries that had been inflicted on me over the years. Many people seem to worry about the state of my health. At the moment I was faintly orange, having recently applied a primer coat of Tan in a Can to disguise my winter pallor. Of course, I'd missed in places, and my ankles were oddly splotched with what looked like tawny hepatitis. I tipped my wide-brimmed straw hat down across my face, trying not to think about the sweat collecting on the underside of my burnt umber knees. Sunbathing has to be the most boring pastime on the planet. On the plus side, I was disconnected from telephones and TV. I hadn't any notion what was happening in the world.

I must have dozed because the next thing I became aware of was the rattle of newspaper and a conversation in Spanish taking place between two people on the chaises to my right. Here's how a conversation in Spanish sounds to someone with my limited vocabulary: blah, blah, blah . . . but . . . blah, blah, blah, blah, . . . because . . . blah, blah, blah . . . here. A woman, whose accent was clearly American, was saying something about Perdido, California, the small town thirty miles south of Santa Teresa. I perked right up. I was in the process of lifting the brim of my hat so I could see who she was when her male companion responded in a rift of Spanish. I adjusted my hat, turning by degrees until he came into view. Shit, it had to be Jaffe. If I made allowances for aging and cosmetic surgery, this guy was certainly a distinct possibility. I can't say he was a dead ringer for the Wendell Jaffe in the pictures, but he was close enough: the age, the build, something about the man's posture and the way he held his head, characteristics he probably wasn't aware were part of the image he projected. He was scanning the newspaper, his eye moving restlessly from one column to the next. He sensed my scrutiny and flashed a cautious look in my direction. His gaze held mine briefly while the woman rattled on. Emotions shifted in his face, and he touched her arm with a warning look at me. The flow of talk was halted temporarily. I liked the paranoia. It spoke volumes about his mental state.

Smoothly I reached down and retrieved my straw tote, fussing in its depths until his attention was focused elsewhere. And me without my camera. I was kicking myself. I pulled out my paperback, which I opened to the middle. I flicked an imaginary bug from my calf and then inspected the site, conveying (I hoped) a complete lack of interest. They took up their conversation in lowered tones. Meanwhile I was running a set of mental flashcards, comparing the guy's face to one in my folder. It was the eyes that betrayed him: dark and deep-set under platinum brows. I studied the woman with him, feeling reasonably certain I'd never seen her before. She was in her forties, very small and dark, tanned to the color of polished pecanwood. She had breasts like paper weights in a halter made of hemp, and the arc of her bikini bottom indicated she'd been waxed where it hurt.

I settled down on my chaise with my hat across my face, eavesdropping shamelessly on the escalating conflict. The two chattered on in Spanish, and the nature of the dialogue seemed to shift from simple upset to intense debate. She broke it off abruptly, withdrawing into one of those injured silences men never seem to know how to penetrate. They lay on adjacent chaises for much of the afternoon, hardly speaking, interaction at a minimum. I would have loved to snap some pictures.

Twice I considered a quick run up to the room, but I thought it would look weird if I came back moments later loaded down with photographic equipment. It seemed better to wait and bide my time. The two were clearly guests of the hotel, and I couldn't imagine them checking out this late in the day. Tomorrow I could take some pictures. Today I'd let them get used to the sight of me.

At 5:00, the wind began to rattle through the palms and a haze of black dust spiraled up from the beach. I could feel the sand blow against my skin like talcum powder. I tasted grit and my eyes were soon watering in response. The few hotel guests within range of me started packing up in haste. I knew from experience that the gusts of soot would abate automatically once the sun began to set. In the meantime, even the towel boy working the concession stand closed his booth and fled for cover.

The man I'd been watching pulled himself to his feet. His companion waved a hand in front of her face, as if to fan away a cloud of gnats. She gathered up their belongings, ducking her head to avoid getting dust in her eyes. She said something to him in Spanish and then moved off toward the hotel at a rapid pace. He took his sweet time, apparently undismayed by the sudden shift in weather. He folded the towels. He screwed the lid on a tube of sunscreen, tucked odds and ends in a beach bag, and ambled toward the hotel as she had only moments before. He seemed in no hurry to catch up with her. Maybe he was a man who liked to bypass confrontation. I gave him some leeway and then stuffed my belongings in my beach tote and followed.

I entered the lower lobby, which was usually left

open to the elements. Bright canvas sofas faced a television set. Chairs were arranged in small conversational groupings for the smattering of guests. The ceiling rose two floors to a railing above that marked the upper lobby with its registration desk. There was no sign of the couple. The bartender was bolting tall wooden shutters into place, barricading the room against the hot, stinging wind. The bar was immediately bathed in an artificial gloom. I went up the wide, polished stairs to the left, checking the main lobby which was located on the floor above. I headed for the hotel entrance on the off chance that the two were staying somewhere else, perhaps retrieving their vehicle from the hotel parking lot. The grounds were deserted, people driven indoors by the mounting fury of the winds. I moved back to the elevators and went up to my room.

By the time I secured the sliding doors to the balcony, the sand was being blown against the glass like a sudden summer rainstorm. Outside, the day was shrouded in a synthetic twilight. Wendell and the woman were somewhere in the hotel, probably holing up in their room just as I was in mine. I pulled out my book, tucked myself under the faded cotton coverlet, and read until my eyes closed in sleep. At 6:00, I woke with a start. The wind was down and the overworked air-conditioning had made the room too cold for comfort. The sunlight was fading to the mellow gold of late day, brushing my walls with a pale wash of maize. Outside, I could hear the maintenance crew begin its daily sweeping. All the walks and patios would be cleared and the piles of black sand would be returned to the beach.

I showered and dressed. I made a beeline for the

lobby and began my circle of the premises, hoping to catch sight of the couple again. I scanned the hotel restaurant, the two bars, the patio, the courtyard. Maybe they were napping or having dinner in their room. Maybe they'd taxied into town for a bite to eat. I snagged a taxi myself and headed into Viento Negro. The town, at that hour, was just coming to life. The sinking sun briefly gilded all the telephone wires. The air was thick with heat and laced with the dry scent of the chaparral. The only contribution from the gulf was the faint, sulfurous smell of wharf pilings and gutted marlin.

I found an empty table for two in an open-air cafe overlooking a half-completed construction site. All the weedy cinder block and rusted fencing didn't dull my appetite in the least. I sat on a rickety metal folding chair with a paper plate of boiled shrimp, which I peeled and dipped in salsa, forking the accompanying black beans and rice into a soft corn tortilla. Canned music played, jittery and tuneless, brass harmonies blasting out of the speakers overhead. The beer was ice cold and the food, while mediocre, was at least cheap and filling.

I went back to the hotel at 8:35. Again, I scanned the lobby and then toured the hotel restaurant and both bars. There was no sign of Wendell or the woman I'd seen with him. I couldn't believe he'd be traveling under the name Jaffe, so there wasn't much point in asking for him at the desk. I hoped they hadn't decamped. I roamed the place for an hour and finally settled on the sofa in the lobby near the entrance. I rummaged in my handbag for my paperback novel and read inattentively until well after midnight.

Finally I gave it up and returned to my room. Surely the two would resurface by morning. Maybe I could find out the name he was currently using. I wasn't sure what I'd do with the information, but I was certain Mac would take an interest.

# 3

THE NEXT MORNING I got up at 6:00 for a run on the beach. The morning after I arrived I'd timed out a mile and a half in each direction. Now I reduced that to quarter-mile loops so I could keep the hotel in view. I kept hoping I would spot them . . . on the terrace above the pool, taking an early morning walk on the sand. Unlikely as it seemed, I was still worried they might have checked out in the night.

After my run I went up to my room, took a quick shower, and dressed. I loaded film in my camera and hung it around my neck by its strap, returning to the sunroom off the upper lobby, where breakfast was being served. I chose a seat near the open door, placing my camera on the seat of the chair next to mine. I kept a restless eye on the elevator doors while I ordered coffee, juice, and cereal. I stretched out the meal as far as I could, but neither Wendell nor the woman made an appearance. I signed the check, grabbed my camera, and went downstairs to the pool. Other guests had appeared. A pride of prepubescent males pushed and shoved each other in the water while a pair of newlyweds played Ping-Pong in the courtyard. I circled the hotel and headed back inside, passing through the bar in the lower lobby as I went up the stairs. My anxiety was rising.

Then I spotted her.

She was standing near the elevator doors, with a couple of different editions of the newspapers in hand. Apparently no one had told her how seldom the elevators worked. She hadn't yet applied makeup, and her dark hair was still tousled and asymmetrical from sleep. She wore rubber thongs and a terry-cloth beach coat loosely belted at the waist. Through her gaping lapels, I caught sight of a dark blue bathing suit. If the two were scheduled to depart that day, I didn't think she'd be dressed for the pool. She glanced at my camera but avoided my eyes.

I took my place beside her, looking up with blank attention as the indicator light moved haltingly from the third floor to the lobby. The elevator doors opened and two people emerged. I hung back discreetly, allowing her to get on the elevator first. The woman pressed 3 and then flashed an inquiring look at me.

"That's fine," I murmured.

She smiled at me vaguely, with no real intention of being friendly. Her narrow face looked pinched, and dark shadows under her eyes suggested she hadn't slept well. The musky scent of her perfume filled the air between us. We rode up in silence, and when the doors slid open I gestured politely, allowing her to get off first.

She turned to the right and headed for a room at the

far end of the corridor, her flip-flops slapping against the tiles as she walked away. I paused, pretending to search my pockets for my key. My room was one floor down, but she didn't have to know that. I needn't have bothered with my wee attempt at deception. She unlocked the door to room 312 and went in without a backward glance. It was then almost ten, and the maid's cart was parked two doors away from the room the woman had entered. The door to room 316 was standing open, the room empty, stripped of occupants.

I headed back to the elevator and went straight to the front desk, where I asked to have my room changed. The clerk was most accommodating, possibly because the hotel was nearly vacant. The room wouldn't be ready for an hour, he said, but I was gracious about the wait. I crossed the lobby to the gift shop and bought myself a copy of the San Diego paper, which I tucked under my arm.

I went up to my room and packed my clothes and my camera in the duffel bag, gathering up toilet articles, shoes, and dirty underwear. I took the duffel with me to the lobby while I waited for the room change, unwilling to give Wendell the opportunity to skip. By the time I went up to claim 316, it was almost eleven. Outside 312, someone had set a room service tray stacked with dirty breakfast dishes. I scanned the toast crusts and coffee cups. These people needed to include a fruit exchange in their overall meal plan.

I left my door ajar while I unpacked. I had now placed myself between Wendell Jaffe, and the exits, as both the stairs and the elevators were several doors to my right. I didn't think he could pass without my being aware of it. Sure enough, at 12:35 I caught a glimpse of him and his lady friend as they went downstairs, both now dressed for a swim. I moved to the balcony with my camera and watched them emerge on the walkway three floors down.

I lifted my camera, following their progress in the viewfinder, hoping they'd alight within zoom range of me. They passed behind a splashy screen of yellow hibiscus. I caught a glimpse of them arranging their belongings on a nearby table, seating themselves with some attention to comfort. By the time they got settled, stretching out on their chaises in preparation for sunning, the flowering shrubs obscured all but Wendell's feet.

After a decent interval, I followed and spent the bulk of the day within a few yards of them. Various pale new arrivals were establishing their minikingdoms, staking out their turf between the bar and the pool. I've noticed that resort guests tend to be territorial, returning to the same recliners day after day, reclaiming bar stools and restaurant tables in hastily improvised routines that would rival all their old, boring habits at home. After one day's observation, I could probably predict how most of them would structure their entire vacations. My guess was they went home feeling ever so faintly puzzled that the trip hadn't generated the kind of rest they were looking forward to.

Wendell and the woman had parked themselves two loungers down from the spot they'd occupied the day before. The presence of another couple suggested they hadn't been quite quick enough for the location they really wanted. Again, Wendell occupied himself with two issues of the news: one in English from San Diego and one in Spanish. My proximity attracted little notice, and

I made a point of making no eye contact with Wendell or the woman. Casually I took pictures, feigning interest in architectural details, arty angles, ocean views. If I focused on anything in range of them, they seemed to sense it, retreating like exotic forms of sea life recoiling in self-protection.

They ordered lunch by the pool. I munched on some wholesome chips and salsa at the bar, nose buried in a magazine but keeping them in view. I sunbathed and read. Occasionally I went over to the shallow end of the pool and got my feet wet. Even with the oppressive July temperatures, the water seemed nippy, and if I lowered myself into the depths by as much as six inches, I suffered shortness of breath and a nearly overwhelming desire to shriek. I didn't really relax my vigilance until I heard Wendell make arrangements to go deep-sea fishing the following afternoon. Had I been truly paranoid, I might have pictured the outing as a cover for his next big getaway, but at that point what did he have to get away *from*? He didn't know me from Adam, and I hadn't given him any reason to suspect that I knew him.

To pass the time, I wrote a postcard to Henry Pitts, my Santa Teresa landlord. Henry's eighty-four years old and adorable: tall and lean, with a great set of legs. He's smart and good-natured, sharper than a lot of guys I know who are half his age. Lately he'd been on a tear because his older brother William, who was now eighty-six, was having a geriatric fling with Rosie, the Hungarian woman who owned the tavern down the street from us. William had come out from Michigan early the previous December, fighting off a bout of depression that descended on him in the wake of a heart attack. William was a trial under the best of circumstances, but his "brush with death" (as he referred to it) had exacerbated all his worst qualities. I gathered that Henry's other siblings—Lewis, who was eighty-seven, Charlie, age ninety-one, and Nell, who turned ninety-four in December—had taken a completely democratic family vote and, in Henry's absence, had awarded him custody.

William's original two-week visit had now expanded to seven months, and the personal proximity was taking its toll. William, a self-absorbed hypochondriac, prissy, temperamental, and pious, had fallen in love with my friend Rosie, who was herself bossy, neurotic, flirtatious, opinionated, penny-pinching, and outspoken. It was a match made in heaven. Love had turned them both rather kittenish, and it was nearly more than Henry could bear. I thought it was cute, but what did I know?

I finished the card to Henry and wrote one to Vera, employing a few carefully chosen Spanish phrases. The day seemed interminable, all heat and bugs, kids shrieking in the pool with ear-splitting regularity. Wendell and the woman seemed perfectly content to lie in the sunshine and brown themselves. Hadn't anyone ever warned them about wrinkles, skin cancer, and sun poisoning? I retreated into the shade at intervals, too restless to concentrate on the book I was reading. He certainly didn't behave like a man on the run. He acted like a man with all the time in the world. Maybe after five years he no longer thought of himself as a fugitive. Little did he know that officially he was dead.

Around five, the *viento negro* began to blow. On a nearby side table, Wendell's newspapers gave a rattle, pages riffled into snapping attention like a set of canvas sails. I saw the woman snatch at them with annoyance, gathering them together with her towel and her beach hat. She slid her feet into her flip-flops and waited impatiently for Wendell to collect himself. He took a final plunge in the pool, apparently washing off the sunscreen before he joined her. I collected my belongings and left in advance, conscious that the two of them were not far behind. As anxious as I was to maintain a connection, I thought it unwise to be any more direct than I'd been. I might have introduced myself, striking up a conversation in which I might gradually bring the subject around to their current circumstances. I'd noticed, however, their scrupulous avoidance of any show of friendliness, and I had to guess they'd have shunned any overtures. Better to feign a similar disinterest than excite their suspicion.

I went up to my room and shut the door behind me, watching through the fish-eye until I saw them pass. I had to assume they'd hole up the way the rest of us did until the winds had died. I took a shower and changed into a pair of dark cotton slacks and the dark cotton blouse that I'd worn on the plane. I stretched out on the bed and pretended to read, dozing intermittently until the corridors were quiet and no noises at all filtered up from the pool. I could still hear blowing sand slant against my sliding glass door in gusts. The hotel's air-conditioning, which was fitful at best, seemed to drone off and on in a fruitless attempt to cut into the heat. Sometimes the room would be refrigerator chilly. The rest of the time the air was merely tepid and stale. This was the kind of hotel that generates worries about exotic new strains of Legionnaires' disease.

When I woke it was dark. I was disoriented at first, unsure where I was. I reached out and turned the light on, checking my watch: 7:12. Oh, yeah. I remembered

Wendell and the fact that I was dogging his trail. Had the pair left the premises? I got up from the bed and padded to the door in my bare feet, peering out. The hall was brightly illuminated, empty in both directions. I slipped my key in my pocket and left the room. I moved down the hall, passing 312, hoping a crack of light beneath the door might indicate that their room was occupied. I couldn't tell one way or the other, and I didn't dare risk plastering my ear to the door.

I went back to my room and slipped my shoes on. Then I went into the bathroom, where I brushed my teeth and ran a comb through my hair. I snagged a shabby hotel towel and took it out on the balcony, placing it on the railing near the right-hand side. I left my room lights on, locked the door behind me, and went downstairs with my binoculars in hand. I checked the coffee shop, the newsstand off the lobby, and the bar downstairs. There was no sign of Wendell or the woman who accompanied him. Once outside on the walkway, I turned and lifted my binoculars, skimming my sights across the hotel's facade. On the top floor, I spotted the towel on my balcony, magnified now to the size of a blanket. I counted two balconies to the left. There was no sign of activity, but Wendell's room lights were dimly visible and the sliding glass door seemed to be halfway open. Were they gone or asleep? I found the house phone in the lobby and dialed 312. No one answered my ring. I returned to my room, tucked my room key, pen, paper, and my soft-sided flashlight in my pants pocket. I doused the lights.

I went out onto my balcony and leaned my elbows on the railing, staring out at the night. I kept my expression contemplative, as though I were communing with nature when I was really trying to figure out how to break into the room two doors over. Not that anyone was watching. Across the face of the hotel, less than half the rooms were lighted, bougainvillea trailing like dark Spanish moss. I could see an occasional guest sitting out on the balcony, sometimes a cigarette ember glowing in the shadows. By now it was fully dark and the grounds were plunged in gloom. The exterior walkways were lined with little low-voltage lamps. The swimming pool glowed like a semiprecious stone, though the filtering system was probably still laboring to remove all the soot. On the far side of the pool, some sort of social event was just getting under way—music, the buzz of conversation, the smoky scent of grilled meat. I didn't think anyone would notice if, chimplike, I swung from one balcony to the next.

I leaned forward as far as I could and peered right. The adjacent patio was dark. The sliding glass door was closed and the drapes were drawn. I had no way of knowing if the room was occupied, but it didn't seem to be. I was going to have to risk it in any event. I swung my left leg over the railing and tucked my foot between the pales, adjusting my position before I swung my right leg into place. The distance to the next balcony was a bit of a stretch. I grabbed the railing and gave it a preliminary yank, testing it against my weight. I was aware of the yawning three-story drop, and I could feel my basic dislike of heights kick in. If I slipped, the bushes wouldn't do much to cushion my fall. I pictured myself impaled on an ornamental shrub. Not a pretty sight, that one—a hard-assed private eye, punctured by a sticker bush. I wiped my palm on my pants and reached across again. I extended my left foot and inserted it between the pales on the next balcony. It's never smart to give a lot of thought to these things.

I made my mind a blank and hauled myself clumsily from my balcony to the next. In silence I crossed my neighbor's patio and went through an identical procedure on the other side, only this time I paused long enough to peer around the corner and satisfy myself that Wendell's room was empty. The drapes were pulled back, and though the room itself was dark, I could see a rectangle of light slanting out of the bathroom. I reached across to his railing, again testing my weight before I ventured the distance.

Once on Wendell's balcony, I took a little time to catch my breath. A breeze touched my face, the chill making me aware that I was sweating from tension. I stood near the sliding glass door and peered in. The bed was a king-size, the cotton spread pulled down. The sheets were atangle, showing the tousled imprint of a little predinner sex. I could smell the lingering musk of the woman's perfume, the damp smell of soap where they'd washed up afterward. I used my little pocket flash to amplify the light seeping in from outside. I crossed to the door and secured the chain, peering through the fish-eye at the empty corridor beyond. I checked the time. It was 7:45. With luck, they'd taxied into town for dinner as I had the night before. I flipped on the overhead light, trusting providence.

I did a visual survey of the bathroom first, since it was closest to the door. She had covered the counter on either side of the sink with a profusion of toiletries: shampoo, conditioner, deodorant, cologne, cold cream, moisturizer, skin toner, foundation, blusher, loose powder, eye shadow, eyeliner, mascara, hairdryer, hairspray, mouthwash, toothbrush, toothpaste, floss, hairbrush, eyelash curler. How did the woman ever manage to leave the room? After doing her "toilette" every morning, it'd be time for bed again. She had washed out two pairs of nylon underpants, which she'd hung over the shower rod. I had pictured her in black lacy bikini briefs, but these were that serviceable, high-waisted style favored by lingerie conservatives. She probably wore bras that looked like corrective appliances after back surgery.

Wendell had been accorded the lid to the toilet tank, where his Dopp kit sat, black leather with a monogram in gold that read *DDH*. That was interesting. All he carried with him was a toothbrush, toothpaste, shaving gear, and contact lens case. He probably borrowed her shampoo and deodorant. I checked my watch again. The time was 7:52. I peered through the fish-eye with caution. So far the coast was clear. My tension had passed, and I suddenly realized I was enjoying myself. I suppressed a quick laugh, doing a little dance step in my tennis shoes. I love this stuff. I was born to snoop. Nothing's as exhilarating as a night of breaking and entering. I turned back to the task, fairly humming with happiness. If I didn't work in behalf of law enforcement, I'd be in jail, I'm sure.

# 4

THE WOMAN TURNED out to be the sort who unpacked all her suitcases, probably within minutes of checking into a room. She'd taken the right side of the double dresser, and she'd filled the space neatly: jewelry and underwear in the top drawer, along with her passport. I scribbled down her name, which was Renata Huff, passport number, birth date, place of birth, the passport agency that had issued the document, and the date of expiration. Without searching further among her personal effects, I checked the top drawer on Wendell's side of the dresser, hitting pay dirt again. His passport indicated that he was using the name Dean DeWitt Huff. I made a note of the data and checked the fish-eye again. The corridor was empty. It was now 8:02, probably time to scram. With every additional minute, there was an accelerating risk, especially since I had no idea what time they'd left. Still, as long as I was there, I thought I'd see if anything else turned up.

I went back and opened the remaining drawers systematically, sliding my hand under and between the neatly stacked articles of clothing. All of Wendell's clothes and his personal effects were still in his suitcase, which was propped open on a stand. I worked in haste, with as much care as I could muster, not wanting them to discern my presence after the fact. I lifted my head. Had I heard a noise or not? I checked the fish-eye again.

Wendell and the woman had just emerged from the elevator and were heading in my direction. She was visibly upset, voice shrill, her gestures theatrical. He was looking grim, his face stony and his mouth set, slapping a newspaper against his leg as he walked.

One of the things I've learned about panic is that it inspires gross errors in judgment. Events take place in a blur in which the instinct for survival—winged flight, in this case—overrules all else. Suddenly you find yourself on the far side of a crisis in worse shape than you were to start. The instant I spotted them, I tucked all my personal items in my pants pocket and slid the security chain off the slide track. I reached for the bathroom light and flipped it out, flipped out the overhead light in the bedroom, and then moved speedily to the sliding glass door to the balcony. Once outside, I glanced back to assure myself that I'd left the room just as I'd found it. Shit! They'd left the bathroom light on. *I'd* flipped it out. As though with X-ray vision, I could picture Wendell approaching on the far side of the door, room key at the ready. In my imagination he was moving faster than I was. I calculated rapidly. It was too late to correct. Maybe they'd forget or imagine that the bulb had burned out.

I crossed to the edge of the balcony, swung my right
leg over, secured my foot between the pales, swung the
other leg over. I reached for the railing on the next balcony, crossing the distance just as the light in Wendell's
room came on. I was acutely aware of the adrenaline
that had juiced my pulse rate up into training range, but
at least I was safe on the adjacent balcony.

Except for the guy standing out there smoking a cigarette.

I don't know which of us was more surprised. *He*
was, no doubt, because I knew what I was doing there
and he did not. I had an additional advantage in that
fear had accelerated all my senses, giving me an exag-
gerated awareness of his persona. The truth about this
man began to flash through the air at me like the sub-
liminal messages suddenly made visible in a sports
training film.

The man was white.

The man was in his sixties and balding. What hair he
had was silver and combed straight back from his face.

He wore glasses with the kind of dark frames that
looked like they'd house hearing aids in the stems.

The man smelled of alcohol, fumes pouring from his
body in nearly radiant waves.

He had blood pressure high enough to make his flushed
face glow, and his pug nose had a ruby cast that gave him
the kindly look of a K mart Santa Claus.

He was shorter than I and therefore didn't seem that
threatening. In fact, he had a puzzled air about him that
made me want to reach out and pat him on the head.

I realized I'd seen the guy twice in my constant cruising of the hotel in search of Wendell and his lady
friend. Both times I'd spotted him in the bar—once

alone, his elbow propped up, his cigarette ember weaving as he orchestrated his own lengthy monologue, once in a party of bawdy guys his age, overweight, out of shape, smoking cigars, and telling the kinds of jokes that inspired sudden martini-generated guffaws.

I had a decision to make.

I slowed myself to a leisurely pace. I reached over and lifted his glasses gingerly from his face, folding the stems so I could tuck them into my shirt pocket. "Hey, stud. How are you? You're lookin' good tonight."

His hands came up in a helpless gesture of protest. I unbuttoned my right sleeve, while I gave him a look of lingering assessment.

"Who are you?" he asked.

I smiled, blinking lazily as I unbuttoned my left sleeve. "Surprise, surprise. Where have you been all this time? I been lookin' for you since six o'clock tonight."

"Do I know you?"

"Well, I'm sure you will, Jack. We're going to have us a good old time tonight."

He shook his head. "I think you've made a mistake. My name's not Jack."

"I call everybody Jack," I said as I unbuttoned my blouse. I let the flaps hang open, revealing tantalizing glimpses of my maidenly flesh. Happily, I was wearing the one bra not held together with safety pins. In that light, how could he tell if it was faintly gray from the wash?

"Can I have my glasses? I don't see very well without them."

"You don't? Well, now that's too bad. What's the

deal here . . . you nearsighted, farsighted, astigmatism, what?"

" 'Stigmatism," he said apologetically. "I'm kind of nearsighted, too, and this one eye is lazy." As if to demonstrate, the gaze in his one eye drifted outward, following the flight path of an unseen bug.

"Well, don't you worry none. I'll stay real close so you can see me good. You ready to party?"

"Party?" The one eye drifted back.

"The boys sent me up. Those fellows you hang out with. Said today's your birthday and everybody pitched in to buy you a present. I'm it. You're a Cancer, is that right?"

His frown was slow and his smile flickered on and off. He couldn't quite comprehend what was happening, but he didn't want to be unkind. He also didn't want to make a fool of himself, just in case this was a joke. "It's not my birthday today."

Lights were being flipped on in the room next door, and I could hear the woman's voice rise in anger and distress.

"Now it is," I said. I pulled out my shirttail and peeled my blouse off like a stripper. He hadn't taken a puff of his cigarette since I arrived. I took the lighted cigarette from his hand and tossed it over the railing, and then I moved closer, squeezing his mouth into a pout like I intended to kiss him. "You got something better to do?"

He laughed uneasily. "I guess not," he said in a little puff of cigarette breath. Yum yum.

I kissed him right on the puss, using some slurpy lip-and-tongue stuff I'd seen in the movies. It didn't seem any sexier when other people did it.

I took his hand and drew him into his hotel room, trailing my blouse along the floor like a feather boa. As Wendell came out onto his balcony, I was in the process of closing the sliding glass door behind us. "Why don't you relax while I clean myself up. Then I can bring a little soap and warm water and we'll clean you up, too. Would you like that?"

"You mean just lie down like this?"

"You always make whoopee with your shoes on, honeybun? Why don't you take them old Bermuda shorts off while you're at it. I have to take care of a little something in the other room, and then I'll be right out. I want you ready now, you hear? Then I'll blow out that big old candle of yours."

The guy was unlacing one sturdy black business shoe, which he pulled off and tossed, peeling off a black nylon sock in haste. He looked like somebody's nice, short, fat granddaddy. Also like a five-year-old, prepared to cooperate if there was a cookie in the offing. I could hear Renata, in the next room, begin to shriek. Then Wendell's voice thundered, his words indistinguishable.

I gave my friend a little finger wave. "Be right back," I sang. I sashayed toward the bathroom, where I set his eyeglasses by the basin, then leaned over and turned on the faucet. Cold water gushed out with a vigorous splashing that masked all other sounds. I shrugged into my blouse, eased over to the door, and went out into the hall, closing the door behind me with care. My heart was thudding, and I felt the cold air in the corridor wash across my bare skin. I moved swiftly to my room, pulled my key out of my pants pocket and jammed it in the keyhole, turned it, opened the door, and shut it behind me. I slid the burglar chain into place and stood there for a moment, my back to the door, pulse racing while I rebuttoned my blouse as quickly as I could. I felt an involuntary shiver run down my frame from head to toe. I don't know how hookers do it. Yuck.

I crossed to the balcony and closed my sliding glass door, which I locked with a snap. I pulled the drapes and then I moved back to the door and looked out through the spyhole. The old drunk was now standing halfway out in the hallway. Mr. Magoo-like, he peered right, squinting without his glasses. He was still in his shorts, one sock off and one sock on. He'd begun to eye my door with interest. Suddenly I wondered if the man was as drunk as he'd first appeared. He glanced around casually, making sure he couldn't be observed, and then he moved over to my fish-eye and tried to peer in. I pulled back instinctively and held my breath. I knew he couldn't see me. From his side it must have been like looking down the wrong end of a telescope.

He gave a shy little knock. "Miss? You in there?"

He placed his eye against the spyhole again, blocking the little circle of light from the hallway. I swear I could smell his breath through the wood. I saw light in the fish-eye again, and I approached with care, pressing my eye to the tiny circle so I could peer out at him. He had backed up and was looking down the hall again with uncertainty. He moved to my left, and after a moment I heard his door close with a thunk.

I tiptoed over to the sliding glass and took a position just to the left, my back against the wall as I peered out. Suddenly ... slyly ... the top portion of the old guy's head appeared as he craned around the wall between his balcony and mine, trying to get a glimpse into my darkened room. "Ooo-whooo," he whispered hoarsely. "It's me. Is it time to party yet?"

This guy's blood was up. It wouldn't be long before he'd paw the ground and snort.

I held myself motionless and waited him out. After a moment he withdrew. Ten seconds later my telephone rang, a room-to-room call, if you really want my guess. I let it ring endlessly while I felt my way into the bathroom and brushed my teeth in the dark. I fumbled back toward the bed, peeled my clothes off, and laid them on the chair. I didn't dare leave my room. I couldn't read because I didn't want to risk turning on the light. In the meantime, I was so wired I thought my hair might be standing straight up on end. I finally tiptoed to the minibar and extracted two small bottles of gin and some orange juice. I sat up in bed and sipped screwdrivers until I felt myself getting sleepy.

When I emerged in the morning, the drunk's door was shut with a DO NOT DISTURB tag hung over the knob. Wendell's door was standing open and the room was empty. The same cart was parked in the corridor between rooms. I peered in and caught sight of the same maid patiently damp-mopping the tile floor. She set the mop aside, leaning it against the wall near the bathroom while she picked up the wastebasket and carried it into the hall.

"*¿Dónde están?*" I said, hoping that I was saying "Where are they?"

She must have known better than to pepper her response with lots of past participles and pluperfects. I wasn't going to get it unless she kept the meaning down to a minimum.

What I believe she said was, "Gone ... they leave
... not here."

"*¿Permanente?* Completely *vamos*?"

"*Sí, sí.*" She nodded vigorously and repeated her
original statement.

"Mind if I take a look?" I didn't really wait for her
permission. I pushed my way into room 312, where I
checked the dresser drawers, the night table, the desk,
the minibar. Goddamn it. They hadn't left me *anything*. Meanwhile, the maid was watching me with interest. She shrugged to herself and moved back into the
bathroom, where she tucked the wastebasket under the
sink again.

"*Gracias,*" I said to her, and backed out of the room.

As I passed the cleaning cart, I caught sight of the
plastic bag attached to one end, filled with newly accumulated trash. I snagged it off the hook and carried it
back to my room, closing the door behind me. I moved
over to the bed and dumped the contents on the spread.
There was nothing of interest: yesterday's papers,
Q-Tips, used tissues, an empty can of hairspray. I
picked through with distaste, hoping my tetanus shots
were up to date. As I gathered the detritus and stuffed
it all back in the bag, I caught sight of the front page,
which was splashed with news of a crime spree. I unfolded the section, flattened the newsprint, and studied
the Spanish.

Living in Santa Teresa, I've learned it's almost impossible not to pick up a smattering of the language
whether you take a Spanish class or not. Many words
have been borrowed, and many simply mirror their
counterparts in English. Sentence construction is fairly
straightforward and pronunciation is consistent. The

story that was spread across page one of *La Gaceta* had
something to do with a homicide *(homicidio)* in the
*Estados Unidos*. I read aloud to myself in the halting
style of a kindergartner, which helped me decipher
some of the meaning of the text. A woman had been
murdered, her body found on a deserted stretch of highway just north of Los Angeles. Four male inmates had
escaped from the juvenile facility in Perdido County,
California, fleeing south along the coast. Apparently,
they'd flagged down the victim and commandeered her
car, shooting her in the process. By the time the body
was discovered, the escapees had reached the Mexican
border, crossing into Mexicali, where they'd killed
again. The *federales* had caught up with them, and in a
wild exchange of gunfire, two youths were killed and
another was severely wounded. Even in black and
white, the photograph of the shooting scene seemed un-
necessarily lurid, with ominous dark splotches on the
shrouded bodies of the deceased. The four juveniles
were pictured in a row of sullen mug shots. Three were
Hispanic. The fourth was identified as a kid named
Brian Jaffe.

I booked the first flight back.

On the plane coming home my sinuses seized up, and
during our descent into Los Angeles, I thought my ear-
drums would burst. I arrived in Santa Teresa at 9:00,
bearing with me all the symptoms of an old-fashioned
cold. My throat was scratchy, my head ached, and my
nasal passages stung like I'd sucked a pint of saltwater
up my nose. I couldn't help but rejoice, anticipating the
use of NyQuil in fully authorized nightly doses.

Once safely home, I locked the door behind me and

hauled a stack of newspapers up my spiral stairs. I emptied my duffel into the dirty clothes hamper, stripped off
my travel clothes, and added them to the mix. I donned
my sweat socks and flannel nightie and tucked myself
into the hand-stitched quilt Henry's sister made for my
birthday, settling in with the accounts of the jailbreak in
the Santa Teresa paper. The story had already been
moved to the second section, page three. I got to read it
all again, only this time in English. Wendell Jaffe's
younger son, Brian, along with three confederates had
made a daring daylight escape from the medium-
security juvenile commitment facility called Connaught.
The dead inmates were identified as Julio Rodriguez,
sixteen, and Earnesto Padilla, whose age was fifteen. I
wasn't sure what extradition agreements the United
States had with Mexico, but it looked like Brian Jaffe
was being sent back to the States as soon as sheriff's
deputies could be dispatched. The fourth escapee, a
fourteen-year-old, was still in critical condition in a
hospital in Mexico. His name was being withheld from
the local papers because of his age. The Spanish-
language paper, as I recollected, had listed him as
Ricardo Guevara. Both the murder victims had been
Americans, and it was possible the *federales* were anxious to relinquish responsibility. It was also possible
that a great whack of cash had been passed under the
table. Whatever the circumstances, the escapees were
lucky not to find themselves permanently incarcerated
down *there*. According to the paper, Brian Jaffe had cel-
ebrated his eighteenth birthday shortly after his capture,
which meant that once he was returned to the Perdido
County Jail, he'd be kept and charged as an adult. I

found a pair of scissors and clipped all the articles, setting them aside to take with me for the office files.

I glanced at the clock on my bedside table. It was only 9:45. I picked up the phone and called Mac Voorhies at home.

# 5

"HI, IT'S KINSEY," I said when Mac picked up on his end.

"You don't sound like yourself. Where're you calling from?"

"Here in town," I said. "I just came down with a cold and I'm feeling like death."

"That's too bad. Welcome home. I wasn't sure when to expect you back."

"I walked in the door forty-five minutes ago," I said. "I've been reading the papers, and I see you had some excitement while I was gone."

"Can you believe it? I don't know what the hell is going on. I haven't heard a word about this family for the last two, three years. Now all the sudden the name's cropping up everywhere."

"Yeah, well, here it comes again. We hit pay dirt on Wendell. I spotted him right where Dick Mills said he'd be."

"Are you sure it's him?"

"Of course, I'm not *sure*, Mac. I never laid eyes on the man before, but judging from the photographs, this fellow comes damn close. For one thing, he's American and he's in the right age group. He's not using the name Jaffe. It's Dean DeWitt Huff, but the height's on the money, and the weight seemed close enough. He's somewhat heavier, but he probably would be in any event. He's traveling with a woman, and the two kept themselves very isolated."

"Sounds pretty sketchy."

"Of course it's sketchy. I could hardly walk up to him and introduce myself."

"How sure are you on a scale of one to ten?"

"Let's put it this way: adjusting for age and some surgical tampering, I'd say a nine. I tried to get some pictures, but he was very paranoid about attention. I had to maintain a very low profile," I said. "By the way, what was Brian Jaffe in jail for, has anybody said?"

"As I understand it, some kind of burglary. Probably nothing sophisticated or he wouldn't have been caught," Mac said. "What about Wendell. Where is he at this point?"

"That's a very good question."

"He got away," Mac said flatly.

"More or less. He and the woman took off in the dead of night, but don't start screaming yet. You want to know what I found? This was in their room after they checked out. A Mexican newspaper featuring Brian Jaffe's capture. Wendell must have spotted it in the late edition because the two of them went off to dinner at the regular time. Next thing I know, they're hightailing it back, and they're both upset. By this morning, they were gone. I found the newspaper in the trash." Even as I played out my recital of the facts, I realized something about the situation was bothering me. It was too coincidental—Wendell Jaffe ensconced in that obscure Mexican resort . . . Brian breaking out of jail and heading straight for the border. I could feel a spark of insight connect the two events. "Oh, wait a minute, Mac. I got a little flash here, catch this. You know what just occurred to me? From the moment I spotted Wendell, he was skimming through the papers, five or six altogether, and he was checking every page. What if he *knew* Brian would be making that escape? He could have been waiting for him. It's possible Wendell even helped set it up."

Mac cleared his throat with a skeptical hum. "That's pretty far-fetched. Let's don't jump to conclusions until we know what's what."

"Yeah, I know. You're right, but it adds up in a way. I'll table it for now, but I may check it out later."

"Any idea where Jaffe went?"

"I talked to the desk clerk in my rudimentary Spanish, but it didn't produce much except a half-concealed smirk. If you want my opinion, I think there's a good chance he's heading back in this direction."

I could practically hear Mac squinting through the telephone lines. "I don't believe it. You really think he'd step a foot in this state? He wouldn't have the *nerve*. The man would have to be nuts."

"I know it sounds risky, but his kid's in trouble. Put yourself in his place. Wouldn't you do the same?"

There was silence. Mac's kids were grown, but I knew he was still protective. "How could he have known what was going on?"

"I don't know, Mac. It's always possible he kept in touch. We don't have a clue where he's been all these years. Maybe he still has contacts in the area. It's probably worth pursuing if we're trying to get a line on his current whereabouts."

Mac cut in. "What's the game plan here? You have a scheme in the works?"

"Well, I think we should find out how soon the kid's being brought back from Mexicali. I can't believe much will happen over the weekend. Monday, I can talk with one of the deputies at the county jail. Maybe we can pick up Wendell's trail from there."

"Sounds like a long shot."

"The long shot was Dick Mills's spotting him in the first place."

"True enough," he conceded, though he wasn't happy about it.

"I've also been thinking we should talk to the local cops. They have the kind of resources I can't touch."

I could hear him hesitate. "Seems early to bring the police into it, but I'll let you use your own judgment. I wouldn't mind the help, but I'd hate to scare him off. *If* he shows, that is."

"I'm going to have to get in touch with old friends of his. We'll just have to run the risk of somebody warning him off."

"You think his pals will cooperate?"

"I have no idea. I gather he ripped off a lot of folks back then. Surely there are some who'd like to see him land in jail."

"You'd think so," he said.

"Anyway, we'll talk Monday morning, and in the meantime, don't fret."

Mac's laugh was bleak. "Let's hope Gordon Titus doesn't get wind of this."

"I thought you said you'd take care of him."

"I was picturing an arrest. Lots of public glory for you."

"Hold on to the thought. We may get there yet."

I spent the next two days in bed, my vacation extending into a lazy, unproductive weekend by virtue of my affliction. I love the solitude of illness, the luxury of hot tea with honey, the canned tomato soup with gooey grilled-cheese sandwiches. I kept a box of Kleenex on my nightstand, and the wastebasket by the bed was soon filled to the rim with a puffy soufflé of used tissues. One of the few concrete memories I have of my mother was her salving my chest with Vicks VapoRub, then covering it with a square of pink rose-sprigged flannel, secured to my pajama top with safety pins. The heat of my body would envelop my nasal passages in a cloud of heady fumes while the ointment on my skin conveyed a mentholated contradiction of searing heat and biting cold.

I dozed fitfully during the day, my body aching with inactivity. For two hours each afternoon, I staggered down my spiral stairs, dragging my quilt behind me like a wedding train. I curled up on my sofa bed and flipped on the television set, watching mindless reruns of "Dobie Gillis" and "I Love Lucy." At bedtime I stood in my bathroom at the sink and filled my little plastic cup with the vile, dark green syrup that would ensure a good night's sleep. I've never once downed a hit of NyQuil without shuddering violently afterward. Nonetheless,

I'm aware that I harbor all the incipient characteristics of an over-the-counter cold medication addict.

Monday morning I woke at 6:00 A.M. only moments before the alarm was set to go off. Once I opened my eyes, I lay in my rumpled nest and stared up at the domed Plexiglas skylight above my bed, trying to gauge the day ahead. The morning sky was thickly overcast, bright, white clouds forming a dense ceiling probably half a mile thick. At the airport, the commuter flights to San Francisco, San Jose, and Los Angeles would be stalled out on the runways, waiting for the fog to lift.

July in Santa Teresa is an unsettling affair. Morning dawns behind a cloud bank that lingers just off the coast. Sometimes the marine layer clears by afternoon. Other times the sky remains overcast and the day stretches on in a nebulous gloom, creating the illusion of storm clouds hovering. The local citizens complain and the *Santa Teresa Dispatch* reports the temperatures in a chiding tone as if the summer season weren't always this way. Tourists, who arrive in search of rumored California sunshine, spread their paraphernalia on the beach—umbrellas and sunscreen, portable radios and swim fins—waiting patiently for a break in the monotonous gray skies. I see their little children hunkered in the surf with toy buckets and shovels. Even from a distance I can sense their goose bumps and pale blue lips, teeth beginning to chatter as the icy water surges around their bare feet. This year the weather had been very strange, varying wildly from one day to the next.

I rolled out of bed, pulled on my sweats, brushed my teeth, and combed my hair, avoiding the sight of my sleep-smudged face. I was determined to run, but my body thought otherwise, and after half a mile I was beset by a coughing fit that sounded like the mating call of some wild beast. I abandoned the notion of a three-mile jog and contented myself with a brisk walk instead. My cold, by then, had settled in my chest, and my voice had dropped into that wonderful, husky FM disc jockey range. By the time I reached home, I was chilled but invigorated.

I took a steaming hot shower to loosen my bronchial passages and emerged from the bathroom feeling somewhat restored. I changed my sheets, emptied trash, ate a breakfast of fruit and yogurt, and went into the office with a file folder full of clippings. I found a parking space down the street, hoofed the block and a half, then hit the stairs. My usual pace is two stairs at a time, but today I had to pause at every landing on the way up. The downside of fitness, which takes years to achieve, is how quickly it vanishes—almost instantly. After three days of inactivity I was back to square one, huffing and puffing like a rank amateur. The shortness of breath inspired a renewed round of coughs. I entered through the side door and paused to blow my nose.

As I passed Ida Ruth's desk, I stopped for a chat. When I first met Lonnie's secretary, I found the double name unwieldy. I tried shortening it to Ida, but I found it didn't suit. The woman is in her mid-thirties, a robust outdoor type who looks as if a day of typing would drive her round the bend. Her hair is white blond, combed away from her face as if blown by a strong wind. Her complexion is sun-scrubbed, her lashes white, her eyes an ocean blue. Her clothing is conservative: straight medium-length skirts, boxy jackets in muted tones, her blouses a boring succession of the long-sleeved, button-down sort. She looks like she'd prefer to be paddling a kayak or climbing t..e face of a rock in some national park. I've heard that in her spare time she does precisely that—backpacking trips to the High Sierras, fifteen-mile day hikes in the local mountain range. She's undeterred by ticks, steep inclines, venomous snakes, poison oak, sticks, sharp rocks, mosquitoes, or any of the other joyous aspects of nature I avoid at all costs.

She flashed a smile when she saw me. "You're back. How was Mexico? You turned orange, I see."

I was in the process of blowing my nose, my cheeks suffused with pink from the climb to the third floor. "Great. I had a ball, picked up a cold on the plane coming back. I've been in bed for two days. That's my faux tan," I said.

She opened her pencil drawer and took out a mint dish filled with big white pills. "Vitamin C. Take a handful. It'll help."

Dutifully I plucked up a pill, which I held to the light. It was easily an inch long and looked like it would require surgical removal if it got lodged going down.

"Go on. Help yourself. And try zinc if your throat hurts. How was Viento Negro? Did you get up to see the ruins?"

I picked up another couple of vitamin C's. "Pretty good. A little windy. What ruins?"

"You're kidding. The ruins are famous. There was a huge volcano that blew ... oh, I don't know ... in 1902? It was something like that. In a matters of hours, the entire town was buried in a blanket of ash."

"I saw the ash," I said helpfully.

Her telephone rang and she took the call while I con-

tinued across the hall, pausing at the water cooler to fill
a paper cup. I tossed down the vitamin C, adding an antihistamine for good measure. Better living through
chemistry. I moved on to my office, unlocked the door,
and opened one of the windows, letting in some fresh
air after the week away. There was a pile of mail on my
desk: a few checks for accounts receivable and the rest
of it junk. I checked my answering machine for
messages—there were six—and I spent the next thirty
minutes getting life in order. I made up a file for
Wendell Jaffe and tucked in the newspaper articles
about his son's escape and recapture.

At 9:00 I put a call through to the Santa Teresa Police
Department. I asked for Sergeant Robb, belatedly aware
that my heart had begun to thump. I hadn't seen Jonah
for a year by my calculation. I'm not sure our relationship could ever have been classified as an "affair." At
the time I first met him, he was separated from his wife,
Camilla. She'd walked out on the marriage, taking both
their daughters, leaving Jonah with a freezer full of
home-cooked meals that she'd placed in recycled TV
dinner trays. In roughly three hundred foil-wrapped tins,
she'd assembled an entrée and two vegetables. The directions taped to the top, always said the same thing:
"Bake in 350 oven for 30 minutes. Remove foil and
eat." Like he was really going to try to eat with the foil
in place. Jonah didn't seem to think that was weird,
which should have been a clue. In theory, he was a free
man. In truth, she kept him on a tight rein. She'd come
back at intervals, insisting that the two of them see a
therapist. She'd find a new marriage counselor for each
reconciliation, thus assuring that no real progress was
ever made. If they came anywhere close to working out

a relationship, she would split again. I finally decided that I had troubles enough, so I removed myself from the situation. Not that either of them seemed to notice. They'd been together since the seventh grade, when both were thirteen years old. One day I would read about them in the local paper, celebrating the wedding anniversary where etiquette suggests gifts made of recycled aluminum.

In the meantime, Jonah was still working the missing persons detail. He came on the line abruptly, using his businesslike policeman's manner. "Lieutenant Robb," he said.

"Oh, wow, it's 'Lieutenant' Robb. You've been promoted. Congratulations. This is a voice from your past. It's Kinsey Millhone," I said.

I enjoyed the moment of startled silence while he computed my identity. I pictured him suddenly sitting back in his chair. "Well, hey there. How are you?"

"I'm fine. How are you?"

"Not bad. You have a cold? I didn't recognize your voice. You sound all stuffed up."

We went through the formalities, exchanging basic information, which didn't take that long. I told him I'd left California Fidelity. He told me Camilla had come back to him. I could see it wasn't any different from missing fifteen episodes of your favorite soap opera. Tuning in again, weeks later, you realize you really haven't lost a beat.

Like a plot synopsis, Jonah began to fill me in. "Yeah, she got a job last month. Working as a court clerk. I think she's happier. She has a little money of her own, and everybody seems to like her. She thinks it's interesting, you know what I mean? Helps her understand my job, which is good for both of us."

"Well, that's great. It sounds good," I said. He must have noticed I didn't press for additional details. I could feel the conversation stalling like a biplane about to crash. It's disconcerting to realize how little you have to say to someone who once occupied such a prominent place in your bed. "You're probably wondering why I got in touch," I said.

Jonah laughed. "Yeah, I was. I mean, I'm glad to hear from you, but I figured there was something up."

"Remember Wendell Jaffe? The guy who disappeared off his sailboat. . . ."

"Oh! Yeah, yeah, yeah. Of course."

"He's been spotted in Mexico. It's possible he's on his way back to California."

"You're kidding."

"No, I'm not." I told him an abbreviated version of my encounter with Wendell, omitting the fact that I'd broken into his room. In talking to cops, I don't always volunteer information. I can be a dutiful citizen when it suits my purposes, but this wasn't one of those occasions. For starters, I was secretly embarrassed that I'd blown the contact. If I'd done the job right, Wendell never would have known anyone was on his tail. I said, "Who should I be talking to? I thought I ought to notify someone, preferably the detective in charge of the case back then."

"That'd be Lieutenant Brown, but he's gone now. He retired last year. You'll probably want to talk to Lieutenant Whiteside in Major Frauds. I can have you transferred if you like. That Jaffe was a bad-ass. Neighbor of mine lost ten grand because of him, and that was *peanuts* compared to most."

"I gathered as much. Did they have any recourse?"

"They put his partner in jail. Once the scam came to light, all the investors brought suit. Since there wasn't any way to get Jaffe served, they ended up publishing the summons and complaint, and finally took his default. Of course, they got the judgment, but there wasn't any way to collect from him. He stripped all his bank accounts before he disappeared."

"So I heard. What a bummer."

"You got *that* right. Plus, he was mortgaged to the eyeballs, so his house wasn't worth a cent. I know people who'd love to think he's still around someplace. He ever showed up, they'd enforce the judgment in ten seconds flat, whip his ass into court, and take everything he had. *Then* he'd be arrested. What makes you think he'd be dumb enough to come back?"

"He's got a kid in big trouble, according to the papers. You know those four inmates who escaped from Connaught? One of them was Brian Jaffe."

"Shit, that's right. I didn't make the connection. I knew Dana in high school."

"That's his wife?" I asked.

"That's right. Her maiden name was Annenberg. She got married right after graduation."

"Can you get me an address?"

"Shouldn't be too hard. She's probably in the book. Last I heard she was down around P/O some place."

P/O was the ready reference locally to the two adjoining towns—Perdido and Olvidado—on Highway 101 thirty miles to the south. The towns looked just the same, except that one favored shrubs along the highway and the other did not. Usually the two were referred to in the same breath—P/O with a hash mark mentally inserted between the initials. I was making notes like crazy on a legal pad.

Jonah's tone underwent a shift. "I've missed you."

I ignored that, conjuring up a piece of fiction to extricate myself before the conversation turned personal. "Oops. I better go. I have a client due in ten minutes, and I want to talk to Lieutenant Whiteside first. Can you have me switched over to his extension?"

"Sure thing," he said. I heard him depress the plunger rapidly several times in succession.

When the operator picked up, he had the call transferred to the detective bureau. Lieutenant Whiteside was away from his desk but was expected back shortly. I left my name and number with a request to have him get back to me.

# 6

AT NOON, FEELING punk, I walked up to the corner minimarket, where I bought a tuna salad sandwich, a bag of potato chips, and a diet Pepsi. I figured this was no time to obsess about being nutritionally correct. I went back to my office and ate sitting at my desk. For dessert I sucked on some cherry cough drops.

Lieutenant Whiteside finally called me at 2:35 with apologies for the delay. "Lieutenant Robb tells me you may have a line on our old friend Wendell Jaffe. What's the story?"

For the second time that day, I went through an abbreviated version of my encounter. From the nature of the silence on his end, I had to guess Lieutenant Whiteside was taking notes.

He said, "You have any idea if he's using an alias?"

"If you don't press for details, I'll confess I did get a wee tiny glimpse at his passport, which was issued in the name Dean DeWitt Huff. He's traveling in the company of a woman named Renata Huff, who must be his common-law wife."

"Why common-law?"

"He's not divorced, as far as I've heard. His first wife had him declared dead a couple of months ago. Oh, wait a minute now, can dead men remarry? I hadn't thought about that. It's possible he isn't really a bigamist. Anyway, according to the data I saw, the passports came out of Los Angeles. He may well be in the country by now. Is there any way to track the names through the passport office down there?"

Lieutenant Whiteside eased in. "Not a bad idea. Spell the last name for me, if you would. Is it H-o-u-g-h?"

"H-u-f-f."

"I'm making myself a memo," he said. "What I'll do is check with Los Angeles and see what passport records show. We can also notify customs officials at LAX and San Diego so they can keep an eye out in case he comes through either port of entry. I can also notify San Francisco just to cover that base."

"You want the passport numbers?"

"Might as well, though my guess is the passports are forged or counterfeit. If he skipped—which is what it looks like—Jaffe may have ID in half a dozen names. He's been gone a long time, and he may have set up more than one set of documents in the event things get tight. That's what I'd do if I was him."

"Makes sense," I said. "I keep thinking if Wendell contacted anyone, it'd be his old partner, Carl Eckert."

"Well, it's possible, I guess, but I'm not really sure what kind of reception he'd get. They used to be close, but when Wendell pulled his little vanishing act, Eckert was the one left holding the bag."

"I heard he went to jail."

"Yes, ma'am, he did. Convicted on half a dozen counts of fraud and grand theft. Then the investors went after him in a class action suit, claiming fraud, breach of contract, and who knows what else. Not that it did any good. By then he'd filed for bankruptcy, so there wasn't much to collect."

"How much time did he serve?"

"Eighteen months, but that's not gonna stop a sleazy operator like him. Somebody was telling me they ran into him not too long ago. I forget now where it was, but he's still in town."

"I'll have to see if I can scare him up."

"Shouldn't be that hard," he said. "Meanwhile, what are the chances of you coming by and working with our police artist on a composite? We just hired a kid named Rupert Valbusa. He's a whiz at this stuff."

"Sure. I could do that," I said. Mentally I was calculating the worrisome issue of Wendell's likeness suddenly being plastered everywhere. "California Fidelity doesn't want him scared off."

"I understand, and believe me, we don't either. I know a lot of people with a vested interest in seeing this guy picked up," Whiteside said. "You have any recent pictures of him?"

"Just some black-and-white photographs Mac Voorhies provided, but those are six and seven years old. What about you? There's not a mug shot, is there?"

"No, but we had a photograph that went out when Jaffe first disappeared. We can probably adjust that one upward for age. What kind of cosmetic work has he had done, could you say?"

"I'd guess chin implant and cheeks, and he's maybe

had his nose refined. From the pictures I was given, it looks like his nose used to be broader across the bridge. Also, his hair is snowy white now, and he's bulked up to some extent. Aside from that, he looks pretty fit. Nobody I'd want to tangle with."

"Tell you what. I'll give you Rupert's number and you two can work out your own arrangements. He doesn't come in on a regular basis, just when we need him to work something up. Soon as he's done, we can issue a 'be on the lookout.' I can contact Perdido County Sheriff's Department, and in the meantime I'll call the local FBI offices. They may want to distribute a bulletin of their own."

"I'm assuming there's still an arrest warrant outstanding."

"Yes, ma'am. I ran a check before I picked up the telephone. The feds may want him, too. We'll just have to see what kind of luck we have." He gave me Rupert Valbusa's telephone number, then added, "The sooner we can get this in circulation, the better."

"Got it. Thanks."

I tried Rupert's number and got his machine. I left him my name, my home telephone number, and a message, encompassing the bare bones of the case. I suggested an early morning meeting if his schedule permitted and asked him to get back to me to confirm. I hauled out the telephone book and checked the white pages under Eckert. There were eleven of them listed, along with two variations: one Eckhardt and one Eckhart, which I didn't think were correct. I tried all thirteen numbers but couldn't stir up a "Carl" among them.

I dialed Information in Perdido/Olvidado. There was

only one Eckert listed and that was under the name Frances, whose tone was one of polite caution when I told her I was looking for Carl.

"There's no one here by that name," she said.

I could feel myself cock an ear, like a dog picking up a signal pitched beyond human hearing. She hadn't said she didn't *know* him. "Are you related to Carl Eckert, by any chance?"

There was a moment of silence. "He's my ex-husband. May I ask what this is about?"

"Sure. My name is Kinsey Millhone. I'm a private investigator up here in Santa Teresa, and I'm trying to track down some of Wendell Jaffe's old friends."

"Wendell?" she said. "I thought he was dead."

"Looks like he's not. In fact, I've been trying to contact old friends and acquaintances on the off chance he might be getting in touch. Is Carl still in the area?"

"Actually, he's up in Santa Teresa, living on a boat."

"Really," I said. "And you're divorced?"

"You bet. I divorced Carl four years ago when he started doing time. I had absolutely no intention of being married to a jailbird."

"I can't say I blame you."

"I'd have done it if anybody blamed me or not. What a smooth-talking skunk he turned out to be. You find him, you can tell him I said so. There's no love lost between us."

"Do you happen to have a work number for him?"

"Of course. I give his number to everyone, especially his creditors. It gives me great pleasure. Now, you'll have to catch him during the day," she went on to caution me. "There's no telephone on the boat, but he's usually there by six every evening. Most nights he has supper at the yacht club and then hangs around until midnight."

"What's he look like?"

"Oh, he's very well known. Anyone could point him out. You just go on over there and ask for him by name. You can't miss him."

"What about the name of the boat and the slip number in case he's not at the club?"

She gave me both the marina and the slip numbers. "The boat's called the *Captain Stanley Lord*. It was Wendell's," she said.

"Really. How did Carl end up with it?"

"I'll let him tell you that," she said, and hung up.

I did a few odds and ends and then decided to pack it in for the day. I'd felt crummy to begin with, and the antihistamine I'd taken earlier was knocking me for a loop. Since there wasn't much else going on, I thought I might as well go home. I hiked the two blocks to my car and headed over to State Street, where I hung a left. My apartment is tucked away on a shady side street just a block off the beach. I found a parking place close by, locked the VW, and let myself in the front gate.

The space I now occupy was formerly a single-car garage, converted into a studio, complete with a sleeping loft and spiral staircase. I have a galley-style kitchen, a living room that serves as guest quarters on occasion, one bathroom down and another one up, all of this fitting together with amazing efficiency. My landlord redesigned the floor plan after an unfortunate explosion two Christmases before, and he'd infused the "day-core" with a nautical motif. There was a lot of brass and teak, windows shaped like portholes, built-ins everywhere. The apartment has the feel of an adult-size playhouse, which is fine with me, as I'm a kid at heart.

When I rounded the corner, moving toward the back-yard, I saw that Henry's back door was open. I crossed the flagstone patio linking my studio apartment to the main house on the property. I tapped on the screen, peering into his kitchen, which looked empty.

"Henry? Are you there?"

He must have been in cooking mode. I could smell the sautéed onions and garlic that Henry seems to use as the basis for anything he makes. It was a good indica-tion that his mood had improved. In the months since his brother William moved in, Henry had ceased cook-ing altogether, in part because William was so finicky about what he ate. In the most self-deprecating manner imaginable, William would declare that a dish had a lit-tle bit too much salt for his hypertension or just that wee touch of fat he wasn't permitted after his gallblad-der removal. Between his fussy bowels and his temper-amental stomach, he couldn't handle anything with too much acid or spice. Then there were his allergies, his lactose intolerance, and his heart, his hiatal hernia, his occasional incontinence, and his tendency to pass kid-ney stones. Henry had taken to making sandwiches for himself, leaving William on his own.

William began to take his meals at the neighborhood tavern his beloved Rosie had owned and operated for years. Rosie, while paying lip service to William's mal-adies, insisted he eat according to her personal gastromedical dictates. She feels a glass of sherry will remedy any known debilitation. God only knew what her spicy Hungarian cooking had done to his digestive system.

"Henry?"

Henry said, "Yo," his voice emanating from the bedroom. I heard footsteps and he came around the corner, his face wreathed in smiles when he caught sight of me. "Well, Kinsey. You're home again. Come on in. I'll be right there."

He disappeared. I let myself into the kitchen. He'd pulled his big soup kettle from the cupboard. There was a bunch of celery in the dish rack, two large cans of crushed tomatoes on the counter, a package of frozen corn and one of black-eyed peas. "I'm making vegetable soup," he called out. "You can join me for supper."

I raised my voice so he could hear me room to room. "I'll say 'yes,' but I gotta warn you you're risking a cold. I came back with a real doozie. What are you doing back there?"

Henry reappeared, bringing a stack of fresh hand towels into the kitchen with him. "Folding laundry," he said. He tucked the towels in a drawer, keeping one out for current use. He stopped and squinted at me. "What's that on your elbow?"

I checked the skin on my forearm. The self-tanning lotion had darkened decidedly. My elbow now looked as if it had been swabbed with Betadine in preparation for surgery. "That's my Tan in a Can. You know I hate to sunbathe. It'll wash off in another week. At least, I'm *assuming* it will. What's been happening around here? You seem cheerier than I've seen you in months."

"Sit down, sit down. You want a cup of tea?"

I took a seat on his rocker. "This is fine," I said. "I'll only stay a minute. I took some medication for my nose and I can barely stand up. I'm thinking to crawl back in bed for the day."

Henry took out a can opener and began to crank open the two tins of crushed tomatoes, which he dumped into the kettle. "You'll never guess what happened. William's moved in with Rosie."

"You mean for good?"

"I hope. I finally understood that what he did with his life was simply none of my business. I kept thinking I had to save him. It was all so inappropriate. It's a bad match, but so what? Let him discover that for himself. In the meantime, it was making me crazy to have him underfoot. All that talk about sickness and death, depression and palpitations and his diet. My God. Let him 'share' that with her. Let them bore each other senseless."

"Sounds like the perfect attitude. When did he move out?"

"Over the weekend. I helped him pack. I even pitched in and moved some of his boxes. It's been heaven ever since." He flashed me a smile as he picked up the celery and pulled the stalks apart. He rinsed three ribs, then took a knife from the rack and began to dice them. "Go on and hit the sack. You look exhausted. Pop back over here at six and I'll feed you some soup."

"I may take a rain check," I said. "With luck, I'll sleep straight through."

I let myself into my apartment and staggered up to the loft, where I pulled my shoes off and buried myself in my quilt.

My phone rang thirty minutes later and I dragged myself up from the drug-induced depths of sleep. It was Rupert Valbusa. He'd had a brief chat with Lieutenant Whiteside, who'd impressed upon him the importance of getting the composite done. He was going out of town for the next five days, but if I was free, he'd be in his studio for another hour. Inwardly I groaned, but I really had no choice. I made a note of the address, which was not far from me in an industrial/commercial area just off the beach. A former Bekins warehouse on lower Anaconda Street had been converted to a complex of artists' studios available for lease. I put my shoes on and did what I could to make myself presentable. I grabbed my car keys, a jacket, and the photographs of Wendell.

Outside, the air was damp with the breezes coming off the ocean. As I drove along Cabana Boulevard, I could see patches of pale blue where the cloud cover was breaking up. By late afternoon we might have an hour of sunshine. I parked on a narrow tree-lined side street, locked my VW, and walked around the warehouse to the north side, entering the building through a door flanked by two impressive metal sculptures. The interior corridors had been painted stark white, hung with framed works of the artists currently in residence. The ceiling in the hallway rose three stories to the roof, where a series of slanted windows admitted broad shafts of daylight. Valbusa was on the top floor. I climbed the three flights of metal stairs at the far end of the hallway, my footsteps ringing dully against the painted cinder block walls. When I reached the landing at the top, I could hear the muffled strains of country music. I knocked on Valbusa's door and the radio was doused.

Rupert Valbusa was Hispanic, stocky, and muscular. I put him in his mid-thirties, with broad shoulders and a barrel chest. His eyes were dark under the unruly ruffle of his brows. His dark hair was thick, cut full around his face. We introduced ourselves, shaking hands at the door before I followed him in. When he turned to walk away I could see a narrow braid extending halfway down his back. He wore a white T-shirt, cutoffs, and a pair of tire-soled leather sandals. His legs were nicely shaped, the contours defined by dark, silky hairs.

His studio was vast and chilly, with a concrete floor and wide counters circling the perimeter. The air smelled of damp clay, and most surfaces seemed to be coated in the chalky residue of dried porcelain. Big blocks of malleable clay had been swaddled in plastic. He had a kick wheel and a power wheel, two kilns, and countless shelves lined with ceramic bowls that had been fired but not yet glazed. At the end of one counter he had a dry copier, an answering machine, and a light box for slides. There were also stacks of dog-eared sketchbooks, jars of drawing pens and pencils, charcoals, and watercolor brushes. Three easels had been set up, bearing abstract oil paintings in various stages of completion.

"Is there anything you don't do?"

"Not all of this is mine. I've taken on a couple of students, though I don't much like to teach. Some of this is their work. You do any art yourself?"

"I'm afraid not, but I envy those who do."

He moved to the nearest counter, where he picked up a manila envelope with a photograph inside. "Lieutenant Whiteside sent this over for you. Looks like he included an address for the guy's wife." He handed me a slip of paper, which I tucked in my pocket.

"Thanks. That's great. It'll save me some time."

"This the dude who interests you?" Rupert passed me the picture. I glanced at the grainy eight-by-eleven black-and-white head shot. "That's him. His name is

Wendell Jaffe. I've got a few more here just to give you some other views."

I pulled out the collection of shots I'd been using for ID purposes and watched as Rupert sorted through them with care, arranging them according to some system of his own. "Good-looking fellow. What'd he do?"

"He and his partner were into real estate development, some of which was legitimate until the bottom dropped. In the end, they ripped off their investors in what's commonly known as a Ponzi scheme, promising big returns when they were really just paying off the old investors with the new investors' money. Jaffe must have realized the end was in sight. He disappeared off his boat in the course of a fishing trip and was never heard from again. Until now, of course. His partner served some jail time, but he's out again."

"This is ringing a bell. I think the *Dispatch* ran an article about Jaffe a couple of years ago."

"Probably. It's one of those big unsolved mysteries that capture the public imagination. An alleged suicide, but there's been a lot of speculation since."

Rupert studied the pictures. I could see his eyes trace the contours of Wendell's face, hairline, the distance between his eyes. He brought the picture up close to his face, angling it toward the window where the light was streaming in. "How tall?"

"About six four. Weight maybe two thirty. He's in his late fifties, but he's in good shape. I saw him in a bathing suit." I wiggled my eyebrows. "Not bad."

Rupert moved over to the copier and ran off two copies of the photograph on what looked like rough-textured beige watercolor paper. He dragged a stool over to the window. "Grab a seat," he said, nodding toward a cluster of unpainted wooden stools.

I hauled one over to the window and perched beside him, watching while he sorted through his drawing pens and pulled four from the jar. He leaned forward and opened a drawer, taking out a box of Prisma color pencils and a box of pastel chalks. He had an air of distraction, and the questions he began to ask me seemed almost ritualistic, his way of preparing for the task at hand. He secured a copy of the photograph to a board with a clip at the top. "Let's start at the top. How's his hair these days?"

"White. It used to be medium brown. It's thinner at the temples than in the photograph."

Rupert picked up the white pencil and masked out the dark hair. The immediate effect was to make Wendell seem twenty years older and very tanned.

I found myself smiling. "Pretty good," I said. "I think he's had his nose trimmed down. Here at the bridge and maybe some shaved along here." Where my finger touched the nubby paper, Rupert would shade and contour with fine strokes of chalk or pencil, both of which he wielded with an air of confidence. The nose on the paper became narrow and aristocratic.

Rupert began to chat idly while he worked. "It's always amazed me how many variations can be wrung from the basic components of the human face. Given that most of us come equipped with the standard-issue features . . . one nose, one mouth, two eyes, two ears. We not only look entirely different from one another, but we can usually identify each other on sight. Do portraits like I do, and you really begin to appreciate the subtleties of the process." Rupert's unhesitating pencil strokes were adding years and weight, transforming a six-year-old image to its current-day counterpart. He paused, indicating the eye socket. "What about the fold in here? Has he had his eyes done?"

"I don't think so."

"Droopiness? Bags? Five years would etch in a few lines, I should think."

"Maybe some, but not a lot. His cheeks seemed more sunken. Almost gaunt," I said.

He worked for a moment. "How about this?"

I studied the drawing. "That's pretty close."

By the time he was finished I was looking at a reasonable facsimile of the man I'd seen. "I think you got it. He looks good." I watched as he sprayed the paper with a fixative.

"I'll run off a dozen copies and get them over to Lieutenant Whiteside," he said. "You want some yourself? I can run you a dozen."

"That'd be great."

# 7

I HAD A quick bowl of soup with Henry and then downed half a pot of coffee, managing in the process to offset my lethargy and kick into high gear again. It was time to make contact with some of the principals in the cast. At 7:00 I drove south along the coastline toward Perdido/Olvidado. It wouldn't be dark for another hour yet, but the light was fading, the air saturated with an ashen wash of twilight. Billows of fog blowing in from the ocean concealed all but the most obvious aspects of the land. Steep hills, pleated with erosion, rose up on my left, while to the right, the heaving gray Pacific was pounding against the shore. The quarter moon was becoming visible in the thick haze of the sky, a pale crescent of light barely discernible in the mist. Along the horizon, the offshore oil platforms lay at anchor like a twinkling armada. The island of St. Michael, and two that are known as the Rose and the Cross, are threaded like beads along the Cross Islands Fault, the entire east-west structural zone undercut by parallel cracks. The Santa Ynez Fault, the North Channel Slope Fault, Pitas Point, Oak Ridge, the San Cayetano, and the San Jacinto faults branch off like tributaries from the granddaddy of them all—the great San Andreas Fault, which cuts obliquely across the Transverse Range. From the air, the San Andreas Fault forms an ominous ridge, running for miles, like the track left by a giant mole tunneling underground.

There was a time, long before the earth's folding caused the mountains to buckle upward, when the Perdido basin was a hundred miles long and much of California was a lowland covered by vast Eocene seas. Back then this whole region was under water as far as the Arizona border. The petroleum deposits were actually derived from marine organisms, the sediment, in places, nearly thirteen thousand feet thick. There are times when I feel the hairs rising up along my arms at the vision of a world so wildly different from ours. I imagine the changes, millions of years speeded up like time-lapse photography, in which the land heaves and snaps, thrusting, plunging, and shifting in a thunderous convulsion.

I glanced out at the horizon. Twenty-four of the thirty-two platforms along the California coast are near Santa Teresa and Perdido counties, nine of them within three miles of shore. I'd heard the dispute about whether those old platforms could withstand a big 7.0-magnitude trembler. The experts were divided. On one side of the debate were the geologists and representatives of the state Seismic Safety Commission, who kept pointing out that the oldest off-shore oil platforms were built between 1958 and 1969 before the petroleum industry adopted uniform design codes. Reassuring us of our comfort and security were spokesmen for the oil companies who owned the rigs. Gosh, it was baffling. I tried to picture the effect: all those rigs collapsing, oil spewing into the ocean in a gathering storm of black. I thought about the current contamination of beaches, raw sewage spilling into oceans and streams, the hole in the ozone, forests being stripped, the toxic-waste dumps, the merry plunder of mankind added to the drought and the famine that nature dishes up annually as a matter of course. It's hard to know what's actually going to get us first. Sometimes I think we should just blow the whole planet and get it over with. It's the suspense that's killing me.

I passed a stretch of state beach and rounded the point, sliding into the town of Perdido from its westernmost edge. I took the first Perdido off ramp, cruising through the downtown business district while I got my bearings. The wide main street was edged with diagonal head-in parking—lots of pickup trucks and recreational vehicles in evidence. A convertible proceeded slowly down the street behind me with its car radio booming. The combination of brass instruments and thunderous bass reminded me of the thumping passage of a Fourth of July parade. The windows on every other business seemed to be decked with handsome canvas awnings, and I wondered if the mayor had a brother-in-law in the business.

The housing tract where Dana Jaffe now lived was probably developed in the seventies when Perdido enjoyed a brief real estate boom. The house itself was a story and a half, charcoal-gray stucco with white wood trim. Most of the homes in the neighborhood had three and four vehicles parked in the driveways, suggesting a population more dense than the "single-family residential" zoning implied. I pulled into the drive behind a late-model Honda.

Twilight was deepening. Zinnias and marigolds had been planted in clusters along the walk. In the dim illumination from an ornamental fixture, I could see that the shrubs had been neatly trimmed, the grass mowed, and some effort made to distinguish the house from its mirror-image neighbors. Trellising had been added along the fence line. The honeysuckle vines trained up the latticework lent at least the illusion of privacy, perfuming the air with incredible sweetness. As I rang the bell, I extracted a business card from the depths of my handbag. The front porch was stacked high with moving cartons, all packed and sealed. I wondered where she was headed.

After a pause, Dana Jaffe answered the door with a telephone receiver tucked in the crook of her neck. She'd toted the instrument across the room, trailing twenty-five feet of cord. She was the kind of woman I've always found intimidating, with her honey-colored hair, her smoothly sculpted cheekbones, her gaze cool and level. She had a straight, narrow nose, a strong chin, and a slight overbite. A glint of very white teeth peeped out from full lips that, at rest, wouldn't quite close. She put the face of the receiver against her chest, muffling our conversation for the person on the other end. "Yes?"

I held out my card so she could read my name. "I'd like to talk to you."

She glanced at the card with a little frown of puzzlement before she handed it back. She held up an index finger, making an apologetic face as she gestured me in. I crossed the threshold and stepped into the living room just ahead of her, my gaze following the path of the telephone cord into a dining room that had been converted into office space. Apparently she did some kind of wedding consulting. I could see bridal magazines stacked everywhere. A bulletin board that hung above the desk was covered with photographs, sample invitations, illustrations of wedding bouquets, and articles about honeymoon cruises. A schedule with fifteen to twenty names and dates indicated upcoming nuptials that she needed to keep abreast of.

The carpeting was white shag, the couch and chairs upholstered in steel blue canvas, with throw pillows in off-white and seafoam green. Aside from a cluster of family photographs in antique silver frames, there were no knickknacks. The room was interspersed with a variety of glossy house plants, big healthy specimens that seemed to saturate the air with oxygen. This was fortunate given all the noxious cigarette smoke in the air. The furnishings were handsome, probably inexpensive knockoffs of designer brands.

Dana Jaffe was pencil thin, wearing tight, faded jeans and a plain white T-shirt, tennis shoes without socks. When I wear the same outfit, it looks like I'm all set to change the oil in my car. On her, the outfit had a careless elegance. She had her hair pulled into a knot at the nape of her neck, tied with a scarf. I could see now that the blond was laced with silver, but the effect was artless, as if she were confident the aging process would only add interest to a face already honed and chiseled. The overbite made her mouth seem pouty and probably kept her from being labeled "beautiful," whatever that consists of. She would be relegated to categories like "interesting" or "attractive," though personally I'd have killed for a face like hers, strong and arresting, with a flawless complexion.

She picked up the cigarette she'd left in the ashtray, dragging on it deeply as she went on with her conversation. "I don't think you'll be happy with that," she was saying. "Well, the style's not going to be flattering. You told me Corey's cousin was on the hefty side. . . . Okay, a blimp. That's exactly what I'm talking about. You don't want to put a peplum on a blimp. . . . A full skirt. . . . Uh-hun, right. That's going to minimize heavy legs and hips. . . . No, no, no. I'm not talking about bulky fullness. . . . I understand. Maybe something with a slightly dropped waist. I think we should find a dress with a shaped neckline, too, because that's going to pull the eye upward. Do you understand what I'm saying? . . . Uhm-hmmm. . . . Well, why don't I go through my books here and I'll come up with some suggestions. You might have Corey pick up a couple of brides magazines from the supermarket. We can talk tomorrow. . . . Okay. . . . All right, fine. I'll call you back. . . . You're entirely welcome. . . . You too."

She replaced the receiver and gave the telephone cord a little looping flap, pulling the length of it toward her. She extinguished the cigarette in an ashtray on her desk and then moved into the living room, smoke still trailing from her mouth. I took a quick moment to scan the room. In the small slice of family room that I could see, there were miscellaneous items of baby paraphernalia: a playpen, a high chair, a wind-up swing guaranteed to put an infant to sleep if it didn't generate a lot of puking first.

"You'd never guess I'm a grandma," she said with irony when she caught my eye.

I had placed my business card on the coffee table, and I saw her glance at it again with curiosity. I tucked in a hasty question before she had a chance to quiz me. "Are you moving? I saw the boxes on the porch. It looks like you're all set."

"Not me. My son and his wife. They've just bought a little house." She leaned over and picked up the card. "Excuse me, I'd like to know what this is about. If it has to do with Brian, you'll need to talk to his attorney. I'm not at liberty to discuss his situation."

"This is not about Brian. It's about Wendell."

Her gaze became fixed. "Have a seat," she said, indicating a nearby chair. She sat down on the edge of the couch, pulling an ashtray in closer to her. She lit another cigarette, her movements brisk, dragging deeply as she arranged both her lighter and the pack of Eve 100's on the table in front of her. "Were you acquainted with him?"

"Not at all," I said. I perched on a chrome-and-gray-leather director's chair that squawked beneath my weight. Sounded like I'd made a rude butt noise as a joke.

She blew two streams of smoke from her nose. "Because he's dead, you know. He's been gone for years. He got into trouble and he killed himself."

"That's why I'm here. Last week, the California Fidelity agent who sold Wendell his life insurance policy . . ."

"Dick What's-his-name . . . Mills."

"That's correct. Mr. Mills was vacationing in a little Mexican resort and spotted Wendell in a bar."

She burst out laughing. "Oh, sure, right."

I stirred uncomfortably. "It's true."

She cut the power on the smile by half. "Don't be silly. What are we talking here, a seance or something? Wendell's *dead*, my dear."

"As I understand it, Dick Mills did quite a bit of business with him. I gather he knew Wendell well enough to make the initial ID. I'm handling the follow-up."

She continued to smile, but it was all form and no content. She blinked at me with interest. "He actually talked to him? You'll have to forgive my skepticism, but I'm having a problem with this. The two of them had a conversation?"

I shook my head. "Dick was on his way to the airport at the time, and he didn't want Wendell to catch sight of him. As soon as he got home, he called one of the CF vice-presidents, who turned around and hired me to fly down there. At this point, the identification isn't positive, but the chances are good. It looks like he's not only alive, but headed back to the area."

"I don't believe it. There's been some mistake." Her tone was emphatic, but her expression suggested she was waiting for the punch line, a half smile flickering. I wondered how many times she'd played the scene in her head. Some police detective or an FBI agent sitting in her living room, giving her the news that Wendell was alive and well . . . or that his body had finally been recovered. She'd probably lost track of what she wanted to hear. I could see her struggle with a number of conflicting attitudes, most of which were bad.

Agitated, she took a drag of her cigarette and then blew out a mouthful of smoke, her mouth curling up in a parody of mirth as she tried on a new reaction. "Let me hazard a guess here. I'll bet there's money involved. A little payoff, is that it?"

"Why would I do that?" I asked.

"What's the point, then? Why tell me about it? I couldn't care less."

"I was hoping you'd let me know if Wendell tried to get in touch."

"You think Wendell would try to get in touch with *me*? This is dumb. Don't be ridiculous."

"I don't know what to tell you, Mrs. Jaffe. I can understand how you feel. . . ."

"What are you *talking* about? The man is dead! Don't you get it? He turned out to be a con artist, a common crook. I've had trouble enough dealing with all the people he cheated. You're not going to turn around now and tell me he's still out there," she snapped.

"We think he faked his own death, probably to avoid prosecution for fraud and grand theft." I reached for my handbag. "I have a picture if you want to see him. This was done by a police artist. It's not exact, but it's close. I saw him myself." I pulled out the photocopy of the picture, unfolded the paper, and passed it over to her.

She studied it with an intensity that was almost embarrassing. "This isn't Wendell. This looks nothing like him." She tossed it back toward the table. The paper sailed off the edge like an airplane taking off. "I thought they did these with computers. What's the matter? Are the cops here too cheap?" She snatched up my business card again and read my name. I could see that her hand had begun to shake. "Look, Ms. Millhone. Maybe I should explain something. Wendell put me through hell. Whether he's dead or alive is immaterial from my perspective. You want to know why?"

I could see she was working herself into a snit. "I understand you had him declared dead," I ventured.

"That's right. You got it. Very good," she said. "I've collected his life insurance, that's how dead he is. This is over and done. Finito, you savvy? I'm getting on with my life. You understand what I'm saying? I'm not interested in Wendell one way or the other. I've got other problems I'm coping with at the moment, and as far as I'm concerned—"

The telephone began to ring and she glanced back with annoyance. "The machine will pick up."

The machine clicked in, and Dana intoned the standard advice about a name, telephone number, and a message. Without even thinking about it, we both turned to listen. "Please wait for the beep," Dana's recorded voice admonished. We paused dutifully, waiting for the beep.

I could hear a woman using the artificial message-giving voice that machines inspire. "Hello, Dana. This is Miriam Salazar. Your name was given to me by Judith Prancer as a bridal consultant. My daughter, Angela, is getting married next April, and I just thought we should have a preliminary conversation. I'd appreciate a call back. Thanks." She left her telephone number.

Dana smoothed her hair back, checking the scarf at the nape of her neck. "Jesus, this has been a crazy summer," she commented idly. "I've had two and three weddings every weekend, plus I'm getting ready for a midsummer bridal fair."

I stared at her, saying nothing. Like many people, she was capable of delivering informational asides while in the midst of a highly charged emotional conversation. I hardly knew where to take the matter next. Wait until she figured out that California Fidelity was going to reclaim the insurance money if Wendell showed up in the flesh.

I shouldn't even have allowed the thought to enter my head, because the minute it occurred to me she seemed to read my mind.

"Oh, wait. Don't tell me. I just collected half a million bucks. I hope the insurance company doesn't think I'm going to give the money *back*."

"You'd have to talk to them about that. Generally, they don't pay death benefits if a guy's not really dead. They're kind of cranky that way."

"Now just a goddamn minute. If he's alive—which I'm not buying for a minute—but if it turned out he was, it's hardly *my* responsibility."

"Well, it certainly isn't *theirs*."

"I've waited years for that money. I'd be dead broke without it. You don't understand the kind of struggle I've been through. I've had two boys to raise with no help from anyone."

"You'd probably be smart to talk to an attorney," I said.

"An attorney? What for? I didn't do anything. I've suffered enough because of Wendell goddamn Jaffe, and if you think for one minute I'm giving the money back, you're crazy. You want to collect, you'll have to get it from him."

"Mrs. Jaffe, I don't make policy decisions for California Fidelity. All I do is investigate and file reports. I have no control over what they do—"

"I didn't *cheat*," she cut in.

"No one's accusing you of cheating."

She cupped a hand around her ear. "Yet," she said. "Don't I hear a big fat 'yet' at the end of that sentence?"

"What you hear me saying is take it up with them. I'm only here because I thought you should be aware of what's going on. If Wendell tries to get in touch . . ."

"Jesus! Would you stop this? What earthly reason would he have to get in touch with me?"

"Because he probably read about Brian's escapades in all the Mexican papers."

That shut her up momentarily. She stared at me with the panicky blank look of a woman with a train bearing down the track at her and a car that won't start. Her voice dropped. "I can't deal with this. I'm sorry, but this is all nonsense as far as I'm concerned. I'll have to ask you to leave." She rose to her feet, and I rose at the same time.

"Hey, Mom?"

Dana jumped.

Her oldest son, Michael, was coming down the stairs. He caught sight of us and paused. "Oh, sorry. I didn't know you were busy down here." He was lanky and slim, with a dark mop of silky hair much in need of a cut. His face was narrow, nearly pretty, with large dark eyes and long lashes. He wore jeans, a sweatshirt emblazoned with a fake college decal, and high-top tennis shoes.

Dana flashed a bright smile at him to disguise her distress. "We're just finishing. What is it, baby? Did you guys want something to eat?"

"I thought I'd make a run. Juliet's out of cigarettes

and the baby needs Pampers. I just wondered if you needed anything."

"Actually, you might pick up some milk for breakfast. We're almost out," she replied. "Get a half gallon of low-fat and a quart of orange juice, if you would. There's some money on the kitchen table."

"I got some," he said.

"You keep that, honey. I'll get it." She moved off toward the kitchen.

Michael continued to the bottom of the steps and snagged his jacket from the newel post where it was draped. He nodded at me shyly, perhaps mistaking me for one of his mother's bridal clients. Despite the fact that I'd been married twice, I've never had a formal wedding. The closest I'd ever come was a bride of Frankenstein outfit one Halloween when I was in the second grade. I had fangs and fake blood, and my aunt drew clumsy black stitches up and down my face. My bridal veil was affixed to my head with numerous bobby pins, most of which I'd lost by the time the evening came to an end. The dress itself was a cut-down version of a ballerina costume ... some kind of *Swan Lake* number with an ankle-length skirt. My aunt had added sparkles, making squiggles with a tube of Elmer's glue that she sprinkled with dime-store glitter. I'd never felt so glamorous. I remember looking at myself solemnly in the mirror that night in a halo of netting, thinking it was probably the most beautiful dress I would ever own. Sure enough, I've never had anything quite like it since, though, in truth, it's not the dress so much as the feeling I miss.

Dana came back into the living room and pressed a twenty into Michael's hand. They had a brief chat about the errand. While I waited for them to finish their business, I picked up one of the silver-framed photos. It looked like Wendell in high school, which is to say dorky-looking with a bad haircut.

Michael left for the store, and Dana moved over to the table where I was standing. She took the picture from my hand and set it back on the tabletop. I said, "Is that Wendell in high school?"

She nodded, distracted. "Cottonwood Academy, which has gone out of business since. His was the last class to graduate. I gave his class ring to Michael. I'll give Brian his college ring when the time comes."

"When what time comes?"

"Oh, some special occasion. I tell them it's something their father and I always talked about."

"That's laying it on a bit thick, isn't it?"

Dana shrugged. "Just because I think Wendell's a schmuck doesn't mean they have to. I want them to have a man to look up to, even if he isn't real. They need a role model."

"So you give them an idealized version?"

"It might be a mistake, but what else can I do?" she said, coloring.

"Yeah, really. Especially when he pulls a deal like this."

"I know I've given him more credit than he deserves, but I don't want to bad-mouth the man to his sons."

"I understand the impulse. I'd probably do the same in your place," I said.

She reached out impulsively and touched my arm. "Please leave us alone. I don't know what's going on, but I don't want them brought into it."

"I won't bother you if I can help it, but you're still going to have to tell them."

"Why?"

"Because Wendell could beat you to it, and you might not like the effect."

# 8

IT WAS NEARLY 10:00 P.M. by the time I hoofed it through the strip lot behind the Santa Teresa Yacht Club. After I left Dana Jaffe, I hit the 101 north, tearing back up the coast to my apartment, where I hastily tried on several hangers' worth of hand-me-downs Vera'd passed along to me. In her unbiased opinion I'm a complete fashion nerd, and she's trying to teach me the rudiments of "shiek." Vera's into these Annie Hall ensembles that look like you're preparing for a life sleeping on sewer grates. Jackets over vests over tunics over pants. The only thing I lack is a grocery cart for the rest of my possessions.

I sorted through the garments, wondering which items were supposed to go with which. I need a personal trainer when it comes to this shit, someone to explain the underlying strategy. Since Vera is twenty pounds heavier and a good five inches taller, I bypassed the slacks, imagining I'd look like Droopy of the Seven

Dwarfs. She'd given me two long skirts with elasticized waists, swearing either would look great with my black leather boots. There was also a forties-looking rayon drop-waist print dress with an ankle-length skirt. I pulled the garment over my head and regarded myself in the mirror. I'd seen Vera wear this, and she'd looked like a vamp. I looked like I was six, playing dress-up in the discards from my aunt's rag bag.

I went back to one of the long skirts, a black washable silk. I think she intended for me to hem the length, but I simply rolled it up at the waist, a little doughnut effect. She'd also given me a tunic top in a color she called taupe (a blend of gray and old cigar butts), with a long white vest that went over both. She'd told me I could dress up the outfit with accessories. Big duh. Like I really had some kind of clue how to make that work. I searched my drawers for jewelry to no avail and finally decided to wear the long crocheted runner my aunt had made for the dresser top. I gave it a little flap to get all the woofies out and then looped it around my neck with the ends hanging down the front. Looked good to me, kind of devil-may-care, like Isadora Duncan or Amelia Earhart.

The yacht club sits on stilts overlooking the beach with the harbormaster's office nearby and the long concrete arm of the breakwater curving out to the left. The sound of the surf was thunderous that night, like the rumble of cars moving over wooden trestles. The ocean was oddly agitated, the far-flung effects from some violent weather pattern that would probably never reach us. A dense haze hung in the air like a scrim through which I caught shadowy glimpses of the moon-tinted horizon. The sand glowed white, and the boulders piled up around the foundations of the building were draped with strands of kelp.

Even from the sidewalk down below, I could hear the trumpeting laughter of the heavy drinkers. I climbed the wide wooden steps to the entrance and in through the glass doors. A second set of stairs ascended to the right, and I made my way up toward the smoke and recorded music in the bar above. The room was L-shaped, diners occupying the long arm, drinkers confined to the short, which was just as well. The noise level was oppressive given the fact that most of the dinner crowd had departed and the bar was only half-filled. The floor was carpeted, the entire upper story wrapped in windows that overlooked the Pacific. By day, club members were treated to panoramic ocean views. At night, the black glass threw back smudged reflections, pointing up the need for the rigorous application of Windex. When I reached the maître d's pulpit, I paused, watching him approach me from across the room.

"Yes, ma'am," he said. I guessed he'd been recently promoted from his job as headwaiter because he held his left arm at an angle, a ready rack for some wine towel he no longer had to tote.

"I'm looking for Carl Eckert. Is he here tonight?"

I saw his gaze flick downward, taking in my scruffy boots, the long skirt, the vest, shoulder bag, and my ill-cut hair, which the sea wind had tossed into moplike perfection. "Is he expecting you?" His tone suggested he'd expect invading Martians first.

I held out a discreetly folded five-dollar bill. "Now he is," I said.

The fellow slipped the bill in his pocket without checking the denomination, which made me wish I had given him a single. He indicated a gentleman sitting at a window table by himself. I had plenty of time to study him as I crossed the room. I put him in his early fifties, still of an age where he'd be referred to as "youthful." He was silver-haired and stocky. His once handsome face had gone soft now along the jawline, though the effect was still nice. While most of the men in the bar were dressed casually, Carl Eckert wore a conservative dark gray herringbone suit, with a light gray shirt and navy wool tie with a grid of light gray. I wound my way among the tables, wondering what the hell I was going to say to him. He saw me headed in his direction and focused on me as I drew within range. "Carl?"

He smiled at me politely. "That's right."

"Kinsey Millhone. May I join you?"

I held out my hand. He half rose from his chair and leaned forward courteously, shaking hands with me. His grip was aggressive, the skin on his palm icy cold from his drink. "If you like," he said. His eyes were blue, and his gaze was unyielding. He gestured toward a chair.

I placed my handbag on the floor and eased onto the seat adjacent to his. "I hope I'm not intruding."

"That depends on what you want." His smile was pleasant but fleeting and never really reached as far as his eyes.

"It looks like Wendell Jaffe is alive."

His expression shifted into neutral and his body went still, animation suspended as if from a momentary power loss. For a split second it flashed on me that he might have been in touch with Wendell since his disappearance. He was apparently willing to take my word for it, which saved all the bullshit Dana'd put me through. He assimilated the information, sparing me additional expressions of shock or surprise. There was no hint of denial or disbelief. He seemed to shift into gear again. He reached in his jacket pocket smoothly and took out a pack of cigarettes, his way of stalling until he could figure out what I was up to. He shook several cigarettes into view and held the pack out for my selection.

I shook my head, refusing.

He put a cigarette between his lips. "Will it bother you if I smoke?"

"Not a bit. Go ahead." Actually I abhor smoking, but I wanted some information and I didn't think it was the time to voice my prejudice.

He struck a paper match and cupped his hands around the flame. He gave the match a shake and dropped it in the ashtray, easing the pack of matches back into his pocket again. I smelled sulfur and that first whiff of smoldering tobacco that to me smells like no other. Early mornings on the road, I catch the same scent drifting through the room vents in those hotels where the smokers aren't properly segregated from the rest of us.

"Would you like a drink?" he asked. "I'm about to order another round myself."

"I'd like that. Thanks."

"What'll it be?"

"Chardonnay would be fine."

He held his hand up for the waiter, who moved over to the table and took the order. Eckert was having Scotch.

Once the waiter disappeared, his attention came back to me and he focused his gaze. "Who are you? A cop? Narc? IRS, what?"

. "I'm a private detective, working for California Fidelity on the life insurance claim."

"Dana just collected on it, didn't she?"

"Two months ago."

A group of guys in the bar burst into sudden harsh laughter, and it forced Eckert to lean forward to make himself heard. "How did all this business come to light?"

"A retired CF insurance agent spotted him in Mexico last week. I was hired to fly down the next day to verify the report."

"And you actually verified that it was Wendell?"

"More or less," I said. "I never met Mr. Jaffe, so it'd be hard for me to swear it was him."

"But you did see him," he said.

"Or someone damn close. He's had surgery, of course. It's probably the first thing he did."

Carl stared at me blankly and then shook his head. A brief smile appeared. "I assume you've told Dana?"

"I just talked to her. She wasn't thrilled."

"I should think not." He seemed to search my face. "What's your name again?"

I took out a business card and passed it across the table. "You knew his kid was in trouble?" I asked.

Behind us, there was another burst of laughter, this one louder than the last. The guys were apparently having another tedious bawdy joke fest.

He glanced at my name on the card and tucked it in his shirt pocket. "I read about Brian in the paper," he said. "This is curious."

"What is?"

"The notion of Wendell. I was just thinking about him. Since his body never surfaced, I guess I always

had my doubts about his death. I never said much. I figured people would think I was unwilling to face the
facts. 'In denial,' they call it. Where's he been all this
time?"

"I didn't have a chance to ask."

"Is he still down there?"

"He checked out of the hotel in the dead of night and
that's the last I've seen of him. He may be on his way
back."

"Because of Brian," he said, instantly making the
connection.

"That's my guess. At any rate, it's the only lead we
have. Not really a lead, but at least a place to start."

"Why tell me?"

"In case he tries to make contact."

The waiter returned with our drinks and Carl looked
up. "Thanks, Jimmy. Put this on my tab, if you would."
He took the bill, tacked on a tip, and scrawled his name
across the bottom before he handed it back.

The waiter murmured, "Thank you, Mr. Eckert. Will
there be anything else?"

"We're fine."

"You have a good night."

Carl nodded absentmindedly, regarding me with speculation.

I reached in my handbag and pulled a copy from the
sheaf of composites Valbusa had done. "I have a picture
if you want to see it." I laid it on the table in front of
him.

Carl stuck his cigarette in the corner of his mouth,
squinting slightly from the smoke as he studied
Wendell's face. He shook his head, his smile bitter.
"What a fuck."

"I thought you might be glad to hear he was alive," I said.

"Hey, I went to jail because of him. Lot of people wanted a piece of my hide. When money goes down the toilet, someone has to take the blame. I didn't mind paying my debt, but I sure as hell hated paying his."

"Must have been hard."

"You have no idea. Once I filed bankruptcy, all the loans went into default. It was a mess. I don't want to get into that."

"If Wendell gets in touch, will you let me know?"

"Probably," he said. "I don't want to talk to him, that's for sure. He was a good friend. At least I thought he was."

There was another burst of laughter. He shifted restlessly and pushed his drink aside. "Let's go down to the boat. It's too fuckin' loud in here."

Without waiting for an answer, he got up and left the table. Startled, I grabbed my handbag and scurried after him.

The noise level dropped dramatically the minute we stepped outside. The air was cold and fresh. The wind had picked up, and the waves crashed against the seawall in a series of blasting sprays. Boom! A feathery plume, like a stalk of pampas grass, would dance along the breakwater and go down again, throwing off a splat of water that landed on the walk as if it were being thrown by the bucket.

When we reached the locked gate leading into Marina 1, he took out his card key and let us through. In a curiously gallant gesture, Carl put his hand on my elbow and guided me down the slippery wooden ramp. I could hear creaking sounds as the boats shifted in the harbor waters, bobbing and swaying with an occasional tinkling of metal on metal. Our footsteps formed an irregular rhythm as we clunked along the walkway.

The four marinas provide slips for about eleven hundred boats, protected from the open waters in an eighty-four-acre area. The wharf on one side is like the crook of a thumb with the breakwater curling toward it in a nearly completed circle in which the boats are nestled. In addition to visitors occupying temporary slips, there are usually a small number of permanent "live-aboards," using their boats as their primary residence. Key-secured restrooms provide toilets and showers, with a holding tank pump-out station located on the south side of the fuel dock. At the "J" dock we took a left, proceeding another thirty yards to the boat.

The *Captain Stanley Lord* was a thirty-five-foot Fuji ketch, derived from a John Alden–designed sailing vessel with the mainmast toward the bow. The exterior was painted an intense dark green with the trim in navy blue. Carl pulled himself up on the narrow deck and then extended a hand, pulling me up after him. In the dark I could make out the mainsheet and the mizzenmast, but not much else. He unlocked the door and slid the hatch forward. "Watch your head," he said as he moved down into the galley. "You know anything about boats?"

"Not much," I said. I eased carefully down four steep carpeted stairs into the galley behind him.

"This one has three headsails: a one fifty Genoa, a one ten working jib, and a storm jib, then the mainsail, of course, and the mizzen."

"Why is it called the *Captain Stanley Lord*? Who's he?"

"It's nautical lore. Wendell's sense of humor, such as it was. Stanley Lord was captain of the *Californian*, allegedly the only boat close enough to the *Titanic* to have helped with the rescue. Lord claimed he never picked up the distress signal, but a later investigation suggested he ignored the SOS. He was blamed for the extent of the disaster, and the scandal ruined his career. Wendell used the same name for the company: CSL Investments. I never did get it, but he thought it was amusing."

The interior had the cozy, unreal feeling of a doll's house, the kind of space I love best, compact and efficient, every square inch put to use. There was a diesel stove on my left, and on my right an assortment of seagoing equipment: radio, compass, a fire extinguisher, monitors for wind velocity and the electrical systems, the heater, main switch, and the engine start battery. I was picking up the faint smell of varnish, and I could see that one of the berth cushions still had a sales tag attached. All the upholstery was done in dark green canvas with the seams piped in white.

"Nice," I said.

He flushed with pleasure. "You like it?"

"It looks great," I said. I moved over to one of the berths and dropped my handbag, sitting down. I stretched my arm out along the cushion. "Comfortable," I remarked. "How long have you had it?"

"About a year," he said. "The IRS seized it shortly after Wendell disappeared. I was a guest of the feds for about eighteen months. After that, I was broke. Once I got a little money ahead, I had to track down the guy who'd bought it from the government. I went through an incredible rigmarole before he'd agree to sell. Not that he had much use for it. It was a mess when he finally turned it over to me. I don't know why people have to be such butts." He peeled off his suit coat and loosened his tie so he could ease the button on his shirt collar. "You want another white wine? I have some chilled."

"Half a glass," I said. He chatted about sailing for a while and then I brought the subject back to Wendell. "Where'd they find the boat?"

He opened a miniature refrigerator and took out a bottle of Chardonnay. "Off the Baja coast. There are huge shifting sand bars about six miles out. It looked like the boat had run aground and drifted loose again with the tide." He stripped the foil off the neck of the wine bottle, took an opener, and augered out the cork.

"He didn't have a crew?"

"He preferred to single-hand. I watched him sail that day. Orange sky, orange water with a slow, heaving swell. Had this weird feeling to it. Like the *Rime of the Ancient Mariner*. You study that in high school?"

I shook my head. "In high school, most of what I studied was cussin' and smokin' dope."

He smiled. "When you leave the Channel Islands, you sail out through a gap in the oil rigs. He turned and waved as he cast off. I watched until he left the harbor, and that's the last I ever saw of him." His tone was hypnotic, mild envy mixed with mild regret. He poured the wine in a stemmed glass and passed it over to me.

"Did you know what he was doing?"

"What *was* he doing? I guess I'm still not sure."

I said, "Apparently, he was skipping."

Eckert shrugged. "I knew he was feeling desperate. I didn't think he meant to pull a fast one. At the time—

especially when his last note to Dana came to light—I tried to accept the idea of his suicide. It didn't seem in character, but everybody else was convinced, so who was I to argue?" He poured half a glass of wine for himself, set the bottle aside, and sat down on the banquette across from mine.

"Not everybody," I corrected. "The police didn't like it much, and neither did CF."

"Will this make you a hero?"

"Only if we get the money back."

"Doesn't seem very likely. Dana's probably got it all spent."

I didn't want to think about that. "How'd you feel about Wendell's 'death' at the time?"

"Terrible, of course. Actually, I missed him, even with the flak I took. Strange thing is, he told me some of it. I didn't believe him, but he tried to let me know."

"He told you he was leaving?"

"Well, he hinted as much. I mean, he never spelled it out. It was one of those statements you can interpret any way you want. He came to me, I think in March, maybe six or seven weeks before he sailed. Said, 'Carl, buddy, I'm bailing. This whole fuckin' gig is comin' down around our heads. I can't take it anymore. It's too much.' Or words to that effect. I thought the guy was just blowing smoke. I knew we had big problems, but we'd been up against it before and we'd always come out okay. I figured this was just one more hairy episode in the 'Carl and Wendell Show.' Next thing I know they find his boat drifting in the ocean. Looking back, you think, well . . . when he said 'bailing' did he mean he'd kill himself or cut out?"

"But you were stuck either way, yes?"

"Yes indeed. First thing they did was start checking back through the books. I guess I could have walked out the door then, with just the clothes on my back, but I couldn't see the point. I had nowhere to go. I didn't have a cent, so I was forced to ride it out. Unfortunately, I had no idea the extent of what he'd done."

"Was it actually fraud?"

"Oh, big time. It was major. The days went by and all this shit came to light. He'd been stripping the company till there was nothing left. In the letter he left, he claimed he'd been pouring every dime back in, but I didn't see any evidence to support the claim. What did I know? By the time I understood just how bad it was, there was no escape. I didn't even have a way to recoup my personal losses." He paused and shrugged. "What can I say? With Wendell gone, there was just us chickens left. I gave 'em everything. I copped a plea and took the jail time just to get it over with. Now you tell me he's alive. What a joke."

"Are you bitter?"

"Of course." He leaned his arm against the back of the banquette and rubbed his forehead idly. "I can understand his wanting out. At first I didn't realize the extent of his betrayal. I felt sorry for Dana and the kids, but I couldn't do anything about it if the guy was dead." He shrugged and sent me a rueful smile, moving with sudden energy. "What the hell. It's over with and you have to move on."

"That seems generous."

He gestured carelessly. He glanced at his watch. "I'm going to have to call this a day. I have a breakfast meeting in the morning at seven o'clock sharp. I need to get some sleep. Shall I walk you out?"

I got up and set my empty wineglass aside. "I can do it," I said. "It's just a straight shot to the gate." I reached out and shook his hand. "I appreciate your time. You'll probably hear from me again. Do you still have my card?"

He pulled a corner of it from his shirt pocket to assure me it was there.

"If Wendell gets in touch, could you let me know?"

"Absolutely," he said.

I eased my way up the galley stairs, ducking my head as I emerged on deck. Behind me, I was conscious of Eckert's continuing gaze, his smile bemused as he watched me depart. Weird, but in retrospect, Dana Jaffe's response had seemed the truer.

# 9

THE WALK BACK to my place took less than ten minutes.
I was still wide awake, braced by the sea air. Instead of
opening the gate and going into the backyard, I turned
and headed down the street to Rosie's Tavern, which
was located half a block away.

In the old days, Rosie's was perpetually deserted,
cavernous and dimly lighted, no doubt under constant
surveillance by the health police. I used to meet clients
there because nobody ever bothered us. As a single
woman, I could drop in anytime it suited me without attracting the unwanted attentions of bounders and cads.
Rosie might harass me, but nobody else would. Recently, the place has been discovered by sports nuts, and
a variety of teams seem to use it as a hangout, especially on occasions when they've just won a trophy and
feel the need for a parade. Rosie, who can otherwise be
unbearably disagreeable, actually seems to enjoy all the
testosterone and hysteria. In an unprecedented move,

she's even taken to displaying their hardware on the shelf behind the bar, which now boasts a permanent exhibit of winged silver angels holding globes above their heads. Tonight, the bowling championship. Tomorrow, the free world.

As usual, the place was jumping and my favorite table in the rear was occupied by a gang of rowdies. There was no sign of Rosie, but William was perched on a stool at the bar, surveying the premises with a look of sublime satisfaction. All the patrons seemed to know him, and there was much good-natured bantering going back and forth.

Henry was seated at a table by himself, his head bent above a pad of paper, where he was mapping out a crossword puzzle entitled "I Spy with My Little Eye." He'd been working on this one for the better part of a week, using espionage novels and old television shows as the underlying theme. He published regularly in the little crossword puzzle books you see in grocery store lines. Aside from the fact that he picks up some extra money, he's actually known by name among crossword puzzle buffs. He was wearing chinos and a white T-shirt, his face creased with concentration. I took the liberty of pulling out an extra chair at his table, turning it around so that the back rested against the table. I straddled the chair and rested my arms along the top rail.

Henry sent an irritated look in my direction and then relaxed when he saw it was me. "I thought you were one of 'them.' "

I looked around at the crowd. "Where'd we go wrong? A year ago there was never anybody in the place. Now it's a zoo. How's it going?"

"I need an eight-letter word that starts with 'I.' It can end in anything . . . more or less."

A word flashed through my head, and I counted on my fingers. "Impostor," I said.

He stared at me blankly, doing the mental arithmetic. "Not bad. I'll take it. How about five letters down—"

"Stop right there," I said, cutting in. "You know I'm terrible at this stuff, and it just makes me tense. I scored once by a fluke. I think I'll retire while I'm ahead."

He tossed his notepad on the table and placed his pencil behind his left ear. "You're right. It's time to pack it in for the day. What are you having? I'll buy you a drink."

"Nothing for me. I'm about partied out, but I'll keep you company if you're having one."

"I'm fine for now. How'd you do with Dana Jaffe? Did you get anyplace?"

"I didn't expect to. I was just making her acquaintance. I also had a chat with Wendell's ex-partner."

"And what did he have to say?"

As I filled him in on my conversations with Dana Jaffe and Carl Eckert, I saw Henry's gaze stray toward the kitchen and I found myself turning automatically. "Well, would you look at that," I said.

William was emerging with a tray full of food, a not inconsiderable burden for a man of eighty-six. As usual, he was decked out in a three-piece suit with a properly starched white shirt and a crisply knotted tie. He looked enough like Henry to be his twin, though in reality the two men were two years apart. At the moment, William was looking very pleased with himself, high-spirited and energetic. It was the first time I'd registered the changes in him. Seven months before, when he'd moved in with Henry, he'd been morbidly self-obsessed, continually cross-referencing his various illnesses and infirmities. He'd brought his medical records with him when he arrived from the Midwest, and he was constantly assessing the state of his health: his heart palpitations, his digestive tract, his allergies, his suspicions about diseases undiscovered yet. A favorite pastime of his was cruising local funerals, where he commiserated with the other mourners to assure himself he wasn't dead yet. After he and Rosie fell in love, he'd begun to lighten up, until now he worked a full day, side by side with her. Sensing that we were watching, he grinned happily. He set down the tray of food and began to unload plates. One of the patrons at the table made some remark to him. William crowed with delight and high-fived the guy on the spot.

"What's he so happy about?"

"He asked Rosie to marry him."

I stared at Henry, startled. "You're kidding. He did? God, that's great. What a hoot! I can't believe it!"

" 'A hoot' is not exactly how I'd refer to it. This just goes to show what happens when you 'live in sin.' "

"They've lived in sin for a *week*. Now he's making her an 'honest' woman, whatever that means. I think it's sweet." I put a hand on Henry's arm, giving it a shake. "You don't really mind, do you? I mean, way down deep."

"Let's put it this way. I'm not as appalled as I thought I'd be. I resigned myself to the possibility the day he moved in. He's too conventional a fellow to flaunt proprieties."

"So when's all this happening?"

"I have no idea. They haven't set the date. He just asked her tonight. She hasn't agreed to it yet."

"The way you were talking, I assumed she had."

"Well, no, but she's hardly going to turn down a gentleman of his caliber."

I gave his hand a smack. "Honestly, Henry. You're a bit of a snob."

He smiled at me, blue-eyed, his brows lifting quizzically. "I'm a complete snob, not a 'bit' of one. Come on. I'll walk you back."

Once home, I took a handful of medication for my assorted cold symptoms, including a hit of Nyquil that guaranteed a good night's sleep. At 6:00 I rolled out of bed groggily and pulled on my jogging clothes, filling out a mental checklist while I brushed my teeth. My chest was still congested, but my nose wasn't running and my cough no longer sounded like my lungs were on the verge of flopping out. My skin color had lightened to the mild gold of apricots and I thought, in another day or so, might revert to my natural skin tone. Never have I so yearned for my former pale complexion.

I bundled up against the early morning chill, my gray sweats nearly the same color as the ocean. The beach sand was a chalky white, speckled with foam from the outgoing tide. Seagulls, gray and white, stood and stared at the water like a flock of yard ornaments. The sky at the horizon was a perfect blend of cream and silver, the mist blocking out all but the darkened outlines of the islands in the channel. This was hurricane season in the far reaches of the Pacific, but so far we hadn't had a hint of tropical surf. The hush was profound, undercut only by the soft rustle of the waves. There was not another soul as far as I could see. The three-mile walk became a meditation, just me and my labored breathing, the feel of my leg muscles responding to the brisk pace. By the time I reached home, I was ready to face the day.

Through the front door, I caught the muffled sound of the telephone. I let myself into my apartment in haste. I caught it on the third ring, out of breath from the exertion. It was Mac. "What's up? This is awfully early for you." I buried my face in my T-shirt, suppressing a cough.

"We had a meeting last night. Gordon Titus has gotten wind of this Wendell Jaffe business and wants to meet with you."

"With me?" I squeaked.

Mac laughed. "He doesn't bite."

"He doesn't have to," I said. "Titus can't stand me, and the feeling is mutual. He treats me like a piece of—"

"Now, now," he broke in.

"I was going to say *dirt*!"

"Well, that's better."

"Human out-your-butt-type dirt," I amended.

"You better get yourself down here as soon as you can."

I sat for a moment making faces at the phone, my usual terribly mature method of dealing with the world. I did not exactly rush out the door as advised. I stripped off my sweat suit and took a hot shower, washed my hair thoroughly, and then got dressed. I had a bite to eat while I scanned the paper for news of interest. I rinsed my dish and my spoon and then took out a small load of trash, which I dumped in the bin by the street. When I ran out of ways to avoid the inevitable, I grabbed my handbag, a steno pad, and my car keys and headed out the gate. This was making my stomach hurt.

The office really hadn't changed much, though I noticed, for the first time, a certain shabbiness throughout. The wall-to-wall carpet was a quality synthetic, but the style had been chosen for its "wearability," a term synonymous with mottled, stain-mimicking patterns guaranteed not to soil. The space itself seemed crowded by the warren of "action stations," dozens of interlocking cubicles for examiners and underwriters. The perimeter was lined with glass-enclosed offices for the company executives. The walls needed fresh paint, and the trim was looking scuffed. Vera glanced up from her desk as I passed. From that angle I was the only witness to her facial antics, eyes crossed, tongue protruding slightly in comical disgust.

We met in Titus's office. I hadn't laid eyes on him since the day of our encounter. I had no idea what to expect, and I couldn't quite decide what behavior to adopt. He simplified the matter by greeting me pleasantly, as if this were our first meeting and we'd never exchanged a cross word. It was a brilliant move really because it freed me of any necessity to defend or apologize, relieving him of the burden of cross-referencing our past relationship. After the first sixty seconds, I found I had disconnected. I realized the man had no power over me at this point. Debts on both sides were paid, and both of us had ended up with exactly what we wanted. He'd removed what he'd seen as "deadwood" from the company payroll. I'd reestablished myself in a work environment I preferred.

Meanwhile, in the present, Mac Voorhies and Gordon Titus were a perfect contrast to one another. Mac's brown suit was as wrinkled as an autumn leaf, while his teeth and the flip of puffy white hair in front were discolored by the staining properties of nicotine. Gordon Titus wore an ice blue dress shirt with the sleeves rolled up. His gray pants were crisply pleated, the shade an eerie match for his prematurely gray hair. His tie formed a fierce punctuation mark emphasizing his office manner, which was terse and businesslike. Even Mac knew enough not to light a cigarette in his presence.

Titus sat down at his desk and opened the file in front of him. Typically, he'd outlined the relevant data about Dana and Wendell Jaffe. Neatly indented paragraphs marched sideways across the page, the paper pockmarked with holes where the nib of his pen had plunged through. He spoke without looking at me, his face as empty of expression as a mannequin's. "Mac's brought me up to date, so we don't need to cover any old ground," he said. "What's the status of the case?"

I hauled out my steno pad and flipped to an empty page, reciting what I knew about Dana's current situation. I detailed as much as possible and then summarized the rest. "She's probably used part of the insurance benefits to finance Michael's house, with another hefty chunk going as a retainer for Brian's attorney."

Titus was making notes. "Have you talked to the company lawyers about our position in this?"

"What's the point?" Mac broke in. "So what if Wendell faked his own death? What crime did he commit? Is that against the law . . . what's it called, faking suicide?" He snapped his fingers, trying to jog his memory.

I said, " 'Pseudocide' is the term I've heard."

"Pseudocide, right. Is it against the law to falsify your own death?" he asked.

"It is if you do it with intent to defraud the insurance company," Titus said with acid.

Mac's expression was impatient. "Where's the fraud? What fraud? At this point, we don't know that he's collected a cent."

Titus's gaze flicked up to Mac. "You're absolutely right. To be precise about it, we're not even sure it's really Jaffe we're dealing with." And then to me, "I want concrete evidence, proof of identity, fingerprints or some damn thing."

"I'm doing what I can," I said, sounding both dubious and defensive. I made a note on a blank page, just to look industrious. The note said, "Find Wendell." Like I was unclear on the concept until Titus spelled it out. "In the meantime, what? You want to go after Mrs. Jaffe?"

Again, Mac's exasperation surfaced. I couldn't figure out what he was so upset about. "Goddamn it, what's she done? She hasn't committed a crime, as far as we know. How can she be held liable for spending money she believes she's legally entitled to?"

"What makes you think she wasn't in on this from the beginning? For all we know, the two colluded," Titus said.

"To what end?" I interjected mildly. "For the last five years the woman's been dead broke, accumulating debts by the bushel basket. Meanwhile Wendell's down in Mexico by the pool with some babe. What kind of deal is that? Even if she collects, all she ends up with is money to pay off the bill collectors."

"You only have her word for that," Titus said. "Besides which we don't really know how Mr. and Mrs. Jaffe accommodated their relationship. Maybe the marriage was over and this was his way of negotiating spousal support."

"Some support," I said.

Titus plowed right over me. "And as you yourself pointed out, it looks like she's managed to buy one kid a house and probably retained the services of a hotshot attorney for the one who's in trouble. The bottom line is, we need to have a conversation with Wendell Jaffe. Now, how do you propose to find him?" The question was abrupt, but the tone was more curious than challenging.

"I figure Brian's the perfect bait, and if Wendell's too paranoid to approach him in jail, he can always contact Dana. Or Michael, his oldest, who has a child Wendell's never seen. Even his ex-partner, Carl, is a possibility." It all sounded weak, but what was I going to do? Fake it, that's what.

Mac stirred. "You can't run a twenty-four-hour surveillance on the whole lot of them. Even if we hire other ops on this, you're talking thousands of dollars going out, and in return for what?"

"True enough," I said. "Do you have a suggestion?"

Mac crossed his arms, turning his attention back to Titus. "Whatever we do, we better get a move on," he said. "My wife could go through half a million clams in a week."

Titus stood up and closed his file with a snap. "I'll call the company attorney and see if he can get us a temporary restraining order. With a TRO, we can get a lock on Mrs. Jaffe's bank accounts and prevent any more monies going out."

"She's going to love that," I said.

"Is there anything specific you want her to do in the meantime, Gordon?"

Titus sent me a chilly smile. "I'm sure she'll think of something." He looked at his watch as a signal that we were dismissed.

Mac went into his office, which was two doors down. There was no sign of Vera. I chatted briefly with Darcy Pascoe, the CF receptionist, and then I went back to Lonnie's office, where I took care of odds and ends. I picked up messages, opened mail, sat on my swivel chair, and swiveled for a while, hoping for inspiration about where I should go next. In the absence of a great idea, I tried the only other action item that occurred to me.

I put in a call to Lieutenant Whiteside at the police department, asking him if I could have the telephone number of Lieutenant Harris Brown, who'd worked on the case when Wendell first disappeared. Jonah Robb had told me Brown had since retired, but he might have information. "Do you think he'd be willing to talk to me?" I asked.

"I have no idea, but I'll tell you what," he said. "His telephone's unlisted, and I wouldn't want to give it to you unless I had his okay. When I can find a minute, I'll give him a call. If he's interested, I'll have him get in touch with you."

"Great. That'd be fine. I'd appreciate the contact."

I hung up the phone and made a note to myself. If I didn't hear in two days, I'd try calling back. I wasn't sure the man would be any help, but you never knew. Some of those old cops loved nothing better than to reminisce. He might have suggestions about places Wendell might be holing up. In the meantime, what? I went back to the Xerox machine and ran off several dozen copies of the flier with Wendell's photograph. I'd added my name and telephone number in a box at the bottom, indicating my interest in the man's whereabouts.

I filled my gas tank and hit the road again, heading back to Perdido, I cruised past Dana's house, did a U-turn at the intersection, and pulled into a parking place across the street. I began a door-to-door canvass, moving patiently from house to house. I worked my way down the block, leaving a flier in the screen door if there was no one home. On Dana's side of the street many couples apparently worked, because the houses were dark and there were no cars in the drive. When I found someone home, the conversations all seemed to share the same boring elements. "Hello," I would say, quickly trying to work in my message before I could be mistaken for a salesperson. "I wonder if you might give me some help. I'm a private investigator, working to locate a man we think might be in the area. Have you seen him recently?" I would hold up the artist's composite of Wendell Jaffe, waiting without much hope while the person's gaze moved across his features.

Much mental scratching of chins. "No, now I don't think so. No, ma'am. What was it the man did? I hope you're not telling me he's dangerous."

"Actually, he's wanted for questioning in a fraud investigation."

Hand cupped behind the ear. "What's that?"

I would raise my voice. "Do you remember a couple of real estate developers a few years back? They had a company called CSL Investments and they put together syndicates—"

"Oh, my Lord, yes. Well, of course I remember them. The one fellow killed himself and the other one went to jail."

On and on it went, with no one contributing any fresh information.

Across the street from Dana and about six doors down, I had better luck. I knocked on the door of a house identical to hers, same model, same exterior, dark gray with white trim. The man who answered was in his early sixties, wearing shorts, a flannel shirt, dark socks, and an incongruous pair of wingtips. His gray hair was all abristle, and he wore a pair of half-glasses at the mid-point on his septum, peering at me blue-eyed above the smudged surface of his lenses. A mask of white whiskers covered the lower part of his face, a possible refusal to shave more than twice a week. He was narrow through the shoulders, and his posture seemed stooped, a curious combination of elegance and defeat. Maybe the hard-soled shoes were a holdover from his former occupation. I was guessing salesman or a stockbroker, someone who spent his life in a three-piece suit.

"What can I do for you?" he said, the question intended more for efficiency than any real assistance.

"I wonder if you could help me. Are you acquainted with Mrs. Jaffe, from across the street?"

"The one whose boy's been screwing up? We know the family," he said cautiously. "What's he done now? Or what *hasn't* he done might be the better question in this case."

"This is actually about his father."

There was a silence. "I thought he was dead."

"That's what everybody thought until recently. Now we have reason to believe he's alive and possibly returning to California. This is an updated likeness along with my business number. I'd appreciate a call if you should spot him in the area." I held the flier out, and he took it.

"Well, I'll be damned. It's always something with that bunch," he said. I watched his gaze trace a triangle from the photograph of Wendell to Dana's house down the street and then back to my face. "This is probably none of my business, but what's your connection to the Jaffes? Are you a relative?"

"I'm a private investigator working for the company that wrote the policy on Wendell Jaffe's life."

"Is that right," he said. He cocked his head. "Why don't you come on in a second? I wouldn't mind hearing this."

# 10

I HESITATED FOR just a second, and a smile creased his face.

"Don't worry about it. I'm not the boogey man. My wife's on the premises, pulling weeds in the garden. Both of us work at home in one capacity or another. If anybody's going to spot Mr. Jaffe, it's most likely us. What's your name again?" He backed into the hallway, motioning for me to follow.

I moved across the threshold behind him. "Kinsey Millhone. Sorry. I should have introduced myself. That's my name there at the bottom of the flier." I held my hand out, and we shook.

"Good to meet you. Don't worry about it. Jerry Irwin. My wife's name is Lena. She saw you bumping doors across the street. I got a study in the back. She can bring us coffee, if you like."

"None for me, thanks."

118

"She's going to love this," he said. "Lena? Hey, Lena!"

We reached his study, a small room paneled in a light veneer, scored and pockmarked to look like knotty pine. An L-shaped desk occupied most of the space, the walls lined with floor-to ceiling metal shelves. "Let me see if I can find her. Have a seat," he said. He headed off down the hall, moving toward the back door.

I sat down on a metal folding chair and did a quick check of my surroundings, trying to get a feel for Irwin in his absence. Computer, monitor, and keyboard. Lots of floppy disks neatly filed. Open banker's boxes filled with some kind of color illustrations, segregated by sheets of cardboard. A low metal bookshelf to the right of the desk held numerous heavy volumes with titles I couldn't read. I leaned closer, squinting. *Burke's General Armory, Armorial General Rietstap, New Dictionary of American Family Names, Dictionary of Surnames, Dictionary of Heraldry.* I could hear him hollering out into the backyard and moments later the sound of conversation as the two moved toward the study where I was waiting. I sat back in the chair, trying to look like a woman unconsumed by nosiness. I stood up as they entered, but Mrs. Irwin shooed me onto my seat again. Her husband tossed the flier on his desk and moved around to his chair.

Lena Irwin was petite and on the plump side for her height, dressed for gardening in Japanese farmer's pants and a blue chambray shirt with the sleeves rolled up. She'd pinned up her gray hair, damp tendrils escaping from various combs and barrettes. The spattering of freckles across her broad cheekbones suggested that her hair might have been red once upon a time. Her prescription sunglasses sat like a bow across her head. Having come in from digging, she had nails that looked as if she'd just had a set of French tips done in dirt. Her handshake was faintly gritty, and her eyes raked my face with interest. "I'm Lena. How're you?"

"I'm fine. Sorry to interrupt your gardening," I said.

Her wave was careless. "Garden's not going anyplace. I was glad to take a break. That sun out there is murder. Jerry mentioned this business about the Jaffes."

"Wendell Jaffe in particular. Did you know him?"

"We knew of him," Lena said.

Jerry spoke up. "We know her to speak to, though we tend to keep our distance. Perdido's a small town, but we were still surprised when we heard she'd moved in over there. She used to live in a nicer area. Nothing fancy, but better than this one by a long shot."

"Of course, we always thought she was a widow."

"So did she," I said. I gave a quick synopsis of the rumored change in Dana Jaffe's marital status. "Did Jerry show you the picture?"

"Yes, but I haven't had a chance to study it."

Jerry straightened the flier on his desk, lining up the page with the bottom edge of his blotter. "We read about Brian in the papers. What a mess that boy's made. We see police over there every time we turn around."

Lena interjected a change of subject. "Would you like a cup of coffee or some lemonade? Won't take but a minute."

"I better not," I said. "I have a lot of ground to cover yet. I'm trying to get these fliers out in case Wendell puts in an appearance."

"Well, we'll certainly keep an eye out. This close to

the freeway, we get a lot of cars through here, especially during rush hour with people looking for a shortcut. The southbound off ramp's just a block in that direction. We have a little strip mall down the street, so we get foot traffic, too."

Lena added her comment, cleaning dirt away from her cuticles. "I run a little bookkeeping business from my office up front, so I'm sitting near a window several hours a day. We don't miss much, as you can probably tell. Well, now. I'm glad we had a chance to meet. I better finish up out back and get some work done since I mentioned it."

"I'll be on my way, then, but I'd sure appreciate the help."

She walked me as far as the front steps, a copy of the flier and my business card in hand. "I hope you don't mind my getting personal, but your first name's unusual. Do you know the origin?"

"Kinsey is my mother's maiden name. I guess she didn't want to lose it, so she passed it on to me."

"The reason I ask is that's what Jerry's been doing since he took early retirement. He researches names and family crests."

"I gathered as much. The name is English, I think."

"And what's the story on your parents? Do they live here in Perdido?"

"Both died years ago in an accident. They lived up in Santa Teresa, but they've been gone now since I was five."

She pulled her glasses down from her head, giving me a long look above the half-moon of bifocal lenses. "I wonder if your mother was related to Burton Kinsey's people up in Lompoc."

"Not as far as I know. I don't remember any mention of a name like that."

She studied my face. "Because you look an awful lot like a friend of mine who's a Kinsey by birth. She has a daughter just about your age, too. What are you, thirty-two?"

"Thirty-four," I said. "But I don't have any family left. My only close relative was my mother's sister, who died ten years back."

"Well, there's probably no connection, but I just thought I'd ask. You ought to have Jerry check his files. He has over six thousand names in his computer program. He could research the family crest and run off a copy for you."

"Maybe I'll do that the next time I'm down. It sounds interesting." I tried to picture the Kinsey family crest emblazoned on a royal banner. I could probably mount it near the suit of armor in the great hall ante-chamber. Might be the perfect touch on those special occasions when one hopes to impress.

"I'll tell Jerry to do the research," she said, having made up her mind. "This is not genealogy . . . he doesn't trace anybody's family tree. What he gives you is information about the derivation of the surname."

"Don't have him go to any trouble," I said.

"It's no trouble. He enjoys it. We work the art show up in Santa Teresa every Sunday afternoon. You ought to stop by and see us. We have a little booth near the wharf."

"Maybe I'll do that. And thanks for your time."

"Happy to be of help. We'll keep an eye out for you."

"That's great, and please don't hesitate to call if you see anything suspicious."

"We surely will."

I gave her a quick wave and then moved down the porch steps. I heard the door close behind me as she went back inside.

By the time I'd distributed fliers up and down the block, a locally owned moving company with a bright red van had arrived at Dana's house and two burly guys were in the process of angling a box spring down the stairs. The screen door was propped open, and I could see them struggle with the turn. Michael was pitching in, probably in an effort to speed the process and thus cut costs. A young woman I guessed to be Michael's wife, Juliet, wandered out of the house from time to time, the baby on her hip. She'd stand out in the grass, in a pair of white shorts, rocking and jiggling the baby while she watched the movers work. The garage doors were open, a yellow VW convertible parked on one side, the backseat piled high with the sorts of odds and ends no one wants to trust to the movers. There was no sign of Dana's car, and I had to guess she was out running errands.

I unlocked my car door and slid onto the driver's seat, where I busied myself. No one seemed to pay any attention to me, too busy loading furniture to notice what I was doing. Within an hour the truck had been packed with whatever furniture the couple was taking with them. Michael, Juliet, and the baby got into the VW and backed out of the driveway. When the van pulled away from the curb, Michael fell in behind it. I waited a few minutes and joined the motorcade myself, keeping several car lengths between us. Michael must have known a shortcut because I soon lost track of him. Fortunately, the van wasn't hard to spot on the highway up ahead. We drove north on 101, passing two off ramps. The truck took the third, turning right, and then left on Calistoga Street, proceeding into a section of Perdido known as the Boulevards. The van finally slowed, pulling into the curb just as the VW appeared from the opposite direction.

The house they were moving into looked as if it had been built in the twenties: rosy-beige stucco exterior with a tiny porch and a patchy front yard. The window trim had been done in a darker shade of rose with a tiny rim of azure. I'd been in half a dozen houses just like it. The interior couldn't have been much more than nine hundred square feet: two bedrooms, one bath, living room, kitchen, and a small utility room in the rear. There was a cracked concrete driveway to the right of the house, a two-car garage visible in the rear, with what looked like a bachelor apartment above.

The movers began to unload the truck. If they noticed my presence, they gave no indication of it. I made a note of the house number and the street before I fired up my engine and returned to Dana's. I had no compelling reason to talk to her again, but I needed her cooperation, and I was hoping to establish a rapport of some kind. I caught her just as she was turning into her drive. She parked the car in the garage, assembling some parcels before she opened the car door. The minute she spotted me, I could see the color tint her cheeks. She slammed her car door, emerged from the garage, and crossed the grass in my direction. She was wearing tight jeans, an old T-shirt, and tennis shoes, her hair held back by a blue-and-white cotton scarf that she had tied around her head. The assorted paper bags in her arms seemed to crackle with her agitation. "What are you doing back here again? I consider this harassment."

"Well, it's not," I said. "We're trying to get a line on Wendell and you're the logical place to start."

Her voice had dropped, and her eyes were glittering with rage and determination. "I will call you if I see him. In the meantime, if you don't stay away from me, I will notify my attorney."

"Dana, I'm not your enemy. I'm just trying to do a job. Why don't you help me? You're going to have to deal with the issue sometime. Tell Michael what's going on. Tell Brian, too. Otherwise I'm going to have to step in and tell them myself. We need your help on this."

Her nose suddenly reddened and a fiery triangle formed around her mouth and chin. Tears leapt into her eyes and she pressed her lips together, sealing back her rage. "Don't tell me what to do. I can handle this myself."

"Look. Can we talk about this inside?"

I saw her glance at the houses across the street. Without a word she turned and proceeded toward the front door, pulling keys from her shoulder bag. I followed her through the entrance and closed the front door behind us.

"I have work to do." She dumped her parcels and handbag on the bottom step and went up the stairs toward the second-floor bedrooms. I hesitated, watching her until she disappeared from view. She hadn't said I couldn't join her. I took the stairs two at a time, peering right at the landing until I located the empty master

suite that Michael and his wife had apparently just vacated. There was a canister vacuum cleaner outside the
door, cord neatly retracted, cleaning tools still attached.
My guess was that Dana had left it there as a tangible
suggestion, hoping someone would vacuum once the
furniture had been moved. No one seemed to have
taken her up on the offer. She was standing in the middle of the bedroom, surveying the premises, trying (I
imagined) to figure out where to begin the cleanup. I
eased into the doorway and leaned against the frame,
trying not to disturb the fragile truce between us. She
glanced over at me without any evidence of her earlier
hostility. "Do you have children?"

I shook my head.

"This is what it looks like when they leave you," she
said.

The room was drab and empty. I could see a king-
size square of clean carpet where the bed had been.
There were stray coat hangers on the floor, and the
wastebasket was jammed with last-minute discards.
Nests of accumulated hair and fuzz rimmed the wall-to-
wall carpeting. There was a broom leaning against the
wall, a dustpan upright beside it. There was an ashtray
on the windowsill, the brim filled with old cigarette
butts, an empty, crumpled pack of Marlboro Lights bal-
anced jauntily on top. Pictures were gone. I had to
guess the young married couple was still at that stage of
decorating where travel or rock posters were affixed to
the walls with tape. I could see the patches left behind.
The curtains were down. The windowpanes were lac-
quered with a gray film of cigarette smoke, and I
guessed the glass hadn't been washed since the "kids"
moved in. Even from a distance, Juliet didn't strike me

as the sort who scrubbed the baseboards on her hands and knees.

That was Mom's job, and I suspected Dana would tackle it with a vengeance once I had finally left her in peace.

"Mind if I use the bathroom?" I asked.

"Help yourself." She grabbed the broom, attacking the corners of the room, coaxing dust away from the walls. While she exhumed the remains of Michael's presence, I moved into the bathroom. The area rug and the towels had been removed. The door to the medicine cabinet was hanging open, the interior empty except for a sticky circle of cough medicine on the bottom shelf. The glass shelves above were tacky with dust. The room echoed oddly without the softening influence of a shower curtain. I used the last scrap of toilet paper and then washed my hands without the benefit of soap, drying them on my jeans in the absence of a hand towel. Someone had even taken the bulb from the fixture.

I moved back into the bedroom, wondering if I should help. There was no sign of a dust cloth or a sponge or any other cleaning implements. Dana was going after the dust as if the process were therapeutic.

"How's Brian doing? Have you seen him yet?"

"He called me last night when he'd been through the booking process. His attorney's been in to see him, but I'm really not sure just what they discussed. I guess there was some kind of problem when they brought him in, and they've put him in isolation."

"Really," I said. I watched her sweep, the broom making a restful *skritching* sound against the carpet.

"How'd he get into trouble, Dana? What happened to him?"

At first I thought she didn't intend to respond. Dust appeared in little puffs as she swept it away from the wall. Once she completed her circuit of the room, she set the broom aside and reached for a cigarette. She took a moment to light it, letting the question sit there between us. She smiled with bitterness. "It started with truancy. Once Wendell died . . . well, disappeared . . . and the scandal hit the news, it was Brian who reacted. We used to have huge battles every morning about his going off to school. He was twelve years old and he absolutely did not want to go. He tried everything. He'd claim he had stomachaches and headaches. He'd throw temper tantrums. Cry. He'd *beg* to stay home, and what was I going to do? He'd say, 'Mom, all the kids know what Daddy did. Everybody hates him and they all hate me, too.' I kept trying to tell him what his dad did had nothing to do with him, it was completely separate and had no bearing on him at all, but I couldn't talk him into it. He never bought it for a minute. And honestly, kids did seem to pick on him. Pretty soon he was getting into horrible fights, cutting classes, skipping school. Vandalism, petty theft. It was a nightmare." She tapped her cigarette against the already laden ashtray, flicking a quarter inch of ash into a tiny crevice between butts.

"What about Michael?"

"He was just the opposite. Sometimes I think Michael used school as a way of blotting out the truth. Brian was oversensitive where Michael made himself numb. We talked to school counselors, teachers. I don't know how many social workers we saw. Everybody had a theory, but nothing seemed to work. I didn't have the money to get us any real help. Brian was so *bright,* and he seemed so capable. It just broke my heart. Of course, in many ways Wendell was like that, too. Anyway, I didn't want the boys to believe he killed himself. He wouldn't do that. We had a good marriage, and he adored them. He was very family-oriented. You can ask anyone. I was sure he'd never deliberately do anything to hurt us. I've always believed Carl Eckert was the one who was fiddling with the books. Maybe Wendell couldn't face it. I'm not saying he didn't have his weaknesses. He wasn't perfect, but he tried."

I let that one sit there, unwilling to challenge her version of events. I could see her faltering attempt to correct the family story. The dead are always easier to characterize. You can assign them any attitude or motive without fear of contradiction.

"I take it the boys are different in more ways than one," I said.

"Well, yes. Obviously, Michael is the steadier, partly because he's older and feels protective. He's always been a very responsible kid, and thank goodness for that. He was the only one I could depend on after Wendell's ... after what happened to Wendell. Especially with Brian so out of control. If Michael has a fault, it's being too earnest. He's always trying to do the right thing, Juliet being a case in point. He didn't have to marry her."

I kept myself still, making no response at all, because I realized she was giving me a critical piece of information about the situation. She assumed I was already in possession of the facts. Apparently, Juliet was pregnant when Michael married her. She went right on, talking as much to herself as to me.

"Lord knows she wasn't pushing for it. She wanted to have the baby, and she needed financial help, but it's not like she insisted on making things legal. That was Michael's idea. I'm not sure it was a good one, but they're doing okay."

"Has it been hard on you to have them living here?"

She shrugged. "For the most part, I've enjoyed it. Juliet gets on my nerves now and then, but mostly because she's so damned uncooperative. She has to do it her way. She's the expert on every subject. This at eighteen, of course. I know it comes out of her own insecurities, but it's irritating all the same. She can't stand my help, and she can't tolerate suggestions. She doesn't have a clue about motherhood. I mean, she's crazy about the baby, but she treats him like a toy. You ought to see her when she bathes him. It's enough to make your heart fail. She'll leave him lying on the counter while she goes off to get his diapers. It's a wonder he hasn't rolled off half a dozen times."

"What about Brian? Does he live here as well?"

"He and Michael shared an apartment until this latest incident. Once Brian was sentenced and started serving his time, Michael couldn't afford to keep it. His job didn't pay much and then with Juliet, he simply couldn't manage. She's insisted on staying home since the day he married her."

I noticed how neatly she substituted emphemisms. We were not discussing an unplanned pregnancy, a hasty wedding, and the subsequent financial muddle. Gone were the jail escape and the major shooting spree. These were episodes and incidents, inexplicable occurrences for which neither boy appeared to be responsible.

She seemed to pick up on my thought process, quickly shifting the subject. She moved out into the hall and grabbed the vacuum, hauling it in behind her on lustily squeaking casters. My aunt always said a canister vacuum was useless compared with an upright. I wondered if this was the central metaphor in Dana's life. She found the closest electrical outlet and pulled out enough cord to plug it in . . . . "Maybe it's my fault what Brian's been through. God knows being a single parent is the hardest job I've ever faced. When you're penniless at the same time, there's no *way* you can win. Brian should have had the best. Instead, he's had nothing in the way of counseling. His problems have been compounded, which is hardly his doing."

"Will you talk to them for me? I don't want to interfere, but I'm going to have to talk to Brian."

"Why? What for? If Wendell shows up, it's got nothing to do with *him*."

"Maybe so, maybe not. The shooting in Mexicali was all over the news. I know Wendell read the papers down in Viento Negro. It seems reasonable to imagine he'd head back in this direction."

"You don't know that for a fact."

"No. But just suppose it's true. Don't you think Brian should be told what's going on? You don't want him doing something foolish."

She seemed to take that in. I could see her turning over the possibilities. She removed the upholstery attachment and clicked the rug and floor nozzle into place, adding the extension wand in preparation for vacuuming. "Hell, why not? Things couldn't get much worse. The poor kid," she said.

I thought it better not to mention that I was picturing him like a piece of bait in a trap.

In the office alcove below, the phone rang. Dana launched into a description of Brian's misfortunes, but I found myself listening to her canned message as it came wafting up the stairs. The live message followed at the sound of the beep, one of her bridal clients with the latest complaint. "Hello, Dana. This is Ruth. Listen, hon, Bethany's been having a little problem with this caterer you recommended? We've asked the woman twice for a written cost-per-person breakdown of the food and drink for the reception, and we can't seem to get a response. We thought maybe you could give her a call and light a little fire under her for answers. I'll be here in the morning and you can call me, okay? Thank you. I'll talk to you then, babe. Bye now."

I wondered idly if Dana ever told these young brides the problems they were going to run into once the wedding was over with: boredom, weight gain, irresponsibility, friction over sex, spending, family holidays, and who picks up the socks. Maybe it was just my basic cynicism rising to the surface, but cost-per-person food and drink breakdowns seemed trivial compared to the conflicts marriage generated.

" . . . a real helper, generous, cooperative. Winsome and funny. He's got a very high IQ." She was talking about Brian, the alleged teen killer. Only a mother could describe as "winsome and funny" a kid who'd recently broken out of jail and gone on a killing rampage. She was looking at me expectantly. "I have to get on with this so I can reclaim my bedroom. You have any other questions before I get on with the vacuuming?"

Offhand, I couldn't think of any. "This is fine for now."

She kicked the switch and the vacuum cleaner shrilled to life, a high keening whine that drowned out any possibility of conversation. As I let myself out the front door, I could hear the droning of the motor as she hauled the suction wand across the floor.

# 11

MY WATCH SHOWED that it was nearly noon. I drove over to the Perdido County Jail.

The Perdido County Government Center was constructed in 1978, a sprawling mass of pale concrete that houses the Criminal Justice Center, the administration building, and the Hall of Justice. I parked my car in one of the spaces provided in the vast marina of asphalt that surrounds the complex. I went into the main entrance, pushing through the glass doors that opened onto the lower lobby. I hung a right. The main jail public counter was located down a short hallway. On the same floor were the Sheriff's Personnel Counter, Records and Licensing, and the West County Patrol Services counter, none of which interested me for the moment.

I identified myself to the civilian clerk and, in due course, was directed to the watch commander's office, where I introduced myself. I showed my identification, including my driver's license and my investigator's license. There was a brief delay while a second clerk picked up the phone and checked to see if the jail administrator was in. The minute I heard the guy's name, I knew my luck had improved. I had gone to high school with Tommy Ryckman. He was two years ahead of me, but we'd misbehaved together rather desperately in the days when one could do that without risking death or disease. I wasn't sure he'd remember me, but apparently he did. Sergeant Ryckman agreed to see me as soon as I'd received my clearance. I was directed down the hall to his small office on the right.

As I entered his office, he unfolded himself from his swivel chair, emerging to an impressive six feet eight, his face wreathed with a grin. "Well, it's been way too long. How the hell are you?"

"I'm great, Tommy. How are you?"

We shook hands across the desk and made effusive noises at each other, trading hasty summaries of the years since we'd met. He was now in his mid-thirties, clean-shaven with glossy brown hair parted on one side and slicked across. His hair was thinning slightly, and his forehead was scored as if by the tines of a fork. He wore glasses with wire frames, and his jaw looked like it would smell of citrus after-shave. His khaki sheriff's department uniform was starched and crisply pressed, the slacks looking like they'd been professionally tailored to fit. He had long arms and big hands, a wedding ring, of course.

He motioned me to a chair and then eased back into his own. Even seated, he had the build of a basketball player, his grasshopper knees visible above the edge of the desk. His black shoes must have been a size 13. His accent was still shaded by a touch of the Midwest, Wisconsin perhaps, and I remembered that he'd arrived at Santa Teresa High halfway through the school year. He had a studio portrait on his desk: a wifey-looking woman and three medium-aged kids, two boys and a girl, all with glossy brown hair neatly slicked down with water, all wearing glasses with clear plastic frames. Two of the kids were of an age where they had goofy teeth.

"You're here with regard to Brian Jaffe."

"More or less," I replied. "I'm actually more interested in the whereabouts of his father."

"So I understand. Lieutenant Whiteside told me what was going on."

"Are you familiar with the case? I've heard some of it, but nothing in any depth."

"A good buddy of mine worked with Lieutenant Brown on that case so I had him fill me in. Just about everybody down here knows that one. Lot of local citizens got sucked into CSL. Lost their shirts, most of them. Sometimes I think it was a textbook scam. My buddy's transferred since then, but Harris Brown's the one you want to talk to if we can't help."

"I've been trying to get in touch with him, but I was told he retired."

"He did, but I'm sure he'd be willing to help any way he can. Does the kid know there's a chance his dad's still alive?"

I shook my head. "I just talked to his mother and she hasn't told him yet. I understand he was just brought back to Perdido."

"That's right. Over the weekend we dispatched a couple of deputies to Mexicali, where the kid was handed over. He was transported by car up here to the main jail. He was booked in last night."

"Any chance I might see him?"

"Not today, I don't think. Inmate mealtime at the moment and after that he's scheduled for a medical exam. You can try tomorrow or the next day as long as he has no objections."

"How'd he manage to escape from Connaught?"

Ryckman stirred restlessly, breaking off eye contact. "We're not going to talk about that," he said. "Next thing you know the information ends up in the paper and then everybody gets it down. Let's just say the inmates discovered a little quirk in the system and took advantage of it. It won't happen again, I can tell you that."

"Will he be tried as an adult?"

Tommy Ryckman did a stretch, extending his arms above his head with a series of popping sounds. "You'd have to ask the DA, though personally, I'd sure like to see it. This kid is devious. We think he was the one who cooked up the escape plan to begin with, but who's going to contradict him at this point? Two guys are dead and the third's in critical condition. He'll claim he's the innocent victim. You know how it goes. These kids never take responsibility. His mother's already hired him a high-priced attorney, bringing some guy up from Los Angeles."

"Probably utilizing some of the benefits from his father's life insurance policy," I said. "I'd love to see Wendell Jaffe make a discreet appearance. I can't believe he'd risk it, but it would sure verify my intuitions."

"Well now, I'll tell you the problem you're going to

have with that. Case like this, a lot of notoriety, court-room's probably going to be closed and under tight se-curity. You know how it goes. Kid's attorney's going to offer up spirited arguments, asserting his client's fitness for treatment under juvenile court law. He'll want a pro-bation officer to investigate. He'll want reports submit-ted with other relevant evidence. He'll raise six kinds of hell, and until the matter's decided, he'll maintain his client is entitled to protection under juvenile statutes."

"I don't suppose there's any way I'd be given access to his juvenile criminal history," I said. I was stating the obvious, but sometimes a cop will surprise you.

Sergeant Ryckman laced his hands across his head, smiling at me with a sort of brotherly indulgence. "We wouldn't do that regardless," he said mildly. "You can always try the paper. Reporters over there can probably get you anything you want. Not sure how they do it, but they have their little ways." He sat forward on his chair. "I was just on my way to lunch. You want to join me in the cafeteria?"

"Sure, I'd like that," I said.

On his feet again, I realized how much he'd grown since I'd seen him last and he was over six feet tall then. Now he was stoop-shouldered and seemed to carry his head tilted to one side, perhaps hoping to avoid being knocked silly by the door frame when he entered or left a room. I would have bet money his wife was only five feet tall and spent her life with his belt buckle staring her in the face. On a dance floor, the two probably looked as though they were engaged in an ob-scene act. "If you don't mind, I got a few things to take care of on the way."

"Fine with me," I said.

We began to traverse the maze of corridors linking the various offices and departments, moving through a series of security checkpoints, like the airlocks on a spaceship. There were video cameras sweeping every corridor, and I knew we were being observed by the deputy manning level-one control. The smells changed subtly from one area to the next. Food, bleach, burning chemicals, as if someone had set fire to the plastic ring on a six-pack of canned sodas, musty blankets, floor wax, rubber tires. Sergeant Ryckman conducted a couple of administrative transactions, apparently minor matters fraught with clerical jargon. There were a surprising number of women working in the processing unit—all ages, all sizes, usually in jeans or polyester pants. There was a nice air of camaraderie among the people I observed. Lots of telephones ringing, lots of movement from department to department, as we cruised through.

Finally, he steered us toward the small employee cafeteria. The menu for the deputies that day was lasagna, grilled ham-and-cheese sandwiches, french fries, and corn. Not quite enough fat and carbs for my taste, but it was coming close. There was also a salad bar, featuring stainless-steel bins of chopped iceberg lettuce, sliced carrots, green pepper rings, and onions. For drinks, one had a choice of orange juice, lemonade, or cartons of milk. The prisoners' menu was listed on the board above the hot table: bean soup, grilled ham-and-cheese sandwiches, beef Stroganoff or lasagna, white bread, french fries, and the ubiquitous corn. Unlike the meals at the jail in Santa Teresa, which were served cafeteria style, the food here was prepared and dished out by inmates onto trays that were loaded, in turn, into big stainless-steel hot carts. I'd seen several being rolled into the industrial-size elevators en route to jail levels three and four.

Ryckman still had the unruly hunger of an adolescent. I watched him pile his tray with a serving of lasagna the size of a brick, two grilled sandwiches, a mound each of corn and french fries, and a hefty side of salad with a dipper of Thousand Island dressing poured on top. He tucked two cartons of low-fat milk into the remaining space on his tray. I followed him in the line, picking up plastic flatware from a bin. I opted for a grilled ham-and-cheese sandwich and a modest log pile of fries, hungrier than I thought possible given the institutional nature of the setting. We found a free corner table and unloaded our trays.

"Were you working in Perdido when Wendell formed CSL?" I asked.

"You bet," Ryckman said. " 'Course, I never invest in deals like that myself. My dad always told me I was better off with my money stashed in a coffee can. Depression mentality, but it's not bad advice. Actually, you better hope the word on Jaffe doesn't get out. I know a couple deputies lost money on that scam. He shows his face, you're gonna have a posse of irate citizens riding down on that dude."

"What's the deal?" I asked. "I don't understand what these guys are about." He squirted ketchup on his fries and passed the dispenser to me. I could tell we shared the same intense interest in junk food.

Ryckman ate quickly, attention focused on his plate as the mountain of food diminished. "System works on trust—checks, credit cards, a contract of any kind. People perpetrating fraud feel no inner moral obligation to make good on their agreements. They operate along a continuum that runs from financial irresponsibility to civil consumer puffing to fraud to criminal lies. You see it all the time. Bankers, real estate brokers, investment counselors ... anyone exposed to large sums of cash. After a while they can't seem to keep their hands off it."

"Too tempting," I remarked. I wiped my hands on a paper napkin, uncertain whether the grease was coming from the sandwich or the pile of french fries. Both were heaven to a person of my low appetites.

"It's more than that. Because it's not just bucks these boys are after as far as I can tell. The money's just a way of keeping score, like they say. You watch these guys operate and pretty soon you realize it's the game they get off on. Same goes for politicians. It's a power trip. Us ordinary mortals are just fuel for their egos."

"I'm surprised anyone in law enforcement fell for his scheme. You guys ought to know better. You probably see enough of it."

He shook his head, chewing on a bite of sandwich. "Always hope to make a killing. A little something for nothing, and I guess we're not above it."

"I had a conversation with Jaffe's ex-partner last night," I said. "He seemed pretty slick."

"He is. Went right back into business, and what the hell are we gonna do? Everybody around here knows the guy went to jail. Day he comes out they're ready to invest again. What makes these cases so hard to prosecute is the victims don't want to believe they've been deceived. The victims all become dependent on the crook who's cheating them. Once they invest, they *need* him to be successful to get their money back. Then, of course, the con man always has last-minute excuses, stalling repayment and dragging his feet. Case like that is a bitch to prove. Lot of time the DA can't even get corroboration."

"I really don't understand it when smart guys get into stuff like this."

"If you look back far enough, you could probably see it coming. You know, old Wendell's got a law degree, but he never passed the bar."

"Really. That's interesting."

"Yeah, he got into some trouble just out of law school and he ended up letting the whole business drop. He's just one of those guys: smart and well educated, but he had a bad streak that showed up even then."

"What kind of trouble?"

"Some prostitute died in the course of rough sex. Jaffe was the john, pleaded down on a charge of manslaughter, and got off on probation. It all got hushed up, of course, but it was ugly stuff. There's no way you practice law with that in your background. Perdido's too small."

"He could have gone somewhere else."

"He didn't seem to think so."

"Seems weird somehow. I haven't been thinking of him as the violent type. How'd he get from manslaughter to fraud?"

"Wendell Jaffe's sly in more ways than one. It's not like the guy lived in a four-thousand-square-foot house complete with swimming pool and tennis court. He bought a nice three-bedroom tract house in a good middle-class neighborhood. He and his wife drove American cars, the stripped-down economy models and not like new ones. His was six years old. Both of his sons went to public schools. Usually, with these guys, what you'll see is a pattern of conspicuous consumption, but Wendell didn't do that. No designer clothes. He and Dana didn't travel much or entertain lavishly. From the point of view of his investors—and this was something he was quick to assure them—he poured every penny right back into the business."

"What was the gimmick? How'd they pull it off?"

"Well, I did a little digging when I heard you were coming down. From what I understand, it was pretty straightforward. He and Eckert had about two hundred fifty investors, some of them putting up twenty-five to fifty thousand dollars apiece. CLS took fees and royalties off the top."

"On the basis of a prospectus?"

"That's right. First thing Jaffe did, he bought a shell of a company and renamed it CSL Inc."

"What kind of company?"

"This was trust-deed investment. Then he made headlines with the purchase of a one-hundred-two-million-dollar complex, which he announced he had sold six months later for a hundred eighty-nine million. Truth was, the deal never went through, but the public didn't know that. Wendell hands his investors this impressive-looking, unaudited financial statement showing assets in excess of twenty-five million dollars. After that, it was a piece of cake. They'd buy real estate and show a paper profit by selling it back to another of their shell companies, inflating the value of the property in the process."

"Jesus," I said.

"It was a typical Ponzi. Some of the people who came on board early were making out like bandits. Returns of twenty-eight percent on their initial investment. It wasn't unusual to see them turn around and invest twice that sum, cashing in on the bonanza of CSL's financial savvy. Who could resist? Jaffe seemed to be earnest, knowledgeable, hardworking, sincere, conservative. There was nothing flamboyant about the man. He paid good salaries and treated his employees decently. He seemed happily married, devoted to his family. He was a bit of a workaholic, but he managed to take occasional time off: two weeks in May on his annual fishing trip, another two weeks in August when he took the family camping."

"God, you really do know this stuff. What about Carl? How'd he fit into this?"

"Wendell was the front man. Carl did everything else. Wendell's talent was the hustle, which he did with the kind of low-key, drop-dead sincerity that made you want to pull your wallet out and give him everything you had. The two of them put together various real estate syndicates. Investors were told their money would be held in a separate account, devoted exclusively to a particular project. In actual fact, the funds for the various projects were commingled, and some funds intended for a new project were used to complete the old."

"And then the bottom dropped out of the market."

Tommy feigned a slam dunk and pointed a finger at me. "You got it. CSL suddenly began to have trouble finding new investors. Eventually, Jaffe must have realized the whole house of cards was collapsing. He also got a notice about an IRS audit, from what I hear tell. That's when he went off on his trip. I'll tell you one thing. This guy was so persuasive that even when it became apparent the investors had lost their shirts, a lot of people still believed in him, convinced that there was some other explanation for the missing funds, which is where Carl Eckert really ate the big one."

"Did Eckert realize what he was doing?"

"If you want my opinion, he did. He's claimed all along he had no idea what Wendell was up to, but Eckert himself did the nuts-and-bolts end of the biz, so he must have been aware. Hell, he had to know. He just maintained his innocence because there wasn't anyone to contradict him."

"Same thing the Jaffe kid is pulling now," I said.

Tommy smiled. "In matters like this, it always helps if your confederates are dead."

It was 1:15 when I left the building, zigzagging my way across the crowded lot to the far corner where I'd parked. Once I left the complex of government offices, I hung a left, heading back toward 101, managing to catch every traffic light between me and the freeway. At every stop, it amused me to watch women drivers take advantage of the moment to check their eye makeup and fluff their hair. I adjusted my rearview mirror, taking a quick look at the state of my own mop. I was nearly certain the little spiky patch near my left ear had grown some.

Almost inadvertently, I glanced at the car behind me. I got a quick hit of adrenaline, as though a hot wire had touched me. Renata was at the wheel, frowning slightly, her attention focused on her mobile phone. She was alone in the car, which didn't look like a rental, unless, of course, Avis and Hertz have taken to using Jaguars for their "full size." The light changed and I pulled away with Renata right behind me, moving at the same pace. I was in the inside lane of two moving in a southerly direction. She angled into the curb lane, her speed picking up as she passed me on the right.

I saw her right rear turn signal start to blink. I eased into the curb lane, taking my place behind her, trying to anticipate what she meant to do. A large shopping mall loomed up on our right. I saw her turn in, but before I could do likewise, someone cut in front of me. I braked abruptly, trying to avoid rear-ending the other driver while I scanned the parking lot ahead. Renata had taken a quick left and then turned down the second aisle, which seemed to extend the entire length of the mall. I turned into the entrance a full minute behind her. I sped through the parking lot on a parallel course, flying over speed bumps like a skier taking moguls. I kept thinking she would park, but she continued along the same path. There were two rows of cars between us, but in the one clear glimpse I caught, she was still on the phone. Whatever her conversation, she must have changed her mind about shopping. I saw her lean to the right, apparently replacing the handset. The next thing I knew, she reached an exit and took a left, easing into the flow of traffic again. I cut out at the exit, falling into the same lane as Renata, only two cars back. I didn't think she'd spotted me, and I wasn't sure she'd recognize me in a setting so different from the one in which she'd last seen me.

She passed the directional sign for Highway 101, cranking up her speed when she hit the on ramp. The driver in front of me began to slow. "Go on, go on," I was urging under my breath. The guy was old and cautious, swinging wide to the left for a right-hand turn into the gas station on the corner. By the time I whipped around him and up the ramp, Renata's Jaguar was no longer visible among the speeding northbound cars. She was the kind of driver who shot any gap she saw, and she'd apparently zigzagged her way out of sight. I drove the next twenty-five miles, straining for sight of her, but she was gone, gone, gone. I realized, belatedly, that I had missed the opportunity to pick off the numbers on her license plate. The only comfort I took was in the simple assumption that if Renata was in the area, Wendell Jaffe probably wasn't far away.

# 12

BACK IN SANTA TERESA, I went straight to the office, where I hauled out my portable Smith-Corona and typed up my notes, recording the events of the past two days as well as names, addresses, and miscellaneous data. Then I calculated the time I'd put in and tacked on gasoline and mileage. I was probably going to bill CF at a flat rate of fifty bucks an hour, but I wanted to have an itemized accounting ready in case Gordon Titus turned all prissy and authoritarian. Down deep, I knew this rapt attention to the paperwork was only a thinly disguised cover for my mounting excitement. Wendell had to be close by, but what was he doing and what would it take to bring him into the light? At least the Renata sighting had confirmed my hunch . . . unless the two of them had split up, which didn't seem likely. He had family here. I wasn't sure she did. On an impulse, I checked the local telephone directory, but there were no Huffs listed. Hers was probably an alias just as his name was. I would have given just about anything to lay eyes on the man, but that was beginning to feel about as likely as a UFO sighting.

At this stage of any investigation, I'm inclined to impatience. It always feels the same way to me—as though this is the case that's finally going to do me in. So far, I haven't blown a gig. I don't always succeed in ways that I anticipate, but I haven't yet failed to bring a case to resolution. The problem with being a PI is there isn't any rule book. There's no set procedure, no company manual, and no prescribed strategy. Every case is different, and every investigator ends up flying by the seat of her (or his) pants. If you're doing a background check, you can always make the rounds, looking up deeds, titles, births and deaths, marriages, divorces, credit information, business and criminal records. Any competent detective quickly learns how to follow the trail of paper bread crumbs left by the private citizen wandering in the bureaucratic forest. But the success of a missing persons search depends on ingenuity, persistence, and just plain old dumb luck. The leads you develop are based on personal contact, and you better be good at reading human nature while you're at it. I sat and thought about what I'd learned so far. It really wasn't much, and I didn't feel I was any closer to homing in on Wendell Jaffe. I began to transcribe my notes onto index cards. If all else failed, maybe I could shuffle them and deal myself a game of solitaire.

The next time I looked up, it was 4:35. My Spanish class met on Tuesday afternoons from 5:00 until 7:00. I really didn't need to leave for another fifteen minutes, but I'd exhausted my little storehouse of clerical skills. I slipped the paperwork in a folder and locked the file cabinet. I locked the office door behind me, went out through the side door, and down the stairs. I had to stand on the street corner for a good sixty seconds, trying to remember where I'd parked my car. It finally occurred to me and I was just setting off when I heard Alison yoo-whooing from the window.

"Kinsey!"

I shaded my eyes against the late afternoon sun. She was on the little third-floor balcony outside John Ives's office, blond hair hanging over the railing like a latter-day Rapunzel. "Lieutenant Whiteside's on the line. You want me to take a message?"

"Yes, if you would, or he can call my machine and leave a message himself. I'm going off to class, but I'll be home by seven-thirty. If he wants me to call back, ask him to leave me a number."

She nodded and waved, disappearing from sight.

I retrieved my car and drove over to the adult ed facility, which was two miles away. Vera Lipton pulled into the parking lot, arriving shortly after I did. She turned into the first half-empty aisle on her right. I'd eased into the second aisle on the left, parking closer to the classroom. Both of us were testing theories about how to make the quickest getaway once Spanish class ended. Most of the available classrooms had been pressed into service, and there were anywhere from a hundred and fifty to two hundred students piling into cars at the same time.

I grabbed my legal pad, my pile of papers, and my copy of *501 Spanish Verbs*. I locked the car in haste and made a diagonal cut across the parking lot, intercepting Vera. We'd first met when I was still doing periodic investigations for California Fidelity Insurance, where she was employed as an adjuster, later promoted to claims manager. She's probably as close to a best friend as I'll ever have, though I don't really know what such a relationship entails. Now that we no longer have adjacent offices, our contact has taken on a "catch as catch can" quality. This was one reason taking a class together seemed so appealing. During the break, we'd do a fast personal update. Sometimes she'd invite me over for supper after class, and we'd end up laughing and chatting into the night. After thirty-seven years of dedicated singlehood, she'd married a family practice physician named Neil Hess, whom she'd tried to fix me up with the year before. What amused me at the time was that I could tell she was smitten, though she'd decided he was inappropriate for reasons I thought bogus. Specifically, she seemed to object to the fact that she was nearly six inches taller. In the end, love won out. Or maybe Neil got lifts.

They'd been married now for nine months—since the previous Halloween—and I'd never seen her looking better. She's a big gal to begin with: maybe five feet ten, a hundred and forty pounds on a good-size frame. She'd never been apologetic about her generous proportions. The truth was, men seemed to regard her as some sort of goddess, striking up conversations with her everywhere she went. Now that she and Neil were working out together—jogging and playing tennis—she'd dropped fifteen pounds. Her once dyed red hair had grown out to its natural color, a honeyed brown that she was wearing shoulder length. She still dressed like a flight instructor: jumpsuits with padded shoulders and tinted aviator glasses, sometimes with spike heels, tonight with boots.

When she caught sight of me, she whipped off her

glasses and stuck them upright on her head like a prescription tiara. She waved enthusiastically. *"¡Hola!"* she called in merry Spanish tones. So far, this was the only word we'd really mastered, and we used it on each other as often as we could. Some guy clipping the hedges looked up expectantly, probably thinking that Vera was addressing him.

*"¡Hola!"* I replied. *"¿Dónde están los gatos?"* Still in search of those elusive black cats.

*"En los árboles."*

*"Muy bueno,"* I said.

"God, doesn't that sound great?"

"Yeah, I'm almost sure that guy over there thinks we're Hispanic," I said.

Vera grinned, flashing him a thumbs-up before she turned back to me. "You're here early for a change. You usually come flying in fifteen minutes late."

"I was doing some paperwork and couldn't wait to quit. How are you? You look great."

We strolled into class, absorbed in chitchat and idle gossip until the instructor arrived. Patty Abkin-Quiroga is petite and enthusiastic, amazingly tolerant of our clumsy lurches through the language. There's nothing so humbling as being a dunce in a foreign tongue, and if it weren't for her compassion, we'd have lost heart after two weeks. As usual, she started the class by regaling us with a long tale in Spanish, something to do with her activities that day. Either she ate a tostado or her little boy, Edwardo, flushed his baby bottle down the toilet and she had to have the plumber come out and take a look.

When I got home after class and let myself into my apartment, I could see the message light blinking on my answering machine. I pressed the button and listened as I moved around my tiny living room, turning on lights.

"Hello, Kinsey. Lieutenant Whiteside over at Santa Teresa Police Department. I got a fax this afternoon from our pals in the Los Angeles Passport Office. They don't show anything on Dean DeWitt Huff, but they do have a record of a Renata Huff at the following address in Perdido." I snatched up a pen and scribbled a note on a paper napkin while he was reciting the particulars. "If I'm not mistaken, that's over in the Perdido Keys. Let me know what you find out. I'm off tomorrow, but I'll be back on Thursday."

I said, "All riiight," giving both raised fists a shake. I did a quick dance, complete with butt wiggles, thanking the universe for small favors. I dumped my plans for dinner up at Rosie's. Instead, I made myself a peanut-butter-and-pickle sandwich on whole-wheat bread, wrapping it in waxed paper and then sealing it in a plastic bag the way my aunt had taught me. In addition to the preservation of fresh sandwiches, my other notable household skill—thanks to her odd notions—is the ability to gift wrap and tie a package of any size without the use of Scotch tape or stickers. This she considered essential preparation for life.

It was ten of eight and still light out when I hit 101 again. I ate my laptop picnic, steering with one hand while I held my sandwich with the other, humming to myself as the flavors mingled on my tongue. My car radio had been ominously silent for days, and I suspected some relevant fuse had given up the ghost deep inside. I flipped the on button anyway, on the off chance it had somehow healed itself in my absence. No such luck. I flipped the radio off, amusing myself instead with recollections of the annual celebration of Perdido/Olvidado township history, which consisted of a dispirited parade, the erection of many food booths, and the local citizens walking listlessly about, spilling mustard and hot dog relish on their P/O T-shirts.

Father Junipero Serra, who was the first president of the Alta California Missions, established nine missions along a six-hundred-and-fifty-mile stretch of California coastland between San Diego and Sonoma. Father Fermin Lasuen, who assumed leadership in 1785, the year after Serra's death, founded nine more missions. There were other less luminous mission presidents, countless friars and padres whose names have vanished from public awareness. One of these, Father Prospero Olivarez, petitioned in early 1781 to build two small sister missions on the Santa Clara River. Father Olivarez argued that adjacent presidios, or forts, established on dual sites would not only serve as protection for the proposed mission to be built in Santa Teresa, but could simultaneously convert, shelter, and train scores of California Indians who could then serve as skilled laborers for the projected construction process. Father Junipero Serra greatly favored the idea and granted enthusiastic approval. Extensive drawings were submitted, and the site was dedicated. However, a series of frustrating and inexplicable delays resulted in postponement of the ground breaking until after Serra's death, at which point the plan was quashed. Father Olivarez's twin churches were never built. Some historians have portrayed Olivarez as both worldly and ambitious, positing that the withdrawal of support for his project was intended to subdue his unbecoming secular aspirations. Ecclesiastical documents that have since come to light suggest another possibility, that Father Lasuen, who was championing the establishment of missions at Soledad, San Jose, San Juan Bautista, and San Miguel, saw Olivarez as a threat to the achievement of his own aims and deliberately sabotaged his efforts until after Father Serra's demise. His own subsequent rise to power was the death knell of Olivarez's vision. Whatever the truth, cynical observers renamed the dual sites Perdido/Olvidado, a mongrelization of Prospero Olivarez's name. Translated from Spanish, the names mean Lost and Forgotten.

This trip, I bypassed the main business district. The architecture in the town itself was a mix of boxy, blocky modern buildings interspersed with Victorian structures. On the far side of 101, between the freeway and the ocean, there were whole sections of the land entirely covered with blacktop, a series of interconnecting parking lots for supermarkets, gas stations, and fast-food establishments. One could drive for blocks through linked acres of asphalt without ever actually going out onto a city street. I took the Seacove off ramp, heading for the Perdido Keys.

Closer to the ocean, the houses seemed to take on the look of a little beach town—board-and-batten with big decks, painted sea blue and gray, the yards filled with impossibly bright purple, yellow, and orange flowers. I passed a house where there were so many wet suits hung to dry on a second-story balcony that it looked as if the guests from a cocktail party had wandered out on the deck for air.

Daylight had faded to indigo, and all the house lights in the neighborhood were coming on when I finally located the street I was looking for. The houses on both sides of this narrow lane backed onto the keys, long fingers of seawater stretching back from the ocean. The rear of each house seemed to boast a wide wooden deck with a short wood ramp leading down to a dock, the channel itself deep enough to admit sizable boats. I could smell the cool marina cologne, and the quiet was underscored by an occasional slap of water and the chorusing of frogs.

I cruised slowly, squinting at house numbers, finally spotting the address Whiteside had given me. Renata Huff's house was a two-story dark blue stucco with white trim. The roof was wood shake, and the rear portion of the property was shielded from the street by a white board fence. The house was dark, and a FOR SALE sign hung from a post in the front yard. I said, "Well, damn it."

I parked the car across the street and approached the house, moving up a long wooden ramp on to the front door. I rang the bell as if I expected to be admitted. I didn't see a lockbox from the real estate company, which might mean that Renata was still in residence. Casually, I checked the houses on either side of hers. One was dark, and the other showed lights only at the rear. I turned then so I could scrutinize the houses across the street. As nearly as I could tell, I wasn't under observation and there didn't seem to be any vicious dogs on the premises. Often, I consider this a tacit invitation to break and enter, but I had spied, through one of the two narrow windows flanking the front door, the telltale dot of red light denoting an alarm system, armed and ready. This was not gracious behavior on Renata's part.

Now what? I had the option to get back in my car

and return to Santa Teresa, but I hated to admit I'd made the trip for naught. I glanced over at the house to the right of Renata's. Through a side window I could see a woman in her kitchen, head bent to some domestic chore. I walked down the ramp and crossed the yard, trying to avoid the flower beds as I made my way to the door. I rang the bell, staring with idle curiosity at Renata's front porch. Even as I watched, her burglar-fooling lights came on. Now it looked like an empty house filled with pointlessly burning lamps.

Somebody flipped on the porch light overhead and opened the door to the length of the chain. "Yes?" The woman was probably in her forties. All I could see of her was her long, dark, curly hair that cascaded past her shoulders, like the wig on a decadent seventeenth-century fop. She smelled like flea soap. I thought at first it was some new designer perfume until I noticed the towel-swaddled dog she was toting under her arm. It was one of those little brown-and-black jobs about the size of a loaf of bread. Muffin, Buffy, Princess.

I said, "Hi. I wonder if you can give me some information about the house for sale next door. I noticed the outside ramp. Do you happen to know if the place is equipped for the handicapped?"

"Yes, it is."

I was hoping for a little more in the way of information. "On the inside, too?"

"That's right. Her husband suffered a real bad stroke about ten years ago . . . a month before they started work on the house. She had the contractor adjust all the plans for wheelchair access, including a lift up to the second floor."

"Amazing," I murmured. "My sister's in a wheelchair, and we've been looking for a place that would accommodate her disability." Since I couldn't see the woman's face, I found myself addressing my remarks to the dog, who really seemed quite attentive.

The woman said, "Really. What's wrong with her?"

"She was in a diving accident two years ago and she's paralyzed from the waist down."

"That's too bad," she said. Her tone suggested the sort of fake concern a stranger's story generates. I could have bet she was formulating questions she was too polite to ask.

Actually, I was beginning to feel pretty bad about Sis myself, though she sounded brave. "She's doing pretty well. She's adjusted, at any rate. We were driving around today, checking out the neighborhood. We've been house hunting now for what seems like ages, and this is the first that's really sparked her interest, so I told her I'd stop by and ask. Do you have any idea what they're asking for the place?"

"I heard four ninety-five."

"Really? Well, that's not bad. I think I'll have our real estate agent set up an appointment to show us through. Is the owner home during the day?"

"That's hard to say. Lately, she's been out of town quite a lot."

"What's her name again?" I asked as if she'd told me once.

"Renata Huff."

"What about her husband? If she's not home, could I have the agent give him a call instead?"

"Oh, sorry. Dean died, Mr. Huff. I thought I mentioned he had a heart attack." The dog began to wiggle, bored with all this talk that didn't directly relate to him.

"That's awful," I said. "How long ago was that?"

"I don't know. Probably five or six years."

"And she hasn't remarried?"

"She never seemed to have the interest, which is surprising. I mean, she is young—in her forties—and she comes from a lot of money. At least that's the story I heard." The dog began to lick upward, trying to hit the woman's mouth. This might have been some kind of doggy signal, but I wasn't sure what it meant. Kiss, eat, get down, stop.

"I wonder why she wants to sell? Is she leaving the area?"

"I really couldn't say, but if you want to leave me your number, the next time I see her, I can tell her you stopped by."

"All right. I'd appreciate that."

"Hang on. Let me get some paper."

She moved away from the door to a drop-leaf table in the foyer. When she came back, she had a pencil and a junk-mail envelope.

I gave her my number, inventing freely. As long as I was about it, I gave myself the prefix for Montebello, where all the rich people live. "Can you give me Mrs. Huff's number in case the agent doesn't have it?"

"I don't have that. I think it's unlisted."

"Oh, the agent probably has it. Let's don't worry about that," I said casually. "In the meantime, do you think she'd mind if I just peeped in a couple of windows?"

"I'm sure not. It's a really nice place."

"Sure looks like it." I remarked. "I notice there's a boat dock. Does Mrs. Huff have a boat?"

"Oh, yes, she has a nice big sailboat . . . a forty-eight-footer. But I haven't seen it out there for a while. She might be having some work done. I know she pulls it out of the water from time to time. Anyway, I better go before the dog gets cold."

"Right. Thanks very much. You've been very helpful."

"No problem," she said.

# 13

TWO REPRODUCTION CARRIAGE lamps cast overlapping circles of light onto the front porch. The front door was flanked by two panels of glass. I put my cupped hands to the window on the right. I found myself peering past the foyer and down a short corridor, which seemed to open to a great room at the rear. The interior of the house had highly polished hardwood floors, bleached and then rubbed with a wash of pale gray. Doorjambs had been removed for easy wheelchair passage. A row of French doors along the rear wall allowed me to see all the way to the wood deck out back.

In the section of the great room defined by lamplight, I could see that the Oriental carpet had been laid flush with the pickled flooring. To my right, a stairway angled up to the second floor. The neighbor had mentioned a lift, but there was none in evidence. Maybe Renata had had the mechanism removed once Mr. Huff expired. I wondered if it was his passport Wendell Jaffe was using. I crossed the porch, moving right to left. From window to window, I could see the house unfold. The rooms were uncluttered, orderly, surfaces gleaming. There was a den at the front and what looked like a guest bedroom, probably with a bath attached.

I left the porch and moved along the left side of the house. The garage was locked, probably protected by the alarm system as well. I checked the gate into the backyard; it didn't seem to have a lock. I pulled a ring that had a length of string attached. The latch was released and I pushed my way in, holding my breath to see if the gate was tied to the security system. Dead silence, except for the squeaking of the gate as it swung on its hinges. I eased the gate shut behind me and moved down the narrow walkway between the garage and the fence. I could see the exhaust vent for a dryer, and I imagined the laundry room was located on the other side of the wall.

The deck was ablaze, two-hundred-watt floods creating a crazy daylight of sorts. I moved along the back of the house, peering in through the French doors. More views of the great room and the dining room next to that, with a slice of kitchen visible beyond. Oh, dear. I could see now that Renata had chosen the kind of wallpaper only decorators find attractive: a poisonous Chinese yellow with vines and puffballs exploding across the surface. There was expensive fabric to match, drapes and upholstery continuing the pattern. It was possible that a fungus had got loose in the room, replicating like a virus until every corner had been invaded. I'd seen pictures of something like this in a science magazine, mold spores blown up to nineteen hundred times their actual size.

I wandered across the deck and down the ramp to the darkened water in the marina. I turned and looked back at the house. There were no outside stairs and no visible way to reach the second-story bedrooms. I went back through the gate, letting the latch close behind me, making sure the street was clear of approaching cars. All I needed was Renata Huff returning home, headlights picking me out of the darkness as she turned into her driveway.

As I passed the mailbox at the curb, my bad angel tapped me on the shoulder and suggested a violation of U.S. postal regulations. "Would you quit that?" I said crossly. Of course, I'd already reached out and pulled the flap down, taking out the sheaf of mail that had been delivered that day. It was too dark on the street to sort out all the good stuff, so I was forced to shove the whole batch of envelopes in my handbag. God, I'm so rotten. Sometimes I can't believe the kind of shit I pull. Here I was, lying to the neighbor, stealing Renata's mail. Were there no depths to which I wouldn't sink? Apparently not. Dimly, I wondered if the penalties for mail tampering were per incident or per piece. If the latter, I was racking up a lot of jail time.

Before I headed home again, I made a detour past Dana Jaffe's house. I doused my headlights, cruising to a stop across the street from her place. I left my keys in the ignition, making my way silently across the street. All the ground-floor lights were on. Traffic at that hour was sparse to nonexistent. There were no neighbors in evidence, no dog walkers on the street. I angled my way across the grass through the darkness. Shrubs growing at the side of the house provided sufficient cover to al-low me to spy without interruption. I thought I might as well add trespass and prowling to my other sins.

Dana was watching television, her face turned toward the console between the windows in front. Shifting lights played across her face as the program continued. She lit a cigarette. She sipped white wine from a glass on the table beside her. There was no sign of Wendell and nothing to suggest she had company in the house. Occasionally she would smile, perhaps in response to the canned laughter I could hear vibrating in the wall. I realized I'd been entertaining a suspicion that she was in league with him, that she knew where he was now and where he'd been all these years. Seeing her alone, I found myself dismissing the idea. I simply couldn't believe she'd collude in Wendell's abandonment of her sons. Both boys had suffered in the last five years.

I went back to my car and fired up my engine, making an illegal U-turn before I flipped on my headlights. Once I reached Santa Teresa, I stopped off at the McDonald's on Milagro and picked up a Quarter Pounder and an order of fries. For the remainder of the drive home, the air in the car was moist with the smell of steamed onions and hot pickles, meat patty nestled in melted cheese and condiments. I parked the car and toted my belated second supper with me through the squeaking back gate.

Henry's lights were out. I let myself into my apartment. I removed the Styrofoam box and set it on the counter. I opened the lid and used the top half of the container as a receptacle for my fries, taking a few minutes to bite open the handful of ketchup packets, which I squeezed over my shoestring potatoes. I perched on a bar stool, munching junk food while I sorted through the mail I'd stolen. It's hard to give up chronic thievery when my crimes net me such a bonanza of information. Purely on instinct, I'd managed to snag Renata's telephone bill with her unlisted number in a box at the top and a neatly ordered list of all the numbers from which she'd charged calls in the past thirty days. The Visa bill, a joint account, was like a little road map of places she and "Dean DeWitt Huff" had stayed. For a dead man, he was apparently having himself a fine old time. There were some nice samples of his handwritting on some of the credit card receipts. The charges from Viento Negro hadn't surfaced yet, but I could track the two of them backward from La Paz, to Cabo San Lucas, to a hotel in San Diego. All port towns easily accessible from the boat, I noticed.

I went to bed at 10:30 and slept solidly, waking at six o'clock, half a second before my alarm was set to go off. I pushed the covers aside and reached for my sweats. After hasty ablutions, I tinked down my spiral staircase and out to the street.

There was an early morning chill, but the air was curiously muggy, residual heat held in by the lowering cloud cover overhead. The early morning light was pearly. The beach looked as fine and as supple as gray leather, wrinkled by the night winds, smoothed by the surf. My cold was rapidly fading, but I didn't dare try jogging the full three miles yet. I alternated between walking and trotting, keeping track of my lungs and the creaking protests in my legs. At that hour, I tend to keep an uneasy eye out for the unexpected. I see the occasional homeless person, sexless and anonymous, sleeping in the grass, an old woman with a shopping cart alone at a picnic table. I'm especially alert to the odd-looking men in scruffy suits, gesturing, laughing, chatting with invisible companions. I'm wary of being incorporated in those strange and fearful dramas. Who knows what part we play in other people's dreams?

I showered, dressed, and ate a bowl of cereal while I scanned the paper. I drove into the office and spent a frustrating twenty minutes hunting for a parking space that wouldn't generate a ticket. I nearly had to break down and try the public lot, but I was saved at the last minute by a woman in a pickup who vacated a spot just across the street.

I went through the mail from the day before. Nothing much of interest, except the notification that I'd won a million dollars. Well, either me or the two other people mentioned. In fine print, it said that Minnie and Steve were actually already collecting their millions in $40,000 installments. I got busy and tore out perforated stamps, which I licked and pasted in various squares. I studied the material, seriously worried I might win the third prize jet ski. What the hell was I going to do with that? Maybe I'd give it to Henry for his birthday. I went ahead and balanced my checkbook, just to clear the decks. While I was eliminating some of those pesky excess dollars, I picked up the receiver and tried Renata Huff's unlisted number, without results.

Something was nagging at me, and it had nothing to do with Wendell Jaffe or Renata Huff. It was Lena Irwin's reference yesterday to the Burton Kinsey family up in Lompoc. Despite my denials, the name had set up a low hum in my memory, like the nearly inaudible buzz of power lines overhead. In many ways, my whole sense of myself was embedded in the fact of my parents' death in an automobile wreck when I was five. I knew my father had lost control of the car when a rock tumbled down a steep hill and crashed into the windshield. I was on the backseat, flung against the front seat on impact, wedged there for hours while the fire department worked to extract me from the wreckage. I remember my mother's hopeless crying and the silence that came afterward. I remember slipping a hand around the edge of the driver's seat, slipping a finger into my father's hand, not realizing he was dead. I remember going to live with the aunt who raised me after that, my mother's sister, whose name was Virginia. I called her Gin Gin or Aunt Gin. She had told me little, if anything, about the family history before or after that event. I knew, because the fact was embedded in the tale, that my parents were on their way up to Lompoc the day they were killed, but I never thought about the reason for the trip. My aunt had never told me the nature of the journey, and I'd never asked. Given my insatiable curiosity and my natural inclination to poke my nose in where it doesn't belong, it was odd to realize how little attention I'd paid to my own past. I'd simply accepted what I was told, constructing my personal mythology on the flimsiest of facts. Why had I never pushed aside that veil?

I thought about myself, about the kind of child I was when I was five and six, isolated, insular. After their deaths, I created a little world for myself in a cardboard box, filled with blankets and pillows, lighted by a table lamp with a sixty-watt bulb. I was very particular about what I ate. I would make sandwiches for myself, cheese and pickle, or Kraft olive pimento cheese, cut in four equal fingers, which I would arrange on a plate. I had to do everything myself, and it all had to be just so.

Dimly, I remember my aunt hovering nearby. I wasn't aware of her worry at the time, but now when I see the image, I know she must have been deeply concerned about me. I would take my food and crawl into my container, where I would look at picture books and nibble, stare at the cardboard ceiling, hum to myself, and sleep. For four months, maybe five, I withdrew into that ecosphere of artificial warmth, that cocoon of grief. I taught myself how to read. I drew pictures, made shadow creatures with my fingers against the walls of my den. I taught myself how to tie my shoes. Perhaps I thought they'd come back for me, that mother, that father, whose faces I could project, home cinema for the orphaned, a girl child who until lately had been safely ensconced in that little family. I can still remember how cold the trailer felt whenever I crawled out. My aunt never interfered with me. When school started in the fall, I emerged like a little animal coming out of its lair. Kindergarten was fearful. I wasn't used to other children. I wasn't accustomed to noise or to regimentation. I didn't like Mrs. Bowman, the teacher, in whose eyes I could read both pity and disapproval, that judgment. I was an odd child. I was timid. I was anxious all the time. Nothing I've faced since has even come close to the horrors of grade school. I can see now how the story, whatever it was, must have followed me like a specter from level to level: penned in my record, appended to my file, from teacher to teacher, through conferences with the principal . . . what shall we do with her? How shall we cope with her tears and her stoniness? So bright, so fragile, stubborn, introverted, asocial, easily upset . . .

When the phone rang I jumped, adrenaline washing

through me like a blast of ice water. I snatched up the receiver, my heart thudding in my throat. "Kinsey Millhone Investigations."

"Hello, Kinsey. This is Tommy down at the Perdido County Jail. Brian Jaffe's attorney just notified our office that you can talk to him if you want. He didn't sound too happy about it, but I guess Mrs. Jaffe insisted."

"She did?" I said, unable to disguise my astonishment.

He laughed. "Maybe she thinks you'll go to bat for him, clear up this misunderstanding about the jailbreak and the little gal who got shot to death."

"Yeah, right," I said. "When should I come down?"

"Any time you want."

"What's the protocol on this? Shall I ask for you?"

"Ask for the senior deputy. Name's Roger Tiller. He knew the Jaffe kid back when he was working truancy patrol. I thought you might like to pick his brain."

"That's great."

Before I could thank him properly, the phone clicked in my ear. I was smiling to myself as I snagged my handbag and headed for the door. The nice thing about cops—once they decide you're okay, there's nobody more generous.

Deputy Tiller and I traversed the corridor, our footsteps out of synch, keys jingling as he walked. The camera up in the corner was keeping track of us. He was older than I'd expected, in his late fifties and heavyset, his uniform fitting snugly on a five-foot-eight frame. I had a quick vision of him at the end of a shift, stripping off his clothes with relief, like a woman peeling off a girdle. His body probably bore the permanent marks of all the buckles and apparatus. His sandy hair was receding, and he had a sandy mustache to match, green eyes, a pug nose, the kind of face that would have seemed appropriate on a kid of twenty-two. His heavy leather belt was making creaking sounds, and I noticed that his posture and his manner changed when he got in range of an inmate. A small group of them, five, were waiting to be buzzed through a metal door with a glass window embedded with chicken wire. Latinos, in their twenties, they wore jail blues and white T-shirts, rubber sandals. In accordance with regulations, they were silent, their hands clasped behind their backs. White wristbands indicated that they were GP, general population, incarcerated because of DUIs and crimes against property.

I said, "Sergeant Ryckman says you met Brian Jaffe when you were working truancy patrol. How long ago was that?"

"Five years. Kid was twelve, ornery as hell. I remember one day I picked him up and took him back to school three different times. I can't even tell you how many meetings we scheduled with the student study team. School psychologist finally threw her hands up. I felt sorry for his mother. We all knew what she was going through. He's a bad apple. Smart, good-looking, had a mouth on him wouldn't quit." Deputy Tiller shook his head.

"Did you ever meet his father?"

"Yeah, I knew Wendell." He tended to talk without making eye contact, and the effect was curious.

Since that subject seemed to go nowhere, I tried another tack. "How'd you get from truancy patrol to this?"

"Applied for administrative position. To be eligible for promotion, everybody gets a year's tour of jail duty. It's the pits. I like the people well enough, but you spend the whole day in artificial light. Like living in a cave. All this filtered air. I'd rather be out on the streets. Little danger never hurts. Helps keep your juices up." We paused in front of a freight-size elevator.

"I understand Brian escaped from juvenile hall. What was he in for?"

Deputy Tiller pressed a button and made a verbal request to have the elevator take us up to level two, where inmates designated as administrative segregation or medical were housed. The elevators themselves were devoid of interior controls, which effectively prevented their being commandeered by inmates. "Burglary, exhibiting or drawing a firearm, resisting arrest. He was actually being held in Connaught, which is medium security. These days, juvenile hall's maximum security."

"That's a switch, isn't it? I thought juvenile hall was for out-of-control minors."

"Not anymore. Old days, those kids were known as 'status offenders.' Parents could have 'em made wards of the court. Now, juvenile hall's turned into a junior prison. Kids are hard-core criminals. Three M's. Murder, mayhem, and manslaughter, lot of gang-related stuff."

"What about Jaffe? What's the story on him?"

"Kid's got no soul. You'll see it in his eyes. Completely empty in there. He's got brains, but no conscience. He's a sociopath. Our best information, it was him engineered the breakout, talked the gangbangers into it because he needed someone to speak Spanish. Once they crossed the border, the plan was they'd split up. I don't know where he was headed, but the others ended up dead."

"All three? I thought the one kid survived the shoot-out."

"Died last night without regaining consciousness."

"What about the girl? Who was responsible for her death?"

"You'd have to ask Jaffe about that since he's the only one left. Real convenient for him, and believe me, he'll take advantage of it." We'd reached the interview room on level two. Tiller took out a ring of keys and turned one in the lock. He pulled the door open on the empty room where I was to meet with Brian. "I used to think these kids could be salvaged if we did our job right. Now seems like we're just lucky to keep 'em off the streets." He shook his head, and his smile was bitter. "I'm getting too old for this stuff. Time to go shuffle me some paperwork. Have a seat. Your boy'll be here in just a minute."

The interview room was six feet by eight with no outside windows. The walls were unadorned, a semi-gloss beige. I could still smell the lingering odor of la-tex paint. I've heard there's a full-time crew whose sole job is to repaint. By the time they complete the work up on level four, it's time to go back to level one and start all over again. There was one small wooden table and two chairs with metal frames, the seats padded in green vinyl. The floor tiles were brown. There was nothing else in the room except the video camera mounted in one corner near the ceiling. I took the chair that faced the open door.

When Brian entered the room, I was surprised first by his size and second by his beauty. For eighteen he was small, and his manner seemed tentative. I'd seen eyes like his before, very clear, very blue, filled with an aching innocence. My ex-husband, Daniel, had a similar characteristic, some aspect of his nature that seemed unbearably sweet. Of course, Daniel was a drug addict. Also a liar and a cheat, in full possession of his faculties, and bright enough to know the differences between right and wrong. This kid was something else. Deputy Tiller claimed he was a sociopath, but I wasn't sure about that yet. He had Michael's pretty features, but he was blond where his brother was dark. Both were lean, though Michael was the taller and he seemed more substantial.

Brian sat down, slouching on his chair, hands held loosely between his knees. He seemed shy, but maybe that was just a trait he affected . . . sucking up to adults. "I talked to my mom. She said you might be in to see me."

"Did she tell you what I wanted?"

"Just something about my dad. She says he might be okay. Is that true?"

"We don't really know at this point. I was hired to find out."

"Did you know my dad? I mean, like before he disappeared?"

I shook my head. "I never met him. I was given some photographs and told where he'd been seen last. I did run into a guy who looked a lot like him, but then he disappeared again. I'm still hoping to track him down, but right now, I don't have any leads. Personally, I'm convinced it was him," I said.

"That's incredible, isn't it? To think he might be alive? I can't get over it. I mean, I don't even know what that'd be like." He had a full mouth and dimples. I found it hard to imagine he could fake such ingenuousness.

I said, "It must seem weird."

"Hey, no lie ... with all this stuff going down? I wouldn't want him to see me like this."

I shrugged. "If he comes back to town, he'll probably be in trouble himself."

"Yeah, that's what Mom said. She didn't seem all that happy. I guess I can't blame her after what she went through. Like, if he's been alive this whole time, it means he laid a bum deal on her."

"You remember much about him?"

"Not really. Michael does, my brother. Did you meet him?"

"Briefly. At your mother's."

"Did you see my nephew, Brendan? He's really cool. I miss him, little pea-head."

Enough of this chitchat. I was getting restless. "Mind if I ask you about Mexicali?"

He shifted uncomfortably. He ran a hand through his hair. "Man, that was bad. Makes me sick to think of it. I didn't have anything to do with killing anybody, I swear. It was Julio and Ricardo had the gun," he said.

"What about the breakout? How did that come to pass?"

"Uhm, hey, you know? Like, I don't think my attorney wants me to talk about that."

"I just have a couple of questions ... in strictest confidence. I'm trying to get a feel for what's going on here," I said. "Whatever you say goes no further."

"I better not," he murmured.

"Was it your idea?"

"Heck no, not me. You probably think I'm a jerk. I was stupid to go along with it . . . I can see that now . . . but at the time I just wanted to get out. I was desperate. You ever been in juvie?"

I shook my head.

"You're lucky."

I said, "Whose idea was it?"

He gave me a direct look, his blue eyes as clear as a swimming pool. "It was Earnesto came up with it."

"Were you pretty good friends?"

"No way! I only knew 'em because we were all in the same cottage at Connaught. That guy, Julio, said he'd kill me if I didn't help. I wasn't going to do it. I mean, I didn't want to go along with it, but he was big . . . real big guy . . . and he said he'd mess me up bad."

"He threatened you."

"Yeah, he said him and Ricardo would turn me out."

"Meaning sexual abuse."

"The worst," he said.

"Why you?"

"Why me?"

"Yeah. What made you so valuable to the enterprise? Why not another Hispanic if they were headed into Mexico?"

He shrugged. "Those guys are twisted. Who knows how they think?"

"What were you planning to do down in Mexico if you didn't speak the language?"

"Bum around. Hide. Cross back into Texas. Mostly I just wanted to get out of California. Court system here is not exactly on my side."

The jail officer knocked, indicating time was up.

Something about Brian's smile had already caused me to disconnect. I'm a liar by nature, a modest talent of mine, but one I cultivate. I probably know more about bullshit than half the people on the planet. If this kid was telling the truth, I didn't think he'd sound nearly so sincere.

# 14

ON THE WAY back to the office, I stopped off at the Hall of Records, which is located in one wing of the Santa Teresa Courthouse. The courthouse itself was reconstructed in the late 1920s after the 1925 earthquake destroyed the existing courthouse as well as a number of commercial buildings downtown. Hammered copper plates on the doors to the Hall of Records depict an allegorical history of the state of California. I pushed through the entrance doors into a large space, dissected by a counter. To the right, a small reception area was furnished by two heavy oak tables with matching leather chairs. The floors were tiled in polished dark red paving stones, the high ceilings painted with faded blue-and-gold designs. Thick beams bore the echo of the repetitive patterns. Graceful wooden columns were visible at intervals, topped with Ionic capitals, again painted in muted hues. The windows were arched, the leaded-glass panes pierced with rows of linked circles. The actual work of the department was accomplished with the aid of technology: action stations, telephones, computers, microfilm projectors. As a further concession to the present, sections of the walls had been paneled with the soundproofing equivalent of pegboard.

I kept my mind blank, struggling with a curious resistance to the piece of digging I was about to do. There were several people at the counter, and for one brief moment I considered postponing the chore until some other day. Then another clerk appeared, a tall, lean fellow in slacks and a short-sleeved dress shirt, wearing a pair of glasses with one opaque lens. "Help you?"

"I'd like to check your records for a marriage license issued in November of 1935."

"The name?" he asked.

"Millhone, Terrence Randall. Do you need her name as well?"

He made a note. "This will do."

He pushed a form across the counter, and I filled in the blanks, reassuring the county about my purposes in asking. It was a silly formality in my opinion since births, deaths, marriages, and property recordings are a matter of public record. The filing system in use was called Soundex, a curious process whereby the vowels in the last name are eliminated altogether and consonants are awarded various numerical values. The clerk helped me convert the name Millhone to its Soundex equivalent, and then he sent me over to an old-fashioned card catalog where I found my parents listed, along with the date of their marriage, and the book and page numbers of the volume where the license was recorded. I returned to the counter with the information in hand. The clerk made a call to some web-footed creature in the bowels of the building, whose job it was to conjure up the relevant records consigned to cassettes.

The clerk sat me down at the microfilm machine, rattling off a rapid series of instructions, half of which I missed. It didn't matter much, as he proceeded to turn the machine on and insert the cassette while he was telling me how to do it. Finally he left me to fast-forward my way through the bulk of the reel to the document in question. Suddenly, there they were—names and incidental personal data neatly entered into a record nearly fifty years old. Terrence Randall Millhone of Santa Teresa, California, and Rita Cynthia Kinsey of Lompoc, California, had married on November 18, 1935. He was thirty-three years old at the time of the wedding and listed his occupation as mail carrier. His father's name was Quillen Millhone. His mother's maiden name was Dace. Rita Kinsey was eighteen at the time of her marriage, occupation unlisted, daughter of Burton Kinsey and Cornelia Straith LaGrand. They were married by a Judge Stone of the Perdido Court of Appeal in a ceremony that took place in Santa Teresa at four in the afternoon. The witness who signed the form was Virginia Kinsey, my aunt Gin. So there they were, those three, standing together in the public register, not knowing that in twenty years husband and wife would be gone. As far as I knew there were no photographs of the wedding, no mementos of any kind. I'd seen only one or two pictures taken of them in later years. Somewhere I had a handful of snapshots of my babyhood and early childhood, but there were none of their respective families. I realized what a vacuum I'd been living in. Where other people had anecdotes, photograph albums, correspondence, family gatherings, all the trappings of family tradition, I had little or nothing to report. The notion of my mother's family, the Burton Kinseys, still residing up in Lompoc conjured up curious emotional contradictions. And what of my father's people? I'd never heard any mention of the Millhones at all.

I felt a sudden shift in my perspective. I could see in a flash what a strange pleasure I'd taken in being related to no one. I'd actually managed to feel superior about my isolation. I was subtle about it, but I could see that I'd turned it into a form of self-congratulation. *I wasn't the common product of the middle class.* I wasn't a party to any convoluted family drama—the feuds, unspoken alliances, secret agreements, and petty tyrannies. Of course, I wasn't a party to the good stuff, either, but who cared about that? I was different. I was special. At best, I was self-created; at worst, the hapless artifact of my aunt's peculiar notions about raising little girls. In either event, I regarded myself an outsider, a loner, which suited me to perfection. Now I had to consider the possibility of this unknown family unit ... whether I would claim them or they would claim me.

I rewound the reel of film and took the cassette up to the counter. I left the building and crossed the street, heading toward the three-story parking structure where I'd left my car. On my right was the public library, where I knew I could rustle up the Lompoc phone book if I was interested. But was I? Reluctantly I paused, debating the issue. It's only information, I said to myself. You don't have to make a decision, you just need to know.

I took a right, going up the outside stairs and into the building. I turned right again, pushing through the turnstiles designed to capture book thieves. The city directories and various telephone books from towns all across the state were shelved on the first floor to the left of the reference desk. I found the telephone book for Lompoc and leafed through the pages where I stood. I didn't want to act as if I cared enough to sit.

There was only one "Kinsey" listed, not Burton but Cornelia, my mother's mother, with the telephone number but no address. I found the Polk Directory for Lompoc and Vandenberg Air Force Base, checking the section where the telephone numbers were listed in order, beginning with the prefix. Cornelia was listed with an address on Willow Avenue. I checked the Polk Directory for the year before and saw that Burton was listed with her. The obvious inference was that she'd been widowed sometime between this year's census and the last. Terrific. What a deal. First time I find out I have a grandfather, he's dead. I made a note of the address on one of the deposit slips at the back of my checkbook. Half the people I know use deposit slips in lieu of business cards. Why don't banks add a few blanks back there for memos? I shoved the checkbook in my bag again and resolutely forgot about it. Later, I'd decide what I wanted to do.

I went back to the law office and let myself in the side entrance. When I opened the door, I found the message light blinking on my answering machine. I pressed the playback button and then went about the business of opening a window while I listened.

"Miss Millhone, this is Harris Brown. I'm a retired Santa Teresa police lieutenant and I just got a call from Lieutenant Whiteside over there who tells me you're trying to locate Wendell Jaffe. As I believe he mentioned, that was one of the last cases I worked before I left the department, and I'd be happy to discuss some of the details with you if you'll give me a call. I'll be in and out this afternoon, but you can probably reach me between two and three-fifteen at . . ."

I snatched up a pen and caught the number as he recited it. I checked my watch. Poot. It was only twelve forty-five. I tried the number anyway on the off chance he'd be there. No such luck. I tried Renata Huff again, but she wasn't home, either. I still had my hand on the receiver when the phone rang. "Kinsey Millhone Investigations," I said.

"May I speak to Mrs. Millhome?" some woman asked in a sing-song voice.

"This is she," I replied with caution. This was going to be a pitch.

"Mrs. Millhome, this is Patty Kravitz with Telemarketing Incorporated? How are you today?" She'd been instructed to smile at this point so her voice would sound very warm and friendly.

I ran my tongue along the inside of my cheek. "Fine. What about yourself?"

"That's good, Mrs. Millhome, we know you're a busy person, but we're conducting a survey for an exciting new product and wonder if you could take a few minutes to answer some questions. If you're willing to assist us, we have a nice prize already set aside for you. Can we count on your help?"

I could hear the babble of other voices in the boiler room behind her. "What's the product?"

"I'm sorry, but we're not allowed to divulge that information. I *am* permitted to indicate that this is an airline-related service and within the next few months will result in the introduction of an innovative new concept in business and leisure travel. Can we take just a few minutes out of your busy schedule?"

"Sure, why not?"

"That's good. Now, Mrs. Millhome, are you single, married, divorced, or widowed?"

I was really liking her sincere, spontaneous manner as she read from the laminated card in front of her. I said, "Widowed."

"I'm sorry to hear that," she said in a perfunctory manner as she breezed right on. "Do you own your home or rent?"

"Well, I used to own two homes," I said casually. "One here in Santa Teresa and one in Fort Myers, Florida, but now that John's passed away, I've had to sell the property down there. The only place I rent is an apartment in New York City."

"Really."

"I do quite a bit of traveling. That's why I'm helping you with the research," I said. I could practically hear her making frantic flagging motions to her supervisor. She had a live one on the line, and she might need help.

We moved on to the matter of my annual income, which I knew would be substantial with that extra million coming in. I proceeded to lie, fib, and equivocate, amusing myself with the questions while I honed my prevarication skills. We quickly worked our way down to the part where I only needed to write a check for $39.99 to claim the prize I'd won: a complete nine-piece set of matching designer luggage, retailing for over $600.00 in most department stores.

My turn to be skeptical. "You're kidding," I said. "And this is not a gimmick? All I pay is thirty-nine ninety-nine? I don't believe it."

She assured me the offer was genuine. The luggage was absolutely free. All I was being asked to cover was the shipping and handling, which I could also charge to my credit card if that was more convenient. She offered to send someone over to pick up the check within the hour, but I thought it was easier to go ahead and put it on my card. I gave her the account number, inventing a nice series of digits, which she dutifully read back to me. I could tell from her tone of voice she could hardly believe her good luck. I was probably the only person that day who hadn't damaged her hearing by promptly hanging up. Before the end of the business day, she and her cronies would be trying to charge off merchandise to that account.

For lunch I ate a carton of nonfat yogurt at my desk and then took a nap, leaning back in my chair. In between car chases and gun battles, we private eye types have occasional days like this. At two I roused myself, reaching over to pluck up the phone, trying Harris Brown again.

The number rang four times and then somebody picked up. "Harris Brown," he said, sounding cranky and out of breath.

I took my feet off the desk and introduced myself.

His tone underwent a shift and his interest picked up. "I'm glad you called. I was surprised to hear the guy had surfaced."

"Well, we still don't have confirmation, but it's looking good to me. How long did you work the case?"

"Oh, geez, probably seven months. I never for a minute believed he was dead, but I had a hell of a time convincing anyone else. I never did manage it, as a matter of fact. It's nice to have an old hunch confirmed. Anyway, tell me what kind of help you need."

"I'm not sure yet. I guess I was hoping to brainstorm," I said. "I've got a line on the woman he was traveling with, a gal named Renata Huff, who has a house down on the Perdido Keys."

He seemed startled by the information. "Where'd you come up with that one?"

"Uhm, I'd prefer not to spell it out. Let's just say I have my little ways," I said.

"Sounds like you're doing pretty good."

"Working on it," I said. "The problem is she's the only lead I have, and I can't figure out who else he'd turn to for help."

"To do what?"

I could feel myself backpedal, uncomfortable articulating my theory about Wendell. "Well, I hesitate to say this, but my hit on this is he heard about Brian . . ."

"The escape and shoot-out."

"Right. I think he's coming back to help his kid."

There was a fractional silence. "Help him how?"

"I don't know yet. I just can't think of any other reason he'd risk coming back."

"I might buy that," he said after giving it some thought. "So you're figuring he'd either contact close family or old pals of his."

"Exactly. I know who his ex-wife is and I've talked to her, but she doesn't seem to have a clue."

"And you believe that."

"Actually, I'm inclined to. I think she's being straight."

"Go on. I'm sorry to interrupt."

"Anyway, when it comes to Wendell, mostly I'm sitting around hoping he'll show his face, which he doesn't seem to be doing. I thought if we could sit down together, we might come up with some other possibilities. Could I impose on your time?"

"I'm retired now, Miss Millhone. Time is all I've got. Unfortunately, I'm tied up this afternoon. Tomorrow's fine if that suits."

"Looks good to me. What about lunch? Are you free by any chance?"

"That'd be doable," he said. "Where are you?"

I gave him my office address.

He said, "I'm out here in Colgate, but I have an errand in town. Is there someplace we can meet?"

"Whatever's convenient for you."

He suggested a large coffee shop on upper State, not the best place for food, but I knew we wouldn't need reservations for lunch. I made a note on my calendar when I hung up the phone. On a whim, I tried Renata's number.

Two rings. She picked up.

Oh, shit, I thought. "May I speak to Mr. Huff?"

"He's not here at the moment. Would you care to leave a message?"

"Is this Mrs. Huff?"

"Yes."

I tried a smile. "Mrs. Huff, this is Patty Kravitz with Telemarketing Incorporated? How are you today?"

"Is this a sales pitch?"

"Absolutely not, Mrs. Huff. I can guarantee it. We're doing market research. The company I work for is interested in your leisure pursuits and discretionary spending. These forms are filed by number, so your answers

are completely anonymous. In return for your cooperation, we have a nice prize already set aside."

"Oh, right. I bet."

Jesus, this lady wasn't very trusting. I said, "It will
only take five minutes of your valuable time." Then I
kept my mouth shut and let her work it out on her end.

"All right, but make it brief, and if it turns out you're
selling something, I'm going to be annoyed."

"I understand that. Now, Mrs. Huff, are you single,
married, divorced, or widowed?" I picked up a pencil
and started doodling on a legal pad, thinking ahead
frantically. What did I really hope to learn from her?

"Married."

"And do you own or rent your home?"

"What does this have to do with travel?"

"I'm getting to that. Is this a primary or vacation residence?"

Mollified. "Oh, I see. It's primary."

"And how many trips have you taken in the past six
months? None, one to three, or more than three?"

"One to three."

"Of the trips taken in the past six months, what percentage were business?"

"Look, would you just get to the point?"

"Fine. No problem. We'll just skip some of these. Do
you or your husband have plans to travel any time in
the next few weeks?"

Dead silence.

I said, "Hello?"

"Why do you ask?"

"Actually, that brings us to the end of my ques-
tionnaire, Mrs. Huff," I said, speaking rapidly and
smoothly. "As a special thank-you, we'd like to provide

you, at no cost, two round-trip tickets to San Francisco and two nights, all expenses paid, at the Hyatt Hotel. Will your husband be home soon to accept the complimentary tickets? There's absolutely no obligation on your part, but he *will* have to sign for them since the survey was in his name. Can I indicate to my supervisor when you might like to have us drop those off?"

"This is not going to work," she said, her voice tinged with irritation. "We expect to be leaving town momentarily, as soon as . . . I'm not sure when he'll be here and we're not interested." With a click, she disconnected.

Shit! I banged the phone down on my end. Where was the man, and what was he up to that might "momentarily" motivate his departure from Perdido? Nobody's heard from him. At least, nobody *I* knew of. I couldn't believe he'd talked to Carl Eckert, unless he'd done so within the last half day. As nearly as I could tell, he hadn't been in touch with Dana or Brian. I wasn't sure about Michael. I'd probably have to check that out.

What the hell was Wendell doing? Why would he come this close to his family without making contact? Of course, it was always possible he'd managed to talk to all three of them, and if that was the case, they were better liars than I was. Maybe it was time for the cops to put a tail on Renata Huff. And it might not hurt to run Wendell's picture in the local papers. As long as he was running, we might as well sic the dogs on him. Meanwhile, come suppertime, I was going to have to make yet another trip to Perdido.

# 15

I set out for Perdido again after supper that evening. The drive was pleasant, the light at that hour a tawny yellow, gilding the south-facing mountain ridges in gold leaf. As I passed Rincon Point, I could still see surfers out in the water. Most were straddling their boards, rocking in the low swell, chatting while they waited, ever hopeful, for a wave. The surf was mild for the moment, but the weather map in the morning paper had showed an eastern Pacific hurricane off the California Baja, and there was talk that the storm system was moving up the coast. I noticed then that the horizon was rimmed with black clouds like a row of brushes, sweeping a premature darkness in our direction. The Rincon, with its rocky projection and its offshore shoals, seems to act like a magnet for turbulent weather.

*Rincón* is the Spanish term for the cove formed by a land point projecting seaward. Here, the coastline is molded into a series of such indentations, and for a stretch, the ocean butts right up against the roadway. At high tide the waves erupt along the embankment, sending up a white wall of frustrated water. Beyond, on my left, fields of flowers had been cultivated on several terraces where the underlying earth was slumping toward the sea. The vibrant red, gold, and magenta of the zinnias glowed in the half-light as if illuminated from below.

It was just after 7:00 when I left Highway 101 at Perdido Street. I sailed through the light at the intersection and crossed Main Street on a northbound path that cut through the Boulevards. I turned left at Median and pulled over to the curb about six houses down. Michael's yellow VW bug was parked in the driveway. The windows along the front of the house were dark, but I could see lights on in the rear, where I imagined the kitchen and one of the two bedrooms.

I knocked at the front door, waiting on the small front porch until Michael responded. He'd changed from his work clothes into stone-washed denim coveralls, the sort of outfit a plumber wears when he's crawling under the house. Having so recently met Brian, I was struck by the similarities. One was blond, one brunette, but both had inherited Dana's sultry mouth and fine features. Michael must have expected me because he evidenced no surprise at my standing on his doorstep.

"Mind if I come in?"

"If you want. Place is a mess."

"That's all right," I replied.

I followed him through the house, moving toward the rear. The living room and the kitchen were still furnished with opened but largely unpacked moving cartons, clouds of crumpled newspaper boiling out of boxes onto the floor.

Michael and Juliet had taken refuge in the larger of the two small bedrooms, a nine-by-twelve space dominated by a king-size bed and a big color television set currently tuned to a baseball game that I gathered was being played in Los Angeles. Pizza boxes, take-out cartons, and soft-drink cans were crowded together on the surface of the dresser and atop the chest of drawers. The whole place had the air of a hostage situation where the cops were sending in fast food to satisfy the terrorists' demands. Everything was untidy, smelling of damp towels, french fries, cigarette smoke, and men's athletic socks. There were wads of Pampers in the trash, a flip-top plastic waste bin with used diapers bulging out.

Michael, his attention focused on the TV set, perched himself on the edge of the king-size bed, where Juliet was stretched out with a copy of *Cosmopolitan*. A half-filled ashtray rested on the spread beside her. She was barefoot, wearing short shorts and a fuchsia tank top. She couldn't have been more than eighteen or nineteen and had already dropped any excess weight she might have picked up during pregnancy. Her hair was chopped short, a crew cut cropped close around the ears in a style the average man hasn't worn for years. If I hadn't known better, I'd have assumed she'd just joined the service and was off to boot camp. Her face was freckled, her blue eyes lined darkly with black, lashes beaded with mascara. Her upper lids were two-toned, blue and green. She wore big dangle earrings, jaunty hoops of pink plastic, apparently purchased to match her tank top. She set the magazine aside, visibly irritated by the volume on the TV set. The picture switched to a cheap-looking commercial for a local car dealership. The jingle blasting out sounded like it had been especially written by the wife of the company president. "God, Michael. Could you turn that fuckin' thing down? What's the matter with you, are you deaf or what?"

Michael pushed the volume button on the remote control. The sound dropped to something slightly less than the levels required for ultrasonic brain surgery. Neither seemed to react to my arrival. I thought I could probably plop down on the bed and join them for the evening without attracting much notice. Juliet finally slid a look in my direction, and Michael made the formal introduction halfheartedly. "This is Kinsey Millhone. She's the private detective looking for my dad." With a nod at her, he added, "This's my wife, Juliet."

I gave Juliet a murmured, "Hi, how are you?"

"Nice to meet you," she said her eyes already straying back to her magazine. I couldn't help noticing that I was competing for her attention with an article about how to be a good listener. She felt for the pack of cigarettes lying near her on the bed. She explored with her index finger, picked up the pack, and peered in. She made a moue of exasperation when she realized it was empty. I found myself transfixed by the sight of her. With that marine corps haircut, she looked like a teenaged boy in eye shadow and dangle earrings. She nudged Michael with her foot. "I thought you said you're going up to the corner for me. I'm out of cigarettes and the baby needs Pampers. Could you make a run? Please, please, please?"

On the television screen, baseball play was resuming.

His sole function as a husband seemed to be fetching cigarettes and Pampers. I gave this marriage another ten months at best. By then she'd be bored with all these nights at home. Oddly enough, as young as Michael was, he struck me as the sort who could really make a go of it. Juliet was the one who'd be testy and petulant, opting out on her responsibilities until the relationship fell apart. Dana would probably end up taking care of the baby.

Michael, his attention still riveted to the set, made a vague reply unattended by any actual move to get up, a fact not lost on her. He was fiddling with the Cottonwood Academy class ring his mother had given him, turning it around and around.

"Mike-cull, if Brendan pees again, what am I supposed to do? I just used the last diaper."

"Hey, yeah, babe. Just a sec, okay?"

Juliet's face got all pouty and she rolled her eyes.

He glanced back at her, sensing her irritation with him. "I can go in a minute. Is the baby asleep? Mom wanted her to see him."

Startled, I realized the "her" referred to me.

Juliet swung her feet over to the side of the bed. "I don't know. I can check. I just put him down a little while ago. He hardly ever goes to sleep with the TV so loud." She got up and crossed the room, moving toward the narrow hallway between bedrooms. I followed, trying quickly to think of a generic baby compliment in case the kid turned out to have a pointy head.

I said, "I better keep my distance. I don't want him to catch my cold or anything." Sometimes mothers actually wanted you to *hold* the little buggers.

Juliet leaned around the door frame into the smaller

of the two bedrooms. A wall of cardboard wardrobe cartons had been shoved into the room, all packed with heavily laden hangers dragging at the metal bars affixed across the tops. The baby's crib had been placed in the center of this fortress of wrinkled cottons and winter clothing. Somehow I pictured the room looking just like this many months from now. It did seem quieter in this jungle of old overcoats, and I imagined in time Brendan would get used to the smell of mothballs and matted wool. One whiff in later life and he'd feel like Marcel Proust. I lifted up on tiptoe, looking over Juliet's shoulder.

Brendan was sitting bolt upright, his gaze pinned on the doorway as if he knew she'd come to fetch him. He was one of those exquisite babies you see in magazine ads: plump and perfect with big blue eyes, two little teeth showing in his lower gum, dimples in his cheeks. He was wearing blue flannel sleepers with rubber-soled feet, his arms held out on either side of his body for balance. His hands seemed to wave randomly like little digital antennae, picking up signals from the outside world. The minute he caught sight of Juliet, his face was wreathed in smiles and his arms began an agitated pumping motion, indicating much baby joy. Juliet's face lost its sullen cast and she greeted him in some privately generated mother tongue. He blew bubbles, flirting and drooling. When she picked him up, he buried his face against her shoulder, bunching his knees up in a squirm of happiness. It was the only moment in recorded history when I found myself wishing I had a critter like that.

Juliet was beaming. "Isn't he beautiful?"

"He's pretty cute," I said.

"Michael doesn't even try to pick him up these days," she said. "This age, he's suddenly very possessive of me. I swear, it just happened a week ago. He used to go right to his daddy without a murmur. Now if I'm about to hand him to anyone else? You ought to see his face. His mouth gets all puckery and his chin starts to tremble. And the wailing, my Lord. He's so pitiful, it would break your heart. Dis little guy wuves his mudder," Juliet went on. Brendan reached a plump hand forward and stuck some fingers in her mouth. She pretended to bite, which stimulated a low throaty chuckle from the child in her arms. Her expression changed, nose wrinkling. "Oh, God, does he have a load in his drawers?" She stuck an index finger into the back rim of his diaper, peering into the gap. "Mike-cull?"

"What?"

She moved back toward the bedroom. "Would you just one time do like I ask? The baby pooped his pants and I'm out of Pampers. I told you that twice."

Michael got up obediently, his eyes still pinned to the television screen. Another commercial came on, and the shift seemed to break the spell.

"Sometime tonight, okay?" she said, hefting the baby on one hip.

Michael reached for his windbreaker, which he snatched from a pile of clothes on the floor. "I'll be right back," he said to no one in particular. As he hunched into his jacket, I realized it would be the perfect opportunity to talk to him.

"Why don't I go, too?" I said.

"Fine with me," he said with a look at Juliet. "You need anything else?"

She shook her head, watching a crew of cartoon bite-'ems demolish grunge from a dinner plate. I would have bet money she hadn't gotten the hang of washing dishes yet.

Once we were out on the street, Michael walked rapidly, head bent, hands in his jacket pockets. He was easily a foot taller, with a loose-limbed gait. The approaching storm had darkened the sky overhead, and a tropical breeze sent leaves scuttling along the gutters. The paper had warned that the system was weakening and would probably bring us little more than drizzle. The air was already turbulent, erratic, and humid, the sky charcoal blue where it should have been pale. Michael lifted his face, and the promise of rain seemed to buffet his cheeks.

I found myself trotting to keep up with him. "Could you slow down a little bit?"

"Sorry," he said, and cut his pace by a third.

The Stop 'N' Go was at the corner, maybe two blocks away. I could see the lights ahead of us, though the street itself was dark. Every third or fourth house we passed would have the porch lights on. Low-voltage lamps picked out the path of a front walk or an illuminated ornamental shrub. Supper smells still lingered in the chill night air: the aroma of baked potatoes and meat loaf with a barbecue sauce on top, oven-fried chicken, sweet-and-sour pork chops. I knew I'd already eaten supper, but I was hungry anyway. "I'm assuming you know your father might be heading back to town," I said to Michael, trying to distract myself.

"Mom told me that."

"You have any idea what you'll do if he gets in touch?"

"Talk to him, I guess. Why? What am I supposed to do?"

"There's still a warrant out for his arrest," I said.

Michael snorted. "Oh, great. Snitch on your dad. You haven't seen him for years, first thing you do is call the cops."

"It does sound shitty, doesn't it?"

"Doesn't just *sound* like that. It *is*."

"Do you remember much about him?"

Michael lifted one shoulder. "I was seventeen when he left. I remember mom cried a lot and we got to stay home from school for two days. I try not to think about the rest of it. I tell you one thing, I used to think, 'Hey, so my old man killed himself . . . what's the big deal,' you know? Then I had *my* son, and it changed my attitude. I couldn't leave that little guy. I couldn't do that to him, and now I wonder how Dad could have done it to me. What kind of turd is he, do you know what I mean? Me and Brian both. We were good kids, I swear."

"Sounds like Brian was devastated."

"Yeah, that's true. Brian always acted like it didn't matter, but I know he took it hard. Most of it rolled right offa me."

"Your brother was twelve?"

"Right. I was a senior in high school. He was in the sixth grade. Kids are mean at that age."

"Kids are mean at any age," I said. "Your mother tells me Brian started getting into trouble about then."

"I guess."

"What sort of things did he do?"

"I don't know, petty stuff . . . skipping school, marking on the walls with spray paint, fistfights, but he was just messing around. He didn't mean anything by it. I'm not saying it was right, but everybody made such a goddamn big deal out of it. Right away they're treating him like a criminal or something, and he's just a *kid*. Lot of boys that age get in trouble, you know what I mean? He was horsing around and he got caught. That's the only difference. I did the same thing when I was his age and nobody called me a 'juvenile delinquent.' And don't give me that junk about 'a cry for help.' "

"I never said a word. I'm just listening."

"Anyway, I feel sorry for him. Once people think you're bad, you might as well be bad. It's more fun than being good."

"I can't think Brian's having any fun where he is."

"I don't know what the story is on that. Brian's talked about that one guy, Guevara I think his name is. He's a real bad dude. They were in the same quad at one point, and Brian said he was always pulling shit, trying to get him in trouble with the deputies. He's the one talked him into busting out."

"Somebody told me yesterday he died."

"Serves him right."

"I take it you've talked to Brian since he got back. Your mother was in for a visit and so was I."

"Just on the phone, so he couldn't say much. Mostly he said don't believe nothin' until I heard it from him. He's burnt."

" 'Burnt' meaning what?"

"What? Oh. He's mad. Judge charged him with escape, robbery, grand theft auto, and felony murder. Can you believe it? What a crocka shit. Busting out of jail wasn't even his idea."

"Why'd he do it, then?"

"They threatened his life! Said if he didn't go with 'em, they were going to kill his ass. He was like a hostage, you know?"

"I didn't realize that," I said, trying to keep my tone neutral. Michael was so busy defending his brother, he didn't seem to catch the skepticism.

"It's the truth. Brian swears. He says Julio Rodriguez shot the lady on the road. He never killed anyone. Said the whole thing made him sick. He had no idea them beaners were going to pull that kind of shit. Premeditated murder. Jesus, come *on*."

"Michael, that woman was killed in the perpetration of a felony, which automatically elevates the charge to murder one. Even if your brother never touched the gun, he's considered an accomplice."

"But that doesn't make him *guilty*. Whole time he was trying to get away."

I bit back the impulse to argue. I could tell he was getting irritated, and I knew I shouldn't push it if I wanted his cooperation. "I guess his attorney will have to sort that out." I decided I better shift the conversation onto neutral ground. "What about you? What sort of work do you do?"

"I work construction, finally making pretty good money. Mom wants me to go to college, but I can't see the point. With Brendan so little, I don't want Juliet to have to work. I don't know what kind of job she could get anyway. She finished high school, but she couldn't make much more than minimum wage, and with the cost of a baby-sitter, it doesn't make any sense."

We'd reached the corner market, ablaze with fluorescent lighting. We let our conversation lapse while Michael moved up and down the aisles, picking up the items he'd been sent to buy. I occupied myself at the magazine rack, scanning the latest issues of various "ladies" publications. Judging by the articles listed on the front covers, we were all obsessed with losing weight, sex, and cheap home decorating tips, in just about that order. I picked up a copy of *Home & Hearth*, leafing through until I came to one of those features called "Twenty-Five Things to Do for Twenty-five Dollars or Less." One suggestion was to use old bedsheets to make little dresses with tie sashes for a set of metal folding chairs.

I glanced up and saw Michael at the front register. He'd apparently paid for his purchases, which the clerk was bagging. I'm not sure what it was, but I suddenly had the sensation that someone else was watching, too. I turned casually, doing a visual survey of the market. To my left I caught a flicker of movement, a blurred face reflected against the glass doors of the refrigerator cases that lined the wall across from the entrance. I turned to look, but the face was gone.

I moved to the entrance and pushed through the door, stepping out into the chill night air. There was no one visible in the parking lot. The street was devoid of traffic. No pedestrians, no stray dogs, no wind stirring in the shrubs. The feeling persisted, and I felt the hair rising up along my scalp. There was no reason to imagine that either Michael or I would warrant anyone's attention. Unless, of course, it was Wendell or Renata. The wind was accelerating, sending a mist across the pavement like the blow back from a hose.

"What's the matter?"

I turned to find Michael standing in the doorway with the loaded grocery bag in his arms. "I thought I saw someone standing in the doorway looking at you."

He shook his head. "I didn't see anyone."

"Maybe it's my inflamed imagination, but I don't often do that sort of thing," I said. I could feel a silver shiver wash across my frame.

"You think it might have been Dad?"

"I can't think who else would take an interest."

I saw him lift his head like an animal. "I hear a car engine running."

"You do?" I listened carefully but heard nothing except the rustle of wind in the trees. "Where's the sound coming from?"

He shook his head. "It's gone now. Over there, I think."

I peered over at the darkened side street he was pointing to, but there were no signs of life. The widely spaced streetlights created shallow pools of wan illumination that served only to heighten the deep shadows in between. A breeze was moving through the treetops like a wave. The rustling conveyed something shy and secretive. I could hear the patter of light rain in the uppermost leaves. Ever so faintly, at a distance, I thought I picked up the sharp tap of heels, someone walking purposefully away into the gloom beyond. I turned back. His smile faded slightly when he saw my face. "You're really spooked."

"I hate the idea of being watched."

Behind us, I noticed the clerk in the store was staring steadily in our direction, probably puzzled by our behavior. I flicked a look at Michael. "Anyway, we better get back. Juliet'll be wondering what's kept us."

We set off, walking rapidly. This time I made no attempt to slow Michael's pace. I found myself glancing back from time to time, but the street always appeared to be empty. In my experience, it's always easier to walk toward the darkness than away from it. It wasn't until the front door closed behind us that I allowed myself to relax. Even then, an involuntary yip seemed to escape my lips. Michael had moved into the kitchen with his grocery bag, but he peered around the doorway. "Hey, we're safe, okay?"

He came out of the kitchen carrying the Pampers and a carton of cigarettes. He headed for the bedroom, and I was not far behind him, doing a quick step to keep up. "I'd appreciate it if you'd let me know if your father tries to get in touch. I'll give you my card. You can call me anytime."

"Sure."

"You might warn Juliet, too," I said.

"Whatever."

He paused dutifully while I fumbled in my handbag for a business card. I used my raised knee as a desk, penning my telephone number on the back of the card, which I then passed to him. He glanced at it with no apparent interest and put it in his jacket pocket. "Thanks."

I could tell from his tone he had no intention of calling me for any reason. If Wendell tried to reach him, he'd probably welcome the contact.

We went into the bedroom, where the baseball game was still in progress. Juliet had moved into the bathroom with the baby, and I could hear her voice reverberating through the bathroom door as she prattled nonsense at Brendan. Michael's attention was already glued to the set again. He'd sunk down on the floor, his back against the bed, turning Wendell's ring, which he wore on his right hand. I wondered if the stone changed colors, like a mood ring, depending on his disposition in the moment. I took the box of Pampers and knocked on the bathroom door.

She peered out. "Oh, good. You got 'em. I appreciate that. Thanks. You want to help with his bath? I decided to put him in the tub, he was such a mess."

"I better go," I said. "It looks like the rain is just about to cut loose."

"Really? It's going to rain?"

"If we're lucky."

I could see her hesitation. "Can I ask about something? If Michael's dad came back, would he try to see the baby? Brendan *is* his only grandchild, and s'pose he never had another chance?"

"It wouldn't surprise me. I'd be careful if I were you."

She seemed on the verge of saying something but apparently decided against it. When I closed the bathroom door, Brendan was gnawing on the washrag.

# 16

DROPS BEGAN TO dot my windshield as I hit the 101, and by the time I found a parking space half a block from my apartment, the rain had settled into a steady patter. I locked the VW and picked my way through accumulating puddles to the front gate, splashing around to my door, which opens onto Henry's back patio. I could see lights on at his place. His kitchen door was open, and I picked up the scent of baking, some rich combination of vanilla and chocolate that blended irresistibly with the smell of rain and drenched grass. A sudden breeze tossed the treetops, sending down a quick shower of leaves and large drops. I veered off toward Henry's, head bent against the downpour.

Henry was easing a blade through a nine-by-nine pan of brownies, making parallel cuts. He was barefoot, wearing white shorts and a vivid blue T-shirt. I'd seen pictures of him in his youth—when he was fifty and sixty—but I preferred the lean good looks he'd acquired in his eighties. With his silky white hair and blue eyes, there was no reason to imagine he wouldn't simply keep on getting better as the years rolled by. I rapped on the frame of his aluminum screen door. He glanced up, smiling with pleasure when he saw that it was me. "Well, Kinsey. That was quick. I just left a message on your answering machine." He motioned me in.

I let myself in and wiped my wet shoes on the rag rug before I slipped them off and left them by the door. "I saw your light on and came over. I was down in Perdido and haven't even been home yet. Isn't this rain great? Where'd it come from?"

"The tag end of Hurricane Jackie, is what I heard. It's supposed to rain off and on for the next two days. There's a pot of tea brewed if you want to grab cups and saucers."

I did as he suggested, pausing at the refrigerator to take out the milk as well. Henry rinsed and dried his knife blade and moved to the kitchen table, brownies still resting in the pan in which they'd baked. At sundown in Santa Teresa, the temperature routinely drops into the fifties, but tonight, because of the storm, the air felt nearly tropical. The interior of the kitchen functioned like an incubator. Henry had hauled out his old black-bladed floor fan, which seemed to scan the room, droning incessantly as it created its own sirocco.

We sat down at the table across from one another, the pan of brownies between us resting on an oven mitt. The top was light brown, as fragile-looking as dried tobacco leaves. His knife had left a ragged line, a portion of brownie jutting up through the broken crust. Just under the surface, the texture was as dark and moist as soil. There were walnuts as thick as gravel, with intermittent small clusters of chocolate chips. Henry lifted out the first square with a spatula and passed it to me. After that show of gentility, we ate directly from the pan.

I poured us each a cup of tea, adding milk to mine. I broke a brownie in half and then broke it again. This was my notion of cutting calories. My mouth was flooded with warm chocolate, and if I moaned aloud, Henry was too polite to call attention. "I made an odd discovery," I said. "It's possible I have family in the area."

"What kind of family?"

I shrugged. "You know, people with the same name, claiming to be related, blood ties and like that."

His blue eyes rested on my face with interest. "Really. Well, I'll be damned. What're they like?"

"Don't know. I haven't met 'em."

"Oh. I thought you had. How do you know they exist?"

"I was doing a door-to-door canvass in Perdido yesterday. A woman said I looked familiar and asked me about my first name. Then she asked if I was related to the Burton Kinseys up in Lompoc. I said no, but then I looked up my parents' marriage license. My mother's father was Burton Kinsey. It's like, in the back of my mind somewhere I think I knew that, but I didn't want to cop to it in the moment. Weird, huh."

"What are you going to do?"

"Don't know yet. Think about it. Feels like a can of worms."

"Pandora's box."

"You got it. Big trouble."

"On the other hand, it might not be."

I made a face. "I don't want to take the chance. I never had family. What would I do with one?"

Henry smiled to himself. "What do you think you'd do?"

"I don't know. It seems creepy. It'd be a pain in the ass. Look at William. He drives you crazy."

"But I love him. That's what it's all about, isn't it?"

"It is?"

"Well, obviously, you're going to do as you see fit, but there's a lot to be said for kith and kin."

I was silent for a while. I ate a section of the brownies about the shape of Utah. "I think I'll let it sit. Once I get in touch, I'll be stuck."

"Do you know anything at all about them?"

"Nope."

Henry laughed. "At least you're enthusiastic about the possibilities."

I smiled uncomfortably. "I just found out today. Besides, the only one I really know of for sure is my mother's mother, Cornelia Kinsey. I guess my grandfather died."

"Ah, your grandmother's a widow. That's interesting. How do you know she wouldn't be perfect for me?"

"There's a thought," I said dryly.

"Oh, come on. What's your worry?"

"Who says I'm worried? I'm not worried."

"Then why don't you get in touch?"

"Suppose she's hateful and grasping?"

"Suppose she's gracious and smart?"

"Right. If she was so fu— gracious, how come she hasn't been in touch for twenty-nine years?" I said.

"Maybe she was busy."

I noticed the conversation was proceeding in fits and

starts. We knew each other well enough that we could leave transitions out. Nevertheless, I felt as if my IQ were plummeting. "Anyway, how would I go about it? What would I do?"

"Call her up. Say hello. Introduce yourself."

I could feel myself squirm. "I'm not going to do that," I said. "I'm going to let it sit." "Dogged" is the word that would probably describe my tone, not that I'm bullheaded about things like this.

"Let it sit, then," he said with the slightest of shrugs.

"I am. I intend to. Anyway, look how much time has passed since my parents were killed. It'd be weird to make contact."

"You said that before."

"Well, it's the truth!"

"So don't make contact. You're absolutely right."

"I won't. I'm not going to," I said irritably. Personally, I found it irksome to be agreed with like that. He could have urged me to do otherwise. He could have suggested a plan of action. Instead he was telling me what I was telling *him*. Everything sounded so much more reasonable when I said it. What he repeated back to me seemed stubborn and argumentative. I couldn't figure out what was wrong with him unless this was some kind of weird response to all the refined sugar in the brownies.

The conversation shifted to William and Rosie. Nothing new to report. Sports and politics we reduced to one sentence each. Shortly thereafter I went home to my place, feeling out of sorts. Henry seemed fine, but it felt as though we'd had a terrible argument. I didn't sleep that well, either.

\* \* \*

It was still raining at 5:59, and I skipped my run. My cold symptoms had improved, but it still didn't seem smart to exercise in a downpour. It was hard to realize that just a week ago I was lying by a pool down in Mexico, swabbing myself with unnatural substances. I lingered in bed, staring up at the skylight. The clouds were the color of old galvanized pipes, and the day fairly cried out for some serious reading. I extended one arm and studied the artificial tan, which had faded by now to a pale peach. I raised one bare leg, noticing for the first time all the streaking around my ankle. Jesus, I could do with a shave. It looked as if I had taken to wearing angora knee socks. Finally, bored with self-inspection, I dragged my butt out of bed. I showered, shaved my legs, and dressed, choosing fresh jeans and a cotton sweater since I'd be lunching with Harris Brown. I took myself out to breakfast, loading up on fats and carbohydrates, nature's antidepressants. Ida Ruth had told me she was coming in late, authorizing my use of her parking spot. I rolled into the office at nine on the dot.

Alison was talking on the telephone when I arrived. She held a hand up like a traffic cop, indicating some kind of message. I paused, waiting for a break in her conversation. "That's fine, no problem. Take your time," she said. She put a palm across the mouthpiece while the other party was apparently taking care of other business. "I put someone in your office. I hope you don't mind. I'll hold your calls."

"What for?"

Her attention jumped back to the telephone, and I assumed the other party had finally returned. I shrugged and walked down the interior corridor to my office, where the door was standing open. There was a woman at the window with her back to me.

I moved to my desk and slung my handbag on the chair. "Hi. Can I help you?"

She turned around and looked at me with the sort of curiosity reserved for celebrities at close range. I found myself looking at her the same way. We were enough alike to be sisters. Her face was as familiar as the faces in a dream, recognizable but not bearing up well to close scrutiny. Our features were not identical by any means. She looked not *like* me, but like the way I felt I looked to others. As I studied her, the resemblance faded. Quickly I could see that we were more dissimilar than similar. She was five feet two to my five feet six, heavier in a way that suggested rich food and no exercise. I'd been jogging for years, and I was sometimes conscious of the ways my basic build had been affected by all the miles I'd put in. She was heavy-breasted, broader in the beam. At the same time, she was better groomed. I had a glimpse of what I might have looked like if I paid the money for a decent haircut, learned the rudiments of makeup, and dressed with flair. The outfit she wore was a cream-colored washable silk: a long, gathered skirt and matching cardigan-style jacket, with a coral-colored silk tank top visible underneath. Through the magic of fashion, some of her chunkiness was hidden, the eye distracted by all the flowing lines.

She smiled and held out her hand. "Hello, Kinsey. Nice to meet you. I'm your cousin, Liza."

"How did you get here?" I asked. "I only found out yesterday I might have relatives in the area."

"That's when we heard, too. Well, that's not quite accurate. Last night Lena Irwin called my sister, Pam, and

we had an instant meeting. Lena was sure you were related. Both my sisters were panting to drive down to
meet you, but we finally decided it'd be too confusing
for you. Besides, Tasha really had to get back to San
Francisco, and Pamela's so pregnant she's about to
pop."

Three girl cousins suddenly. That was a bit much. I
shifted the subject. "How do you know Lena?"

Liza waved dismissively, a gesture I'd used a hundred times myself. "Her family's up in Lompoc. The
minute she said she'd met you, we knew we had to
come down. We haven't said a word to Grand, but I
know she'll want to meet you."

"Grand?"

"Oh, sorry. That's our grandmother, Cornelia. Her
maiden name was LaGrand, and we've always just
shortened it. Everybody calls her Grand. It's been her
nickname since childhood."

"How much does she know about me?"

"Not that much, really. We knew your name, of
course, but we really weren't sure where you'd ended
up. The whole family scandal was so ridiculous. I don't
mean at the time. Good heavens, from what I've been
told, it split the sisters down the middle. Am I inter-
rupting your work? I should have asked before."

"Not at all," I said with a quick look at my watch. I
had three hours before my lunch appointment. "Alison
told me she'd hold the calls, but I couldn't think what
could be so important. Tell me about the sisters."

"There were five of them altogether. I guess they had
a brother, but he died in infancy. They were completely
divided by the breach between Grand and Aunt Rita.
You really never heard the story?"

"Not at all," I said. "I'm sitting here wondering if you really have the right person."

"Absolutely," she said. "Your mother was a Kinsey. Rita Cynthia, right? Her sister's name was Virginia. We called her Aunt Gin, or Gin Gin sometimes."

"So did I," I said faintly. I'd always thought of it as my pet name for her, one that I invented.

Liza went on. "I didn't know her that well because of the estrangement between those two and Grand, who'll be eighty-eight this year and sharp as a tack. I mean, she's virtually blind and her health's not that good, but she's great for her age. I'm not sure the two of them ever spoke to Grand again, but Aunt Gin would come back to visit and all the sisters would converge. The big horror was that somehow Grand would get wind of it, but I don't think she ever did. Anyway, our mother's name is Susanna. She's the baby in the family. Do you mind if I sit?"

"I'm sorry. Please do. You want coffee? I can get us some."

"No, no. I'm fine. I'm just sorry to barge in and bury you under all this. What was I saying? Oh, yes. Your mother was the oldest and mine's the youngest. There are only two surviving—my mother, Susanna . . . she's fifty-eight. And then the sister one up from her, Maura, who's sixty-one. Sarah died about five years ago. God, I'm sorry to spring all this on you. We just assumed you knew."

"What about Burton . . . Grandfather Kinsey?"

"He's gone, too. He only died a year ago, but of course he'd been sick for years." She said it like I should have known the nature of his illness.

I let that pass. I didn't want to focus on the fine

points when I was still struggling with the overall picture. "How many cousins?"

"Well, there're the three of us, and Maura has two daughters, Delia and Eleanor. Sarah had four girls."

"And you're all up in Lompoc?"

"Not quite," she said. "Three of Sarah's four are on the East Coast. One's married, two in college, and I don't know what the other one's doing. She's sort of the black sheep of the family. Maura's kids are both in Lompoc. In fact, Maura and Mom live within five blocks of each other. Part of Grand's master plan." She laughed and I could see that we had the same teeth, very white and square. "We better do this in small doses or you'll die of the shock."

"I'm close to that as it is."

She laughed again. Something about this woman was getting on my nerves. She was having way too much fun, and I wasn't having any. I was trying to assimilate the information, trying to cope with its significance, trying to be polite and make all the right noises. But I felt foolish, in truth, and her breezy, presumptive manner wasn't helping much. I shifted on my chair and raised my hand like a kid in a classroom. "Could I ask you to stop and go back to the beginning?"

"I'm sorry. You must be so confused, you poor thing. I wish Tasha'd done this. She should have canceled her plane. I knew I'd probably botch it, but there just wasn't any other choice. You do know about Rita Cynthia's elopement. They must have told you *that* part." She made a statement of it, equating the story with the news that the world was round.

I shook my head again, beginning to feel like a bauble-head in somebody's rear car window. "I was five when my parents died in the accident. After that, Aunt Gin raised me, but she gave me no family history whatsoever. You can safely operate on the assumption that I'm dead ignorant."

"Oh, boy. I hope I can remember it all myself. I'll just launch in, and anything you don't get, please feel free to interrupt. First of all, our grandfather Kinsey had beaucoup bucks. His family ran a diatomite mining and processing operation. Diatomite is basically what they use to make diatomaceous earth. Do you know what that is?"

"Some kind of filtering medium, isn't it?"

"Right. The diatomite deposits up in Lompoc are among the biggest and purest in the world. The Kinseys have owned that company for years. Grandmother must have come from money, too, though she doesn't talk much about it so I don't really know the story on that. Her maiden name was LaGrand. She's always been called Grand, ever since I can remember. I already told you that. Anyway, she and Granddaddy had six kids— the boy who died and then the five girls. Rita Cynthia was the oldest. She was Grand's favorite, probably because they were so much alike. I guess she was spoiled . . . or so the story goes, a real hell-raiser. She *totally* refused to conform to Grand's expectations. Because of that, Aunt Rita's become like this family legend. The patron saint of liberation. The rest of us—all the nieces and nephews—took her as a symbol of independence and spirit, someone sassy and defiant, the emancipated person our mothers wished they'd been. Rita Cynthia thumbed her nose at Grand, who was a piece of work in those days. Rigid and snobbish, judgmental, controlling. She raised all the girls to be little robots of gentility.

Don't get me wrong. She could be very generous, but there were usually strings attached. Like she'd give you the money for college, but you had to keep it local or go where she said. Same with a house. She'd give you the down payment and even cosign the loan, as long as you found a place within six blocks of her. It really broke her heart when Aunt Rita left."

"I don't understand what happened."

"Oh, boy. Right. Okay, let me get to the point. First of all, Rita made her debut in 1935. July fifth—"

"My mother was a debutante? She actually made a debut and you can recite the *date*? You must have quite a memory."

"No, no, no. It's all part of the story. Everybody knows that in our family. It's like *Goldilocks and the Three Bears* or *Rumpelstiltskin*. What happened was Grand had a set of twelve sterling silver napkin rings engraved with Rita Cynthia's name and the date of her debut. She was going to make it a tradition for each of the girls in turn, but it didn't really work out. She threw this big coming-out party and set it up so Rita could meet all these incredibly eligible bachelors. Real lah-de-dah social register types."

"In *Lompoc*?"

"Oh, golly, no. They came from everywhere. Marin County, Walnut Creek, San Francisco, Atherton, Los Angeles, you name it. Grand had her heart set on Rita's 'marrying well,' as they used to say in those days. Instead, Rita fell in love with your father, who was serving at the party."

"As a waiter?"

"Exactly. Some friend of his worked for the caterer and asked him to help out. Aunt Rita started seeing

Randy Millhone on the sly. This was right in the middle of the Depression, and his real job was working for the post office here in Santa Teresa. It's not like he was really a waiter," she said.

"Oh, thank God," I said dryly, but the irony was lost on her. "What'd he do for the post office?"

"He was a mail carrier. 'An uncivil servant,' Grand used to say with her nose all turned up. As far as she was concerned, he was poor white trash . . . too old for Rita and way too low class. She found out they were dating and threw a pluperfect fit, but there was nothing she could do. Rita was eighteen and headstrong as they come. The more Grand protested, the more she dug her heels in. By November, she was gone. Just ran off and married him without telling a soul."

"She told Virginia."

"She did?"

"Sure. Aunt Gin was one of the witnesses at the wedding."

"Oh. I didn't know that, but it does make sense. The point is, when Grand found out, she was so furious she cut her off without a dime. She wouldn't even let her keep the silver napkin rings."

"A fate worse than death."

"Well, it must have seemed like it at the time," she said. "I don't know what Grandmother did with the rest of 'em, but there was one we all used to vie for at family gatherings. Grand had this whole collection of assorted napkin rings . . . different styles and monograms, all British silver," she said. "Before dinner, if she thought you'd been rude or disobedient or something? She'd make you use the Rita Cynthia napkin ring. She meant it to be mean. You know, like it was her way of shaming anyone who got out of line—ridiculing all the girls—but we ended up fighting to have possession. We considered it a coup to get to use that one. Rita Cynthia was the only member of the family who ever really got away, and we thought she was great. So secretly we'd all get together and have this pitched battle for which of us would get to be Rita Cynthia. Whoever won would misbehave something fierce, and sure enough, Grand would descend like a witch and make 'em use the Rita Cynthia napkin ring. Big disgrace, but we thought it was such a *hoot*."

"Didn't anyone object to your making such a big deal of it?"

"Oh, Grand didn't know. She could hardly see by then, and besides, we were very careful. That was the best part of the game. I'm not even sure our mothers noticed. Or if they did, they probably applauded secretly. Rita was their favorite, and Virginia ran a close second. That was the hardest part about Aunt Rita's defection. We not only lost her, but for the most part, we lost Gin as well."

"Really," I said, but I could barely hear myself. I felt as though I'd been struck. Liza couldn't have guessed how the story was affecting me. My mother was never even a real person to them. She was a ritual, a symbol, something to be fought over like a bunch of rowdy dogs with a bone. I paused to clear my throat. "Why were they driving up to Lompoc?"

This time Liza was puzzled. I could see it in her eyes.

"My parents were killed on the way to Lompoc," I said carefully, as if translating for a foreigner. "If they'd broken with the family, why were they going up there?"

"I hadn't thought about that. I guess it was part of the reunion Aunt Gin was setting up."

I must have stared at her in some significant way because her cheeks tinted suddenly. "Maybe we should wait until Tasha comes back. She flies down for a visit every couple of weeks. She can fill you in on this stuff much better than I can."

"But what about the years since then? Why didn't anybody get in touch?"

"Oh, I'm sure they tried. I mean, I know they wanted to. They talked back and forth with Aunt Gin on the phone, so everybody knew you were here. Anyway, what's done is done. I know Mom and Maura and Uncle Walter will be thrilled to hear we've met, and you really must come up."

I could feel something strange happening to my face. "None of you felt any reason to come down when Aunt Gin died?"

"Oh, God, you're upset. I feel awful. What's wrong?"

"Nothing. I just remembered I have an appointment," I said. It was only nine twenty-five. Liza's entire revelation had taken less than half an hour. "I guess we'll have to finish this on another occasion."

She was suddenly busy with her handbag and her map. "I better hit the road, then. I probably should have called first, but I thought it would be such a fun surprise. I hope I haven't blown it. Are you okay?"

"I'm fine."

"Please call. Or I'll call you and we'll get together again. Tasha's older. She knows the story better and maybe she can fill you in. Everyone was crazy about Rita Cynthia. Honestly."

Next thing I was aware of, cousin Liza was gone. I

closed the door behind her and went over to the window. A white wall wound along the properties in the back, bougainvillea spilling across the top in a tumbling mass of magenta. In theory, I'd suddenly gained an entire family, cause for rejoicing if you happen to believe the ladies' magazines. In reality, I felt as if someone had just stolen everything I held dear, a common theme in all the books you read on burglary and theft.

# 17

THE COFFEE SHOP Harris Brown had selected for our brainstorming session was a maze of interconnecting rooms with a huge oak tree growing up the middle. I parked in the side lot and walked into the entrance T. There were benches on either side of a corridor intended as an area where people could sit while they waited for their names to be called. Business had fallen off, and now there was just the length of empty space with potted rubber plants and what looked like a lectern at the end. A row of windows on either side of the entranceway gave an unobstructed view of patrons dining at tables in flanking wings of the restaurant.

I gave my name to the hostess. She was a black woman in her sixties, with a manner about her that suggested she was wasting her education. Jobs are hard to find in this town, and she was probably grateful to have the work. As I approached her station I could see her reach for a menu.

"My name's Kinsey Millhone. I'm having lunch with a man named Harris Brown, but I'm hoping to find the restroom first. Could you show him to a table if he arrives before I get back? I'd appreciate it."

"Certainly," she said. "You know where the ladies' room is?"

"I can find it," I said, incorrectly as it turned out.

I should have had a little map or dropped bread crumbs behind me. First, I found myself heading into a closet full of floor mops and then through a door leading to the alleyway out back. I retraced my steps and turned myself around. I could see a sign then in the shape of an arrow pointing to the right: "Telephones. Restrooms." Ah, a clue. I found the proper door, with a ladies' high heel in silhouette. I did my business with dispatch, moving back to the entrance. I arrived as the hostess was returning to her position. She pointed to the dining area to her left, a wing of the restaurant parallel to the entrance. "Second table on the right."

Almost without thinking, I glanced through the two adjacent windows, spotting Harris Brown as he stood to remove his sport coat. Instinctively I backed up a step, obscuring myself behind a potted plant. I looked at the hostess and jerked a thumb in his direction. "*That's* Harris Brown?"

"He asked for Kinsey Millhone," she said.

I peered around the plant at him, but there was no mistake. Especially since he was the only man in there. Harris Brown, retired police lieutenant, was the "drunk" I'd seen on the Viento Negro hotel balcony less than a week ago. Now what was that about? I knew he'd worked the fraud investigation, but that was years ago. How had he picked up Wendell Jaffe's trail, and what was he doing down in Mexico? More to the point, wasn't he going to turn around and ask me the very same thing? He was bound to remember my handy-dandy hooker act, and while that in itself wasn't anything to be ashamed of, I wasn't quite sure how to explain what I'd been up to. Until I knew what was going on, it seemed less than cool to have a conversation with the man.

The hostess was watching me with bemusement. "You think he's too old for you? I could have told you that."

"You know him?"

"He used to come in here all the time when he was working for the police department. Brought his wife and kids in every Sunday after church."

"How long have you worked here?"

"Honey, I own the place. My husband, Samuel, and I bought it in 1965."

I could feel myself flush, though she couldn't have guessed the reason.

Dimples formed in her cheeks, and she flashed a smile at me. "Oh, I get it now. You thought I took this job because I'd fallen on hard times."

I laughed, embarrassed that I was so transparent. "I figured you were probably happy to have the work."

"Make no mistake about it, I am. I'd be happier still if the business picked up. At least I got old friends like Mr. Brown in there, though I sure don't see him as often as I used to. What's the deal? Somebody set you up on a blind date with him?"

I felt a momentary confusion. "You just said he was married."

"Well, he was till she died. I thought maybe some-body fixed you up and you didn't like his looks."

"It's a little trickier than that. Uhm, I wonder if you could do me a favor," I said. "I'm going out to the lot to that public telephone booth. When I call and ask for him, could you let him use this phone?"

She gave me a look. "You're not going to hurt his feelings, are you?"

"I promise I won't. This has nothing to do with dat-ing, I assure you."

"As long as it's not a put-down. I won't participate in that."

"Scout's honor," I said, holding fingers to my temple.

She handed me a take-out menu that was printed on heavy paper. "Telephone number's at the top," she said.

"Thanks."

I kept my face turned away studiously as I left the restaurant, crossing to the pay phone in the corner of the lot. I propped the menu against the phone box and then fished out a quarter, which I put in the slot. After two rings the hostess answered.

"Hello," said I. "I'm looking for Harris Brown—"

"I'll go get him," she said, putting me on hold. In her absence, I was treated to the weather report on a local radio station.

After a pause Brown picked up the line, sounding just as cranky and impatient as he had when I talked to him the first time. His manner would have been perfect for a bill collector. "Yes?"

"Hi, Lieutenant Brown. This is Kinsey Millhone."

"It's Harris," he said shortly.

"Oh, sorry, Harris. I thought maybe I could catch you before you left this morning, but I must have missed you. Something unavoidable has come up, and I'm going to have to give you a rain check on lunch. Can I call you later in the week and maybe set something up then?"

His disposition improved, which was really worrisome when you consider I was bowing out of lunch with no advance notice whatsoever. "No problem," he said. "Just give me a call when it suits." Casual, good-natured.

A little warning bell went off, but I soldiered on. "Thanks. I really appreciate this, and I'm sorry for the inconvenience."

"Don't worry about it. Oh. Tell you what, though. I was hoping to have a quick chat with Wendell's ex-partner. I figure he might know something. Have you had any luck reaching him?"

I nearly blurted out the information, but I caught myself. Ah. Got it. This guy was hoping to jump the gun, bypassing me, so he could get to Wendell himself. I raised my voice. "Hello?" I let two seconds pass. "Helllooo."

"Hello?" he repeated back to me.

"Are you there? Hello?"

*"I'm here,"* he yelled.

"Could you speak up? I can't hear you. We have a terrible connection. What's wrong with this phone? Can you hear me?"

*"I can hear you fine. Can you hear me?"*

*"What?"*

*"I said do you happen to know how I can contact Carl Eckert? I can't seem to find out where he's living these days."*

I banged the mouthpiece on the little shelf the telephone company provides in any public booth. "Hell-llooo! I can't hear you!" I sang. "Hello?" Then, as if annoyed, I said, "Well, goddamn it!" And slammed the receiver down.

I picked it up again once the connection was broken. I stayed where I was, my face averted, pretending to converse with animation while I kept an eye on the restaurant entrance. Moments later I saw him come out, cross the parking lot, and get into a battered Ford. I might have followed him, but to what end? At this point, I couldn't believe he was going any place interesting. The man wouldn't be that tough to connect with again, especially since I had a piece of information he was hoping to get.

As I opened my car door, I could see the hostess watching me through the plate glass window. I debated about going back with some cock-and-bull story, anything to forestall her tipping him off to my deception. On the other hand, I didn't want to make more of the incident than I had to. He probably only went in there every two or three months. Why call attention to a matter I wanted her to forget?

I went back to my office, circling the block endlessly until I found a parking place. I'm afraid to calculate how much time I waste this way on any given day. Sometimes I pass Alison or Jim Thicket, the paralegal, driving in the other direction, as intent as I am on ferreting out a space. Maybe Lonnie would win a big case and sport us all to a little lot of our own. I finally broke down and pulled into the public parking garage beside the library. I'd have to keep an eye on the clock and fetch my car again before the first free ninety minutes ran out. God forbid I should pay a buck an hour for parking if I didn't have to.

As long as I was close, I ducked into the minimart and bought myself a bag lunch. The weather report I'd picked up while on hold was full of cagey meteorological phrases, citing lows and highs and percentages. From this I gathered the weatherperson didn't know any better than I did what would happen next. I walked over to the courthouse and found an unoccupied spot under shelter. The sky was overcast, the air faintly chilly, trees still dripping with rain from the night before. For the moment it was clear, and the grass in the sunken garden smelled like a soggy bouquet garni.

A white-haired female docent led a group of tourists through the big stone-and-stucco archway toward the street beyond. I used to lunch here with Jonah in the days of our "romance." Now it was difficult to remember just what the attraction was about. I ate my lunch, then gathered up my crumpled papers and my empty Pepsi can, depositing the paper bag in the nearest waste container. As if on cue, I saw Jonah moving toward me across the saturated courthouse lawn. He looked surprisingly good for a man who probably wasn't very happy: tall and trim, with a wash of silver showing in his dark hair just above his ears. He hadn't seen me yet. He walked with his head down, a brown bag visible in one hand. Though I was tempted to flee, I found myself nearly rooted in place, wondering how long it would take for him to realize I was standing there. He lifted his face and looked at me without a hint of recognition. I waited, motionless, feeling oddly ill at ease. When he was ten feet away, he stopped in his tracks. I could see the tiny flecks of wet grass plastered to his shoes. "I don't believe it. How are you?"

I said, "Fine. How are you?"

His smile seemed pained and slightly sheepish. "I guess we just did this couple days ago on the phone."

"We're allowed," I said mildly. "What are you doing here?"

He looked down at the brown paper bag in his hand as if perplexed. "I'm supposed to meet Camilla for lunch."

"Oh, that's right. She works here. Well, that's convenient for you both with the station half a block away. You can give each other rides to work." Jonah knew me well enough to ignore my sarcasm, which in this case was automatic and didn't mean that much.

"You never met Camilla, did you? Why don't you hang around for a bit? She'll be here any minute, as soon as court's recessed."

"Thanks, but I have something to take care of," I said. "Anyway, I can't believe she'd be that interested. Maybe some other time." Jesus, Jonah, get a clue, I thought. No wonder Camilla was always mad at him. What wife wants to meet the woman her husband was boffing during past marital separations?

"Anyway, it's nice to see you. You're looking good," he said as he moved away.

"Jonah? I do have a question. Maybe this is something you can help me with."

He paused. "Fire away."

"You know much about Lieutenant Brown?"

He seemed puzzled by the subject. "Sure, I know some. What in particular?"

"Remember I told you CF hired me to check out this Wendell Jaffe sighting down in Mexico?"

"Yeah."

"Harris Brown was down there. In the room next door to Jaffe's."

Jonah's face went blank. "Are you sure?"

"Trust me, Jonah. This is not something I could be mistaken about. It was him. I was this close." I held my hand to my face, implying nose to nose. I repressed the fact that I'd kissed him right in the chops. That was still enough to make me shiver some in retrospect.

"Well, I suppose he could be investigating on his own time," he said. "I guess there's nothing wrong with that. It's been a lot of years, but he always had a reputation as a bird dog."

"In other words, he's persistent," I said.

"Oh, shit, yes. He spots a perp in the distance, he'll hold a point till he drops."

"If he's retired, can he still use the NCIC computer?"

"Technically, probably not, but I'm sure he still has friends in the department who'd help him out if he asked. Why?"

"I don't see how he could find Wendell without access to the system."

Jonah shrugged, unimpressed. "That's not information we have or we'd have pulled him in. If the guy's still alive, we'd have a lot of questions for him."

"He had to get his information somewhere," I said.

"Come on. Brown's been a detective thirty-five, forty years. He knows how to get information. The guy's got his sources. Maybe somebody tipped him off."

"But what's it to him? Why not pass the information on to someone in the department?"

He studied me, and I could see his mental gears engage. "Off-hand, I can't tell you. Personally, I think you're making too much of this, but I can check it out."

"Discreetly," I cautioned.

"Absolutely," he said.

I began to walk backward at a slow pace. I finally turned and moved on. I didn't want to be caught up in Jonah's orbit again. I've never really understood the chemistry between the two of us. While the relationship seemed to be dead now, I wasn't sure what had triggered the spark in the beginning. For all I knew, mere proximity might set the whole thing off again. The man wasn't good for me, and I wanted him at a distance. When I looked back, I saw that he was staring after me.

By two-fifteen my office phone rang. "Kinsey? This is Jonah."

"That was quick," I said.

"That's because there isn't much to report. Word has it he was taken off the case because his personal involvement interfered with his work. He sank his entire pension into CSL and lost his shirt. Apparently, his kids were up in arms because he'd blown all his retirement monies. His wife left him, and then she got sick. Eventually she died of cancer. His kids still don't speak to him. It's a real mess."

"Well, that's interesting," I said. "Is it possible he's been authorized to pursue the case?"

"By who?"

"I don't know. The chief? The CIA? The FBI?"

"No way. I never heard of that. The guy's been retired for over a year. We got a budget barely pays for the paper clips. Where's he getting his funds? Believe me, Santa Teresa Police Department isn't going to spend money chasing after some guy who *might* have been guilty of a crime five or six years back. If he showed up, we'd chat with him, but nobody's going to put in a lot of time on it. Who cares about Jaffe? There was never even a warrant out for his arrest."

"Guess again. There's a warrant out now," I said tartly.

"This is probably just something Brown is doing on his own."

"You'd still have to wonder where he gets his information."

"Might have been the same guy told California Fidelity. Maybe the two of 'em know each other."

That sparked a response. "You mean Dick Mills? Well, that's true. If he knew Brown was interested, he might have mentioned it. I'll see if I can get a line on it from that end. That's a good suggestion."

"Let me know what you find out. I'd like to hear what's going on."

As soon as he hung up, I put a call through to California Fidelity and asked for Mac Voorhies. While I was waiting for him to free up from another call, I had a chance to reflect on the wickedness of my lying ways. I didn't actually repent, but I had to consider all the tricky repercussions. For example, I was going to have to tell Mac *something* about my encounter with Harris Brown down in Viento Negro, but how could I do that without confessing my sins? Mac knows me well enough to realize that I bend the rules on occasion, but he doesn't like to be confronted with any *instances* thereof. Like most of us, he enjoys the colorful aspects of other people's natures as long as he doesn't have to deal with any consequences.

"Mac Voorhies," he said.

I hadn't quite made up my cover story at that point, which meant I was going to have to fall back on that old hoary ruse of telling some, but not all, of the truth as I knew it. The best strategy here is to conjure up strong *feelings* of honesty and virtue even if you don't have the goods to back 'em up. I've noticed, too, that if you pretend to confide in others, they tend to accord great truth value to the contents of the revelation.

"Hi, Mac. This is Kinsey. We've had an interesting development I thought you ought to be aware of. Apparently, five years ago when Wendell's disappearance first came to light, an STPD fraud detective named Harris Brown was assigned to the case."

"Name sounds familiar. I must have dealt with him once or twice," Mac put in. "You having trouble with the guy?"

"Not in the way you might think," I said. "I called him a couple days ago and he was very cooperative. We were supposed to meet for lunch today, but when I got there, I took one look at the man and realized I'd seen him in Viento Negro, staying in the same hotel as Wendell Jaffe."

"Doing what?"

"That's what I'm trying to find out," I said. "I'm not a big fan of coincidence. The minute I realized it was the same guy, I backed out of the restaurant and bagged the appointment. I managed to cover myself so I didn't blow the contact. Meantime, I asked a cop I know to check it out in the department, and he tells me Brown lost a bundle when Wendell's financial scheme collapsed."

Mac said, "Huhn."

"The cop suggested Brown and Dick Mills might have a prior relationship. If Dick knew Harris Brown had some kind of ax to grind, he might have told him about Wendell the same time he told you."

"I can ask Dick."

"Would you do that? I'd really appreciate it, if you don't mind," I said. "I really don't know the guy. He's probably more likely to 'fess up to you."

"No problem. Fine with me. What about Wendell? You got a line on him yet?"

"I'm getting closer," I said. "I know where Renata is, and he can't be that far off."

"You heard the latest on the kid, I guess."

"You mean Brian? I haven't heard a thing."

"Oh, yeah. You'll love this. I caught it in the car coming back from lunch. There was a computer glitch at the Perdido County Jail. Brian Jaffe was released this morning and nobody's seen him since."

# 18

I HIT THE road again. I was beginning to think the real definition of Hell was this endless loop between Santa Teresa and Perdido. As I came around the corner into Dana Jaffe's neighborhood, I spotted a Perdido County Sheriff's Department car parked in front of her house. I parked across the street and down a few houses, watching the front porch for signs of life. I'd probably been sitting there for ten minutes or so when I caught sight of Dana's neighbor, Jerry Irwin, returning from his afternoon jog. He ran on the balls of his feet, almost on tippy-toe, with the same stooped posture he favored in his leisure moments. He was wearing plaid Bermuda shorts and a white T-shirt, black socks, and running shoes. His color was high and his gray hair was matted with sweat, his glasses secured with a length of rubber tubing that made a circular indentation. He finished the last half a block with a little burst of speed, his gait the mincing, irregular hopping of someone running barefoot over hot concrete. I leaned over and rolled down the window on the passenger side.

"Hey, Jerry? How're you? Kinsey Millhone here."

He leaned forward, gasping, hands on his skinny knees while he caught his breath. A whiff of sweat wafted through the window. "Fine." Huff, puff. "Just a minute here." He was never going to look like an athlete doing this. He seemed like a man on the brink of a near death experience. He put his hands on his waist and leaned back, saying, "Whooo!" He was still breathing hard, but he managed to collect himself. He peered in at me, face wrinkling with the effort. His glasses were beginning to fog up. "I was going to call you. Thought I saw Wendell hanging around earlier."

"Really," I said. "Why don't you hop in?" I leaned over and popped up the lock, and he opened the car door, sliding onto the seat.

" 'Course I can't be sure, but it sure looked like him, so I called the cops. Deputy's over there now. Did you see that?"

I checked Dana's porch, which was still deserted. "So I see. You heard about Brian?"

"Kid must lead a charmed life," Jerry remarked. "You think he's headed for home?"

"Hard to say. It'd be foolish . . . that's the first place the cops are going to check," I said. "But he may not have any other choice in the matter."

"I can't believe his mother would tolerate that."

We both peered at Dana's, hoping for activity. Guns going off, vases flying through the window. There was nothing. Dead silence, the facade of the dark gray house looking cold and blank. "I drove down to see her, but I thought I better wait until the deputy leaves. When did you see Wendell? Was it just recently?"

"Might have been an hour ago. Lena was the one who spotted him. She called me in quick and had me take a look. We couldn't quite agree if it was him or not, but I thought it was worthwhile to report. I didn't really think they'd send somebody out."

"They might have dispatched a deputy after Brian came up missing. I didn't hear the newscast myself. Did you happen to catch it?"

Jerry shook his head, pausing to wipe his sweaty forehead on his T-shirt. The car was beginning to smell like a locker room. "Might be why Wendell came back," he said.

"That occurred to me, too."

Jerry gave a little sniff to his armpit and had the decency to wince. "I better head for the shower before I stink up your car. You let me know if they catch him."

"Sure. I'll probably cruise by Michael's house just to make the rounds. I'm assuming the cops will advise him about aiding and abetting."

"For all the good it'll do."

I left the car windows down after Jerry got out. Another ten minutes passed and the sheriff's deputy emerged from Dana's. She followed him out, and the two of them stood on the front porch, conversing. The deputy was staring out at the street. Even at a distance, his expression seemed stony. Dana looked trim and long-legged in a short denim skirt, a navy T-shirt, and flats, her hair pulled back with a bright red scarf. The deputy's stance suggested the effect wasn't lost on him. They seemed to be winding up their conversation, body language cautious and just a shade antagonistic. Her telephone must have rung because I saw her give a quick look in that direction. He gave her a nod and moved down the steps while she banged through the screen door and into the house.

As soon as he'd pulled away from the curb, I got out of my car and crossed the street to Dana's. She'd left the front door open, the screen on the latch. I knocked on the door frame, but she didn't seem to hear me. I could see her pacing, head tilted, handset anchored in the crook of her neck. She paused to light a cigarette, drawing deeply. "You can have her take the pictures if you want," she was saying, "but a professional is going to do a better job—" She was interrupted by the party on the other end, and I could see a frown of annoyance form. She removed a fleck of tobacco from her tongue. Her other line began to ring. "Well now, that's true, and I know it seems like a lot of money. About that, yes. . . ."

Her other line rang again.

"Debbie, I understand what you're saying. . . . I understand that and I empathize, but it's the wrong place to pinch pennies. Talk to Bob and see what he says. I've got another call coming in. . . . All right. Bye-bye. I'll call you back in a bit."

She pressed the button for the other line. "Boutique Bride," she said. Even through the screen door, I could see her manner shift. "Oh, hello." She turned her back to the door, voice dropping into a range I couldn't readily overhear. She set her half-smoked cigarette on the lip of an ashtray and checked her reflection in a wall-hung mirror near the desk. She smoothed her hair back and corrected a little smudge of eye makeup. "Don't do that," she said saying. "I really don't want you to do that. . . ."

I turned and scanned the street, debating whether I should knock on the door again. If Brian or Wendell was lurking in the bushes, I didn't see them. I peered back through the screen door as Dana wound down her conversation and replaced the phone on the desk.

When she caught sight of me through the screen, she gave a little jump, hand coming up automatically to her heart. "Oh, my God. You scared me to death," she said.

"I saw you on the phone and didn't want to interrupt. I heard about Brian. Mind if I come in?"

"Just a minute," she said. She moved to the screen and unlatched the thumb lock. She opened the screen and stepped back so I could enter. "I'm worried sick about him. I have no idea where he'd go, but he *has* to turn himself in. They're going to charge him with escape if he doesn't show up soon. A sheriff's deputy was just here, acting like I'd stashed him under the bed. He didn't say as much, but you know how they act, all puffy and officious."

"You haven't heard from Brian?"

She shook her head. "His attorney hasn't, either, which isn't good," she said. "He needs to know his legal position." She moved into the living room and took a seat on the near end of the couch. I moved to the far end, perching on the arm.

I tossed in a question just to see what she'd say. "Who was that on the phone?"

"Wendell's old partner, Carl. I guess he caught the news. Ever since this business with Brian came up, my phone's been ringing off the hook. I've heard from people I haven't talked to since grade school."

"You keep in touch with him?"

"He keeps in touch with me, though there's no love lost. I've always felt he was a terrible influence on Wendell."

"He paid a price for it," I said.

"Didn't we all?" She shot back.

"What about Brian's release? Has anybody figured out how he got out of jail? It's really hard to believe the computer made an error of that magnitude."

"This is Wendell's doing. No doubt about it," she said. I could see her look around for her cigarettes. She moved over to the desk, stubbing out the butt she'd left burning in the ashtray. She picked up a pack of cigarettes and a lighter, coming back to the couch. She tried to light one and changed her mind, her hands shaking badly.

"How would he get access to a sheriff's department computer?"

"I have no idea, but you said so yourself: Brian was his reason for returning to California. Now that Wendell's back, Brian's out of jail. How else do you figure it?"

"Those computers are bound to be well secured. How could he get an authorized jail release message sent through the system?"

"Maybe he took up hacking in the five years he was gone," she said sarcastically.

"Have you talked to Michael? Does he know Brian's out?"

"That's the first place I called. Michael went to work early, but I talked to Juliet and really put the fear of God in her. She's crazy about Brian, and she doesn't have a grain of sense. I made her swear she would call me if either of them heard from him."

"What about Wendell? Would he know how to reach Michael at the new address?"

"Why not? All he has to do is call Information. The new number's listed. It isn't any big secret. Why? Do you think Brian and Wendell would try to connect at Michael's?"

"I don't know. Do you?"

She thought about it for a moment. "It's possible," she said. She pressed her hands between her knees to still their shaking.

"I probably ought to go," I said.

"I'm staying close to the phone. If you learn anything, will you let me know?"

"Of course."

I left Dana's and headed over to the Perdido Keys. My prime worry at the moment was the whereabouts of Renata's boat. If Wendell had really found a way to arrange Brian's release, his next move would be getting the kid out of the country.

I pulled into a McDonald's and used the pay phone in the parking lot, dialing Renata's unlisted number without luck. I could hardly remember when I'd eaten last, so while I was on the premises I availed myself of the facilities, then picked up lunch: A QP with cheese, a Coke, and a large order of fries, which I took out to the car. At least the smell of fast food obliterated the last traces of Jerry Irwin's sweat.

When I reached Renata's, her big double garage door was wide open and there was no Jaguar in evidence. I did catch a glimpse of the boat at the dock, two wooden masts visible above the fence. The house itself showed no interior lights, and there was no indication of activity. I parked my VW about three doors away and demolished my meal, remembering as I finished that I'd already eaten lunch. I checked my watch. Ah, but that was hours ago. Well, two of them, at any rate.

I sat in my car and waited. Since my car radio wasn't working and I hadn't brought anything to read, I found myself ruminating about the sudden acquisition of family relationships. What was I going to do about them? Grandmother, aunts, cousins of every description . . . not that they'd lost sleep over me. There was something troubling about the feelings being stirred up. Most of them were bad. I'd never devoted any thought to the fact that my father was a mail carrier. I had known, of course, but the information had no impact, and I usually had no reason to reflect on the significance. All that news being delivered . . . the good and the bad, debts and remittances, accounts payable, accounts receivable, dividend checks, canceled notes, word about babies being born and old friends dying, the Dear John letters breaking off engagements . . . that was the task he'd been charged with in this world, an occupation my grandmother apparently judged too lowly for consideration. Maybe Burton and Grand truly felt it was their responsibility to see that my mother chose well in this matter of a husband. I felt defensive of him, brooding and protective.

With Liza's revelation, I'd caught a glimpse of whole dramas that had been acted out without my knowledge: quarrels and rituals, the gentle cooing of women, raucous laughter, cozy chats in the kitchen over cups of coffee, holiday dinners, babies born, advice offered up, the hand-embroidered linens passed down from one generation to the next. It was a ladies' magazine picture of the family: abundant, cinnamon-scented, filled with pine boughs and ornaments, football games on the color TV set in the den, uncles dazed by too much to eat, children glassy-eyed and hyper from all the naps they'd skipped. My world seemed bleak by comparison, and for once the Spartan, stripped-down life-style I so cherished seemed paltry and deprived.

I stirred on my seat, nearly paralyzed with boredom. There was no reason to believe Renata Huff would show up. Surveillance is a bitch. It's tough to sit and stare at the front of a house for five or six hours at a stretch. It's hard to pay attention. It's hard to give a shit. Usually I have to think of it as a Zen meditation, imagining I'm in touch with my Higher Power instead of just my bladder.

Daylight began to fade. I watched the color of the sky shift from apricot to blush. The temperature was dropping almost palpably. Summer evenings are usually chilly, and with this storm system lurking off the coast, the days seemed as short as some premature autumn. I could see a fog bank moving in, a wall of dark clouds against the rapidly accumulating cobalt blue of the twilight sky. I crossed my arms in front of me for warmth, slouching down on my seat. Another hour must have passed.

I felt my awareness flicker, and my head jerked involuntarily as I lurched out of sleep. I sat up straight and made a conscious effort to keep myself awake. This lasted about a minute. Various body parts began to hurt, and I thought about how babies cry when they're tired. Staying awake becomes a physical agony when the body needs rest. I shifted, turning sideways. I pulled my knees up and swung my feet onto the passenger seat, resting my back against the car door where the armrest protruded. I felt like I was drunk, my eyes rolling in their sockets as I fought to keep them open. I imagined the chemicals from all that junk food coursing through my body with this narcotic effect. This was never going to do. I had to have fresh air. I had to get up and move.

I checked my glove compartment for my penlight and set of key picks. I tucked my handbag on the floor out of sight and grabbed a jacket from the backseat. I got out, locked the car door, and crossed the street at an angle, moving toward Renata's with a devilish urge to snoop. Really, it wasn't my fault. I can't be held responsible when boredom sets in. For the sake of good manners, I rang the doorbell first, knowing in my heart that not a soul would come to answer. Sure enough, no response. What's a poor girl to do? I let myself through the side gate and moved around to the rear.

I moved down to the dock, which seemed to rock beneath me. Renata's boat, ironically, had been named the *Fugitive*, a forty-eight-foot ketch, sleek white, with an aft center cockpit and an aft cabin. The body was fiberglass, the deck oiled teak, the trim a varnished walnut, fittings of chrome and brass. The boat would probably sleep six in comfort, eight in a pinch. There were numerous vessels moored on either side of the key, lights shimmering against the black depths of the barely rippling water. What could be better for Wendell's purposes than to have ready access to the ocean through the keys? He might have been sailing in and out of here for years, wholly anonymous, wholly undetected.

I made a feeble effort to "halloo" the boat, which

produced no results. This was not surprising, as the boat was dark and shrouded in canvas.

I went on board, clambering over cables. I unzipped the cover in three places, pushing sections back. The cabin was locked, but I used my penlight to peer through the hatches, sweeping my beam through the galley below. The interior was immaculate: beautiful inlaid woods, muted upholstery in soft sunset hues. Supplies had been laid in, canned goods and bottled water in neatly stacked cardboard boxes, waiting to be stowed. I lifted my head and scanned the houses on either side. I couldn't see a soul. I checked the houses across the way. There were numerous lights on, occasional glimpses of the residents, but no indication that I was being watched. I crawled along the deck toward the bow until I reached the hatch above the V-berth. The bed was neatly made, and there were personal effects visible: clothing, paperback books, framed photographs that I couldn't quite make out.

I moved back to the galley and sat on the aft deck, working at the tubular lock that was set into the wood between my knees. A lock of this type usually has seven pins and is best attacked with a commercially available pick tool, which was part of the set I had with me. This small hand-held device is the approximate size of an old-fashioned porcelain faucet handle of the sort where HOT and COLD are printed across the surface in blue. The tool contains seven thin metal fingers that adjust themselves to correspond to the cut depth of a key. An in-and-out motion is applied, while a slight turning force is applied at the same time, a rubber sleeve providing friction that holds the fingers firmly in place.

Once the lock opens, the tool can be used as an actual key.

The lock finally yielded, but not without a few well-chosen curses. I tucked the tool in my jeans and slid back the hatch, easing myself down the galley steps. Sometimes I'm sorry I didn't hang in with the Girl Scouts. I might have qualified for some keen merit badges, breaking and entering being one. I moved through the cabin, using my penlight, searching every drawer and cubbyhole I could find. I'm not even sure what I was looking for. A compleat travel itinerary would have been a boon: passports, visas, charts marked with conspicuous red arrows and asterisks. Confirmation of Wendell's presence would have been lovely, too. There was nothing of interest. About the time I ran out of steam, I also ran out of luck.

I flipped off the penlight and I was just coming up the galley steps, emerging from the cabin, when Renata appeared. I found myself staring down the barrel of a .357 Magnum revolver. The damn gun was huge and looked like something an old western marshal might carry in a holster hanging halfway to his knees. I stopped in my tracks, instantly aware of the hole a gun like that can make in parts of the anatomy essential to life. I felt my hands come up, the universal gesture of goodwill and cooperation. Renata was apparently unaware of this, as her attitude was hostile and her tone of voice belligerent. "Who are you?"

"I'm a private investigator. My ID's in my handbag, which is out in the car."

"You know I could kill you for trespassing on this boat."

"I'm aware of that. I'm kind of hoping you won't."

She stared at me, perhaps trying to decipher my tone, which was probably not as respectful as she might have wished. "What were you doing back there?"

I turned my head slightly, as if looking at the "back there" might help me recall. I decided it was the wrong time to bullshit. "I was looking for Wendell Jaffe. His son was released from the Perdido County Jail this morning, and I thought the two might be planning to connect." I thought we'd have to stop and play out some kind of nonsense along the lines of "Who's Wendell Jaffe?" but she seemed willing to play the scene the way I'd set it. I didn't articulate the rest of my suspicion, which was that Wendell, Brian, and Renata probably intended to defect on this very boat. "By the way, just to satisfy my curiosity, was Wendell the one who set up that jail release?"

"Possibly."

"How'd he manage that?"

"Haven't I seen you somewhere before?"

"Viento Negro. Last week. I tracked you to the Hacienda Grande."

Even in the shadows I saw her eyebrows lift, and I decided to leave her with the impression that it was my superior detecting that unearthed them. Why mention Dick Mills when his spotting Wendell was dumb luck on his part? I wanted her to think of me as Wonder Woman, bullets ricocheting off my wristbands.

"I tell you what," I said conversationally. "You don't really need to keep that gun on me. I'm unarmed myself, and I'm not going to do anything rash." Slowly I lowered my hands. I expected her to protest, but she didn't seem to notice. She seemed undecided about what to do next. She could, of course, shoot me, but dead bodies are tricky to dispose of and, if not dispatched properly, tend to generate a lot of questions. The last thing she wanted was the sheriff's deputy at her door. "What do you want with Wendell?"

"I work for the company that insured his life. His wife just collected half a million bucks, and if Wendell's not dead, they want their money back." I could see her hand tremble slightly, not from fear, but from the weight of the gun. I thought it was time to take action.

I let out a piercing shriek and whacked her mightily across the wrist, using my arms as a sledgehammer like the guys do in the movies. I suspect it was the shriek that made her loosen her grip. The gun flipped up like a pancake and then hit the deck, clattering across the floor of the cockpit. I pushed Renata backward, knocking her off balance while I snatched it up. She went down on her backside. Now I held the gun. She scrambled to her feet, and her hands came up. I liked this better, though I was just as baffled as she had been about what to do. I'm capable of violence when I'm under attack, but I wasn't going to shoot her while she stood there, staring me in the face. I just had to hope *she* didn't know that. I assumed an aggressive stance, feet spread, gun held with both hands, my arms stiff. "Where's Wendell? I need to talk to him."

She made a little squeaking sound in her throat. A fiery patch formed around her nose, and then her whole face screwed up as she started to weep.

"Cut the crap, Renata, and give me the information or I will shoot your right foot on the count of five." I aimed at her right foot. "One. Two. Three. Four—"

"He's at Michael's!"

"Thank you. I appreciate that. You're too kind," I replied. "I'll leave the gun in your mailbox."

She shuddered involuntarily. "Keep it. I hate guns."

I tucked the gun in my waistband at the small of my back and hopped nimbly to the dock. When I looked back at her, she was clinging weakly to the mast.

I left my business card in her mailbox and tucked another one in her door. Then I drove to Michael's.

# 19

I COULD SEE lights on in the rear. I bypassed the doorbell and walked around to the backyard, peeking in every window I passed. The kitchen revealed nothing except counter surfaces piled with dirty dishes. Cardboard moving boxes still formed the bulk of the furnishings, the crumpled paper now massed like a cloud bank in the corner. When I reached the master bedroom, I saw that Juliet, in a grip of home decorating tips, had draped hand towels over tension rods, effectively obscuring my view. I returned to the front door, wondering if I'd be forced to knock like a mere commoner. I tried the knob and discovered to my delight that I could walk right in.

The television set in the living room had gone on the blink. In lieu of a color picture, there was a display of dancing lights equal to an aurora borealis. The sound that accompanied this remarkable phenomenon suggested tough guys with guns and a thrilling car chase. I peered toward the bedrooms, but I couldn't hear much above the squealing of car brakes and the firing of Uzis. I took out Renata's gun, pointing it like a flashlight as I eased my way cautiously to the back of the house.

The baby's bedroom was dark, but the door to the master bedroom was open a crack and light slanted into the hall. I gave the door a little push with the barrel of my gun. It swung back with a creak, the hinge singing on its pin. Before me, on a rocking chair, Wendell Jaffe was sitting with his grandson in his lap. He made a sharp, startled sound. "Don't shoot the baby!"

"I'm not going to shoot the baby. What's the matter with you?"

Brendan was grinning at the sight of me, flailing his arms in a vigorous nonverbal greeting. He wore a flannel sleeper with blue bunnies, and his back end was bulky with a disposable diaper. His blond hair was still damp from a recent bath. Juliet had brushed it up in a delicate question mark on top. I could smell the baby powder halfway across the room. I put the gun away, tucking it in my blue jeans at the small of my back. This is not a cool place to carry, and I was perfectly aware that I risked shooting myself in the butt. On the other hand, I didn't want the gun shoved down in my handbag, where it would be even less accessible than it was wedged up against my rear.

As family reunions go, this didn't seem to be that good. So far, Brendan was the only one who was having any fun. Michael stood to one side, leaning against the chest of drawers, his expression withdrawn. He studied Wendell's class ring, which he seemed to use like a meditation, turning it on his finger. I've seen professional tennis players do that, focusing on the strings of a tennis racket to maintain concentration. Michael's sweatshirt, soiled jeans, and mud-caked boots suggested that he hadn't cleaned up after work. I could still see the ridge in his hair where he'd worn his hard hat that day. Wendell must have been waiting when he walked in the door.

Juliet was huddled at the head of the bed, looking tense and small in a tank top and cutoffs. Her feet were bare, legs drawn up, her arms wrapped around her knees. She was keeping herself out of the way, letting the drama play out as it would. The only illumination in the room was a table lamp, something imported from Juliet's childhood bedroom at home. The shade was ruffled and hot pink. At the base there was a doll with a stiff pink skirt, her body wired to the fixture, her arms extended. She had a rosebud for a mouth, and her lashes formed a thick fringe above eyes that would open and shut mechanically. The light bulb couldn't have been more than forty watts, but the room seemed warm with its ambient glow.

Juliet's features were etched in sharp contrasts, one cheek hot pink, the other cast in shadow. Wendell's face looked craggy and wooden in the light, his high cheekbones carved. He seemed haggard, and the sides of his nose were shiny from cosmetic surgery. Michael, on the other hand, had the face of a stone angel, cold and sensual. His dark eyes seemed luminous, his tall, lanky frame easily the equal to his father's, though Wendell was heavier and he lacked Michael's grace. The three of them were caught in a curious tableau, the kind of picture a psychiatrist might ask you to explain to gain insight into your mind-set.

"Hello, Wendell. Sorry to interrupt. Remember me?"

Wendell's gaze shifted to Michael's face. He cocked his head in my direction. "Who's this?"

Michael stared at the floor. "Private investigator," he said. "She talked to Mom about you a couple nights ago."

I gave Wendell a little wave. "She works for the insurance company you cheated out of a half a million bucks," I inserted.

"*I* did?"

"Yes, Wendell," I said facetiously. "As odd as it sounds, that's what life insurance is about. Being dead. So far, you're not holding up your end of the bargain."

He was looking at me with a mixture of caution and confusion. "Don't I know you?"

"We crossed paths at the hotel in Viento Negro."

His eyes locked on mine in a moment of recognition. "Were you the one who broke into our room?"

I shook my head, inventing lies on the spot. "Uhn-uhn, not me. That was an ex-cop named Harris Brown."

He shook his head at the name.

"He's a police lieutenant, or he was," I went on.

"Never heard of him."

"Well, he's heard of you. He was assigned to the case when you first disappeared. Then he was taken off for reasons unknown. I thought you might explain."

"Are you sure he was looking for me?"

"I don't think his being there was a coincidence," I said. "He stayed in three fourteen. I was in three sixteen."

"Hey, Dad? Could we finish this?"

Brendan began to fuss, and Wendell patted at him without much effect. He picked up a small stuffed puppy dog and waggled it in Brendan's face while he continued his conversation. Brendan grabbed the animal by the ears and pulled it in close. He must have been teething because he gnawed on its rubber face with all the raw enthusiasm I reserve for fried chicken. Somehow his antics became an odd counterpoint to Wendell's conversation with Michael.

He apparently picked up from a point he'd been making prior to my arrival. "I had to get out, Michael. It had nothing to do with you. It was my life. It was me. I'd just screwed up so bad there wasn't any other way to handle it. I hope you'll understand someday. There's no such thing as justice in the current legal system."

"Oh, come on. Spare me the speech. What is this, a political science class? Just cut the shit and don't talk to me about fucking *justice*, okay? You didn't hang around long enough to find out."

"Please. Michael. Let's stop this. I don't want to fight. There isn't time for that. I don't expect you to agree with my decision."

"It isn't just me, Dad. What about Brian? He's the one suffered all the damage."

"I'm aware he's off course, and I'm doing what I can," Wendell said.

"Brian needed you when he was twelve. It's too late now."

"I don't think so. Not at all. You're wrong about that, trust me."

Michael seemed to wince, and his eyes rolled toward the ceiling. "*Trust* you? Dad, you are so full of shit! Why should I trust *you*? I'm never going to trust you."

Wendell seemed disconcerted at the harshness of Michael's tone. He didn't like being contradicted. He wasn't accustomed to having his judgment questioned, especially by a kid who was seventeen when he left. Michael had become an adult in his absence, had in fact stepped in to fill the very gap that Wendell had left. Maybe he pictured himself coming back to mend the breach, cleaning up old business, setting everything to rights. Maybe he'd thought an impassioned explanation might somehow compensate for his abandonment and neglect. "I guess there's no way we can agree," he said.

"Why didn't you come back and face what you did?"

"I couldn't come back. I didn't see a way to make it work."

"Meaning you weren't interested. Meaning you didn't want to be asked to make any sacrifices in our behalf. Thanks a bunch. We appreciate your devotion. It's typical."

"Now, son, that's not true."

"Yes, it is. You could have stayed if you wanted, if we *meant* anything to you. But here's the truth. We didn't matter to you, and that was just our tough luck, right?"

"Of course you matter. What do you think I've been talking about?"

"I don't know, Dad. As far as I can tell, you're just trying to justify your behavior."

"This is pointless. I can't undo the past. I can't change what happened back then. Brian and I are going to turn ourselves in. That's the best I can do, and if that's not good enough, then I don't know what to say."

Michael broke off eye contact, shaking his head with frustration. I watched him consider and discard a retort.

Wendell cleared his throat. "I have to go. I told Brian I'd be there." He got to his feet, shifting the baby against his shoulder. Juliet swung her legs over to the side of the bed and got up, prepared to take Brendan from his grandfather's arms. It was clear the conversation had upset her. Her nose was pink, her mouth swollen with emotion.

Michael shoved his hands down in his pockets. "You didn't do Brian any favor with that fake jail release."

"That's true, as it turned out, but there was no way we could know that. I've changed my mind about a lot of things. Anyway, this is something your brother and I have to work out between us."

"You've got Brian in worse trouble than he was in before. You don't move fast, the cops'll pick him up and throw him back in the slammer and he won't see daylight 'til he's a hundred and three. And where will you be? Off on a fuckin' boat without a care in the world. Good luck."

"Doesn't it occur to you that I'll have to pay a price, too?"

"At least you don't have a murder charge hanging over your head."

"I'm not sure there's any point in going on with this," Wendell said, ignoring the actual content of Michael's remark. The two of them seemed to be talking at cross purposes. Wendell was trying to reassert his parental authority. Michael wasn't having any of that shit. He had a son now himself, and he knew how much his father had forfeited. Wendell turned away. "I have to go," he said, holding one hand out to Juliet. "I'm glad we had a chance to meet. It's too bad the circumstances weren't happier."

"Are we going to see you again?" Juliet said. Tears were spilling down her cheeks. Mascara had formed a sprinkling of soot beneath her eyes. Michael seemed watchful, his expression haunted, while grief poured from Juliet like water bursting through a wall.

Even Wendell seemed affected by her open display of feeling. "Absolutely. Of course. That's a promise."

His gaze lingered on Michael, perhaps hoping for some sign of emotion. "I'm sorry for the pain I caused you. I mean that."

Michael's shoulders hunched slightly with the effort to stay disconnected. "Yeah. Right. Whatever," he said.

Wendell hugged the baby to him, his face buried in Brendan's neck, drinking in the sweet, milky smell of the child. "Oh, you sweet boy," he said, his voice tremulous. Brendan was staring fascinated at Wendell's hair, which he grabbed. Solemnly he tried to put a fistful in his mouth. Wendell winced, gently extracting the baby's fingers. Juliet reached for Brendan. Michael watched, his eyes pooling with silver before he looked away. Sorrow rose from his skin like steam, radiating outward.

Wendell passed the baby to Juliet and kissed her on the forehead before he turned to Michael. The two grabbed each other in a tight embrace that seemed to go on forever. "I love you, son." They rocked back and forth in an ancient dance. Michael made a small sound at the back of his throat, his eyes squeezed shut. For that one unguarded moment, he and Wendell were connected. I had to look away. I couldn't imagine what it must feel like to find yourself in the presence of a parent you thought was dead. Michael pulled back. Wendell took out a handkerchief and swiped at his eyes. "I'll be in touch," he whispered, and then let out a breath.

Without looking at them, he turned and left the room. His guilt probably felt oppressive, like a weight on his chest. He moved through the house, heading for the front door with me right behind him. If he was aware of my presence, he didn't object.

The outside air had picked up a sting of moisture, wind tossing through the trees. The streetlights were almost entirely blocked by branches, shadows blowing across the street like a pile of leaves. I intended to bid the man a fare-thee-well, get in my car, and then play tag with him, following at a discreet distance until he led me to Brian. As soon as I got a fix on the kid's location, I was calling the cops. I said good night and moved off in the opposite direction.

I'm not sure he even heard me.

Preoccupied, Wendell took out a set of car keys and crossed the grass to a little red Maserati sports car that was parked at the curb. Renata apparently had a fleet of expensive autos. He unlocked the car and let himself in, quickly sliding in under the steering wheel. He slammed the car door. I unlocked my VW and jammed my key in the ignition in concert with his. I could feel Renata's gun pressing into the small of my back. I pulled it out of my waistband. I torqued myself around to the backseat, where I snagged my handbag and deposited the gun into the depths. I heard Wendell's engine grind. I fired mine up and sat there with lights out, waiting for his front and rear lights to come on.

The grinding continued, but his engine didn't turn over. The sound was high-pitched and unproductive. Moments later I saw him fling open his car door and emerge. Agitated, he checked under the hood. He did something to the wires, got back into the car, and started grinding again. The engine was losing hope, batteries surrendering any juice they had. I put the VW in gear and flipped my lights on, pulling forward slowly until I was next to him. I rolled my window down. He leaned over from the driver's seat and rolled his down.

I said, "Hop in. I'll take you to Renata's. You can call a tow truck from her place."

He debated for a moment, with a quick glance at Michael's. He didn't have much choice. The last thing in the world he wanted was to go back in with a chore as mundane as a call to triple A. He got out, locked his car, and came around the front, getting into mine. I turned right on Perdido Street and took a left before I reached the fairgrounds, thinking to hit the frontage road that ran along the beach. I could have hopped on the freeway. Traffic wasn't heavy. The street leading to the Keys was just one ramp away, and just as easily reached by this route.

I turned left when I reached the beach. The wind had picked up considerably, and there were massive black clouds above the pitch black of the ocean. "I had a nice chat with Carl Monday night," I said. "Have you talked to him?"

"I was supposed to meet with him later, but he had to go out of town," Wendell said, distracted.

"Really. He thought he'd be too mad to talk to you."

"We have business to settle. He has something of mine."

"You mean the boat?"

"Well, that, too, but this is something else."

The sky was charcoal gray, and I could see flashes out at sea, an electrical storm sitting maybe fifty miles out. The light flickered among the darkening cloud banks, creating the illusion of artillery too far away to hear. The air was filled with a restless energy. I glanced over at Wendell. "Aren't you even curious how we picked up your trail? I'm surprised you haven't asked."

His attention was fixed on the horizon, which was illuminated intermittently as the storm progressed. "It doesn't matter. It was bound to happen sometime."

"You mind telling me where you've been all these years?"

He stared out the side window, his face averted. "Not far. You'd be surprised how few places I've been."

"You gave up a lot to get there."

Pain flickered across his face like lightning. "Yes."

"Have you been with Renata the whole time?"

"Oh, yes," he said with just a hint of bitterness. A small silence fell, and then he stirred uneasily. "Do you think I'm wrong to come back like this?"

"Depends on what you were hoping to accomplish."

"I'd like to help them."

"Help them do what? Brian's already on his path, and so is Michael. Dana coped as well as she could, and the money's been spent. You can't just step back into the life you left and make all the stories come out differently. They're working out the consequences of your decision. You'll have to do that, too."

"I guess I can't expect to mend all my fences in the course of a few days."

"I'm not sure you can do it at all," I said. "In the meantime, I'm not going to let you out of my sight. I lost you once. I don't intend to lose you again."

"I need some time. I have business to take care of."

"You had business to take care of five years ago!"

"This is different."

"Where's Brian?"

"He's safe."

"I didn't ask *how* he was, I said 'where.' " The car began to lose speed. I looked down with bafflement, pumping the accelerator as the car slowed. "Jesus, what's this?"

"You out of gas?"

"I just filled the tank." I steered toward the right curb as the car drifted to a halt.

He peered over at the dashboard. "Gas gauge says full."

"What'd I just tell you? Of course it's full. I just filled it!"

We had reached a full stop. The silence was profound, and then the underlying thrum of wind and surf filtered into my consciousness. Even with the moon obscured by storm clouds, I could see the whitecaps out in the water.

I hauled my handbag from the backseat and fumbled in the front pocket until I found my penlight. "Let me see what's going on," I said, as though I had a clue.

I got out of the car. Wendell got out on his side and moved around to the rear in concert with me. I was glad of his company. Maybe he knew something about cars that I didn't—no big trick. In situations like this, I always like to take action. I opened the back flap and stared at the engine. Looked like it always did, about the size and shape of a sewing machine. I expected to see sprung parts, broken doohickies, the flapping ends of a fan belt, some evidence of rogue auto parts adrift from their moorings. "What do you think?"

He took the penlight and leaned closer, squinting. Boys know about these things: guns, cars, lawn mowers, garbage disposals, electric switches, baseball statistics. I'm scared to take the lid off the toilet tank because that ball thing always looks like it's on the verge of exploding. I leaned over and peered with him. "Looks a little bit like a sewing machine, doesn't it?" he remarked.

Behind us, a car backfired and a rock slammed into my rear fender. Wendell made sense of it a split second before I did. We both hit the pavement. Wendell grabbed me, and the two of us scrambled around to the side of the car. A second shot was fired, and the bullet *ping*ed off the roof. We ducked, hunched together. Wendell's arm had gone around me protectively. He flipped the switch on the penlight, making the pitch dark complete. I had a terrible desire to lift up to window level and peek out across the street. I knew there wouldn't be much to see: dark, a dirt bank, swiftly passing cars on the freeway. Our assailant must have followed us from Michael's house, first incapacitating Wendell's car and then mine.

"This has got to be one of your pals. I'm not this unpopular in my set," I said.

Another shot was fired. My rear window turned to cracked ice, though only one chunk fell out.

Wendell said, "Jesus."

I said, "Amen." Neither of us meant it as profanity.

He looked at me. His previous lethargy had vanished. At least his attention had been sharpened by the situation. "Someone's been following me the last few days."

"You have a theory?"

He shook his head. "I made some phone calls. I needed help."

"Who knew you were going to Michael's?"

"Just Renata."

I thought about that one. I'd taken her gun, which I

remembered now was in my handbag. In the car. "I have a gun in the car if you can reach it," I said. "My handbag's on the backseat."

"Won't the inside light come on?"

"In *my* car? Not a chance."

Wendell opened the door on the passenger side. Sure enough, the interior light came on. The next bullet was swift and nearly caught him in the neck. We ducked down again, silent for a moment while we thought about Wendell's carotid artery.

I said, "Carl must have known you'd be at Michael's if you told him you'd meet him afterward."

"That was before his plans changed. Anyway, he doesn't know where Michael lives."

"He says his plans changed, but you don't know that for a fact. It wouldn't take a rocket scientist to call Information. All he had to do was ask Dana. He's kept in touch with her."

"Hell, he's in love with Dana. He's always been in love with her. I'm sure he was delighted to have me out of the picture."

"What about Harris Brown? He'd have a gun."

"I told you before. I never heard of him."

"Wendell, quit bullshitting. I need some answers here."

"I'm telling you the truth!"

"Stay down. I'm going to try the car door again."

Wendell flattened himself as I gave the door a yank. The next shot *thunk*ed into the sand close by. I flipped the seat forward and grabbed my bag, hauled it out of the backseat, and slammed the door again. My heart had rocketed. Anxiety was coursing through my body as if a sluice gate had opened. I needed to pee like crazy, except for the fact that my kidneys had shriveled. All my other internal organs had circled, like wagons under serious attack. I pulled out the revolver, with its white pearlite grips. "Gimme some light over here."

Wendell flipped on the penlight, shielding it like a match.

I was looking at the sort of single-action six-shooter John Wayne might have favored. I popped open the cylinder and checked the load, which was full. I snapped the cylinder shut. The gun must have weighed three pounds.

"Where'd you get that?"

"I stole it from Renata. Wait here. I'll be back."

He said something to me, but I was already duck-walking my way out into the darkness, angling toward the beach and away from our assailant. I cut left, circling out a hundred yards around the front of the car, hoping I wasn't visible to anybody interested in target practice. My eyes were fully adjusted to the dark by now, and I felt conspicuous. I looked back, trying to measure the distance I'd come. My pale blue VW looked like some kind of ghostly igloo or a giant pup tent. I reached a left-turning curve in the road, crouched, and crossed in a flash, easing back toward the point from which I imagined our attacker was firing.

It probably took ten minutes until I reached the spot, and I realized I hadn't heard a shot fired the whole time. Even in the hazy visibility of the half-dark around me, the area felt deserted. I was now directly across from my car on the two-lane road, keeping myself low to the ground. I popped my head up like a prairie dog.

"Wendell?" I called.

No answer. No shots fired. No movement in any direction and no more sense of jeopardy. The night felt flat and totally benign at this point. I stood upright. "Wendell?"

I did a 360 turn, sweeping my gaze across the immediate vicinity, and then sank down again. I looked both ways and crossed the street at a quick clip, keeping low. When I reached the car, I slid past the front bumper into home base. "Hey, it's me," I said.

There was only sea wind and empty beach.

Wendell Jaffe was gone again.

# 20

IT WAS NOW ten o'clock at night, and the roadway was deserted. I could see lights from the freeway tantalizingly close, but no one in their right mind was going to pick me up at that hour. I found my handbag by the car and hefted it over my shoulder. I went around to the driver's side and opened the car door. I reached in, leaning forward to snag the keys from the ignition. I could have locked the car, but what would be the point? It wasn't running at the moment, and the rear window was shattered, open to the elements and any pint-size little car thieves.

I hiked to the nearest gas station, which was maybe a mile away. It was very dark, street lamps appearing at long intervals and even then with only dim illumination. The storm had apparently stalled off the coast, where it lingered, brooding. Lightning winked through the inky clouds like a lamp with a loose connection. The wind whuffled across the sand while dried fronds rattled in the palm trees. I did a quick self-assessment and decided I was in pretty good shape, given all the excitement. One of the virtues of physical fitness is that you can walk a mile in the dark and it's no big deal. I was wearing jeans, a short-sleeved sweatshirt, and my tenny bops, not the best shoes for walking, but not agonizing, either.

The station itself was one of those places open twenty-four hours a day, but it was run largely by computer, with only one fellow in attendance. Naturally he couldn't leave the premises. I got a handful of change and headed for the public phone booth in the corner of the parking lot. I called AAA first, gave them my number, and told them where I was. The operator advised me to wait with the car, but I assured her I had no intention of hiking back in the dark. While I waited for the tow truck, I put a call through to Renata and told her what was happening. She didn't seem to bear me any grudges after our tussle on the boat deck for possession of the gun. She said Wendell wasn't home yet, but she'd hop in the car and cruise the route between the house and the frontage road where I'd last seen him.

The tow truck finally appeared about forty-five minutes later. I hopped in with the driver and directed him to my disabled car. He was a man in his forties, apparently career tow truck, full of sniffs, tobacco chaws, and learned assessments. When we reached the vehicle, he stepped down from the truck and hiked his pants up, circling the VW with his hands on his hips. He paused and spat. "What's the deal here?" He might have been asking about the shattered rear window, but I ignored that for the moment.

"I have no idea. I was tooling along about forty miles an hour and the car suddenly lost power."

He reached toward the car roof where a large-caliber slug had punched a hole the size of a dime. "Say, what *is* this?"

"Oh. You mean *that*?" I leaned forward, squinting in the half-light.

The hole looked like a neat black polka dot against the pale blue paint. He stuck the tip of one finger into it. "This here looks like a *bullet* hole."

"Gosh, it does, doesn't it?"

We circled the car, and I echoed his consternation at all the hurt places we came across. He quizzed me at length, but I fended off his questions. The guy was a tow truck driver, not a cop, I thought. I was hardly under oath.

Finally, head shaking, he slid onto the driver's seat and tried starting the car. I suspect he would have taken great satisfaction if the engine had fired right up. He struck me as the sort of fellow who didn't mind women looking foolish. No luck. He got out, went around, and peered in the back end. He grunted to himself, fiddled with some car parts, and tried the starter again without producing results. He towed the VW to the gas station, where he left it in a service bay and then departed with a sly glance backward and a shake of his head. No telling what he thought of little ladies these days. I had a chat with the attendant, who assured me the mechanic would be in by seven the next morning.

By now it was well after midnight and I was not only exhausted, but I was stranded as well. I could have called Henry. I knew he'd have hopped in his car and driven down to fetch me at any hour without complaint.

The problem was I simply couldn't face the drive, yet another lap in the track I was running between Santa Teresa and Perdido. Happily, the area wasn't short of motels. I spotted one on the far side of the freeway, within easy walking distance, and hoofed it across the overpass. In preparation for such emergencies, I always carry a toothbrush, toothpaste, and clean underpants shoved down in my handbag.

The motel had one vacancy. I paid more than I wanted, but I was too tired to argue. For the extra thirty dollars I was accorded one tiny bottle each of shampoo and conditioner. A matching container held just enough "body" lotion to moisturize one limb. The problem was you couldn't get the stuff out. I finally gave up the idea of being moist and went to bed stark naked and dry as a stick. I slept like a zombie without any medication and decided, with regret, that my cold was gone.

I woke up at 6:00, wondering briefly where I was. Once I remembered, I sank down under the covers and went back to sleep, not waking again until 8:25. I showered, donned my clean underwear, and then put on yesterday's clothes again. The room was paid for until noon, so I kept my key and grabbed a quick cup of coffee from the vending machine before I hiked back across 101 to my car.

The mechanic was eighteen years old, with frizzy red hair, brown eyes, a pug nose, a gap between his front teeth, and a thick Texas accent. The coverall he was wearing looked like a romper suit. When he saw me, he beckoned me over by doing curls with his index finger. He'd put the car up on the hydraulic lift, and we peered at the underside together. I could already picture dollars flying out the window. He wiped his hands on a rag and said, "Lookit."

I looked, not understanding at first what he was pointing to. He reached up and touched a vise clamp that had been affixed to a line. "Somebody put this little dingus on your fuel line. I bet you onny got about three blocks before the engine give out."

I laughed. "And that's all it was?"

He unscrewed the clamp and dropped the little dingus in the palm of my hand. "That's all. Car should run fine now."

"Thanks. This is great. How much do I owe you?"

"Thanks is good enough where I come from," he said.

I drove back to my motel room, where I sat on the unmade bed and called Renata. Her machine picked up and I left a message, asking her to give me a call. I tried Michael's house next, surprised when he snatched up the phone after half a ring.

"Hi, Michael. This is Kinsey. I thought you'd be at work. Have you heard from your father?"

"Nuhn-uhn, and Brian hasn't, either. He's called this morning to say Dad never showed. He really sounded worried. I called in sick so I could hang by the phone."

"Where is Brian?"

"He won't tell me. I think he's afraid I'll turn him in to the cops before he and Dad connect up. You think Dad's okay?"

"That's hard to say." I filled him in on events from the night before. "I left a message for Renata, and I hope to hear back. When I talked to her last night, she said she'd see if she could find him. She may have picked him up somewhere out on the road."

There was a brief silence. "Who's Renata?"

Oops. "Ahh. Nnnn. She's a friend of your dad's. I think he's been staying at her place with her."

"She lives here in Perdido?"

"She has a house on the Keys."

Another silence. "Does my mom know?"

"I don't think so. Probably not."

"Man, oh, man. What a jerk." Silence again. "Well. I guess I better let you go. I want to keep the line free in case he tries to get in touch."

I said, "You've got my number. Will you let me know if you should hear from him?"

"Sure," he said tersely. I suspected any lingering sense of loyalty to his father had been erased with the news about Renata.

I tried calling Dana. Her machine picked up. I listened to strains of the wedding march, drumming my fingers until I heard the beep. I left word for her to call me, keeping my message brief. I was still kicking myself for mentioning Renata in my conversation with Michael. Wendell had generated enough hostility in the kid without my adding the issue of his common-law wife. I tried reaching Lieutenant Ryckman at the Perdido County Jail. He was out, but I had a quick chat with Senior Deputy Tiller, who told me there was a big department shake-up over Brian's unauthorized release. Internal Affairs was scrutinizing every employee who had access to the computer. Another call came through, and he had to ring off. I said I'd try Ryckman again when I got back to Santa Teresa.

I'd just about exhausted my list of local calls. I checked out of the motel and was on the road by 10:00. I was hoping that by the time I reached the office in

Santa Teresa I'd have some return messages, but I unlocked my door to find the green light glowing blankly
on my answering machine. I spent the morning with my
usual office routines: business calls and mail, a few
bookkeeping entries, one or two bills to pay. I made a
pot of coffee and then called my insurance adjuster to
report last night's incident. She told me to go ahead and
get the rear window replaced at the auto glass shop I'd
used before. It was clear I couldn't ride around without
protection because I'd be ticketed.

In the meantime I was half tempted to leave the bullet holes where they were. Make too many claims and
you get your policy canceled or your rates elevated to
astronomical rates. What did I care about bullet holes?
I was sporting a few of those myself. I called and made
an appointment to have the window taken care of late
afternoon.

Shortly after lunch, Alison buzzed me to say Renata
Huff was in the reception area. I went out to the front.
She was sitting on the little sofa, head back, eyes
closed. She was not looking good. She wore chinos,
bunched together and belted at the waist, and a black
V-neck top with an orange anorak over it. Her dark
curls were still damp from a recent shower, but her eyes
were darkly circled and her cheeks seemed gaunt from
stress. She pulled herself together with an apologetic
smile at Alison, who seemed especially perky by comparison.

I took Renata back to my office, sat her on my visitor's chair, and poured us both some coffee. "Thank
you," she murmured, sipping gratefully. She closed her
eyes again, savoring the rich liquid on her tongue. "This
is good. I need this."

"You look tired."

"I am."

It was really the first time I'd had a chance to study her closely. Her face in repose was not what I'd call pretty. Her complexion was lovely—clear olive tones without flaw or blemish—but her features seemed wrong: brows dark and untamed, dark eyes too small. Her mouth was large, and her short-cropped hair made her jaw look squared off. Her expression ordinarily had a petulant cast, but in the rare moments when she smiled, her whole face was transformed—exotic, full of light. With her coloring, she could wear hues a lot of women couldn't get away with: lime green, hot pink, royal blue, and fuchsia.

"Wendell got home about midnight last night. This morning I went out to run errands. I couldn't have been gone for more than forty minutes. When I came home, everything he owned was gone and so was he. I waited for an hour or so and then got in my car and came up here. My real inclination was to call the police, but I thought I'd try you first and see what advice you might have to give."

"About what?"

"He stole money from me. Four thousand dollars in cash."

"What about the *Fugitive*?"

She shook her head wearily. "He knows I'd kill him if he took that boat."

"Don't you have a speedboat, too?"

"It's actually not a speedboat. It's an inflatable dinghy, but it's still at the dock. Anyway, Wendell doesn't have keys to the *Fugitive*."

"Why not?"

Her cheeks tinted slightly. "I never trusted him."

"You've been together five years and you didn't trust him with the keys to your boat?"

"He had no business on the boat without me," she said in an irritated tone.

I had to let that one pass. "So what's your suspicion?"

"I think he went back for the *Lord*. God only knows where he means to go after that."

"Why would he steal Eckert's boat?"

"He'd steal anything. Don't you get that? The *Lord* was his boat to begin with, and he wanted it back. Besides, the *Fugitive*'s a coastal cruiser. The *Lord*'s a blue water boat, better suited to his purpose."

"Which is what?"

"Getting as far away from here as possible."

"Why come to me?"

"I thought you'd know where the *Lord* was slipped. You said you talked to Carl Eckert on the boat. I didn't want to waste a lot of time at the harbormaster's office trying to track him down."

"Wendell told me Carl Eckert was out of town last night."

"Of course he's gone. That's the point. He won't even miss the boat until he gets back." She checked her watch. "Wendell must have left Perdido about ten this morning."

"How'd he manage that? Did he get the car fixed?"

"He took the Jeep I keep parked on the street. Even if it took him forty minutes to get up here, the Coast Guard still has a chance to head him off."

"Where would he go?"

"Back to Mexico, I'd guess. He knows the waters

around the Baja, and he's got a counterfeit passport that identifies him as a Mexican citizen."

"I'll get my car," I said.

"We can take mine."

We clattered down the steps together, me in front, Renata bringing up the rear. "You should notify the police about the Jeep."

"Good point. I'm hoping he left it somewhere in the marina parking lot."

"Where'd he go last night, did he say? I lost track of him around ten. If he got home at midnight, what'd he do for two hours? It doesn't take that long to walk a mile and a half."

"I'm not sure. After you called, I got in my car and went looking for him. I scoured every street between my place and the beach, and there was no sign of him. From what he said later, I got the impression somebody came and got him, but he wouldn't say who. Maybe one of his boys."

"I don't think so," I said. "I talked to Michael a little while ago. He says Brian called this morning. Wendell was supposed to be there last night, but he never showed."

"Wendell's never been good at promises."

"Do you know where Brian is?"

"I have no idea. Wendell made sure I knew as little as possible. That way if I was ever questioned by the police, I could claim ignorance."

This was apparently Wendell's standard operating procedure, but I wondered if this time keeping everybody ignorant was going to work against him.

We'd reached the street by then. Renata had defied all the parking gods and snagged a place right in front where the curb was painted red. And did she have a ticket? Of course not. She unlocked the Jag, and I let myself into the passenger seat. Renata took off with a little chirp of her tires. I found myself holding on to the chicken stick. "Wendell might have gone to the cops," I said. "From what he told Michael, he intended to turn himself in. With somebody shooting at him, he might have felt safer in the slammer."

She made a little snort of contempt, flashing me a cynical look. "He had no intention of turning himself in. That was bullshit. He mentioned he was going to see Dana, but that might have been bullshit, too."

"He went to Dana's last night? What was that about?"

"I don't know that he went, but he said he wanted to talk to her before he left. He felt guilty about her. He hoped to get things squared away before he took off. He probably wanted to have his conscience clear."

"You think he left without you?"

"I certainly think he has it in him. Spineless bastard. He never faced the consequences of his own behavior. Never. At this point, I don't care if he ends up in jail." She seemed to be catching every traffic light. If there was no cross traffic visible, she would sail through on red, skipping four-way stops altogether in her haste to reach the marina. Maybe she thought traffic laws were meant only as suggestions, or maybe the traffic laws simply didn't apply to her that day.

I studied her profile, wondering how much information I could pump her for. "Do you mind if I ask about the logistics of Wendell's disappearance?"

"Like what?"

I shrugged, not quite sure where to start. "What arrangements did he make? I don't see how he could have managed it alone." I could see her hesitate, so I tried a gentle coaxing, hoping she would open up. "I'm not just being nosy. I'm thinking whatever he did then, he might try again."

I didn't think she'd answer, but she finally slid a look in my direction. "You're right. He couldn't pull it off without help," she said. "I single-handed my ketch down along the coast of Baja and picked him up in the dinghy after he abandoned the *Lord*."

"That was risky, wasn't it? What if you'd missed him? The ocean's a big place."

"I've sailed all my life, and I'm very good with boats. The whole plan was risky, but we pulled it off. That's the point, isn't it?"

"I guess so."

"What about you? Do you sail yourself?"

I shook my head. "Too expensive."

She smiled faintly. "Find a man with some money. That's what I've always done. I learned to ski and play golf. I learned to fly first class traveling around the world."

"What happened to your first husband, Dean?" I asked.

"He died of a heart attack. He was actually number two."

"How long has Wendell been traveling on his passport?"

"The whole five years. Ever since we took off."

"And the passport office never checked?"

"They slipped up on that, which is what gave us the idea in the first place. Dean died in Spain. Somehow the papers were never processed here. When his passport expired and the time came to renew, Wendell filled out the application and we substituted his picture. He and my husband were close enough in age to use Dean's birth certificate if the documentation was ever questioned."

We reached Cabana Boulevard and turned right, the marina visible, with its forest of naked masts, to our left. The day was thickly overcast, a mist floating on the dark green waters of the harbor. I could smell brine shrimp and diesel fuel. A strong wind was blowing off the ocean, bringing with it the smell of a distant rain. Renata turned into the marina parking area and found a space in the tiny lot just outside the kiosk. She parked the Jag and the two of us got out. I led the way since I knew where the *Captain Stanley Lord* was slipped.

We passed a funky little seafood restaurant with a few outside tables and the naval reserve building. "Then what?"

She shrugged. "After we got the passport? We took off. I would come back at intervals, usually by myself, but occasionally with Wendell. He stayed on the boat. I was free to come and go as I pleased since no one knew of our connection. I kept an eye on the boys, though they didn't seem to be aware of it."

"So when Brian first got in trouble with the law, Wendell knew all about it?"

"Oh, yes. At first he didn't worry. Brian's run-ins with the law seemed like childish pranks. Truancy and vandalism."

"Boys will be boys," I said.

She ignored that. "We were off on a round-the-world cruise when things got out of hand. By the time we came home, Brian was in bigger trouble than we knew. That's when Wendell really went to work."

We passed a yacht brokerage and a fish market. The navy pier extended to our left, a big marine travel rig in place. A boat had just been hoisted out of the water, and we had to wait impatiently while the long-legged mobile rig crept across the walkway and down the short avenue to our right. "Doing what? I still don't understand how he managed it."

"I'm not sure myself. It had something to do with the name of the boat." The breakwater was nearly deserted, the threatening weather probably driving boats into port and people under cover. "Not directly," she went on. "From what he told me, Captain Stanley Lord was always blamed for something he didn't do."

"He ignored the SOS from the *Titanic*, is what I heard," I said.

"Or so people claimed. Wendell had done a lot of research on the incident, and he felt Lord was innocent."

"I don't get the connection."

"Wendell was in trouble with the law once himself. . . ."

"Oh, that's right. I remember. Somebody mentioned that. He'd graduated from law school. He was convicted of manslaughter, wasn't he?"

She nodded. "I don't know the details."

"He told you he wasn't guilty?"

"Oh, he wasn't," she said. "He took the blame for somebody else. That's how he was able to get Brian out of jail. By calling in his marker."

I stared at her without slowing my pace. "Did you ever hear of a guy named Harris Brown?"

She shook her head in the negative. "Who's he?"

"An ex-cop. He was originally assigned to the fraud investigation after Wendell disappeared, but then he was pulled off. Turns out he'd invested a lot of money in Wendell's company, and the scam wiped him out. I was thinking he might have used some of his old connections to help Brian. I just can't figure out why he'd do it."

The ramp for Marina 1 was another fifty yards down on the left, the gate locked as usual. Seagulls were pecking intently at a fishing net. We stood there for a moment, hoping somebody with a key card would pass through so we could slipstream in behind them.

Finally I grabbed on to the fence post and held on while I climbed around on the outside of the barrier, working my way along the fencing until I reached the other side. I opened the gate for her and let her through, and we started off down the dock. Conversation between us dwindled. I turned into the sixth line of slips on the right, marked J, counting down visually to the slot where the *Lord* was tied up.

Even from a distance, I could see the slip was empty and the boat was gone.

# 21

RENATA'S MOOD DARKENED as we moved up the ramp toward the harbormaster's office, which was located above a ship's chandler selling marine hardware and supplies. I half expected an outburst of some kind, but she was remarkably silent. She waited on a small wooden balcony outside while I went through the explanations with the clerk at the counter. Since we weren't the legal owners of the missing boat and since there was no way we could prove Eckert hadn't taken the boat himself, it soon became clear that for the time being, nothing much could be done. The clerk took the information, as much to appease me as anything else. When and if Eckert showed, he could file a report. The harbormaster would then notify the Coast Guard and the local police. I left my name and telephone number and asked if they'd have Eckert get in touch if they heard from him.

Renata followed me downstairs, declining to accom-

pany me as I walked over to the yacht club next door.
I was hoping somebody there might know where Eckert
had gone. I pushed in through the glass doors and went
upstairs, pausing outside the dining room. From the
second-floor deck, she looked cold and tired, sitting on
the low concrete wall that bordered the breakwater. At
her back the ocean thundered monotonously, wind tearing at her hair. In the shallows a yellow Labrador
charged through the surf, chasing pigeons off the beach
while the seagulls wheeled above him and screamed
with amusement.

The yacht club dining room was empty except for the
bartender and a fellow with a vacuum cleaner, mowing
the wall-to-wall carpeting. Again I left my name and
number, asking the bartender to have Carl Eckert get in
touch with me if he came in.

As we walked back to the car, Renata gave me a bitter smile. "What's so funny?" I asked.

"Nothing. I was just thinking about Wendell. He has
all the luck. It'll be hours before anybody starts to look
for him."

"There's nothing we can do, Renata. It's always possible he'll show up," I said. "Actually, we can't really
be sure he left. Hell, we can't even prove Wendell took
the boat."

"You don't know him like I do. He rips everybody
off one way or another."

We cruised through the parking lot in search of her
missing Jeep, but it was nowhere in sight. She drove me
back to the office, where I retrieved my VW and drove
out to Colgate. I spent the next two irksome hours getting the rear window replaced. While I was waiting, I
sat in the chrome-and-plastic reception area, drinking

free bad coffee from a foam cup while I leafed through tattered back issues of *Arizona Highways*. This lasted four minutes before I left the building. As was my habit of late, I found a public telephone booth and conducted a little business from the parking lot. Once I got the hang of it, I could probably dispense with an office altogether.

I put a call through to Lieutenant Whiteside in Fraud and brought him up to date. "I think it's time to run mug shots in the paper," he said. "I'll contact the local TV station, too, and see what they can do for us. I want the public aware these guys are out there. Maybe someone will dime 'em out."

"Let's hope."

Once my rear window had been installed, I tooled on back to the office and spent the next hour and a half at my desk. I felt I should stay near the phone in case Eckert called in. In the meantime, I gave Mac a buzz and filled him in on what was happening. I no sooner put the phone down than it rang. "Kinsey Millhone Investigations. Kinsey Millhone."

An instant of silence and then a woman said, "Oh. I thought this was an answering machine."

"No, this is me. Who is this?"

"This is your cousin Tasha Howard, up in San Francisco."

"Ah, yes. Tasha. Liza mentioned you. How are you?" I said. Mentally I'd begun to drum my fingers, hoping to get her off the line in case Wendell phoned in.

"I'm fine," she said. "Something's come up and it occurred to me you might be interested. I just had a chat with Grand's attorney down in Lompoc. The house where our mothers lived is either being moved or torn down. Grand's been fighting with the city for the last several months, and we're supposed to hear something soon about the disposition of the matter. She's trying to have the house protected under the local historical preservation act. The original structure dates back to the turn of the century. The house hasn't been lived in for years, of course, but it could be restored. She owns another lot where she can put the house if she can get the city to agree. Anyway, I thought you might want to see the place again since you were there once yourself."

"I was there?"

"Oh, sure. You don't remember? The four of you— Aunt Gin, your parents, and you—came up when Burt and Grand were off on the big cruise for their forty-second anniversary. It was really meant for their fortieth, but it took 'em two years to get organized. All the cousins got to play together, and you fell off the sliding board and cut your knee. I was seven, so you must have been about four, I'd say. Maybe a little older, but I know you weren't in school yet. I can't believe you don't remember. Aunt Rita taught us all to eat peanut-butter-and-pickle sandwiches, which I've adored ever since. You were supposed to come back in the next couple of months. It was all set up for when Burt and Grand got home."

"Only my parents never made it," I said, thinking, Jesus, the peanut-butter-and-pickle sandwiches aren't even mine anymore.

"I suppose not," she said. "Anyway, I thought if you saw the house, it might jog your memory. I have to come down on business, and I'd be happy to give you the nickel tour."

"What sort of work do you do?"

"I'm an attorney. Probate and estate administration, wills, intervivos trusts, tax planning. The firm has an office up here and another one in Lompoc, so I end up flying back and forth all the time. What's your schedule look like in the next few days? Are you free any time soon?"

"Let me think about that. I appreciate the offer, but I'm currently tied up with a case. Why don't you go ahead and give me the address? If I have a chance to get up there, I can take a look and if not, well . . . so be it."

"I suppose that would do," she said reluctantly. "I was actually hoping I could see you. Liza wasn't entirely happy with the way she handled the situation. She thought maybe I could smooth the waters a bit."

"No need for that. She did fine," I said. I was keeping my distance, and I'm sure the maneuver wasn't lost on her. She gave me the address and a sketchy set of directions, which I jotted on a sheet of scratch paper. I was already struggling with an urge to toss it in the trash. I started making good-bye noises, using that airy tone that says, Okay, thanks a lot, nice talking to you.

Tasha said, "I hope this doesn't seem too personal, but I get the impression you're really not interested in cementing any family ties."

"I don't think that's too personal," I said. "I guess I'm in the process of assimilating the information. I don't really know what I want to do about it yet."

"Are you angry with Grand?"

"Of course I am, and why wouldn't I be? She threw my mother out. That estrangement must have gone on for twenty years."

"That wasn't all Grand's doing. It takes two to make a rift."

"Right," I said. "At least my mother was on her way to make amends. What did Grand ever do? She sat back and waited, which I notice she's still doing."

"What does that mean?"

"Well, where's she been all these years? I'm thirty-four years old. Until yesterday I never even knew she existed. She could have gotten in touch."

"She didn't know where you were."

"Bullshit. Liza told me everybody knew we were down here. For the last twenty-five years I've been an hour away."

"I don't mean to argue about this, but I really don't believe Grand was aware of that."

"What did she think happened, I was eaten by bears? She could have hired a detective if she'd cared enough."

"Well. I see your point, and I'm sorry about all this. We didn't make the contact to cause you pain."

"Why did you, then?"

"We were hoping to connect. We thought enough time had passed to heal old wounds."

"Those 'old wounds' are news to me. I just heard about this shit yesterday."

"I can appreciate that, and you're entitled to feel what you feel. It's just that Grand's not going to live forever. She's eighty-seven now, and she's not in the best of health. You still have a chance to enjoy the relationship."

"Correction. *She* has a chance to enjoy the relationship. I'm not sure I would."

"Will you think about it?"

"Sure."

"Do you mind if I tell her we've spoken?"

"I don't see how I can prevent it."

There was a fractional silence. "Are you really this unforgiving?"

"Absolutely. Why not? Just like Grand," I said. "I'm sure she'll appreciate the attribute."

"I see," she said coolly.

"Look, this is not your fault, and I don't mean to take it out on you. You're just going to have to give me some time here. I've made my peace with the fact that I'm alone. I like my life as it is, and I'm not at all sure I want to change."

"We're not asking you to change."

"Then you better get used to me the way I am," I said.

She had the good grace to laugh, which in an odd way helped. Our good-byes were slightly warmer. I said all the right things, and by the time I hung up my churlishness was already fading to some extent. Content so often follows form. It's not just that we're nice to the people we like . . . we like the people we're nice to. It works both ways. I guess that's what good manners are about, or so my aunt always claimed. In the meantime, I knew I wouldn't be driving up to Lompoc any time soon. To hell with that.

I went across the hall to the restroom, and when I got back the phone was ringing. I made a lunge and snatched up the receiver from the far side of the desk, easing my way around until I reached my swivel chair. When I identified myself, I could hear breathing on the line and for one split second I thought it was Wendell.

"Take your time," I said. I closed my eyes and crossed my fingers, thinking, Please, please, please.

"This is Brian Jaffe."

"Ah. I thought it might be your father. Have you heard from him?"

"Nuhn-uhn. That's why I called. Have you?"

"Not since last night."

"Michael says the car Dad came to his place in is still parked at the curb."

"He was having car trouble, which is why I gave him a lift. When did you last see him?"

"Day before yesterday. He came by in the afternoon and we talked. He said he'd be back last night, but he never showed."

"He may have tried," I said. "Someone took some shots at us and he disappeared. This morning we found out the *Lord* was gone."

"The boat?"

"Right. That's the one your father was on when he vanished."

"Dad stole a boat?"

"Well, it looks that way, but nobody really knows at this point. Maybe that's the only way he could think of to get out. He must have felt he was in real jeopardy."

"Hey, yeah, getting shot at," Brian said facetiously.

I fleshed out the story for him, hoping to ingratiate myself. I nearly mentioned Renata, but I bit the words off in time. If Michael hadn't known about her, chances were that Brian didn't, either. As usual, given my perverse nature, I was feeling protective of the "villain" of the piece. Maybe Wendell would have a change of heart and return the boat. Maybe he'd talk Brian into "coming in," and the two would turn themselves over to the cops. Maybe the Easter bunny would bring me one of those spun-sugar eggs with a hole you could peek in, revealing a world much better than this.

Brian breathed in my ear some more. I waited him out. "Michael says Dad has a girlfriend. Is that true?" he said.

"Ah, mmm. I don't know what to say about that. He was traveling with a friend, but I really don't know what their relationship consists of."

"Right." He snorted with disbelief. I'd forgotten he was eighteen years old and probably knew more about sex than I did. He certainly knew more about violence. What made me think I could fool a kid like him?

"You want Renata's number? She may have heard from him."

"I got a number to call and this machine picks up. If Dad's around, he calls back. Is this the one you have?" He recited Renata's unlisted number.

"That's it. Look, why don't you give me your current location. I'll pop over there and we can talk. Maybe between us we can figure out where he is."

He thought about that. "He told me to wait. He said don't talk to anyone until he gets here. He's probably on his way." He said this without conviction in a tone edged with uneasiness.

"That's always possible," I said. "What's the plan?" Like I really thought Brian would spill the beans to me.

"I have to go."

"Wait! Brian?"

The phone clicked down in my ear.

"Goddamn it!" I sat and stared at the receiver, willing it to ring. "Come on, come on."

I knew perfectly well the kid wasn't going to call

again. I became aware of the tension rippling through
my shoulders. I got up and moved around the desk,
finding a bare expanse of carpeting where I could
stretch out on my back. The ceiling was singularly
uninformative. I hate waiting for things to happen, and
I don't like being at the mercy of circumstance. Maybe
I could figure out where Brian was being hidden.
Wendell didn't have much in the way of personal resources. He had very few friends and no confederates
that I knew of. He was also being very secretive, apparently not even trusting Renata with the information
about Brian. The *Fugitive* might have been a great place
for him to hole up, but she and Brian would both have
to be extraordinarily talented liars to pull that one off.
From what I could tell, he'd seemed genuinely ignorant
of her existence, and she seemed uninterested in his. I
suspected if Renata had known where Brian was, she'd
have blown the whistle on him. She was certainly angry
enough at Wendell's desertion.

Wendell almost had to have Brian tucked away in a
motel or hotel someplace. If he was able to pop in to
see Brian on a near daily basis, the place probably
wasn't that far away. If Brian was left on his own for
long periods, he'd have to have access to food without
exposing himself to public scrutiny. Maybe a motel
room with a kitchen so he could cook for himself. Big?
Small? There were maybe fifteen to twenty motels in
the vicinity. Was I going to have to drive down there
and canvass every single one? That was an unappealing
possibility. Canvassing is the equivalent of cold calls in
the sales field. Once in a while you might hit pay dirt,
but the process is tedious. Then again, Brian was really
my only access to Wendell. So far, the *Dispatch* didn't

seem to be picking up on Brian's jail release, but once pictures of the two appeared in the papers, the situation was going to heat up. Brian might have pocket money, but he probably didn't have unlimited funds. If Wendell was determined to rescue his kid, he had better be quick about it, and I had, too.

I checked my watch. It was now 6:15. I hauled myself off the floor and made sure my answering machine was in message mode. I pulled out the newspaper clippings that detailed the original escape. The mug shot of Brian Jaffe wasn't flattering, but it would serve my purposes. I grabbed my portable Smith-Corona typewriter and my handbag and headed for the door. I clattered down the stairs, typewriter bumping against my leg, and then trotted two blocks to the spot where my car was parked. I decided at the last minute to take a quick detour along the beach. By taking the long way around to a freeway entrance, I'd end up passing the marina, where I could check up on Carl Eckert. It was entirely possible that he'd returned from out of town and nobody'd bothered to let me know. I was also thinking about the little harborside snack shack where I could pick up some killer burritos to munch on in the car. Kinsey Millhone dining al fresco again.

All the slots in the small no-pay parking lot were full, so I was forced to take a ticket and actually drive through to the pay lot. I locked my car, glancing to my left as I passed the kiosk. Carl Eckert was sitting in his car, a little red sports job of some exotic sort. He looked like a man in shock, pasty-faced and sweating, his pupils dilated. He surveyed his surroundings with an air of confusion. He was wearing a snappy dark blue business suit, but his tie had been loosened and his collar button opened. His silvery hair was unkempt, as if he'd been running his hands through it.

I slowed my pace, watching. He couldn't seem to decide what to do. I saw him reach for his car keys as if to turn the ignition. He pulled his hand back, reached into his pants pocket, and took out a handkerchief, which he used to mop at his face and neck. He shoved the handkerchief in his suit coat, then took out a pack of cigarettes and shook one into view. He pushed in his car lighter.

I crossed to his car, hunkering down on the driver's side so that my gaze would be level with his. "Carl? Kinsey Millhone."

He turned and stared at me without comprehension.

"We met at the yacht club the other night. I was looking for Wendell Jaffe."

"The private investigator," he said finally.

"That's right."

"Sorry it took me so long, but I've had some bad news."

"I heard about the *Lord*. Can I do anything?"

The lighter popped out. He lit his cigarette with hands that shook so badly he could barely make the lighter meet the tip. He sucked in smoke, choking on it in his desperation for a hit of nicotine. "Son of a bitch stole my boat," he said, coughing violently. He started to say something more, but then he stopped himself and looked off across the parking lot. I'd caught the glint of tears, but I couldn't tell if they were from the smoke or the loss of his boat.

"Are you okay?" I asked.

"I live on that boat. Everything I have is tied up in the *Lord*. It's my life. He had to have known that. He'd be a fool not to know. He loved the boat as much as I did." He shook his head in disbelief.

"That's a rough one," I said.

"How'd you hear about it?"

"Renata showed up at my office after lunch," I said. "She said he'd cleared out of her place and she was worried he'd try to make a run for it. Her boat was at the dock, so I guess she thought of yours."

"How'd he get in? That's what I can't figure out. I had all the locks changed the minute I bought that boat."

"Maybe he broke in. Or he might have picked the lock," I said. "At any rate, by the time we got here, it was gone."

He stared at me. "Is that the woman? Renata? What's her last name?"

"Why?"

"I'd like to talk to her. She might know more than she's saying."

"Yeah, she might," I said. I was thinking about the shooting the night before, wondering if Carl could account for his whereabouts. "When did you get back? I heard you were out of town last night, but no one seemed to know where you were."

"Wouldn't have done much good. I was hard to reach. I had a bunch of meetings up in SLO-town in the afternoon. I was at the Best Western overnight, checked out before eight this morning, and threw my bag in the trunk. I sat in another bunch of meetings today and started home around five."

"It must have been a shock."

"Jesus, I'll say. I can't believe it's gone."

SLO-town was the shorthand for San Luis Obispo, a

small college town ninety miles north of us. It sounded like he'd been completely tied up for the last two days, or had his alibi all rehearsed. "What will you do now? Do you have a place to stay?"

"I'll try one of those places unless the tourists beat me to it," he said with a nod toward the motels that lined Cabana Boulevard. "What about you? I take it you never caught up with him."

"Actually, I ran into him at Michael's last night. I was hoping we could talk, but something else came up. We were separated inadvertently, and that's the last I saw of him. I heard he was supposed to meet you, as a matter of fact."

"I had to cancel at the last minute when this other business came up."

"You never saw him at all?"

"We only chatted by phone."

"What'd he want? Did he say?"

"No. Not a word."

"He told me you had something that belonged to him."

"He said that? Well, that's odd. I wonder what he meant." He gave his watch a glance. "Oh, shit. It's getting late. I better get a move on before all the rooms get snapped up."

I stepped away from the car. "I'll let you go, then," I said. "If you hear anything about the *Lord*, will you let me know?"

"Sure thing."

The car started with a rumble. He backed out of the slot and pulled up beside the kiosk with his ticket extended to the woman in the booth. I went on about my business, moving toward the snack shack with a quick backward glance. He'd adjusted his rearview mirror to keep an eye on me. The last thing I saw of him was his vanity license plate, which read SAILSMN. That was cute. I thought he'd probably done a little sales job on me. He was lying about something. I just wasn't sure what it was.

# 22

BY THE TIME I reached the beachside neighborhood on the periphery of Perdido where all the motels are situated, the ocean was tinted by an eerie gray-green haze. As I watched, an odd refraction of fading sunlight created the fleeting mirage of an island hovering above the sea, mossy and unreachable. There was something otherworldly in its gloom. I've seen something like it in the endless passageway created when two mirrors reflect one another, shadowy rooms curving back out of sight. The moment passed, and the image turned to smoke. The air was hot and still, unusually humid for the California coast. The area residents would have to search their garages tonight, looking for last summer's electric floor fans, wide blades sueded with dust. Sleep would be a restless confection of sweat and tangled sheets without hope of refreshment.

I parked on a side street just off the main thoroughfare. All the motel lights had come on, creating an artificial daylight: neon greens and blues blinking out competing invitations to passing travelers. There were countless people milling along the sidewalks, all in shorts and tank tops, looking for relief from the heat. The Frostee Freeze would probably set a sales record. Cars cruised in an endless search for parking spaces. There wasn't actually any sand in the streets, but there was the feeling of blown sand, something scrubby and windswept, a scent in the air of salt corrosion and fishing nets. The few funky bars were crowded with college students, bass-heavy music pulsing through the open doorways.

One thing I needed to keep in mind: Brian Jaffe grew up in this town. His picture had been splashed across the local papers, and he probably wasn't free to spend a lot of time on the streets—too much risk of being recognized. I added free cable TV to my mental list of motel attributes. I didn't think Brian's father would dare leave him in a dive. The bleaker the accommodations, the more likely the kid was to seek amusement elsewhere.

I started with motels on the main drag and worked my way out into the surrounding neighborhood. I don't know how motel builders get their training, but they all seem to take the same motel-naming class. Every seaside community seems to sport the same assortment. I went in and out of the Tides, the Sun 'N' Surf, the Breakwater, the Reef, the Lagoon, the Schooner, the Beachside, the Blue Sands, the White Sands, the Sandpiper, and the Casa Del Mar. I flashed the photostat of my PI license. I flashed the grainy black-and-white newspaper photograph of Brian Jaffe. I couldn't believe he'd be registered under his own name, so I tried variations: Brian Jefferson, Jeff O'Brian, Brian Huff, Dean Huff, and Wendell's favorite, Stanley Lord. I knew the date Brian had been erroneously released from jail, and I reasoned that he'd checked into a motel the same day. He was a single, and his bill was probably paid in advance. My guess was he kept to himself and hadn't done a lot of coming and going. I was hoping someone could identify him from the picture and my description. Motel managers and desk clerks shook their heads in ignorance. I left a business card with each, extracting weighty promises that they'd get in touch if someone resembling Brian Jaffe checked into their establishments. Oh, sure. Absolutely. I wasn't all the way out the door when they dropped the cards in their respective trash baskets.

At the Lighthouse—Direct Dial Phones*Color Cable TV*Weekly & Monthly Rates*Heated Pool*Complimentary Morning Coffee—on the twelfth try, I got a nod instead of a negative. The Lighthouse was a three-story oblong of boxy cinder block with a pool in the center. The exterior was painted sky blue and had a thirty-foot stylized image of a lighthouse affixed to the front. The desk clerk was in his seventies, energetic and alert. He was as bald as a doorknob, but he seemed to have all his own teeth. He tapped the clipping with an index finger crooked with arthritis.

"Oh, yes, he's here. Michael Brendan. Room one ten. I wondered why he looked familiar. An older gentleman signed the register and paid a week in advance. To tell you the truth, I wasn't sure of the relationship."

"Father and son."

"That was their claim," the clerk said, still dubious. He scanned the details of the escape and the subsequent killing of the female motorist whose car was stolen. "I remember reading about this. Looks like that young fellow got himself in a peck of trouble and he's not out yet. You want me to call the police?"

"Make that the county sheriff's department and give me ten minutes with him first. Ask them to use restraint. I don't want this turned into some kind of bloodbath. The kid is eighteen. It's not going to look good if he's gunned down in his pajamas."

I left the lobby and moved through a passageway to the courtyard. It was fully dark by then, and the lighted swimming pool glowed aquamarine. Reflections from the water shimmered against the building, blots of light in a constantly shifting pattern of white. Brian's room was on the first floor, with sliding glass doors that opened onto a small patio, which in turn opened onto the pool. Patios were separated from each other by low-growing shrubbery. Each was numbered, so finding his wasn't difficult. I caught sight of him through mesh drapes only partially drawn. The sliding doors were closed, and I had to guess the air-conditioning was cranked up to high.

He was dressed in sweatshirt-gray gym shorts and a tank top. He looked tanned and fit, slouched on the one upholstered chair in the room, feet propped on the bed as he watched television. I went around to the end of the building and entered the corridor, passing a door marked EMPLOYEES ONLY. On impulse, I tried the knob and found it turning in my hand. I peered in. The room was the equivalent of a huge walk-in closet, with linen shelves along three walls. Sheets, towels, and cotton bedspreads were stacked in neat packets. There were also mops, vacuums, irons, ironing boards, and miscellaneous cleaning supplies. I pulled out an armload of fresh towels and carried them with me.

I found Brian's room along the inside corridor and knocked, standing at an acute angle to the fish-eye in the door. The sound from the television set was doused. I stared off down the hall, allowing him time to cross to the door. He must have tried peering at me through the lens. A muffled "Yes?"

*"Criada,"* I called. The word was Spanish for "maid." I learned that the first week of class because so many of the women taking Spanish were hoping to learn to speak to their Hispanic maids. Otherwise the maids did anything they felt like, and the women were reduced to following them around the house, ineffectually trying to demonstrate cleaning techniques the maids pretended not to "get."

Brian didn't get it, either. He opened the door to the width of the chain, peering through the crack. "What?"

I held a batch of towels up, concealing my face. "Towelettas," I sang in Spanglish.

"Oh." He closed the door and slid the chain off the track. He stepped back, leaving the door open between us. I moved into the room. He didn't look at me. He indicated the bathroom to the left, his attention already riveted on the screen again. The show seemed to be an old black-and-white movie: men with high cheekbones and pomaded waves, women with eyebrows plucked to the size of hairline fractures. All the facial expressions were tragic. He crossed back to the set and turned up the sound. I went into his bathroom and checked it out as long as I was there. No visible guns, claw hammers, or machetes. Lots of sun block and hair mousse, a hairbrush, a blow dryer, and a safety razor. I didn't think the kid had enough hair on his face to shave it. Maybe he was just practicing, like prepubescent girls with little training bras.

I set the towels on the counter and went out to the bedroom, where I took a seat on the bed. At first, my presence didn't seem to register. Terminal disease music was swelling, and the lovers stood together with their two perfect faces side by side. His was prettier than hers. When Brian finally saw me, he was cool enough to suppress any surprise. He picked up the remote control and muted the sound again. The scene continued in silence, many animated speeches. I've often wondered if I could learn to read lips that way. The lovers on the screen were speaking directly into each other's faces, which made me worry about bad breath. Her mouth was moving, but Brian's words came out. "How'd you find me?"

I tapped my temple, trying to divert my gaze from the television set.

"Where's Dad?"

"We don't know yet. He may be sailing down the coast to pick you up."

"I wish he'd get on with it." He leaned back in his chair and raised his arms, lacing his fingers so his hands were resting across the top of his head. The gesture made his biceps bulge. He propped a foot up on the edge of the bed, kicked his chair back an inch. The tufts of hair in his armpits seemed oddly sexual. I wondered if I was reaching an age where all young boys with hard bodies would seem sexual to me. I wondered if I'd been that age all my life. He reached over and picked up a pair of clean socks, which had been rolled and folded to form a soft wad. He threw the ball of socks against the wall and caught it on the fly when it bounced back at him.

"You haven't heard from him?"

"Nope." He flung the wad again and caught it.

"You said you saw him day before yesterday. Did he say anything to indicate he might be leaving?" I asked.

"No." He dropped the wad from his right hand, straightening his arm abruptly so that the socks bounced off the anterior aspect of his elbow. He caught it as it popped up, and he let it fall again. He had to watch very carefully so he wouldn't miss. Bounce. Catch. Bounce. Catch.

"What did he say?" I asked.

He missed.

He shot me a look, annoyed at the distraction. "Fuck, I don't know. He's selling me this whole line of horse-shit about how there's no justice in the legal system. Then he turns around and tells me we have to turn ourselves in. I go, 'No way, Dad. I'm not going to do it, and there's no way you can make me.' "

"What'd he say to that?"

"He didn't say anything." He tossed the sock ball against the wall again and caught it on the fly.

"You think he might have gone ahead and taken off without you?"

"Why would he do that if he was going to turn himself in?"

"Maybe he got scared."

"So he leaves me to face all this shit by myself?" His look was incredulous.

"Brian, I hate to say this, but your father isn't exactly famous for sticking it out. He gets nervous and he bolts."

"He wouldn't leave me," he said sullenly. He tossed the socks in the air, leaned forward, and caught the wad behind his back. I could see the title of the book now: *Tricks with Socks: 101 Ways to Amuse Yourself with Underwear.*

"I think you ought to go ahead and turn yourself in."

"I will when he gets here."

"Why don't I believe that? Brian, I hate to sound pompous, but I have a responsibility here. You're wanted by the cops. I don't turn you in, that's called 'aiding and abetting.' I could lose my license."

He was on his feet in an instant, half lifting me, hauling me off the bed by my shirt, fist cocked back, ready to bust my teeth out. Our faces were suddenly six inches apart. Like the lovers. Anything cute about this kid was gone. Someone else stared down at me, a person within a person. Who could have guessed that this vicious "other" was hidden behind Brian's blue-eyed, California perfection? The voice wasn't even his: a low-pitched gravelly whisper. "Listen, you bitch. I'll tell you about aiding and abetting. You want to take me in? Just try. I'll kill your ass before you can lay a finger on me, you got that?"

I stilled myself, scarcely daring to breathe. I made my body invisible, beaming myself into hyperspace. He was nearly cross-eyed with rage, and I knew he'd strike out if he were pressed. His chest was heaving, adrenaline pumping hard through his nervous system. He was the one who killed the woman when the four of them escaped. I'd have bet money on that. Give a kid like this a weapon, give him a victim, some subject to vent his rage on, and he'd attack in a white heat. I said, "Okay, okay. Don't hit me. Don't hit."

I thought the rush of feelings would make him extraordinarily alert. Instead, emotion seemed to slow his senses, dulling his perceptions. He pulled back slightly. He brought my face into focus, frowning. "What?" His manner seemed dazed, as if his hearing had gone out on him.

My message had finally reached him, through some impossible maze of supercharged neurons. "I just want you safe when your dad comes back."

"Safe." The very concept seemed alien. He shivered, tension rippling through his body. He released me, backed away, and sank onto the chair, breathing heavily. "God. What's the matter with me? God."

"You want me to go in with you?" My shirt was permanently pleated across the front where he'd gripped it in his fist.

He shook his head.

"I can call your mother."

He bowed his head, running his hand through his hair. "I don't want her. I want him," he said. The voice belonged to the Brian Jaffe I knew. He wiped his face against his sleeve. I thought he was close to tears, but his eyes were dry ... empty ... the blue as cold as a gel pack. I sat and waited, hoping he would say something more. Gradually his breathing returned to normal and he began to look like himself again.

"It'll look better in court if you return voluntarily," I ventured.

"Why should I do that? I got a legitimate jail release." The tone was petulant. The other Brian was gone, receding into the dark recesses of his underwater hole like an eel. This Brian was just a kid who thought everything should go his way. On the playground, he was the kind of kid who'd cry, "You cheated!" any time he lost a game, but he would always be the cheater, in truth.

"Oh, come on, Brian. You know better than that. I don't know who screwed with the computer, but believe me, you're not supposed to be out on the street. You've got murder charges filed against you."

"I didn't *kill* anybody." Indignant. By that, he probably meant he didn't *mean* to kill her when he pointed the gun. And why should he feel guilty afterward when it wasn't his fault? Dumb bitch. She should have kept her mouth shut when he asked for the car keys. Had to argue with him. Women all the time argued.

"Good for you," I said. "In the meantime, the sheriff's on his way over here to pick you up."

He was astonished at the betrayal, and the look he gave me was filled with outrage. "You called the *cops*? Why'd you do that?"

"Because I didn't believe you'd turn yourself in."

"Why should I?"

"See what I mean? You got an attitude. Like somehow the rules don't apply to you. Well, guess what?"

"Guess what yourself. I don't have to take any crap from you." He got up from the chair, grabbing his wallet from the top of the TV as he passed. He reached the door and opened it. A sheriff's deputy, a white guy, was standing on the threshold, his hand raised to knock. Brian wheeled and moved rapidly toward the sliding glass door. A second deputy, black, appeared on his patio. Frustrated, Brian flung his wallet to the floor with such force that it bounced like a football. The first deputy reached for him, and Brian wrenched his arm away. *"Get the fuck off me!"*

The deputy said, "Son. Now, son. I don't want to have to hurt you."

Brian was breathing heavily again, backing up, his gaze raking the air from face to face. He was hunched over, and he had his hands out as if to ward off attacking animals. Both deputies were big, made of dense flesh and tough experience, the first in his late forties, the other maybe thirty-five. I wouldn't have wanted to truck with either one of them.

The second deputy had his hand on his gun, but he hadn't drawn it. These days a confrontation with the law ends in death, pure and simple. The two officers exchanged a look, and my heart began to bang at the specter of sudden violence. The three of us were immobilized, waiting to see what the next move might be. The first deputy went on in a low tone. "It's all right. Everything's cool. Let's just keep calm here and everything's going to be fine."

Uncertainty flickered in Brian's eyes. His breathing slowed, and he regained his composure. He straightened up. I didn't think it was over, but the tension evaporated. Brian tried a deprecating smile and allowed himself to be handcuffed without resistance. He avoided my gaze, which suited me just fine. There was something embarrassing about having to watch him submit. "Bunch of dumb fucks," he murmured, but the deputies ignored him. Everybody has to save face. No offense in that.

Dana appeared at the jail while Brian was being processed through booking. She was dressed to the teeth, in a gray rayon-linen-blend power suit, the first time I'd seen her wearing anything other than jeans. It was eleven o'clock at night, and I was standing in the hall with another cup of bad coffee when I heard the snapping of her high heels down the corridor. I took one look at her and knew she was furious, not with Brian or the cops, but with me. I had followed the sheriff's car over to the jail, parking in the lot while they drove into the sally port. I had even put the call through to Dana Jaffe myself, thinking she should be informed about her little boy's arrest. I was not in the mood to take shit from her, but it was clear she intended to spew.

"You have caused trouble since the moment I ·laid eyes on you," she spat. Her hair was pulled back in a shiny chignon, not a strand out of place. Snowy blouse, silver earrings, her eyes lined with black.

"Do you want to hear the story?"

"No, I don't want to hear the story. I want to tell you one," she snapped. "I have a fucking restraining order on my bank accounts. Every cent I have is inaccessible. I have no money. Do you get that? None! My kid is in trouble, and what the hell can I do? I can't even get through to his lawyer."

Her linen suit was immaculate, not a wrinkle on it anywhere; tough with linen, I've heard, even in a blend. I stared down at the contents of my cup. The coffee was cold by now, the surface bespeckled with little clots of powdered milk. I was really hoping I wouldn't fling it all in her face. I watched my hand carefully to see if it would move. So far, so good.

In the meantime, Dana was going on and on, heaping invective at me for God knew what offenses. I pushed the mute button with my internal remote. It was just like watching some silent TV show. Some part of me was listening, though I tried not to let the sound penetrate. I noticed my coffee-flinging inclination was picking up momentum. I used to be a biter in kindergarten, and the impulse was the same. When I was a cop, I'd had to arrest a woman once for flinging a drink in another woman's face, which the law regards as assault and battery. California Penal Code 242: "A battery is any willful and unlawful use of force or violence upon the person of another." Battery is a consummated assault and is a necessarily included offense where battery is charged. "The force or violence necessary to constitute a battery need not be great nor need it necessarily cause pain or bodily harm, nor leave a mark," I recited to myself. Except maybe on her suit, I added. Tee hee.

I heard footsteps approaching in the corridor behind me. I glanced back and spotted Senior Deputy Tiller, with a file folder in his hand. He nodded at me briefly and disappeared through the doorway.

"Excuse me, Tiller?"

He stuck his head back out the door. "You call me?"

I glanced at Dana. "Sorry to interrupt, but I have to talk to him," I said, and followed him into the office. Her look of annoyance indicated she wasn't nearly done with me yet.

# 23

TILLER LOOKED UP quizzically from the file drawer where he was tucking the folder. "What was that all about?"

I closed the door, lifting a finger to my lips. I pointed to the back. His eyes strayed to the hallway. He closed the file drawer and jerked his head toward the rear. I followed him through a maze of desks. We reached a smaller office, which I took to be his. He closed a second door behind us and motioned me onto a chair. I tossed my empty coffee cup in the trash can and sat down with relief. "Thanks. This is great. I couldn't think how else to get away from her. She must have needed someone to crank on, and I was elected."

"Well, I'm glad to oblige. You want another cup of coffee? We got a fresh pot back here. That probably came from the vending machine."

"Thanks, but I'm coffeed out for the time being. I'd like to sleep at some point. How are you?"

"Fine. I just came on, working graveyard. I see you got our boy back in the can." He sat down on his swivel chair and leaned back with a creaking sound.

"Wasn't that hard to do. I figured Wendell had to have him somewhere close, and I did a little legwork. Boring, but not tough. What's the deal on this end? Do they know yet how he got sprung?"

Tiller shrugged, uncomfortably. "They're looking into it." He changed the subject, apparently reluctant to share the details of the in-house investigation. Under the harsh fluorescent lights, I could see that his sandy hair and his mustache were threaded with silver, his eyes wreathed in creases. The boyish contours of his face had begun to shrink, leaving puckers and wrinkles. He must have been close to Wendell's age without the youth-perpetuating benefits of Wendell's cosmetic surgery. I was staring idly at his hands when I felt a little question mark appear above my head. "What is that?"

He caught the look and held out his hand. "What, the class ring?"

I leaned forward, peering. "Isn't that Cottonwood Academy?"

"You know the school? Most people never heard of it. Went out of business, I don't know how many years back. These days you don't find many all-male institutions. Sexist, they call it, and they may be right. Mine was the last class to graduate. Only sixteen of us. After that, kapoot," he said. His smile was tinged with pride and affection. "What's your connection? You must have a good eye. Most class rings look the same."

"I just saw one recently from a Cottonwood graduate."

"Really. Who's that? We're still a real tight bunch."

"Wendell Jaffe."

His gaze stuck to mine briefly, and then he looked away. He shifted on his chair. "Yeah, I guess old Wendell did go there," he said, as if it had just occurred to him. "You sure you don't want some more coffee?"

"It was you, wasn't it?"

"Me, what?"

"Brian's jail release," I said.

Tiller laughed, jolly ho-ho, but it didn't sound sincere. "Hey, sorry. Not me. I wouldn't even know how to go about it. You put me near a computer, my IQ drops about fifteen percentage points."

"Oh, come on. What's the scoop? I'm not going to tell anyone. What do I care? The kid's back. I swear I won't say a word." I shut my mouth then and let the silence accumulate. Basically he was an honest soul, capable of an occasional unlawful act, but not comfortable about it, unable to deny his culpability when confronted. His fellow cops love guys like him because they're quick with a confession, eager for the relief. He said, "No, really. You're barking up the wrong tree here." He did a neck roll, trying to relieve the tension, but I noticed he hadn't terminated the conversation. I prodded him a bit. "Did you help Brian the first time, when he escaped from juvie?"

His expression became bland, and his tone shifted into officiousness. "I don't think this line of talk is going to be productive," he said.

"All right. Let's forget about the first escape and just talk about the second. You must have owed Wendell a big one to risk your job that way."

"I think that's enough. Let's just say we drop it."

This had to be the manslaughter charge that Wendell

had pleaded to, a felony conviction that would have barred Tiller from his job in law enforcement. "Tiller, I heard the story about the manslaughter charge. You're safe with me. I promise. I just want to know what happened. Why did Wendell take the fall?"

"I don't owe you an explanation."

"I never said you did. I'm asking for myself. It isn't anything official. It's a piece of information."

He was silent for a long time, staring down at his desktop. Maybe his was one of those fairy-tale families where you have to ask three times before your wish is granted.

"Tiller, please? I don't want any details. I understand your hesitation. Just the broad strokes," I said.

He sighed deeply, and when he finally spoke, his voice was so low I had to squint to hear him. "I don't really think I can say why he did it. We were young. Best friends. Twenty-four, twenty-five, something like that. He'd already decided the law was corrupt and he wasn't going to sit for his bar exams. All I ever wanted was to be a cop. The situation came up. The girl died by accident, though it was all my fault. He happened to be there, and he took the blame. He was innocent. He knew it. I knew it. He took the rap, that's all. I thought it was an incredible gesture."

It sounded weak to me, but who knows why people do what they do? A certain earnest idealism takes hold of us when we're young. That's why so many draftees are eighteen and dead. "But surely he didn't have any real hold over you. The statutes would have run out on a charge like that years ago, and it was his word against yours. So he claims you did something. You claim you didn't. He'd already been convicted. After all this time, I don't understand what the big deal was."

"No deal. It wasn't like that. He didn't threaten me. I was paying off an obligation."

"But you didn't have to do what he asked."

"No sir, I did what I wanted, and I was happy to do it for him."

"But why take the chance?"

"You never heard about honor? I owed him. It's the least I could do. And it's not like I baked a file in a cake. Brian's a bad egg. I'll admit that. I don't like the kid, but Wendell told me he'd get him out of the state. He said he'd take full responsibility, so I figured good riddance."

"I think he had a change of heart on that score. Well, actually I've heard mixed reports," I said, correcting myself. "He told both Michael and Brian he was going to turn himself in. He was apparently trying to talk Brian into following suit. But his girlfriend claims he had no intention of going through with it."

Tiller rocked on his swivel chair, staring off in the middle distance. He shook his head, mystified. "I just don't see how he's going to pull it off. What's he doing?"

"You heard about the boat?"

"Yeah, I heard. Question is, what's he think he's going to do with it? I mean, how far can he get?"

"I guess we'll just have to wait and see about that," I said. "Anyway, I gotta go. I have a thirty-mile drive ahead of me and it's past my bedtime. Is there another way out of here? I don't want to run into Dana Jaffe again. I've about had it with that bunch."

"Through the next department. Come on. I'll show

you," he said, getting to his feet. He moved around the
desk and took a left through an interior corridor. I followed. I thought he'd caution me to silence, extracting
a promise about the confidentiality of our conversation,
but he never said a word about it.

It was nearly 1:00 A.M. by the time I rolled into Santa
Teresa. There was very little traffic and few pedestrians.
Streetlights drew a pattern of overlapping pale gray circles on the sidewalk. Businesses were locked, but
lighted. Occasionally I spotted one of the homeless
seeking out the shelter of some darkened alleyway, but
for the most part the streets were deserted. The temperature was finally beginning to drop, and a mild ocean
breeze was offsetting the humidity to some extent.

I was feeling itchy and restless. Nothing was really
happening. With Brian in jail and Wendell still missing,
what was there to investigate? The hunt for the *Captain
Stanley Lord* was currently in the hands of the Harbor
Patrol and the Coast Guard. Even if I could charter a
plane and do an aerial search—an expense Gordon Titus
was never going to authorize—I wouldn't know one
boat from another at altitude. In the meantime, there
had to be something I could do.

Without even meaning to, I made a detour, easing
through all the motel parking lots between my place and
the marina. I spotted Carl Eckert's sports car at the
Beachside Inn: a one-story motel, arranged in a T-shape
with the short bar along the front. The parking slots
were lined up, one for each room, the numbers marked
on the pavement so that no one would poach. Every
room on this side of the building was dark.

I drove through to the alley and circled back to Ca-

bana. I parked on the street, a few doors down from
Eckert's motel. I slipped my penlight in my jeans
pocket and returned on foot, grateful that my tennies
were rubber-soled and silent. The parking area was illuminated for the safety of the occupants, the fixtures
aimed so as to cast light away from the windows. I
could see my own shadow, like an elongated companion, follow me across the lot. Carl had secured the tonneau cover across the open body of his car. I did a
thorough visual scan, taking in the darkened windows
and the dimly lighted parking area. There were no signs
of movement within range of me. I didn't even see the
gray flickering light against the motel drapes that would
indicate a television set in use. I took a deep breath and
started popping snaps on the tonneau, loosening the
driver's side first. I slid my hand down along the inside,
feeling through the map pockets in the door. He kept his
interior immaculate, which meant he probably had a
system for all the gas slips and detritus. I felt a spiral-
bound notebook, a road map, and some kind of paper
booklet. I brought everything to the surface like a net
full of fish. I paused to check my surroundings, which
seemed as benign as before. I flicked the penlight across
the spiral notebook. He was keeping track of his gasoline mileage.

The booklet I found was his business log, noting
odometer readings, destinations, purpose of meetings,
names and titles of those in attendance. Personal and
business expenses were neatly separated into columns. I
had to smile to myself. This from a con artist who'd
spent months in jail. Maybe prison had some rehabilita-
tive effect. Carl Eckert was behaving like a model citizen. At least he wasn't trying to cheat the IRS, as far as

I could tell. Tucked in a slot at the back of the log was his itemized Best Western hotel bill, two gasoline receipts, five credit card vouchers, and—what ho!—the speeding ticket he'd picked up last night on the outskirts of Colgate. According to the time so obligingly noted by the CHP officer who issued the citation, Carl Eckert could easily have sped the remaining distance to Perdido in plenty of time to take potshots at Wendell and me.

"You want to tell me what the fuck you're doing out here?"

I jumped, papers flying, barely managing to suppress a shriek. I put a hand to my chest, heart pounding. It was Carl in his stocking feet, his hair rumpled from sleep. God, I hate sneaks! I leaned over and started picking up papers. "Jesus! Warn a person. You nearly scared me to death. What I'm doing is blowing your alibi for last night."

"I don't need an alibi for last night. I wasn't doing anything."

"Well, somebody was. Did I mention the fact that my car engine cut out, leaving Wendell and me stranded on a very dark beach road?"

"No. You didn't mention that. Go on," he said cautiously.

"Go on. That's good. Like this is news to you. Somebody was shooting at us. Wendell disappeared shortly afterward."

"You think *I* did that?"

"I think it's possible. Why else would I be out here in the dead of night?"

He shoved his hands down in his pockets and looked around at the darkened windows, realizing that our voices would carry into every room. "Let's talk about this inside," he said, and padded off toward his room. I trotted along behind him, wondering where all this was going.

Once inside, he flipped on the bed table lamp and poured himself a tumbler full of Scotch from a bottle on the desk. He held it up, a silent query. I shook my head to decline. He lit a cigarette, this time at least remembering not to bother offering me one. He sat on the edge of the bed, and I sat on the upholstered chair. The room didn't look that different from the one Brian Jaffe had occupied. Like any other liar once confronted, Carl Eckert was probably preparing another set of lies. I settled in like a kid waiting for a bedtime story. He thought for a little while, adopting his sincere look. "Okay, I'll level with you. I did drive down from SLO-town last night, but I didn't go to Perdido. I got back to the hotel after a day of meetings and checked with my service. There was a message from Harris Brown, so I called him back."

"Well, you've got *my* attention. I've been wondering how Harris Brown fits into the picture. Fill me in. I'd love it."

"Harris Brown is an ex-cop—"

"I know that part. He was assigned to the case and taken off because he lost his life savings, investing in CSL, blah, blah, blah. What else? How'd he pick up Wendell's trail down in Viento Negro?"

Carl Eckert smiled slightly, like he thought I was cute. Sometimes I am, but I wasn't sure this was one of those occasions. "Some pal of his called. An insurance agent."

"Right. That's great. I know the guy. I wasn't sure,

but that was my guess," I said. "Obviously Harris Brown knew Wendell, but did Wendell know him?"

Eckert shook his head. "I doubt it. I was the one who brought Brown in as an investor back then. They might have dealt with each other by phone, but I'm pretty sure they never met. Why?"

"Because Brown was in the room right next to his, hanging out in the bar. Wendell didn't seem aware of him, and that puzzled me. What next? Harris Brown calls you last night and you call him back. Then what?"

"I was supposed to connect up with him this afternoon on the way back from SLO-town, but he was suddenly in a hurry and said he had to see me right away. I got in the car and met him at his house in Colgate."

I stared at him, uncertain whether to believe him or not. "What's his address?"

"Why do you ask?"

"So I can verify what you're saying."

Eckert shrugged and looked it up in a small leather address book. I made a careful note. If the man was bluffing, he was good. "Why the rush?" I said.

"You'd have to ask him that. He had some bug up his butt and insisted I come down last night. I was annoyed and time was short. I had a breakfast meeting at seven, but I didn't want to argue the point. I jumped in my car and came barreling down, which is when the CHP stopped me and gave me the ticket."

"What time did you get to his place?"

"Nine. I was only there an hour. I was probably back in my hotel in SLO-town by eleven-thirty."

"By your account," I said. "Actually either one of you could have driven to Perdido in plenty of time to use Wendell and me as target practice."

"Either of us could have, but I didn't. I can't speak for him."

"You didn't see Wendell at all last night?"

"I already told you that."

"Carl, what you already did is called lying through your dentures. You swore you were out of town when you were here in Colgate. Why should I believe this?"

"I have no control over what you believe."

"What was the deal with Brown once you got there?"

"We talked and I came back."

"All you did was talk? About what? Why couldn't you talk on the phone?"

He looked away from me long enough to flick the ash off his cigarette. "He wanted his money back. I delivered it."

"His money."

"The pension monies he invested in CSL."

"How much?"

"A hundred grand."

"I don't get it," I said. "He lost that money five years ago. What made him think he could suddenly collect?"

"Because he found out Wendell was alive. Maybe he had a conversation with him. How the hell do I know?"

"During which he learned what? That there were funds available?"

He stubbed out one cigarette and lit another, squinting at me stubbornly through the smoke. "You know, this is really none of your business."

"Oh, stop that already. I'm not a threat to you. I've been hired by California Fidelity to find Wendell Jaffe so we can prove he's alive. All I care about is the half a million dollars we paid off on his life insurance. If you have a cache of money somewhere, that's really not my concern."

"Then why should I tell you anything?"

"So I can understand what's going on. That's all I care about. You had the money Harris Brown was demanding, so you drove down last night. What happened then?"

"I gave him the money and drove back to San Luis Obispo."

"You keep cash like that around?"

"Yes."

"How much? You don't have to answer. This is pure curiosity on my part."

"Altogether?"

"Just the ballpark," I said.

"About three million dollars."

I blinked. "You keep that kind of money around in *cash*?"

"What else can I do with it? I can't put it in the bank. They'd report it to the government. We've got a judgment out against us. The minute anybody finds out about it, the litigants will swoop down on it like a bunch of vultures. Anything they don't get, the IRS will come after."

I could feel indignation rising up like acid indigestion. "Of course they'd swoop down. That's the money you cheated them out of."

The look he gave was pure cynicism. "You know why they invested in CSL? They wanted something for nothing. They expected to make a killing and got killed instead. Come on, use your head. Most of 'em knew it was a crooked deal from the get-go, including Harris.

He was just hoping to collect his share before the whole scheme collapsed."

"I can see we're not talking the same language here. Let's skip past the rationale and get down to the facts. You kept three million in cash on the *Lord*?"

"You don't have to take that tone with me."

"Excuse me, right. Let me try it again." I adjusted my tone, gearing down from judgmental to neutral. "You kept three million dollars in cash hidden on the *Lord*."

"Right. Wendell and I were the only ones who knew about it. Now you," he said.

"And that's what he came back for?"

"Of course. After five years on the road, he was flat broke," Carl said. "He not only came back for it, that's what he sailed away with when he stole that boat. Half of that belonged to me, which he bloody well knew."

"Oh, wow, babe. I got news for you. You got hosed."

"You're telling me? I can't believe he'd do such a thing to me."

"Well, he did it to everyone about equally," I said. "What about his kids? Did they figure into this, or was it just the money he came back for?"

"I'm sure he was concerned about his sons," Carl said. "He was a very good father."

"The kind of parent every kid needs," I said. "I'll pass that on to them. It'll help with their therapy. What are you going to do now?" I got up from the chair.

His smile was bitter. "Get down on my knees and pray the Coast Guard catches up with him."

From the doorway, I turned. "One more thing. There was talk about Wendell turning himself in to the cops. Do you think he meant that?"

"It's hard to say. I think he was hoping to join his family again. I'm just not sure there was any room for him."

I finally crawled into bed at 2:15, brain buzzing with information. I thought what Eckert said was probably true, that there was no longer room for Wendell in the family he'd left. In some curious way we were in the same position, Wendell Jaffe and me: trying to understand what our lives might have been if we could have enjoyed the benefits of family life, looking at the mislaid years and wondering how much we'd missed. At least, I assumed that was some of what was running through his mind. There were obvious differences. He had voluntarily surrendered his family, while I'd never known mine existed. More telling was the fact that he wanted his family back and I wasn't sure I did. I couldn't understand why my aunt had never told me. Maybe she'd tried to spare me the pain of Grand's rejection, but all she'd really done was postpone the revelation. Here I was, ten years after her death, having to sort it all out for myself. Ah, well. She wasn't very good at that stuff, anyway. I drifted in and out of sleep.

My alarm went off at 6:00, but I didn't have the heart to get up and jog three miles. I turned off the buzzer and squirmed down in the sheets, sinking back into sleep. I was awakened by a phone call at 9:22. I reached for the receiver, brushing hair from my eyes. "What."

"This is Mac. Sorry if I woke you. I know it's Saturday, but I thought this was important."

His voice sounded odd, and I could feel caution flashing in me like a yellow traffic light. I pulled the sheet around me and sat up in bed. "Don't worry about it. That's okay. I was up till all hours and decided to sleep in. What's happening?"

"The *Lord* was found this morning about six miles offshore," he said. "It looks like Wendell pulled off another disappearing act. Gordon and I are down here at the office. He'd like to have you come in as soon as possible."

# 24

I PARKED IN the lot behind the office and went up the back stairs to the second floor. Most of the businesses in the building were shut down, which gave the premises a curious air of abandonment. I'd brought along my steno book, hoping to impress Gordon Titus with my professionalism. The notebook was empty except for an entry that read "Find Wendell." Back to that again. I couldn't believe it. We were so close to reeling him in. What was gnawing at me was the fact that I'd seen him with his grandson. I'd heard him talk to Michael, ostensibly making amends. As big a shit as he was, I had a hard time believing it was all a front. I was willing to imagine him changing his mind about surrendering to the cops. I could picture him stealing the *Lord* so he could sail down the coast and rescue Brian from a jail sentence. What I couldn't accept was the idea that he'd betray his family all over again. Even Wendell, God bless him, wasn't that mean-spirited.

The CF offices were officially closed, but there was a big jumble of keys in the lock, visible through the glass. Darcy's desk was unoccupied, but I caught a glimpse of Gordon Titus in Mac's glass-enclosed office, which was the only one showing any lights. Mac passed with two mugs of coffee in hand. I tapped on the glass. He set the mugs on Darcy's desk and unlocked the door for me. "We're in my office."

"So I see. Let me grab a cup of coffee and I'll be right there."

He picked up the mugs and moved on without comment. He seemed depressed, not a reaction I'd anticipated. I'd half expected fireworks. He'd seen the case as his way of going out in a blaze of glory, retiring from CF with a big gold star pasted to the front of his personnel file. He wore a pair of red-and-green-plaid pants and a red golfing shirt, and I wondered if his current emotional state was generated by the forfeiture of his weekend tee time.

All the workstations were empty, phones silent. Gordon Titus sat at Mac's desk, immaculately dressed, hands folded, his facial expression bland. I have a hard time trusting anyone so unflappable. While he appeared to be levelheaded, I suspected that he truly didn't care about most things. Poise and indifference so often look the same. I poured myself a mug of coffee and added nonfat milk before I opened Mac's office door and braved the chill effect of Titus's personality.

Mac was now seated on one of his two upholstered visitors' chairs, apparently unaware of how neatly Titus had displaced him. "I tell you one thing," Mac was saying, "and Kinsey can pass this on to Mrs. Jaffe for a fact. I'll have a lock on that money till Wendell dies of old age. If she has any hopes of seeing even one red cent, she'll have to drag his dead body up the steps and lay it across my desk."

"Good morning," I murmured to Titus. I took the other chair, which at least lined me up on the same side of the desk as Mac. He shook his head and sent me a dark look. "The son of a bitch has done it to us again."

"I gathered as much. What's the story?" I asked.

"You tell her," Mac said.

Titus pulled a ledger over in front of him. He opened it and leafed through, looking for a blank page. "What do we owe you to date?"

"Twenty-five hundred. That's ten days on a flat. You're lucky I didn't charge you for the mileage. I'm making two and three trips to Perdido every day, and that adds up."

"Twenty-five hundred dollars and for what?" Mac said. "We're right back where we started. We've got nothing but air."

Titus ran his finger down a column and penciled in a figure before he turned to another part of the book. "Actually, I don't think this is as bad as it seems. We have enough witnesses who'll testify that Jaffe was alive and well as recently as this week. We'll never see a dime of the money Mrs. Jaffe's already spent—we might as well write that off—but we can settle for the balance, thus cutting our losses." He glanced up. "That should be the end of it. She's hardly going to wait five years and make another claim."

"Where'd they find the boat?"

He began to write, not looking up. "A southbound tanker saw it as a radar blip right in the middle of a shipping lane last night. The guy on watch flashed a warning light, but there was no response. The tanker notified the Coast Guard, who went out at first light."

"The *Lord* was still in the area? That's interesting."

"It looks like Wendell sailed the boat as far as Winterset and then headed out toward the islands. He left the sails up. There was no big sea running, but with the storms coming through, the normal northwesterlies were countered by the hurricane effect. The *Lord* probably has a seven-knot hull speed, and with the right puff of wind it should have gone much farther. When they found the boat, it was stalled and drifting. The jib was backwinded, sheeted to the windward side, in effect, blowing the bow down off the wind while the main and the mizzen were trying to put it up wind. The boat must have lay hove to until discovery."

"I didn't know you sailed."

"I don't anymore. I did once upon a time." Brief smile, the most I'd ever gotten from him.

"Now what?"

"They'll tow it to the closest harbor."

"Which is what, Perdido?"

"Probably. I'm not certain where jurisdiction lies. Some crime scene unit will go over it. I don't think they'll find much, and frankly, I don't see that it's any longer our concern."

I looked over at Mac. "I take it there's no trace of Wendell."

"All his personal possessions were on the boat, including four thousand in cash and a Mexican passport, which doesn't prove a thing. He could have half a dozen passports."

"So we're supposed to think, what . . . that he's dead or gone?"

Mac gestured his irritation, showing the first signs of his usual impatience. "The guy's gone. There's no suicide note, but this is exactly what he pulled last time."

"God, Mac. How can you be so sure about that? Maybe it's a cover. Something to divert our attention."

"From what?"

"From what's really going on."

"Which is what?"

"Beats me." I said. "I'm just telling you what occurs to me. Last time he did this, he abandoned the *Lord* off the coast of Baja and set off in a dinghy. Renata Huff intercepted him, and the two sailed away on the *Fugitive*. This time she was sitting in my office within an hour of his disappearance. This was noon yesterday."

Mac wasn't buying it. "She was under surveillance from the time she left your office. Lieutenant Whiteside decided it made sense to keep an eye on her. All she did was go home. She's been there, off and on, ever since."

"My point exactly. Last time he made a run for it, he had a coconspirator. This time, assuming that's what he's up to, who's he got on his side? Carl Eckert and Dana Jaffe surely wouldn't come to his rescue, and who else is there? Actually, now that I think about it, his son, Brian was still free yesterday, and there's always Michael. Wendell might have had other friends. It's also possible he tried the gig alone this time, but it just doesn't *feel* right."

Titus spoke up. "Kinsey thinks he's actually dead," he said to Mac, his mouth turning up with amusement. He tore along the line of perforation, removing a check from the ledger.

"We're *supposed* to think he's dead!" Mac said. "That's what he did the last time, and we fell for it like a ton of bricks. He's probably on a boat right this minute, sailing off to Fiji, laughing up his ass at us."

Gordon closed the ledger and pushed the check in my direction.

"Wait a minute, Mac. Someone took some shots at us Thursday night. Wendell made it home, but suppose they flushed him out the next day? Maybe they caught up with him and killed him." I picked up the check and glanced at it casually. The amount was twenty-five hundred dollars, made out to me. "Oh, thanks. This is nice. I usually don't bill until the end of the month."

"This is final payment," he said. He folded his hands in front of him on the desk. "I have to admit I wasn't in favor of hiring you, but you've done a very nice job. I don't imagine Mrs. Jaffe will give us any more trouble. As soon as you submit your report, we'll turn the matter over to our attorney and he can see to the affidavits. We probably won't need to take the matter to court. She can return any remaining monies and that will be the end of it. In the meantime, I see no reason we can't do business together in the future, on a case-by-case basis, of course."

I stared at him. "This can't be the end of it. We don't have any idea where Wendell is."

"Wendell's current whereabouts are immaterial. We hired you to find him and you did that . . . quite handily, I might add. All we needed to do was show that he was alive, which we've now done."

"But what if he's dead?" I said. "Dana would be entitled to the money, wouldn't she?"

"Ah, but she'd have to prove it first. And what's she have? Nothing."

I looked over at Mac, feeling dissatisfied and confused.

He was avoiding my gaze. He shifted on his chair, clearly uncomfortable, probably hoping I wouldn't make a fuss. I got a quick flash of his complaints about CF in my office that first day. "Does this seem right to you? This seems weird. If it turns out something's happened to Wendell, the benefits would be hers. She wouldn't have to give back any money."

"Well, yes, but she'd have to refile," Mac said.

"But aren't we in business to see that claims are settled fairly?" I looked from one to the other. Titus's face was blank, his way of disguising his perpetual dislike, not just of me, but of the world in general. Mac's expression was tinged with guilt. He was never going to stand up to Gordon Titus. He was never going to complain. He was never going to take a stand. "Isn't anybody interested in the truth?" I asked.

Titus stood up and put on his jacket. "I'll leave this to you," he said to Mac. And to me, "We appreciate the fact that you're so conscientious, Kinsey. If we're ever interested in having someone go out and establish the company's liability to the tune of half a million dollars, you'd be the first investigator we'd think of, I'm sure. Thank you for coming in. We'll look for your report first thing Monday morning."

After he left, Mac and I sat in silence for a moment, not looking at each other. Then I got up and walked out myself.

I hopped in my car and headed for Perdido. I had to know. There was no way in the world I was going to let this one go. Maybe they were right. Maybe he'd run off. Maybe he'd been faking every shred of concern for his ex-wife and his kids, for his grandson. He was not a tower of strength. As a man, he possessed neither scruples nor a sense of moral purpose, but I couldn't make my peace with events as they stood. I had to know where he was. I had to understand what had happened to him. He was a man with far more enemies than friends, which didn't bode well for him, which seemed ominous and unsettling. Suppose somebody had killed him. Suppose the whole thing was a setup. I'd already been paid off with a check and a handshake. My time was my own, and I could do as I pleased. Before this day was over, I was going to have some answers.

Perdido's population is roughly ninety-two thousand. Happily, some small percentage of the citizens had called Dana Jaffe the minute news about the finding of the *Lord* came to light. Everybody likes to share the misery of others. There's a breathless curiosity, mixed with dread and gratitude, that allows us to experience misfortune at a satisfying distance. I gathered Dana's phone had been ringing steadily for more than an hour by the time I arrived. I hadn't wanted to be the one to tell her about Wendell's possible defection. News of his death would have cheered her no end, but I thought it unfair to share my suspicions when I had no proof. Without Wendell's body, what good would it do her? Unless she killed him herself, of course, in which case she already knew more than I did.

Michael's yellow VW was parked in the driveway. I knocked on the front door, and Juliet let me in. Brendan slept heavily against her shoulder, too tired to protest the discomfort of a vertical rest.

"They're in the kitchen. I have to get him down," she murmured.

"Thanks, Juliet."

She crossed the room and went upstairs, probably grateful for the excuse to escape. Some woman was in the process of leaving a telephone message in her most solemn tone. "Well, okay, hon. Anyway, I just wanted you to know. If there's anything we can do, you just call us now, you hear? We'll talk to you soon. Bye-bye now."

Dana was sitting at the kitchen table, looking pale and beautiful. Her silver-blond hair looked silky in the light, gathered at the nape of her neck in a careless knot. She wore pale blue jeans and a long-sleeved silk shirt in a shade of steel blue that matched her eyes. She stubbed out a cigarette, glancing up at me without comment. The smell of smoke lingered in the air, along with the faint smell of sulfur matches. Michael was pouring coffee for her from a newly made pot. Where Dana seemed numb, Michael seemed to be in pain.

I'd been around so much lately that no one questioned my unsolicited presence on the scene. He poured a mug of coffee for himself and then opened the cabinet and took out a mug for me. A carton of milk and the sugar bowl were sitting in the middle of the kitchen table. I murmured a thank-you and sat down. "Anything new?"

Dana shook her head. "I can't believe he did it."

Michael leaned against the counter. "We don't know where he is, Mom."

"And that's what drives me insane. He makes just enough of an appearance to screw us up and then he's off again."

"You talked to him?" I asked.

A pause. She dropped her gaze. "He stopped by," she said, her tone faintly defensive. She shifted on her chair, reached for the pack of cigarettes, and lit another one. She'd look old before her time if she didn't knock that off.

"When was this?"

She frowned. "I don't know, not last night, but the night before. Thursday, I guess. He went to Michael's to see the baby afterward. That's how he got the address."

"You have a long talk with him?"

"I wouldn't call it 'long.' He said he was sorry. He'd made a hideous mistake. He said he'd do anything to have the five years back. It was all bullshit, but it sounded good and I guess I needed to hear it. I was pissed, of course. I mean, I said, 'Wendell, you can't *do* this! You can't just waltz back in after everything you've put us through. What do I care if you're sorry? We're all sorry. What horseshit.' "

"You think he was sincere?"

"He was always sincere. He couldn't hold on to the same point of view from one minute to the next, but he was always sincere."

"You didn't talk to him after that?"

She shook her head. "Believe me, once was enough. That should have put an end to it, but I'm still mad," she said.

"So there was no reconciliation."

"Oh, God, no. There's absolutely no way I'd do that. Sorry doesn't cut any ice with me." Her eyes came up to mine. "What now? I guess the insurance company wants their money back."

"They won't press for what you've spent, but they really can't let you walk away with half a million bucks. Unless Wendell's dead."

She became very still, breaking off eye contact. "What makes you say that?"

"It happens to everyone eventually," I said. I pushed my coffee mug away and got up from the chair. "Call me if you hear from him. He's got a lot of people interested. One, at any rate."

"Would you walk her to the door, babe?" Dana said to Michael.

Michael moved away from the counter and walked me to the front door. Lean and brooding.

"You okay?" I asked.

"Not really. How would you feel?"

"I don't think we've gotten to the end of it yet. Your father did what he did for reasons of his own. His behavior was not about you. It was about him," I said. "I don't think you should take it personally."

Michael was shaking his head emphatically. "I never want to see him. I hope I never have to see his face again."

"I understand how you feel. I'm not trying to defend the man, but he's not all bad. You have to take what you can. One day maybe you can let the good back in. You don't know the whole story. You only know this one version. There's far more to it—events, dreams, conflicts, conversations you were never privy to. His actions are coming out of that," I said. "You have to accept the fact that there was something larger at work and you may never know what it was."

"Hey, know what? I don't care. Honest to God, I don't."

"You don't maybe, but one day Brendan might. These things tend to drift down from one generation to the next. Nobody deals well with abandonment."

"Yeah."

"There's a phrase that runs through my head in situations like this: 'the vast untidy sea of truth.' "

"Meaning what?"

"The truth isn't always nice. It isn't always small enough to absorb at once. Sometimes the truth washes over you and threatens to take you right down with it. I've seen a lot of ugly things in this world."

"Yeah, well, I haven't. This is my first and I don't like it much."

"Hey, I hear you," I said. "Take care of your kid. He's really beautiful."

"He's the only good thing that's come out of this."

I had to smile. "There's always you," I said.

His eyes were hooded and his return smile was enigmatic, but I don't think the sentiment was lost on him.

I drove from Dana's to Renata's house. Whatever the flaws in Wendell Jaffe's character, he'd managed to connect himself to two women of substance. They couldn't be more different—Dana with her cool elegance, Renata with her dark exoticism. I parked out in front and made my way up the walk. If the police were still running surveillance, they were being damn clever. No vans, no panel trucks, no curtains moving in the houses across the way. I rang the bell and waited, staring off at the street. I turned back and cupped a hand to the glass, peering in through the front door panes. I rang the doorbell again.

Renata finally appeared from the back of the house. She was wearing a white cotton skirt and a royal blue cotton T-shirt, white sandals emphasizing the deep olive tan on her legs. She opened the door, pausing for a moment with her cheek against the wood. "Hello, I heard on the radio they found the boat. He isn't really gone, is he?"

"I don't know, Renata. Honestly. Can I come in?"

She held the door open for me. "You might as well."

I followed her down the hallway to the living room, which was built across the back of the house. French doors opened onto a view of the backyard patio, which was small, mostly concrete with a fringe of annuals. Beyond the patio, a slope led down to the water. The *Fugitive* was visible, still moored at the dock.

"Would you like a bloody Mary? I'm having one." She moved to the wet bar and opened the lid of the ice bucket. She used a pair of silver tongs to lift cubes of ice, which she dropped, clinking, into her old-fashioned glass. I always wanted to be the kind of person who did that.

"You go ahead. It's a little early for me."

She squeezed lime over the ice and added an inch of vodka. She took a jug of bloody Mary mix from the minirefrigerator, gave it a whirl to shake it, and poured it over the vodka. Her movements were listless. She looked haggard. She wore very little makeup, and it was clear she'd been crying. Maybe she'd only pulled herself together, answering the door when I rang. She gave me a pained smile. "To what do I owe the pleasure?"

"I was at Dana's. As long as I was down in Perdido anyway, I thought I'd ask if I could go through some of Wendell's belongings. I keep thinking he might have forgotten something. He might have left some piece of information. I don't know how else to get a line on him."

"There aren't any 'things,' but you're welcome to have a look around if you like. Have the police been over the boat, dusting for prints or whatever it is they do?"

"All I know is what I heard this morning from the insurance company. The boat's apparently been found, but there's no sign of Wendell. I don't know about the money yet."

She brought her drink with her, crossing to a big upholstered chair. She took a seat, gesturing for me to join her in the matching chair. "What money?"

"Wendell didn't tell you about that? Carl kept three million dollars hidden somewhere on the boat."

It took about five seconds for the information to register. Then she threw her head back and started laughing, not exactly a happy sound, but better than sobbing. She collected herself. "You are *kidding*," she said.

I shook my head.

Another brief laugh and then she shook her head. "Well, that's incredible. There was that much money on the *Lord*? I can't believe it. Actually this helps me because it all makes sense."

"What does?"

"I couldn't understand his obsession with the damn boat. The *Lord* was all he talked about."

"I don't understand what you're saying."

She stirred her drink with a swizzle stick, which she licked elaborately. "Well, he loved his kids, of course, but he'd never let that interfere with his life before. He was low on money, which was never an issue as far as I was concerned. God knows I have enough for both of us. About four months ago, he started in on this talk about coming back. He wanted to see his boys. He wanted to see his grandson. He wanted to make it up to Dana for the way he'd treated her. I think what he really wanted was to get his hands on that cash. You know what? I'll bet he did it. No wonder he was so fucking secretive. Three million dollars. I'm amazed I didn't guess."

I said, "You don't seem amazed. You seem depressed."

"I suppose I am now you mention it." She took a long swallow from her glass. I had to guess she'd had more than one drink before I showed up. Tears welled in her eyes. She shook her head.

"What?" I asked.

She leaned back, resting her head against the chair, her eyes closed. "I want to believe in him. I want to think he cares about something besides money. Because if that's really the kind of man he is, then what's that say about me?" Her dark eyes came open.

"I'm not sure what Wendell Jaffe does has anything to do with anything," I remarked. "I said the same thing to Michael. Don't take it personally."

"Will the insurance company pursue him?"

"Actually, CF has nothing at stake at this point. I mean, aside from the obvious. Dana's the one who got the insurance money, and they'll deal with her in due course. Aside from that, they're out of it."

"What about the police?"

"Well, they might go after him—frankly, I hope they do—but I don't know how much manpower they'd be willing to devote. Even if we're talking fraud and grand theft, you have to catch the guy first. Then try to prove it. After all these years? You'd have to ask yourself what's the object of the exercise."

"I'll bite. What *is* the object of the exercise? I thought you worked for the insurance company."

"I did. I don't now. Let's put it this way. I have a vested interest. This is all my life has been about for the last ten days, and I won't leave it open-ended. I have to finish it out, Renata. I have to know what happens."

"God, a zealot. Just what we need." She closed her eyes again and rolled the icy glass against her temple as if to cool a raging fever. "I'm tired," she said. "I'd like to sleep for a year."

"Do you mind if I look around?"

"Be my guest. You're welcome to look. He picked the place clean, but I really haven't bothered to check myself. You'll have to pardon my disheveled emotional state. I'm having trouble comprehending the fact that after five years he left me."

"I'm not convinced that's what's going on, but look at it this way. If he did it to Dana, why not do it to you?"

She smiled with her eyes closed, and the effect was odd. I wasn't sure she really heard me. She might have already been asleep. I lifted the glass from her hand and set it on the glass-topped table with a click.

I spent the next forty-five minutes searching every nook and cranny in the house. In situations like this, you never know what you might find: personal papers, notes, correspondence, telephone numbers, a diary, an address book. Anything might help. She was right about Wendell. He'd really picked her clean. I was forced to shrug. I might have found some fabulous secret concerning his whereabouts. You never know until you look.

I came down the stairs and moved quietly through the living room. Renata stirred, her eyes coming open as I passed the couch. "Did you have any luck?" Her voice was thick with alcohol-induced weariness.

"No. But it was worth a try. Will you be all right?"

"You mean once I recover from the humiliation? Sure, I'll be fine."

I paused. "Did a guy named Harris Brown ever call Wendell?"

"Oh, yes. Harris Brown left a message, and Wendell called him back. They had a quarrel on the phone."

"When was this?"

"I don't remember. Maybe yesterday."

"What'd they quarrel about?"

"Wendell didn't tell me that. Apparently there were a lot of things he never got around to 'sharing.' If you find him, don't tell me. I think I'll have the locks changed tomorrow."

"That's Sunday. It'll be expensive."

"Today, then. This afternoon. As soon as I get up."

"Call me if you need anything."

"I need some laughs," she said.

# 25

THE ADDRESS I had for Harris Brown was in a small Colgate housing tract, one lane of dinky cottages on the bluffs overlooking the Pacific. I counted eight houses altogether on a dirt lane lined with eucalyptus. Board-and-batten, peaked roofs with twin dormers and screened-in porches across the front. Close to shacks now, they were probably built for the domestic staff on a once grand estate, the main house long demolished by the passage of time. Unlike the neighboring exteriors, which were pale pink and green, Harris Brown's house was ... well ... brown, perhaps a waggish form of self-referencing. It was hard to tell if the property had been shabby to begin with or if the general state of dilapidation was the function of his being widowed. Sexist creature that I am, it was hard to imagine a woman living here without keeping it better. I went up to the porch.

The front door was standing open, the wooden screen

door hooked shut. I could have popped it open with a penknife, but I knocked instead. Classical music was booming from a radio in the kitchen. I could see a section of the counter from the front doorstep, brown-and-white-checked cafe curtains above the sink. I smelled chicken being fried in bacon grease, the sizzling and popping a succulent counterpoint to the music. If Harris Brown didn't show up quickly, I'd begin to pick and whimper at the screen. "Mr. Brown?" I called.

"Hello?" he answered back. He appeared in the kitchen doorway, leaning sideways from the stove. He had a towel around his waist and a two-pronged fork in one hand. "Oh. Hang on." He disappeared, apparently adjusting the flame under the skillet. If he would just offer me some chicken, I wouldn't care what he'd done. Food first, then justice. That's the proper ordering of world events.

He must have put a lid on the skillet because the sizzling sound was abruptly dampened. He moved to the far wall and turned down the radio, and then he came toward the door, wiping his hands on the towel. I was standing against the light, so I figured he really couldn't see much of me until he got up close.

He peered at the screen. "Can I help you?"

"Hi. Remember me?" I said. I suspected he'd been a cop so long he'd never forget a face, though he probably recognized me without being able to recall the context. What added another layer of confusion was the fact we'd chatted on the phone within the last few days. If he knew my voice, I didn't think he'd attach it to the hooker on the balcony in Viento Negro, but it would nag at him.

"Refresh my memory."

"Kinsey Millhone," I said. "We were supposed to have lunch."

"Oh, right, right, right. Sorry. Come on in," he said. He unhooked the screen door and held it open, his expression attentive. "We've met, haven't we? I know your face from some place."

I laughed sheepishly. "Viento Negro. The hotel balcony. I said the boys sent me up, but I'm afraid I was fibbing. I was really looking for Wendell, the same as you."

He said, "Christ." He walked away from the door. "I got chicken on the stove. You better come on back here."

I eased the screen shut behind me, taking in the room at a glance as I passed through. Scruffy linoleum on the floor, big overstuffed chairs from the thirties, shelves piled haphazardly with books. Not only messy, but not clean. No curtains, no table lamps, a fireplace that didn't function.

I reached the kitchen and peered in. "It looks like Wendell Jaffe's disappeared again."

Harris Brown was back at the stove, skillet lid held aloft while a cloud of steam escaped. A glass pie plate full of seasoned flour sat on the edge of the stove. The surface of the unused griddle looked as though snow had fallen on it where he'd trailed the pieces from the pie plate to the skillet. If he stuck me in the neck with the fork he held, it would look like I'd been bitten by a snake. He poked at the pieces. "Really. I hadn't heard. How'd he manage that?"

I stayed where I was, leaning against the door frame. The kitchen was the one room that seemed to get all the sunlight. It was also cleaner than the rest of the house.

The sink had been scoured. The refrigerator was round-shouldered, old and yellowing, but it wasn't smudged with prints. The shelves were open, filled with mismatched crockery. "I don't know," I said. "I thought you might tell me. You talked to him the other day."

"Says who?"

"His girlfriend. She was there when he called you back."

"The infamous Mrs. Huff," he said.

"How'd you find her?"

"That was easy. You told me her name in our first telephone conversation."

"Ah, that's right. I bet I even mentioned she lived in the Keys. I'd forgotten."

"I don't forget much," he said, "though I notice age is catching up with me."

Inwardly I was gritched. The man seemed too casual. "I talked to Carl last night. He told me he paid the hundred grand he owed you."

"That's right."

"Why'd you quarrel with Wendell?"

He turned over some chicken pieces, mahogany brown with a spice-speckled crust. Looked done to me, but when he stuck it with his fork, blood-tinged liquid oozed out of the joint. He lowered the flame and replaced the lid. "I quarreled with Wendell before I got the money. That's why I laid into Eckert and made him drive down that night."

"I don't understand the connection."

"Wendell tells me he's going to blow the whistle. He wants to 'clear his conscience' before he goes to jail. What a crock of shit. I can't believe it. He's going to tell 'em about the money he and Eckert have been hoarding. The minute he says it, I know that's the end of it. I'm finished. By the time the court gets done, I'll never see a cent. I get straight on the horn to Eckert and tell him he better get himself down here with the cash in hand. I mean, *pronto*."

"Why hadn't you pressed for the money before?"

"Because I thought it was gone. Eckert claimed the two of them had blown every penny. Once I heard Wendell was alive, I threw the whole story out the window. I put the screws to Eckert, and it turns out they had a bundle. Wendell only took a million or so when he left. Eckert had the rest. Can you believe that? He'd had it the whole time, just taking out what he needed. He was clever, I'll say that. He lived like a pauper, so who would have guessed?"

"Weren't you a party to the lawsuit?"

"Well, sure, but that kind of money won't survive intact. You know what I'd get? Maybe ten cents on the dollar, and that's if I'm lucky. You got the IRS first and two hundred fifty investors? Everybody wants a piece. I didn't give a shit if he turned in the money, as long as I got mine up front. To hell with everybody else. I earned that dough, and I went to great lengths to collect."

"And what was the deal? What did you do in exchange?"

"I didn't do anything. That's the point. Once I had the money I didn't care about those two."

"You had no further interest."

"That's right."

I shook my head, confused. "I don't get this. Why would Carl Eckert pay you that much? If you want to get right down to it, why would he pay you at all? Was it blackmail?"

"Of course it wasn't blackmail. Jesus Christ, I'm a cop. He didn't *pay* me a cent. He made good on my losses. I invested a hundred grand and that's what I got back. To the nickel," he said.

"Did you tell Carl Eckert about Wendell turning in the money?"

"Sure I did. Wendell was going to the cops that night. I'd already talked to Carl. He was supposed to stop by with the money Friday morning, so I knew he had it with him. I wanted to make sure I had the money in my pocket before old looney tunes Wendell started blabbing. What a dope he was."

"Why do you say 'was'?"

"Because he's gone again, right? You just said so yourself."

"Maybe getting your money back wasn't enough."

"What the hell does that mean?"

I shrugged. "You might have wanted him dead."

He laughed. "You're really stretching for that one. Why would I want him dead?"

"The way I heard it, he ruined your relationship with your kids. Your marriage broke up. Your wife died shortly after that."

"Oh, hell. My marriage was lousy to begin with, and she was sick for years. Losing the money was what pissed my kids off. Once I slipped 'em each twenty-five grand under the table, they warmed right up."

"Nice kids."

"At least I know where I stand," he said dryly.

"You're telling me you didn't kill him."

"I'm telling you I didn't have to. I figured Dana Jaffe

would do that once she found out about this other woman. It's enough he'd abandon her and the kids, but to do it over some little piece of fluff like that? Seems a bit much."

Since my apartment is only a block from the ocean, I left my car parked in front and walked back to the marina. I loitered outside the locked gate leading down to Marina 1. I could have climbed around the outside as I'd done with Renata, but there was enough foot traffic at that hour to wait for someone with a key. The day was turning grim. I didn't think it would rain, but the clouds were a thick, brooding gray and the sea air was chilly. These Santa Teresa summers are really such a treat.

Finally a guy came along in shorts and a sweatshirt. He had his card key in hand and he unlocked the gate. He even held it for me when he saw that I was interested in sliding through.

"Thanks," I said, falling into step with him as he proceeded along the walkway. "You know Carl Eckert, by any chance? He owns the boat that was stolen Friday morning."

"I heard about that. Yeah, I know Carl by sight. I think he went down to get it, as a matter of fact. I saw him motor out in his dinghy a couple of hours ago." The guy took the second left turn onto the line of slips marked D. I continued on to J, which was on the right-hand side. Sure enough, Eckert's slip was still empty, and there was no way to predict just what time he'd get back.

It was nearly one o'clock, and I'd never had lunch. I walked back to my place and brought my typewriter in from the car. I made myself a sandwich—hot hard-boiled egg, sliced across a slathering of Best Foods mayo. Whole-wheat bread, lots of salt, a vertical cut. Rules are rules. I hummed to myself, licking my fingers as I set up my Smith-Corona. I ate at my desk, typing intermittently in between big gooey bites. I worked my way through a pack of index cards, reducing everything I knew to three-by-five notes. I sorted them into various categories and tacked them on the bulletin board hanging over my desk. I turned on my desk lamp. I got myself a diet Pepsi at one point. As if it were some kind of board game, I played and replayed the same set of cards. I didn't even know what I was doing, just looking at the information, arranging and rearranging, hoping I'd see a pattern emerge.

The next time I looked at my watch it was 6:45. I felt anxiety stir. I'd meant to spend only a couple of hours at my desk, making use of the time until Eckert got back. I shoved a few bucks in my jeans pocket and grabbed a sweatshirt, pulling it over my head as I went out the door. I half trotted back to the marina, through that artificial twilight that gloomy weather generates. I caught up with a woman going down the ramp toward Marina 1. She glanced at me idly as she unlocked the gate. "Forgot my key," I murmured as I followed her in.

The *Lord* was back in its slip, shrouded in blue canvas covers. The cabin was dark, and there was no sign of Eckert. There was an inflatable dinghy bobbing in the water behind it, attached by a line. I stared at it for a while, exploring the possibilities. I walked back to the yacht club, which was blazing with lights. I pushed in through the glass doors and went up the stairs.

I spotted him across the dining room. He was sitting

at the bar, wearing jeans and a denim jacket, his silver hair ruffled from the hours on the boat. The jacket-and-tie dinner crowd was already heavy, the bar itself jammed with drinkers, air dense with cigarette smoke. The maître d' looked up at me, feigning startlement at my attire. In truth, he was probably just annoyed that I hadn't paused to genuflect as I passed. I waved toward the windows, letting my face light up as if with recognition. He glanced in that direction. There wasn't any dress code in the bar, and he knew it. Half the people in there wore polo shirts and long pants, windbreakers, deck shoes.

Carl Eckert turned, catching sight of me when I was ten feet away. He murmured something to the bartender and then picked up his drink. "Let's grab a table. I think there's one outside." I nodded and followed as we picked a path through the crush.

Both the noise and the temperature dropped considerably once the door closed behind us. We were out on the deck, where only a few hardy souls were huddled. It was getting darker by the minute, though the sun was actually setting behind clouds. Below us, the ocean bucked and heaved, waves breaking on the sand with a constant thunder and swish. I loved the smell out here, though the air was damp and uninviting. Two tall propane heaters generated a rosy, oblong glow without doing much to warm the air. We sat near one nonetheless.

Carl says, "I ordered you some wine. The guy should be out with it in a minute."

"Thanks. You got your boat back, I see. What'd they find? I'd guess nothing, but one can always hope."

"Actually, they found traces of blood. Couple of little

smears on the railing, but they don't know if it's Wendell's."

"Oh, right. Like it might be yours."

"You know the police. They're not going to jump to conclusions. For all we know, Wendell did it himself, trying to create the suspicion of foul play. Did you see Renata? She just left."

I shook my head, noticing the change of subject he'd engineered. "I didn't know you two knew each other."

"I know Renata. I can't say we're friends. I met her years ago when Wendell first fell in love with her. You know how it is when a good friend has a mate you don't really get along with. I couldn't understand why he wasn't happy with Dana."

I said, "Marriage is a mystery. What's she doing up here?"

"I'm not sure. She seemed down in the mouth. She wanted to talk about Wendell, but then she got upset and walked out."

"I don't think she's handling this business well," I said. "What about the money? Is it gone?"

His laugh was a dry, flat sound. "Of course. For a while I had hopes that it might still be on the boat. I can't even call the cops. That's the irony."

"When did you last talk to Wendell?"

"Must have been Thursday. He was on his way to Dana's."

"I saw him after that at Michael's. We left together, but his car wouldn't start. I'm sure now somebody tampered with it because mine was tampered with, too. I was giving him a lift when my engine cut out. That's when somebody started shooting at us."

Behind us, the door opened with a burst of noise. The

waiter came out with a glass of Chardonnay on a tray. He had another Scotch and water for Carl. He set both drinks on the table, along with a bowl of pretzels. Eckert paid in cash, tossing out an extra couple of bills as a tip. The waiter thanked him and withdrew.

When the door closed again, I shifted the conversation. "I talked to Harris Brown."

"Good for you. How is he?"

"He seems fine. For a while I thought maybe he was a likely candidate for Wendell's murder."

"Murder. Oh, right."

"It does make sense," I said.

"Why does that make sense? It makes just as much sense to think he's gone off again," Carl said. "Why not suicide? God knows the people here didn't exactly welcome him with open arms. What if he killed himself? Have you considered that?"

"What if he was taken up in a spaceship?" I countered.

"Make your point. I can feel myself getting irritated with the subject. It's been a long day. I'm bushed. I'm out at least a million bucks. Not fun, I can tell you."

"Maybe you killed him."

"Why would I kill him? The fucker stole my money. If he's dead, how am I ever going to get it back?"

I shrugged. "To begin with, it wasn't *your* money. Half of it belonged to him. I only have your word for the fact that the money's missing. How do I know you didn't take it off the boat yourself and hide it somewhere else? Now that Harris Brown knows about it, you may be worried he'll hit you up for more than the hundred thousand he's claiming."

"Take my word for it. The money's gone," he said.

"Why would I take your word for anything? You were filing bankruptcy while two hundred and fifty investors were getting a judgment against you for money they couldn't collect. Turns out you had it all the time, playing poor while you had millions stuffed under the mattress."

"I know it looks like that."

"It doesn't just *look* like that. That's how it *was*."

"You can't possibly think I had a motive for killing Wendell. You don't even know if he's dead. Chances are he's not."

"I don't know what the chances are one way or the other. Let's just look at it this way. You had the money. He came back to collect his share. You'd had the cash so long you were beginning to think you were the only one entitled to it. Wendell's been 'dead' for five years. Who's really going to care if he's 'dead' for the rest of time? You'd be doing Dana a big favor. Wendell turns up alive, she has to give the money back."

"Hey, I talked to the guy on Thursday. That's the last I ever saw of him."

"That's the last anybody ever saw of him except Renata," I said.

He got up abruptly and headed for the door. I was right on his heels, banging through the door behind him. People turned to watch as he pushed his way across the crowded bar with me in his wake. He clattered down the stairs, around the corner, and out through the front door. Oddly enough, I wasn't worried, and I didn't care if he got away. Something was stirring at the back of my mind. Something about timing, about Wendell and the sequence of events. The dinghy bobbing in the water, trailing along behind the *Lord* like a little duckling.

I couldn't put my finger on it yet, but I was going to get it soon.

I could see Carl ahead of me, pausing at the locked gate. He was fumbling for his card key, and I trotted down the ramp behind him. He looked back in haste, and then his eyes flickered up toward the breakwater behind me. I glanced up. There was a woman at the railing. She was barefoot, in a trench coat, staring down at us. Her bare legs and the pale oval of her face were like punctuation against the darkness. Renata.

I said, "Hang on a minute. I want to talk to her."

Eckert ignored me, pushing on through the gate while I retraced my steps. The curving wall along the breakwater is about eighteen inches wide, a ledge of hip-high concrete. The ocean crashes perpetually against the barrier, water shooting straight up. A line of spray is forced along the wall and around the bend, which is marked by a row of flagpoles. The wind off the ocean blows a constant mist in this direction, waves splatting onto the walkway on the harbor side. Renata had hopped up on the wall and she was walking the curve, waves catching at her shoulder almost playfully. Her raincoat was getting soaked—dark tan on the ocean side, lighter tan on the left where the fabric was still dry. It was like getting rained on, that spray. I could feel it on my face.

"Renata!"

She didn't seem to hear, though she was only fifty yards ahead of me. The walk was slippery from seawater, and I had to watch my step. I broke into a trot, moving gingerly, hopping over puddles as I tracked her progress. The tide was in. I could see the ocean churning, a massive black presence disappearing into blackness. All the flags were snapping. There were lights at intervals, but the effect was ornamental.

"Renata!"

She glanced back then and saw me. She slowed her pace, waiting until I caught up with her before she started up again. She stayed one pace ahead of me. I was on the walkway below while she kept to the top of the wall so that I was forced to look up at her. I could see now that she was crying, mascara smudges below her dark eyes. Her hair was a series of dripping strands that hugged her face and clung to her neck. I tugged at her coat hem and she stopped, looking down. "Where's Wendell? You said he took off Friday morning, but you're the only one who ever claimed to have seen him after Thursday night." I needed details. I really wasn't sure how she'd managed to pull it off. I thought about how haggard she'd looked when she showed up in my office. Maybe she'd been up all night. Maybe she was making me part of her alibi. "Did you kill him?"

"Who cares?"

"I'd like to know. I really would. CF took me off the case this morning and the cops don't give a shit. Come on. Just between us. I'm the only one who believes he's dead, and nobody's listening to me."

The answer was delayed as if traveling from a distance. "Yes."

"You killed him?"

"Yes."

"How?"

"I shot him. It was quick." She made a gun barrel of her index finger, firing it at me. The recoil was minimal.

I scrambled up on the wall beside her, so that our

faces were level. I liked it better that way. I didn't have to raise my voice to be heard above the surf. Was she drunk? I could smell alcohol on her person, even downwind. "Was that you shooting at us at the beach?"

"Yes."

"But I had your gun. I took it away from you on the boat."

Her smile was wan. "I had a collection to choose from. Dean kept six or eight. He was very paranoid about burglars. The one I used on Wendell was a little semiautomatic with a suppressor. The shot didn't even make as much noise as a hardcover book falling on the floor."

"When did you do it?"

"That same night, Thursday. He walked home from the beach. I had my car. I got home first, so I was there to meet him when he got in. He was exhausted and his feet hurt. I made him a vodka tonic and took it out to him on the deck. He took a long swallow. I put the gun against his neck and fired. He barely jumped, and I was quick enough to keep the drink from spilling. I dragged him down the dock to the dinghy and hauled him in. I covered him with a tarp and putt-putted out of the Keys. I took my time about it so I wouldn't attract attention."

"Then what?"

"Once I was out about a quarter mile, I weighted his body down with an old twenty-five-horsepower motor I was getting rid of anyway. I kissed him on the mouth. He was already cold and he tasted like salt. I heaved him overboard and he sank."

"Along with the gun."

"Yes. After that I shifted into high gear and jammed it from Perdido up to Santa Teresa, where I eased into the marina, attached the dinghy to the *Lord*, and motored it out to sea. I brought the boat down along the coast and hauled the sails up. I got back in the dinghy and puttered into the Keys again while the *Lord* headed out into the ocean."

"But why, Renata? What did Wendell ever do to you?"

She turned her head, staring out at the horizon. When she looked back, I saw that she was smiling slightly. "I lived and traveled with the man for five years," she said. "I provided him money, a passport, shelter, support. And how does he repay me? By going back to his family . . . by being so ashamed of me, he wouldn't even admit my existence to his grown sons. He had a midlife crisis. That's all I was. Once it was over he was going back to his wife. I couldn't lose him to her. It was too humiliating."

"But Dana wasn't ever going to take him back."

"She would have. They all do. They say they won't, but when it comes right down to it, they can't resist. I'm not sure I blame them. They're just so bloody grateful when hubby finally comes crawling back. It doesn't matter what he's done. Just so he shows up again and says he loves her." The smile had faded, and she was starting to cry.

"Why the tears? He wasn't worth it."

"I miss him. I didn't think I would, but I do." She pulled the belt on her coat and let it slip off her shoulders. She was naked underneath, slim and white, shivering. Like an arrow of flesh.

"Renata, don't!"

I saw her turn and propel herself into the boiling ocean. I pulled my shoes off. I yanked my jeans down

and pulled the sweatshirt over my head. It was cold. I
was already soaked with spray, but for a moment I hesitated. Below me, out about ten yards now, I could see
Renata swimming, slender white arms cutting through
the water methodically. I didn't want to go into the water at all. It looked deep and cold and black and bitter.
I flew forward, feeling birdlike, wondering if there was
any chance of staying airborne forever.

I hit the water. It was stunning, and I gasped and then
heard myself sing aloud with the surprise. The cold
took my breath away. The weight of the water forced
my lungs to labor. I caught my breath and started moving. Salt stung my eyes, but I could see the white of
Renata's hands, face bobbing through the water a few
yards in front of me. I'm an adequate swimmer, but not
a strong one by any means. To swim for any length of
time, I'm usually forced to shift from stroke to stroke—
the crawl, the sidestroke, the breaststroke, rest. The
ocean was buoyant, nearly playful by nature, a big liquid death, cold as torture, unforgiving.

"Renata, wait!"

She looked back, apparently surprised that I had
braved the water. Almost as a courtesy, she seemed to
slow down a bit, allowing me to catch up with her before she started off again. I was already winded from
exertion. She seemed tired, too, and maybe that's why
she consented to the rest. For a moment we bobbed together, water lifting us up and down like some kind of
bizarre attraction at an amusement park.

I went under, coming up again face first, washing the
hair back out of my eyes. I wiped my nose and mouth,
tasting brine. Pickled by death, I'd become a human olive. "What happened to the money?"

I could see her arms move in the water, the motion keeping her near the surface of the water. "I didn't know about the money. That's why I laughed so hard when you told me."

"It's gone now. Somebody took it."

"Oh, who cares about that, Kinsey? Wendell taught me a lot. I hate to sound trite about it at a time like this, but money really can't buy happiness."

"Yeah, but at least you can afford to rent a little bit."

She didn't even bother to laugh politely. I could tell her energy was flagging, but not nearly to the extent mine was.

"What happens when you can't go on swimming?" I asked.

"Actually, I've done some research. Drowning isn't such a bad way to go. There's bound to be a moment of panic, but after that, it's euphoric. You simply slide into the ether. Like going to sleep, except you have nice sensations. It's the oxygen deprivation. Suffocation, in effect."

"I don't trust the reports. Gotta be from people who didn't really die, and what do they know? Besides, I'm not ready. Too many sins on my conscience," I said.

"You better save your strength then. I'm going on," she said, and moved off through the water. Was the woman a fish? I could barely move. The water did seem warmer, but that was worrisome. Maybe this was stage one, the preliminary illusion just before the final full-blown hallucination. We swam. She was stronger than I was. I went through all the strokes I knew, trying to keep up with her. For a while, I counted. One, two. Breathe. One, two. Breathe. "Oh, Jesus, Renata. Let's rest." I stopped, winded, and turned over on my back, looking up at the sky. The clouds actually seemed lighter than the night around us. Almost as a form of indulgence, she slowed again, treading water. Out there in the darkness, the waves were pitiless, inviting. The cold was numbing.

"Please come back to shore with me," I said. My chest was burning. I was panting in the water, but I couldn't get enough air. "I don't want to do this, Renata."

"I never asked you to."

She started swimming again.

I experienced a failure of will. My arms felt like lead. For a moment I thought about trying to keep up, but I was close to collapse. I was cold and tired. My arms were getting heavier, burning down the length of them from total muscle fatigue. I could barely breathe. I'd begun to miscalculate, gulping down saltwater every time I tried for air. I might have been crying, too. Hard to tell out there. I trod water for a bit. I felt like I'd been swimming forever, but when I turned and looked at the shore lights, it was clear we'd gone only half a mile, if that. I couldn't imagine what it'd be like swimming to exhaustion—in the dark, in black water, until fatigue overtook us. I couldn't save her. There was no way I was going to match her, swimming stroke for stroke. And what would I do if I caught up with her, wrestle her into submission? Not likely. I hadn't practiced any lifesaving skills since I was certified back in high school. She was on her way out. It wasn't going to make a bit of difference to her if she took me out with her. Once people get into killing mode, they don't always know how to stop. At least I understood now what had happened to Wendell and what would happen to her. I had to stop. I trod water, conserving energy. I simply couldn't go on. I couldn't even think of anything pithy or profound to say to her. Not that she was paying attention. She had her own destination, just as I had mine. I heard her briefly, but it didn't take long before the splashing sounds were swallowed up by the night. I rested for a while and then turned and started back to shore.

# Epilogue

WENDELL JAFFE'S BODY emerged from the Pacific nine days later, washing up on Perdido Beach, trailing kelp like a net. Some peculiar combination of tides and storm surf had freed him from the ocean bottom and brought him ashore. Of the family survivors, I think Michael took it hardest. Brian had issues of his own to deal with, but he could at least take comfort in the fact that his father hadn't willfully abandoned him. Dana's financial problems were resolved by the hard proof of Wendell's death. It was Michael who was left with all the unfinished business.

As for me, having cost California Fidelity half a million dollars, I thought it was safe to assume I wouldn't be doing business with *them* anytime soon. That should have been the end of it, but a few facts began to filter in as the months went by. Renata's body never surfaced. I heard, inadvertently, that when her estate was probated, both her house and her boat were mortgaged to the hilt and all her bank accounts had been stripped. That bothered me. I found myself picking at the past, like a little knot in a piece of thread.

Here's what I think about when I wake in the dead of night. I'm not sure anybody really knows what happened to Dean DeWitt Huff. She claims he died of a heart attack in Spain, but did anyone ever check it out? And the husband before that? Whatever happened to him? I'd been viewing this as Wendell Jaffe's story, but suppose it was hers? The missing millions never showed. Suppose she knew about the money and persuaded him to come back? Suppose she had a boat anchored out there somewhere in the dark? She could have dived off her own dock if she wanted to drown. You really want to kill yourself, why drive thirty miles to do it? Unless you need a reliable witness—like me. Once I made my report to the police, the case was considered closed. But is it?

I've never believed the perfect crime was possible. Now I'm not so sure. She told me Wendell taught her a lot, but she never really said what it was. Please understand: I don't have the answers. I'm simply posing the questions. God knows I have questions about my own life to answer yet.

Respectfully submitted,
Kinsey Millhone

Turn the page for a preview
of the next exciting Kinsey Millhone mystery,

# K IS FOR KILLER

# by Sue Grafton

Published by Ballantine Books.
Available at your local bookstore.

# 1

THE STATUTORY DEFINITION of homicide is the "unlawful killing of one human being by another." Sometimes the phrase "with malice" is employed, the concept serving to distinguish murder from the numerous other occasions in which people deprive each other of life—wars and executions coming foremost to mind. "Malice" in the law doesn't necessarily convey hatred or even ill will, but refers instead to a conscious desire to inflict serious injury or cause death. In the main, criminal homicide is an intimate, personal affair insofar as most homicide victims are killed by close relatives, friends, or acquaintances. Reason enough to keep your distance, if you're asking me.

In Santa Teresa, California, approximately eighty-five percent of all criminal homicides are resolved, meaning that the assailant is identified, apprehended, and the question of guilt or innocence is adjudicated by the courts. The victims of unsolved homicides I think of as the unruly dead; persons who reside in a limbo of their own, some state between life and death, restless, dissatisfied, longing for release. It's a fanciful notion for someone not generally given to flights of imagination, but I think of these souls locked in an uneasy relationship with those who have killed them. I've talked to homicide investigators who've been caught up in similar reveries, haunted by certain victims who seem to linger among us, persistent in their desire for vindication. In the hazy zone where wakefulness fades into sleep, in that leaden moment just before the mind sinks below consciousness, I can sometimes hear the murmuring. They mourn themselves. They sing a lullaby of the murdered. They whisper the names of their attackers, those men and women who still walk the earth, unidentified, unaccused, unpunished, unrepentant. On such nights, I do not sleep well. I lie awake listening, hoping to catch a syllable, a phrase, straining to discern in that roll call of conspirators, the name of one killer. Lorna Kepler's murder ended up affecting me that way, though I didn't learn the facts of her death until months afterward.

It was late February and I was working late, little Miss Virtue organizing itemized expenses and assorted business receipts for my tax return. I'd decided it was time to handle matters like a grown-up instead of shoving everything in a shoe box and delivering it to my accountant at the very last minute. Talk about cranky! Each year, the man positively bellows at me and I have to swear I'll reform, a vow I take seriously until tax time rolls around again and I realize my finances are in complete disarray.

I was sitting at my desk in the law firm where I rent office space. The night outside was chilly by the usual California definition, which is to say fifty degrees. I was the only one on the premises, ensconced in a halo of warm, sleep-inducing light while the remaining offices remained dark and quiet. I'd just put on a pot of coffee to counteract the narcolepsy that afflicts me at the approach of money matters. I laid my head down on my desk, listening to the soothing gargle of the water as it filtered through the coffee maker. Even the smell of mocha java was not sufficient to stimulate my torpid senses. Five more minutes and I'd be out like a light, drooling on my blotter with my right cheek picking up inky messages in reverse.

I heard a tap at the side entrance and I lifted my head, tilting an ear in that direction like a dog on alert. It was nearly nine o'clock and I wasn't expecting any visitors. I roused myself, left my desk, and moved out into the hallway. I cocked my head against the side door leading out into the hall. The tap was repeated, much louder. I said, "Yes?"

I heard a woman's muffled voice in response. "Is this Millhone Investigations?"

"We're closed."

"What?"

"Hang on." I put the chain on the door and opened it a crack, peering out at her.

She was on the far side of forty, her outfit of the urban cowgirl sort: boots, faded jeans, and a buckskin shirt. She wore enough heavy silver and turquoise jewelry to look like she would clank. She had dark hair nearly to her waist, worn loose, faintly frizzy, and dyed the color of oxblood shoes. "Sorry to bother you, but the directory downstairs says there's a private investigator up here in this suite. Is he in by any chance?"

"Ah. Well more or less," I said, "but these aren't actual office hours. Is there any way you can come back tomorrow? I'll be happy to set up an appointment for you once I check my book."

"Are you his secretary?" Her tanned face was an irregular oval, lines cutting down along each side of her nose, four lines between her eyes where the brows were plucked to nothing and reframed in black. She used the same sharpened pencil to line her eyelids, too, though she wore no other makeup that I could see.

I tried not to sound irritated sice the mistake is not uncommon. "I'm 'him,'" I said. "Millhone Investigations. The first name is Kinsey. Did you tell me yours?"

"No, I didn't and I'm sorry. I'm Janice Kepler. You must think I'm a complete idiot."

Well not *complete*, I thought.

She reached out to shake hands and then realized the crack in the doorway wasn't large enough to permit contact. She pulled her hand back. "It never occured to me you'd be a woman. I've been seeing the Millhone Investigations on the board down in the stairwell. I come here for a support group once a week down a floor. I've been thinking I'd call, but I guess I never worked up my nerve. Then tonight as I was leaving, I saw the light on from the parking lot. I hope you don't mind. I'm actually on my way to work so I don't have that long."

"What sort of work," I asked stalling.

"Shift manager at Frankie's Coffee Shop on upper State Street. Eleven to seven, which makes it hard to take care of any daytime appointments. I usually go to bed at eight in the morning and don't get up again until late afternoon. Even if I could just *tell* you my problem, it'd be a big relief. Then if it turns out it's not the sort of work you do, maybe you could recommend someone else. I could really use some help, but I don't know where to turn. Your being a woman might make it easier." The penciled eyebrows went up in an imploring double arch.

I hesitated. Support group, I thought. Drink? Drugs? Codependency? If the woman was looney-tunes, I'd really like to know. Behind her, the hall was empty, looking flat and faintly yellow in the overhead light. Lonnie Kingman's law firm takes up the entire third floor except for two public restrooms; one marked M and one W. It was always possible she had a couple of M confederates lurking in the commode, ready at a signal to

366

jump out and attack me. For what purpose, I couldn't think. Any money I had, I was being forced to give to the Fed's at pen point. "Just a minute," I said.

I closed the door and slid the chain off its track, opening the door again so I could admit her. She moved past me hesitantly, a crackling brown paper bag in her arms. Her perfume was musky, the scent reminiscent of saddlesoap and sawdust. She seemed ill-at-ease, her manner infected by some edgy combination of apprehension and embarrassment. The brown paper bag bulged with papers of some sort. "This was in my car. I didn't want you to think I carried it around with me ordinarily."

"I'm in here," I said. I moved into my office with the woman close on my heels. I indicated a chair for her and watched as she sat down, placing the paper bag on the floor. I pulled up a chair for myself. I figured if we sat on opposite sides of my desk she'd check out my deductible expenses, which were none of her business. I'm the current ranking expert at reading upside down and seldom hesitate to insert myself into matters that are not my concern. "What support group?" I asked.

"It's for parents of murdered children. My daughter died here last April. Lorna Kepler. She was found in her cottage over by the Mission."

I said, "Ah yes. I remember, though I thought there was some speculation about the cause of death."

"Not in my mind," she said tartly. "I don't know *how* she died, but I know she was murdered just as sure as I'm sitting here." She reached up and tucked a long ribbon of loose hair behind her right ear. "The police never did come up with a suspect and I don't know what kind of luck they're going to have after all this time. Somebody told me for every day that passes, the chances diminish, but I forget the percentage."

"Unfortunately, that's true."

She leaned over and rooted in the paper bag, pulling

367

out a photograph in a bi-fold cardboard frame. "This is Lorna. You probably saw this in the paper at the time." She held out the picture and I took it, staring down at the girl. Not a face I'd forget. She was in her early twenties with dark hair pulled smoothly away from her face, a long swatch of hair hanging down the middle of her back. She had clear hazel eyes with a nearly Oriental tilt, dark, cleanly arched brows, a wide mouth, straight nose. She was wearing a white blouse with a long snowy white scarf wrapped several times around her neck, a dark navy blazer, and faded blue jeans on a slender frame. She stared directly into the camera, smiling slightly, her hands tucked down in her front pockets. She was leaning against a floral print wall, the paper showing lavish pale pink, climbing roses against a white background. I returned the picture, wondering what in the world to say under the circumstances. "She's very beautiful," I murmured. "When was that taken?"

"About a year ago. I had to bug her to get this. She's my youngest. Just turned twenty-five. She was hoping to be a model, but it didn't work out."

"You must have been young when you had her,"

"Twenty-one," she said. "I was seventeen with Berlyn. I got married because of her. Five months gone and I was big as a house. I'm still with her daddy, which surprised everyone, including me, I guess. I was nineteen with my middle daughter. Her name's Trinny. She's real sweet. Lorna's the one I nearly died with, poor thing. Got up one morning, day before I was due, and started hemorrhaging. I didn't know what was happening. Blood everywhere. It was just like a river pouring out between my legs. I've never seen anything like it. Doctor didn't think he could save either one of us, but we pulled through. You have children, Ms. Millhone?"

"Make it Kinsey," I said. "I'm not married."

She smiled slightly. "Just between us, Lorna really

was my favorite, probably because she was such a problem all her life. I wouldn't say that to either of the older girls, of course." She tucked the picture away. "Anyway, I know what it's like to have your heart ripped out. I probably look like an ordinary woman, but I'm a zombie, the living dead, maybe a little bit cracked. We've been going to this support group ... somebody suggested it and I thought it might help. I was ready to try anything to get away from the pain. Mace—that's my husband—went a few times and then quit. He couldn't stand the stories, couldn't stand all the suffering compressed in one room. He wants to shut it out, get shed of it, get clean. I don't think it's possible, but there's no arguing the point. To each his own, as they say."

"I can't even imagine what it must be like," I said.

"And I can't describe it either. That's the hell of it. We're not like regular people anymore. You have a child murdered and from that moment on, you're from some other planet. You don't speak the same language as other folks. Even in this support group, we seem to speak different dialects. Everybody hangs on to their pain like it was some special license to suffer. You can't help it. We all think ours is the worst case we ever heard. Lorna's murder hasn't been solved, so naturally we think our anguish is more acute because of it. Some other family, maybe their child's killer got caught and he served a few years. Now he's out on the street again and that's what they have to live with—knowing some fella's walking around smoking cigarettes, drinking beers, having himself a good old time every Saturday night while their child is dead. Or the killer's still in prison and'll be there for life, but he's warm, he's safe. He gets three meals a day and the clothes on his back. He might be on death row, but he won't actually *die*. Hardly anybody does unless they *beg* to be executed. Why should they? All thoses soft-hearted lawyers go to work. System's set up to keep 'em all alive while our kids are dead for the rest of time."

"Painful," I said.

"Yes, it is. I can't even tell you how much that hurts. I sit downstairs in that room and I listen to all the stories and I don't know what to do. It's not like it makes my pain any less, but at least it makes it part of *something*. Without the support group, Lorna's death just evaporates. It's like nobody cares. It's not even something people talk about anymore. We're all of us wounded so I don't feel so cut off. I'm not separate from them. Our emotional injuries just come in different forms." Her tone throughout was nearly matter-of-fact and the dark-eyed look she gave me then seemed all the more painful because of it. "I'm telling you all this because I don't want you to think I'm crazy ... at least any more than I actually am. You have a child murdered and you go berserk. Sometimes you recover and sometimes you don't. What I'm saying is, I know I'm obsessed. I think about Lorna's killer way more than I should. Whoever did this, I want him *punished*. I want this laid to rest. I want to know why he did it. I want to tell him face-to-face exactly what he did to my life the day he took hers. They psychologist who runs the group, she says I need to find a way to get my power back. She says it's better to get mad than go on feeling heartsick and defenseless. So. That's why I'm here. I guess that's the long and short of it."

"Taking action," I said.

"You bet. Not just talking. I'm sick and tired of talk. It gets nowhere."

"You're going to have to do a bit more talking if you want my help. You want some coffee?"

"I know that. I'd love some. Black is fine."

I filled two mugs and added milk to mine, saving my questions until I was seated again. I reached for the legal pad on my desk and I picked up a pen. "I hate to make you go through the whole thing again, but I really need to have the details, at least as much as you know."

"I understand. Maybe that's why it took me so long to come up here. I've told this story probably six hundred times, but it never gets any easier." She blew on the surface of her coffee and then took a sip. "That's good coffee. Strong. I hate drinking coffee too weak. It's no taste. Anyway, let me think how to say this. I guess what you have to understand about Lorna is she was an independent little cuss. She did everything her way. She didn't care what other people thought and she didn't feel what she did was anybody else's business. She'd been asthmatic as a child and ended up missing quite a bit of school, so she never did well in her classes. She was smart as a whip, but she was out half the time. Poor thing was allergic to just about everything. She didn't have many friends. She couldn't spend the night at anybody else's house because other little girls always seemed to live with pets or house dust, mold or whatnot. She outgrew a lot of that as she matured, but she was always on medication for one thing or another. I make a point of this because I think it had a profound affect on the way she turned out. She was antisocial; bull-headed and uncooperative. She had a streak of defiance, I think because she was used to being by herself, doing what *she* wanted. And I might have spoiled her some. Children sense when they have the power to cause you distress. Makes them tyrants to some extent. Lorna didn't understand about pleasing other people, ordinary give and take. She was a nice person and she could be generous if she wanted, but she wasn't what you'd call loving or nurturing." She paused. "I don't know how I got off on that. I meant to talk about something else if I can think what it was."

She frowned, blinking, and I could see her consult some interior agenda. There was a moment or two of silence while I drank my coffee and she drank hers. Finally, her memory clicked in and she brightened, saying, "Oh yes. Sorry about that." She shifted in her chair and took up the narrative. "Asthma medication sometimes caused her insomnia. Everybody thinks anti-histamines make you drowsy, which they can, of course, but it isn't the deep sleep you need for ordinary rest. She didn't like to sleep. Even grown, she got by on as little as three hours sometimes. I think she was afraid of lying down. Being prone always seemed to aggravate her wheezing. She got in the habit of roaming around at night when everybody else was asleep."

"Who'd she hang out with? Did she have friends or just ramble on her own?"

"Other night owls I'd guess. An FM disc jockey for one, the guy on that all-night jazz station. I can't re-member his name, but you might know if I said it. And there was a nurse on the night shift at St. Terry's. Se-rena Bonney. Lorna actually worked for Serena's hus-band at the water treatment plant."

I made a note to myself. I'd have to check on both if I decided to help. "What sort of job?"

"It was just part-time . . . one to five for the city, doing clerical work. You know, typing and filing, an-swering the telephone. She'd be up half the night and then she could sleep late if she wanted."

"Twenty hours a week isn't much," I said. "How could she afford to live?"

"Well, she had her own little place. This cabin at the back of somebody's property. It wasn't anything fancy and the rent on that was cheap. Couple of rooms, with a bath. It might have been some kind of gardener's cot-tage to begin with. No insulation. She had no central heating and not a lot of kitchen to speak of; just a mi-crowave oven and a two-burner hot plate, refrigerator the size of a little cardboard box. You know the kind. She had electricity, running water, and a telephone, and that was about the extent of it. She could have fixed it up real cute, but she didn't want to bother. She liked it

372

simple, she said, and besides it wasn't all that permanent. Rent was nominal and that's all she seemed to care about. She liked her privacy and people learned to leave her pretty much alone."

"Hardly sounds like an allergen-free environment," I remarked.

"Well, I know and I said as much myself. Of course by then she was doing better. The allergies and asthma were more seasonal than chronic. She might have an occasional attack after exercise or if she had a cold or she was under stress. The point is she didn't want to live around other people. She like the feel of being in the woods. The property wasn't all that big . . . six or seven acres with a little two-lane gravel road coming in along the back. I guess it gave her the sense of isolation and quiet. She didn't want to live in some apartment building with tenants on all sides—bumping and thumping and playing loud music. She wasn't friendly. She didn't even like to say 'hi' in passing. That's just how she was. She moved into the cabin and that's where she stayed."

"You said she was found at the cabin. Do the police think she died there as well."

"I believe so. She wasn't found there for some time. Nearly two weeks, they think, from the state she was in. I hadn't heard from her, but I didn't think much about it. I'd talked to her on a Thursday night and she told me she was taking off. I assumed she meant that night, but she didn't say as much, at least not that I remember. If you recall spring came late last year and the pollen count was high, which meant her allergies were acting up. Anyway, she called and said she'd be out of town for two weeks. She was on vacation from work and she said she was going up to the mountains to see whatever snows were left. Ski country was the only place she found relief when she was suffering. She said she'd call when she got back and that was the last I talked to her."

I'd begun to scribble notes. "What date was this?"

"April nineteenth. The body was discovered May fifth."

"Where was she going? Did she give you her destination?"

"She mentioned the mountains, but she never did say where. You think that makes a difference?"

"I'm just curious," I replied. "April seems late for snow. It could have been a cover story if she was going somewhere else. Did you get the impression she was concealing something?"

"Oh, Lorna's not the kind who confided details. My other two, if they're going off on vacation, we all sit around poring over the travel brochures and hotel accommodations. Like right now, Berlyn's saved her money for a trip and we're always talking about this cruise versus that, oohing and ahhing. The fantasy's half the fun is the way I look at it. Lorna said that just set up a lot of expectations and then reality would disappoint. She didn't look at anything the way other people did. At any rate, when I didn't hear from her, I figured she was out of town. She wasn't one to call much anyway and none of us would have any reason to go to her place if she was gone." She hesitated, embarrassed. "I can tell I feel guilty. Just listen to how much explanation I'm going into here. I just don't want it to seem like I didn't care."

"It doesn't sound like that."

"That's good because I loved that child more than life itself." Tears rose briefly, almost like a reflex, and I could see her blink them away. "Anyway, it was someone she'd done some work for, who finally went back there."

"What was her name?"

"Oh. Serena Bonney."

I glanced at my notes. "She's the nurse?"

"That's right."

374

"What kind of work had Lorna done for her?"

"She housesat. Lorna looked after Mrs. Bonney's dad sometimes. As I understand it, the old fella wasn't well and Mrs. Bonney didn't like leaving him by himself. I guess she was trying to make arrangements to leave town and wanted to talk to Lorna befores she made reservations. Lorna didn't have an answering machine. Mrs. Bonney called several times and then decided to leave a note on her front door. Once she got close, she realized something was wrong." Janice broke off, not with emotion, but with the unpleasant images that must have been conjured up. After two weeks undiscovered, the body would have been in very poor shape.

"How did Lorna die? Was there a determination as to the cause of death?"

"Well, that's the point. They never did find out. She was lying facedown on the floor in her underwear, with her sweat clothes strewn nearby. I guess she'd come back from a run and stripped down for her shower, but it didn't seem like she'd been assaulted. It's always possible she suffered an asthma attack."

"But you don't believe it."

"No, I don't, and the police didn't either."

"She was into exercise? I find that surprising from what you've told me so far."

"Oh, she liked to keep in shape. I do know there were times when a workout made her wheezy and short of breath, but she had one of those inhalers and it seemed to help. If she had a bad spell, she'd cut back on exercise and then take it up again when she was feeling better. Doctors didn't want her to act like an invalid."

"What about the autopsy?"

"Reports right in here," she said, indicating the paper bag.

"There were no signs of violence?"

Janice shook her head. "I don't know how to say this.

375

I guess because of putrefaction they weren't even sure it was her at first. It wasn't until they compared her dental records that she was identified."

"I'm assuning the case was handled as a homicide."

"Well, yes. Even with the cause of death undetermined, it was considered suspicious. They investigated as a homicide, but then nothing turned up. Now it seems like they dropped it. You know how they do those things. Something else comes along and they concentrate on that."

"Sometimes there isn't sufficent information to make a finding in a situation like that. It doesn't mean they haven't worked hard."

"Well, I understand, but I still can't accept it."

I noticed that she had ceased to make eye contact and I could feel the whisper of intuition crawling up along my spine. I found myself focussing on her face, wondering at her apparent uneasiness. "Janice, is there something you haven't told me?"

Her cheeks began to tint as if she were being overtaken by a hot flash. "I was just getting to that."

# K IS FOR KILLER
## by Sue Grafton

**Published by Ballantine Books.**
**Available at your local bookstore.**